STORMBREWER

Mary Walz

To my husband, Dave, who fifteen years ago married a not-very-nerdy young woman, and got her reading fantasy, introduced her to things like Dungeons and Dragons and LARP, and basically helped her grow into the nerd she is today. I love you.

PROLOGUE

TONIGHT WAS THE perfect evening for a sail, or so my brother Jade thought. And I certainly couldn't tell him how wrong he was.

The sky was mostly clear, dotted by just a few puffy clouds, their undersides tinged pink as the sun slid slowly towards the horizon. A brisk wind blew in from the west, making the sails billow. Jade was rather proud of his new boat, so when he'd invited me along for a sail a few days before, I'd agreed to come.

That was before I realized what the weather was going to do.

Now I could feel it. I could sense the massive bank of dark clouds that brewed just beyond our line of sight and could feel the wind currents picking up. I shivered. *If it's just a short sail, we might be all right.* I'd have to find an excuse to ask Jade to turn around early, because I couldn't tell him the truth. Especially not with Gabrielle here.

Standing at the wheel, his arm around his wife, Jade was a picture of poise and calm. They were both beautiful, their features illuminated by the evening light, her slender form next to Jade's tall, muscular physique looking like it could blow away. We'd known Gabrielle—or Gabby, as Jade had us calling her now— since I was about seven, when Father's job moved us from Sylvenburgh to Kirstein. Her family lived a few doors down from our new home. She was right between my brothers in age, and they'd both had crushes on her at various points in their lives. Jade, of course, won that battle, and the two of them had been married for just over two years now. The wedding was a dream come true for my mother, whose illness had just begun to take a turn for the worse at the time.

I doubted Mother would approve of them now, though. There was no talk of children, and Gabrielle was no simpering housewife. They spent their money on extravagant things like sailboats and their time on organizations that I was only just beginning to understand.

"Ruby," Gabrielle said to me, "you haven't congratulated your brother yet."

I turned back from the bow and grinned at her. "Which brother? I have two of them, you know." My last words were muffled as a gust of wind whipped my blond curls directly into my face. Jade laughed and ran a hand through his own hair—blond like mine but cut short enough that his curls were nonexistent.

"This one, obviously." She snorted and turned to Jade. "Where is your brother, anyway?"

Jade shrugged. "I invited him, but he said he was busy. He's probably out smoking teakflower with his new friends, as usual."

Gabby frowned. "A shame. I still don't understand what happened to him."

Jade and I both nodded. Just over three years had passed since our brother returned from a job with scars on his face and the light gone from his eyes. The scars were nearly gone now, but the person we'd known had yet to return. Within a month, our normally competitive brother had been demoted to a mere clerical job at work, due to poor performance and constant tardiness. Most nights, he would stumble into the house in the wee hours of the morning, reeking of alcohol or strung out on teakflower, occasionally accompanied by an equally intoxicated woman. Neither Jade nor I had any idea what happened to him.

"He would have made a wonderful Witch Slayer," Gabby went on. "Which, of course, is what you should be congratulating Jade on, Ruby. He became a full member just this afternoon."

Jade grinned, his blue eyes glinting. "Time to start slaying some witches."

"You did a splendid job of that during your initiation," Gabby replied. "You should have seen your brother, Ruby. Put a knife right in that elfieblood's gut and twissssted." She drew the last word out, moving her hands to simulate the motion.

I felt the blood drain from my face, and Jade chuckled. "I don't think Ruby here is the slaying type, Gabby. You're scaring her."

"What, you don't want to join us when you're a little older?" Gabby grinned.

I shook my head. "As Jade says, I'm not into killing." My voice shuddered, and I toyed with my hair. I'd learned to just smile and nod at talk of capturing magic users and rendering them mute and disabled. It was unavoidable in my family. However, now that Gabrielle was a part of it, the talk had shifted from stories of capture to outright murder. I frowned at Jade. "Does your job allow that? Killing witches for sport?"

"If I'm on the job, I'm meant to turn them in, not kill them, so long as I can avoid it. But no one can tell me what to do when I'm off the job." Jade eyed me. "Don't tell Father."

Gabby snorted. "Your father—second captain of the Breoch Guard, renowned hunter of magic, the same fellow who once turned in two dozen hildakins in a single day—disapproves of the Witch Slayers?"

"He thinks we're a little extreme," Jade replied. "The law doesn't forbid being born with a talent, he says, it only forbids using it."

"You're going to have to move past that sort of thinking, my dear. That's not how the Witch Slayers operate. The only way to eliminate the scourge of magic is to eliminate *all* witches. Whether they use their magic or not."

"Yes, I know that, but that's why Father thinks…" A shadow fell over our boat as Jade spoke, and he frowned. "Huh. That doesn't look good."

The large bank of clouds was visible now, hanging ominously on the horizon. The wind picked up, and our boat began to list to the right. "We'd better get turned around," Jade mumbled.

My heartbeat picked up as I stared up into the clouds. They were blowing in fast, and I knew they'd be over us in a matter of minutes. *We don't have enough time to get to shore.*

There was, of course, one way to stop the storm. But it was suicide, especially in present company.

Jade and Gabby worked to turn the boat around, and the first few raindrops fell just as they set us to head back to land. The rain came hard and fast, heavy droplets that soaked through our clothes in a matter of seconds. But it wasn't the rain that worried me. It was the wind.

Strong gusts tore at our sails and threatened to send us back to sea. The waves picked up and slammed themselves against the boat. One particular wave spilled over the side; the next tilted us far to the right. Gabby screamed as she nearly went over the edge.

This is ridiculous.

I knew exactly how to stop this. The words were burning on my tongue, words that I knew were damning and yet might well save us. If I did nothing, we could die. If I acted…well, I knew the consequences.

I turned away from my brother and sister-in-law, took a deep breath and whispered a phrase, summoning the wind to do my bidding and driving the remainder of the storm far to the east, away from us. *"Arius Dominus Karnium."*

In seconds, the storm passed, clouds moving away from our boat with unnatural speed. Gabby gripped the railing, gasping and trying not to cry. Jade put an arm around her and then glanced up at the sky, eyebrows knitted. "How…how did that happen?" he asked. It was then that I realized there were no other boats nearby. His eyes met mine then looked at his wife. "One of you did that."

Gabby's head snapped up, and she pulled out of his embrace. "You've got to be joking," she said, her voice wobbling. "You think *I* did that? Jade, I was the one who convinced you to join the Witch Slayers! You think I, of all people, am an elfieblood?"

Jade's eyes narrowed, and then both of them turned to me.

My mouth was dry; my heart pounded in my chest. I stared at my brother, unable to move or think. "I…"

Gabby spoke first. "Your sister is a *witch?*" Her voice turned acidic. "You have *magic* in your family?"

Jade gawked at me. "Apparently," he said softly.

"You have magic in your family, and you didn't think to *tell* me?" Gabby tossed her auburn hair out of her face and stared up at him. "No, no, this isn't happening. How do I know you're not a witch yourself? One of your parents must be, which means that when we have children, there's a chance that…" Her voice broke, and she glared. "Why didn't you *tell* me?" Her words came out as a screech.

Jade's eyes had not left me. "Because I had no idea Ruby was like this! And if one of my parents is a witch, then I don't know about that, either." He turned to face Gabby and crossed his arms. "You think I'd hide something like that from you? You think I'd even consider dating someone whose entire family is made up of Witch Slayers, if there was a chance I was a witch myself? I'm not the one hiding things around here." His gaze returned to me. "Why didn't *you* tell us, Ruby?"

I gaped at him. "Why…why do you think?" My words came out ragged, halting. "Jade, you've known me my whole life, and suddenly you're looking at me like I'm some sort of monster!"

"That's exactly what you are." Gabby's lip curled in disgust. "I can't believe I've known you all these years, only to find out now that you're a filthy little witch. And you know what we do to witches, now don't you?" My breath caught in my throat as she drew a dagger from her belt. Then she turned to Jade. "You do it."

Jade's eyes widened. "You're asking me to kill my own sister?"

"I'm telling you to slay a witch like a good Witch Slayer!" Gabby thrust the handle of the knife towards him.

Jade glanced at me and then shook his head. "No way. If you're so intent on her being dead, you do it."

"She's your sister, therefore *you* need to purge your family of this...this stain!" Gabby's green eyes narrowed. "If you value me as your wife, you will do this."

"Since when do I take orders from you? I thought we were in this together, as partners! You're not my superior."

"If you don't deal with her, then you're not worthy to call yourself a Witch Slayer. And you're not worthy of me, either." Gabby's voice turned to ice. "Spare her, and I will step off this boat, go back to my parents' home, and never set foot in our house again. Choose, Jade. Me or her."

Jade glanced between the two of us again and shook his head. "All right, how about this? No one kills Ruby. But when we get back to shore, I'll turn her in, as per my job."

"Jade, no!" The world began to spin. "I'm your sister!"

His jaw tightened. "You broke the law, Ruby. Rules are rules."

"But...I saved your lives! Don't you understand? We'd all be dead if I hadn't moved that storm along."

He turned away from me and looked at Gabby. "Do we have a deal?"

Gabby huffed. "I suppose so."

"Then let's move."

Jade took his place at the wheel, and I stood at the front of the boat blinking back tears, trying to control my pounding heart. *I need to get away.* I knew all too well what awaited me if I did not.

I went through a list of all my friends who I might be able to stay with if I ran away from home but came up lacking. *None of them would shelter me if they knew the truth.* I chased away a rogue thought that perhaps I should run off into the Shrouded Woods and join the riffraff that I knew lived there. I was aware the Woods were home to thieves and troublemakers, but I also knew that my father had gone into them hunting magic users at least once. *Maybe someone there could help me?*

When we reached the docks, though, I knew it was too late.

Kirstein harbour's busy docks were crawling with Breoch Guard. As soon as they spotted our ship, a dozen guns were pointed at us, and orders were yelled to come into harbour immediately. My heart in my throat, I watched as my brother obeyed. A young guard approached our boat once we were within speaking distance. "Jade?" he said.

Jade nodded. "Albert. What is this?"

"Magic out on the water, that's what. Someone chased away a storm. We're looking for the culprit."

"Well, you have her." Jade pointed at me. "My sister, Ruby."

My heart dropped into my stomach.

Albert's gaze turned to me, and he looked me over, surprise evident on his face. Then he chuckled. "You're a hard man, Jade, turning in your own family. All right, get your boat tied up."

My head began to spin as Jade got to work. *There's no way out.* I had water on one side, Breoch Guard on the other.

My brother worked methodically, avoiding my gaze. Gabby, on the other hand, glared at me, her eyes glittering with hatred. As soon as the boat was secure, one of the guards stepped onto the deck and grabbed my arm. Several others stood behind him, guns trained on me. My vision blurred with tears as the guard hauled me off the boat.

People began to crowd around as I was led to the waiting carriage, gawking at me as word spread on the docks of my capture. My wet dress had plastered itself to my body, making my curves more obvious, and a group of older men let out catcalls. One woman pulled her children close as I passed; on my other side, a child broke free of her father's grasp and spat at me. "Elfieblood, elfieblood!" she cried out in a singsong voice. My face burned, but I wasn't sure if it was from anger or shame. I forced myself to keep my head up, scanning the crowd, looking for an escape, a sympathetic passerby, *anything* to get me out of this.

Then my eyes landed on a familiar face. "Father!" I screamed. "Father, don't let them take me! I won't do it again, I swear!" My voice broke, tears running down my face. "Call them off, Father, please!"

But my father did not meet my eyes. He kept his head down, gaze averted. *He doesn't want the people to know it's him I'm screaming for,* I realized. My father, the second captain of the Breoch Guard, had a witch for a daughter. His fellow Guard would doubtlessly shame him for that.

Just before they hauled me into the carriage, I screamed out one last name in a desperate hope that my other brother was somewhere within earshot, and that, despite his past entanglements with the Breoch Guard, he would save me.

"Jasper!"

There was, of course, no answer.

CHAPTER 1

Six Months Later

BANISHING DAY WAS a joke on Yarel island. But I still wanted to see the fireworks.

There were, of course, no celebrations here. The day was a slap in the face to us, a reminder of what we'd become. What they'd turned us into.

I could feel the moods of the others when we'd gotten up earlier that morning to collect eggs from beneath the stubborn chickens. The tension and despair that I'd found to be so common here were thicker this morning, palpable, like clouds gathering on a horizon.

We'd set about our usual day. Those of us who were new arrivals attended a sign class each morning, taught by Starla and Matt and a rather bored guard. The rest of the day was spent working the massive garden that sprawled across our section of the island. It was too early in the year to be picking much more than peas, so we pulled weeds and tended to the strawberry plants, some of which showed their first signs of green fruit. We thinned out carrot seedlings and put fertilizer into the ground where we'd plant tomatoes next month. The garden was the easy work, we teens were told, and they gave us the easy jobs because we were likely still getting used to life without our dominant hands. The adults on the other side of the fence— who we rarely got to see— were given the hard jobs. But even those were preferable to the alternative.

I felt my own mood begin to dampen as we filed into the dining hall for supper. I'd been able to keep a better head than most since my arrival. Perhaps it was just that I was new. Or perhaps it was that this place, prison or not, was peaceful. But at every meal, I was reminded of the injustice of what had been done to me.

Working with one hand, I was adjusting to. Not being able to speak was frustrating, but I'd always been quiet. But eating without being able to taste my food properly was an insult that reared its head three times a day.

I sat between Alisa and Kaden and shoveled the tasteless food into my mouth, using my fork to move it to the back of my throat once I'd chewed it. We all did this; it was a trick we'd learned early on.

The thought of this evening's fireworks in Sylvenburgh came to mind again, and I nudged Alisa, pointing outside. *"I'm going to watch the fireworks,"* I told her using sign language. *"Will you come?"*

Alisa wrinkled her nose and shook her head. On my other side, Kaden looked absolutely disgusted with me. A few of the others were watching, and they shook their heads too.

I knew why they didn't want to join, of course. Why witness the celebration of the very law that had put us here, robbed of our hands and tongues? It made no sense. And yet, it was hard for me to resist. *I'll just have to go by myself,* I decided.

An hour later, the sky was nearly dark, and I sat on a cliff overlooking the water. I wasn't sure if I'd be able to see the fireworks from here, but I had to try. I could see the dark forests that edged this part of mainland Breoch easily enough. Sylvenburgh was a little inland from here, but a few of its taller towers were visible from this vantage point, their spires poking above the treetops.

I heard a noise from behind and turned to see Starla watching me. She gestured at the spot next to me, and I nodded. *"Sit,"* I signed.

Starla sat down, and I studied her. She had been assigned to watch over the teens, so she was one of the only adult krossemages I'd met. I guessed her to be in her late thirties; her black curls had yet to grey, but I could see the beginnings of smile lines around her mouth. She was likely pretty at one time, I thought, before the fire took her.

I had no idea what had happened to Starla before she came here— none of us did— but her face was marred with burn scars, which stood out pink and puckered against her light brown skin. Most of the left side of her face was permanently reddened, her eye drooping and near useless. Scars snaked down her left arm onto her one remaining hand, and she'd lost her left foot, which was now replaced by a peg leg. I imagined that they'd put her in charge of the teens because she wouldn't be much use doing hard labour.

"You're here to watch the fireworks?" Starla signed.

I eyed her and nodded. *"The others think I'm crazy for liking them."*

She shrugged. *"I used to like watching fireworks with my family when I was young, so they bring back good memories for me."*

As Starla signed, I heard the unexpected screech of a raptor, and I looked up to see a red-tailed hawk perched in a tree nearby. *"That's odd. I didn't think hawks were out this late."*

Starla nodded. *"That bird has been following me around for the last few days. No idea why."*

A burst of colour in the night sky interrupted our conversation, and the hawk let out another screech before flying away. We sat back and watched the fireworks light up the night. Starla was afraid of fire when it was close to her; I'd figured out this much by watching her hesitate when she had to blow out candles or bank the fire at night— but she seemed to be able to enjoy it from a distance.

I felt my chest constrict as I remembered watching these same fireworks as a child, my two brothers huddled up against me as we sat on the rooftop of our home. I didn't miss home— at least, not what it had become— but it was hard not to think of the days when we'd felt like a family.

The fireworks began to fizzle out, and Starla stood. Then she frowned and walked over to the edge of the cliff, where she looked back at me. *"Is that a boat coming toward our island?"*

I joined her at the cliff's edge and followed her gaze to where the moonlight glinted off something small that approached the beach immediately below us. *"Hard to say from up here. It could just be a big log."*

"If it is a boat, then whoever's in it isn't using the docks, which tells me

they're trying to sneak onto the island."

I snorted. *"Now why would anyone want to do that? Sneaking off the island in a rowboat, I could see. But sneaking* on*?"*

Starla nodded. *"It doesn't make any sense."* As she signed, I became aware of haunting piano music coming from behind me, a simple yet poignant melody that I knew by heart. I looked down at the ramshackle farmhouse where all the teens lived, then glanced at Starla. She gave me a smile. *"Let's go,"* she signed. *"She's waiting for you."*

"You think she'll want to play with me? I'm pretty sure she's mad at me right now."

Starla shrugged. *"There's only one way to find out."*

I wasn't sure if the folks who set this place up left the old piano in the farmhouse out of laziness because they thought it might be a source of entertainment, or, conversely, as a sadistic reminder that none of us would be able to play well ever again, but we krossemages were a resilient bunch. We had found ways around the limitations that were forced on us, sometimes working together on tasks that required two hands. And that was exactly how Kaden and I overcame the challenge the piano presented.

We first met a few weeks after I'd arrived on the island. It was a cold, late fall evening, and we teens were huddled in the farmhouse living room, having finished our work for the day. Evenings were incredibly boring when it was too cold to be outside, I'd quickly learned. Most of the other kids knew enough sign language that they could sit in groups and socialize, while others practiced doodling or writing with stolen pencils. A fellow about my age named Tass had mastered doing pushups with the stump of his right hand resting on a book and spent most evenings in a corner alternating between those and crunches, intent on getting stronger. There were a few dusty, dog-eared books that had made their way into the farmhouse, but those were read in secret, as most of them had been stolen from the guards.

It was likely boredom that propelled me towards the old piano that evening. I didn't know enough sign language yet to talk to the others fluently. So I pulled out the dusty old bench and lifted the lid of the piano. The keys were yellowed, a few of them chipped. I put my fingers on the cool ivory and tentatively tested out a chord.

Nearly everyone looked up as I then played a series of chords. The piano was a bit out of tune, but I smiled nonetheless. I found myself playing the lower part of a popular childhood duet, without thinking.

Then I felt someone settle next to me on the bench. I looked over to see a girl who I'd only noticed from a distance, wiry with mahogany skin, a narrow face and tight black curls. She gave me a grin and began playing the upper part of the song. When we were finished, everyone in the room slapped their thighs wildly in the only sort of applause they could give.

Ever since then, Kaden and I had been nearly inseparable. We'd been each other's solace for the first months of my time here, most of our days spent on the piano, lying on the beach at night watching the stars, or in conversations signed with increasing speed.

Kaden was more volatile than me; she was full of big emotions, and when she was angry, everyone knew about it. But she also smiled big and laughed easily, and signed in sweeping, dramatic gestures. She was a little over a year younger than me, and neither of us talked about what would happen when I turned eighteen in a year and a half. It was possible we might both get posted to the adult side of the farm and reunite once she aged out of the teen section, but we might very well not be that lucky.

The hope, of course, was that we'd manage to escape before then. To our knowledge, no one had ever gotten away from the farm before. But there were rumours of people who'd escaped the pursuit of the Breoch Guard. There was one particular story, told in hastily signed conversations out of sight of the guards, about a girl who could cast with her mind, who'd run away from her school, outwitted the Guard numerous times, and had eventually been captured and taken aboard a Guard ship, only to evade their grasp once again. And if a teenage girl could do that much, I figured fleeing the island couldn't be that hard. And so Kaden and I concocted elaborate, unlikely escape plans, writing them on stolen scraps of paper, in hopes of one day making a run for it.

Now I could hear her playing away on the piano as I approached the farmhouse, Starla behind me. Kaden was a much better pianist than me; she could make incredible music with just her left hand and knowledge of how to use the foot pedals. But when I was there, I could play chords to round out her melodies. We worked better as a team.

I made my way into the large but sparsely furnished living room where Kaden was playing. With the warmer and longer evenings, many of the other teens were still outdoors.

Those who were gathered glanced up as I entered. Some smiled, others glared. There were a few who definitely didn't approve of my choice to go watch the fireworks. Ignoring them, I slid onto the bench next to Kaden and began adding my chords into the song. Kaden gave me a quick glance and frowned but continued playing.

I could hear murmuring behind me and glanced back to see that a pair of guards had made their way into the farmhouse to watch Kaden and me. They were both young; one was lean and dark haired, and the other was blond. I shot them a wary glance.

The dark-haired one laughed. "By all means, keep playing," he said. "You're doing a great job."

I raised an eyebrow; these were certainly relief guards. Normal guards watched the perimeter of the farmhouse in the evenings but left the interior to Starla and Matt, the man who supervised the boys. They would only come inside if there was a disturbance, and they certainly wouldn't go complimenting us on our piano playing. *They probably wouldn't be watching the beach too closely, either,* I mused. *Which would make tonight the perfect time for someone to sneak onto the island in a little rowboat.*

Kaden glanced at me, shrugged, and returned to playing. I joined her, trying to ignore the odd feeling I had about what Starla and I had witnessed. *It was probably nothing,* I assured myself. *And there's no point in getting worried about it.*

Half an hour later, I was sitting on my narrow cot in the large room where all the girls slept. Alisa and Shawnie were perched on the cot opposite from me, his arm slung casually around her shoulders. We weren't supposed to date, but the only adult who ever came up this way was Starla, and she didn't seem to care, so long as Shawnie headed up to the boys' dorm at curfew. Alisa and Shawnie were two of the oldest teens on the farm; they were both nearly eighteen and had both been here since they were thirteen. Shawnie played with Alisa's short, dark hair, his olive skin contrasting with her fair, freckled complexion. *"How were the fireworks?"* Alisa signed to me.

I shrugged. *"They were pretty. A bit further away than I'd like, though."*

"I still don't understand why you needed to go watch them." Kaden plopped down on the cot on the other side of me and frowned.

I sighed. *"It's complicated."* I could try explaining my reasons to her, but I doubted she'd understand.

I tried to make the best of our situation, reminding myself of all the things that I'd hated about my life before I was hauled off to the farm. Alisa threw herself into taking care of the younger girls, acting like a second mother to several of them. But Kaden was angry about what had been taken from her. And she had no problem letting that anger show.

"They're a symbol of what was done to us," Kaden went on, glancing at her stump. *"How can you enjoy them?"*

Unable to find the words to explain, a familiar ball of anxiety began to roll in my stomach. *She's mad at me. I hate when people are mad at me.*

"Oh, leave her alone, Kaden," Alisa scolded. *"Everyone deals with these things differently."*

Kaden rolled her eyes and flopped down on the cot.

"I saw something else while I was watching the fireworks," I told them, trying to change the subject ever so slightly. *"A rowboat coming toward the island. At least that's what I think it was."*

Shawnie shrugged. *"So? It's an island. Boats are the only way to access it."*

"Yes, but this boat wasn't heading for the docks, it was headed for the beach just below the bluffs. If it was a rowboat, then whoever was in it was trying to sneak onto the island."

His eyes narrowed. *"Why would anyone do that?"*

"Exactly what I was wondering."

Our conversation was cut short by Starla banking the fire, which meant it was time to head to our cots. Alisa and Shawnie slid off her bed and went to the landing to say goodnight. On my other side, Kaden refused to look at me. I reached a foot toward her cot to poke her with my toe, and she turned toward me, her expression still disdainful. *"That boat could be useful,"* I told her.

Instantly, her expression changed, and she sat up. *"For running away, you mean?"*

I nodded, thankful that I'd managed to distract her from her annoyance. *"We should go down to the beach in the morning and see if it's still there. Maybe we can steal it and hide it somewhere until we're ready to run away."*

Her eyes narrowed. *"But where would we hide a boat?"*

"I don't know. But I'm sure we can figure something out." I gave her a small smile. *"Perhaps it's a good thing I watched the fireworks?"*

Kaden rolled her eyes again, but she returned my smile before lying back down. I felt a weight lift off my chest as I pulled the scratchy wool blanket over myself.

Some time later, I was pulled from my sleep by the sound of someone crying out and gasping. I heard Starla rise and walk over to the cot. *Nightmares.* We all had them here; it was completely normal to wake up in the night to cries and howls and sobbing. Mostly we ignored it, allowing whoever it was the dignity of pretending they hadn't woken us.

There were exceptions, though. Kaden and I would comfort one another when we woke up to the other's cries, and there were a few other girls who were also often there for one another. And then, of course, there was Starla, who nearly always woke up and came to comfort us. Starla, it seemed, did not have the nightmares anymore. Perhaps it was her age, or perhaps it was that life on the farm was considerably better than whatever she'd been taken from.

I imagined that many of the others had nightmares about losing their hands and tongues. I suppose I'd been lucky in that regard. It was only in the last few years, I understood, that anyone who was made into a krossemage was given a strong drink before the amputation. And being tiny like I was, that drink rendered me nearly unconscious. I had very little memory of what came after.

The pain the next morning, however, I did remember— the stickiness of blood in my mouth without being able to taste its iron tang, the phantom pains that went on for weeks, all accompanied by a searing, pounding headache from the alcohol. So my own nightmares were not about the amputation; they were always about the boat trip that had preceded it. In my dreams, I relived the storm that nearly capsized our boat, the casual banter about slaying magic users, the hate in Gabby's eyes when she realized I was one. Jade torn between the two of us, his family ties challenged by his new allegiances. And Father looking away as I was hauled off, ashamed of the magic that ran in my blood.

Ashamed of me.

I imagined I'd rather have nightmares about having my hand cut off.

Starla, hearing the girl with the nightmare was breathing normally now, returned to her cot. I closed my eyes again, my thoughts drifting to a song I wanted to teach Kaden. I had nearly fallen back asleep when I heard a new set of footsteps.

A moment later, a hand clapped over my mouth. My eyes flew open, and I let out a small, involuntary cry. "Shhh," a male voice hissed in my ear. "Don't make a sound. I'm here to get you out, Ruby."

My eyes widened at the sound of my name. The young man's features were hard to see in the near-dark, but I thought I saw the outline of a mop of curls.

"It's Jasper," he whispered. "Come on, let's get you out of here."

CHAPTER 2

JASPER? **MY HEAD** spun as I let him pull me to my feet and out of the girls'
dorm. I followed him mechanically, unsure whether I should fight or acquiesce.
It can't actually be Jasper, can it? How did he get here? I found myself thinking
of the boat that Starla and I spotted earlier. *Was that him?*

Jasper— if it really was Jasper— paused on the landing, where moonlight
shone through the large window, illuminating his features. I stared at him for a
moment, dazed. His hair was longer than I remembered, and his beard had grown
large and bushy, but I certainly recognized the blue eyes, the boyish smile. *It
really is him!* Without thinking, I threw my arms around my brother.

He returned my embrace for a few moments, holding me tight against him as
if afraid I would slip from his grasp. "I'm so glad I found you, Ruby," he
whispered as he pulled away. "We need to get out of here, now."

Wait. I pulled away from him and stared back at the girls' dorm. *I need to
bring Kaden.* I tugged on Jasper's sleeve and pointed to her cot.

He glanced back and shot me a confused look. "What?"

I pointed again, and he sighed. "I don't know what you want, Ruby. Come
on." He motioned urgently at the stairs. I looked from him to the dorm, my heart
in my throat. Tears pricked at my eyes. *This might be my only chance at escape.
But I can't just abandon Kaden. She'll have no idea where I went.* I looked to
Jasper once more and then started back toward the dorm.

His hand closed around my wrist. "Listen, Ruby," he hissed, "I'm not sure
what you're trying to go back for, but we don't have time for this. If you go back
into that room, you'll risk waking people up. Now let's *go.*" He began to pull me
toward the staircase.

I had little choice but to stumble after him. *I'll come back for you,* I promised
Kaden silently as we made our way down the stairs and out of the farmhouse.

We crept through the dark towards the sea, the moon shining bright and full above
us. Jasper led me to a willow tree whose branches grew out over the water. "In
here," he whispered, disappearing between the hanging branches. I followed him
and found a tiny rowboat waiting for us. I raised my eyebrows; it seemed we'd
been right about the mysterious object on the water.

Jasper waded in and pulled the boat with him so only the bow remained on
land. "Climb in."

"You there! What are you doing?" a male voice called out from beyond the
shore.

Jasper swore. "Get down, Ruby. Hide in the boat; I'll deal with him."

Jasper dashed out of the tree cover. I ducked into the boat and watched
through the willow branches as a young guard charged in our direction. Jasper

stayed crouched in the shadows until the guard was within striking distance, then he sprung. The guard cried out as Jasper tackled him head-on, knocking him to the ground easily with a kick to the knee and then pinning him.

"Help!" the guard began to cry, only to have his voice muffled by what I imagined was Jasper's hand. He grunted and thrashed about, clearly helpless against my brother's weight and superior training. I heard the guttural sound of choking, then the guard was quiet.

When Jasper joined me once again, I gaped at him. "He's not dead," he assured me. "Just unconscious. Someone will have heard that though; we need to move." He climbed in behind me and took the oars, using them to push off. The cool night air bit into my skin through my nightgown, and I shuddered. "Right," Jasper said, reaching behind him. "Here, put this on." He passed me a cloak. I took it from him, and my eyes widened in recognition. *It's my travelling cloak from home.* "Don't worry, I brought you other clothes. I have a camp set up in the woods."

More shouts sounded from the retreating shoreline, and Jasper huffed. "Here they come." He began to row faster, panting from exertion. My heart in my throat, I turned around and watched as several of the guards ran down the dock and piled into a rowboat. *If only I could help somehow.*

Then I recalled the plans I'd made with Kaden.

As the men pushed off from the dock, I tentatively raised my left hand. I moved my wrist in a small, familiar motion and closed my eyes. Instantly, I felt the wind in my mind, its power tugging at my consciousness. I nudged it in the direction of the approaching boat, and bid it to blow harder, keeping the guards successfully at bay.

When I opened my eyes, Jasper was staring at me. "Did you do that? You can't cast with your mind, can you?"

I hesitated for a moment, debating whether to trust him with this information, and then waved my remaining hand.

"Right. You're left handed. I forgot."

I shrugged. Most of the time *I* forgot I was left-handed; the teachers in school had insisted I learn to use my right hand. Father and Jade must have forgotten as well, seeing as neither of them told the guards who took me away.

Jasper adjusted his angle so he was not rowing directly into the wind. "I suppose that's a flaw in the krossemage system, huh? Doesn't account for folks like you."

I nodded, keeping my eyes on the boat behind us.

"We'll beat them to the shore, but they've got enough gain on us that they might be able to follow on foot," Jasper said. "At least they don't have guns." He paused. "Wait."

Jasper pulled the oars across the boat and reached under his seat. When he sat up, he was holding a small flintlock. He aimed it at the guards' boat, and my eyes widened. *Is he going to start shooting?*

The shot rang out across the water. The men began to curse, and I turned to squint into the night, unable to see exactly what had happened.

Then I saw them bailing water out of the rowboat, and I realized Jasper had shot a hole in its side. He sighed and returned the gun to its place. "Well, that bought us a bit of time, at least. Once we're ashore, we'll have to make a run for the woods."

He returned to rowing, keeping an eye on the boat that sank behind us. When we reached the shore a few minutes later, Jasper leapt out and pulled the boat onto land, then reached out and grabbed my hand. "Come on," he said, motioning to the forest just beyond the beach.

He began to run, and I let him pull me along. Tears pricked at my eyes once again, and I tried, but failed, to hold back a sob. Jasper heard me and gave my hand a squeeze. "Ah, Ruby. You're safe now. You're away from that place, and I'm going to get you fixed up, I promise."

My eyes narrowed. *Get me fixed up?*

"I'll explain once we get to camp," he said. "Come on, we need to hurry."

We ducked into the woods, and Jasper's pace slowed a bit, though he was still moving faster than I'd have liked, leading us through a maze of twists and turns. I nearly tripped on a tree root, and branches whipped at my face. The moon shone down through the trees, casting odd shadows.

After what felt like a good hour of stumbling through the forest, we broke into a small clearing where a tent and fire ring were set up. A horse, which looked to be asleep, stood tethered nearby. Jasper motioned that I should sit on a fallen log as he lit a small lantern. "I'd get us a fire going, but that'd give us away."

I nodded.

"Sorry I wasn't able to get to you sooner," he went on, sitting down next to me. "I wish I'd been there when they took you. I might've been able to stop them, or convince Jade not to turn you in…" He shook his head. "Can't do much about the past, though. I got you out, and now we need to get you fixed up. Do you know where the Isle of Dundere is?"

I nodded, recalling the small island colony to the northeast of Breoch.

"Well, rumour has it that the governor of Dundere is a healer."

I cocked my head. *Healing magic exists?*

Jasper caught my expression. "I know, I'd never heard of healers either until a few years back. But then I met a few folks who were willing to travel all the way to Dundere to visit a healer, so that a blind girl could get her sight restored. I don't know if it worked, but I'm sure hoping so, given that my plan is to take you to see her as well." His shoulders hunched. "Getting you there might be tricky though. There aren't as many ships that travel the route as I thought, and the ones that take passengers are expensive. Most of them would refuse to take you as a passenger once they noticed your…condition. I could pass you off as my personal servant, but then they'd put you to work scrubbing decks and catching rats and cleaning out the bilge. And I've heard rumours about how the crew sometimes treats female krossemages." He shook his head in disgust, and I shuddered.

"There's one other option," he continued. "I know of a certain ship that might take us both as passengers, but I'm not sure how often it sails or where it stops. But I do know of a fellow who would likely have that information, and who might be able to get us onto that ship. Problem is, I don't know where he lives— somewhere in the Shrouded Woods, I think?"

I frowned. *We're going into the Shrouded Woods?*

"Fortunately, I remember hearing that his brother is the vice-principal of

Sylvenburgh Academy. So the plan is to head there in the morning, see if this fellow can put us in contact with his brother, and then hope they can get us onto the ship. There are a lot of unknowns, but it's the best I can do for now." He glanced up at the moon that shone through the branches above us. "We should get some sleep."

I nodded, stifling a yawn, and he motioned at the tent. "Go on in. I'll join you in a few minutes."

Obediently, I shuffled over to the tent and crawled inside. There were plenty of blankets piled in one corner; I grabbed a few of them and wrapped myself up. I could hear Jasper putting things away outside. A few minutes later, he extinguished the lantern, then joined me in the tent, now in his own nightclothes.

Jasper's breathing evened out quickly, and I was left alone with my thoughts. Here I was, free from the prison that had been my home for the past six months, and perhaps on my way to being healed. But a thousand questions danced about in my mind. *Where will we go after Dundere?* Clearly home was not an option. *Who are these folks Jasper wants to ask for help? And what am I going to do about Kaden? She'll be so scared when she wakes up and realizes I'm gone.*

This time, when the tears pricked at my eyes, I let them come, sobbing quietly into my blanket. I'd been told I was safe. But if this was true, why was I more terrified now than I'd been since my arrival at the farm?

I awoke the next morning to the sound of Jasper putting logs on the fire and sat up to stretch my legs; I wasn't used to sleeping on the ground, and a rock had dug into the side of my thigh while I slept.

I emerged from the tent to see the fire already burning nicely, a large pot suspended over the flames. Jasper was hunched over it; he looked up and gave me a quick smile when he saw me. "Morning, Ruby. Ready to head to Sylvenburgh?"

I pointed at my rumpled nightgown.

He nodded. "I have some clothes for you. We're going to go to the Academy in disguise. I'll be a Breoch Guard, and you'll be my assistant." He glanced down at the pot. "Can you eat oatmeal?"

I nodded; that was one of the easier things for me to eat.

"Good. I'm not the best cook. I hope it tastes all right."

I let out a bitter laugh at his words. He glanced at me and blinked for a moment, then shook his head. "Of course. I forgot. Well, perhaps it's for the best that you can't taste if you have to endure my cooking." He attempted a smile as he ladled porridge into my bowl. He passed it to me and then got a bowl for himself.

There were still many questions in my mind, and when I finished eating, I stood, picked up a stick, and began to write in the dirt.

How did you find me?

"I learned about the farm in Guard training. All the teenagers who are…well, you know," he gestured at my stump, "get sent to that camp. So when I found out you'd been taken, I knew that's where you'd end up." He sighed then. "It took me a while to get myself together enough to make a decent rescue plan. I was a bit of a mess at that point."

I nodded knowingly and raised an eyebrow.

"But I managed to get myself sober and off of teakflower, because now I had something motivating me. And once my head was in a better place, I started planning. I knew the best way to get to you would be to go in disguised as one of the guards. And I figured Banishing Day, when the substitute guards were on duty, would be the best time."

I nodded, taking in his story. *I'm glad you're doing better,* I wrote in the dirt.

He nodded and offered a thin smile. "We don't need to leave camp until after lunch. I want to get us to the Academy as classes are ending. There's a river a little ways to the left of here, so you can wash up there. I'll fetch your clothes for you." He stood and retrieved a small pack from one of the horse's side bags. "I figure the blue outfit would be the most ideal for a Guard assistant."

I nodded and began rifling through the familiar dresses. There was the soft brown wool dress that was well suited for travelling, a flowered white dress that I'd often worn to school functions, a pink silk number that seemed far too fancy for travel, and the crisp blue pinafore and white blouse that he'd mentioned, along with several pairs of stockings and shoes. I took the suitcase with me and followed the noise of the water until I found the river. It was clear and not too fast moving, and I shivered as I dipped a toe in. I was used to bathing in cold water— that's all we had on the farm— but this was chilly even for me.

Quickly, I stripped out of my nightgown and plunged into the water, gasping. I only stayed in long enough to wash up and then made my way to the bank, shivering, to dry off.

Putting on the outfit that Jasper provided proved difficult. I'd learned how to fasten buttons with one hand, but the pinafore had a tie in the back that I couldn't manage myself. I ran a brush through my hair, then returned to camp with the pinafore untied and gestured to Jasper that I needed help.

He nodded. "Just let me finish this." He was in the middle of trimming his beard down to a more reasonable length, using a mirror he'd brought. "There. I think I look a bit less like a ruffian now."

I smiled, then gestured for him to pass me the mirror. There were none on the farm, and I hadn't seen my reflection in months. Studying myself now, I could see that my cheekbones were more prominent than before. My skin, which was once pale, had taken on a tan from all the time working outside. *And my hair...* I sighed and shook the short blond curls.

"It'll grow back," Jasper said as he tied up my pinafore. "Hair does that. See?" He ran a hand through his mop of curls and grinned.

I nodded and looked in the mirror once more. "I think our hair is about the same length now," Jasper mused.

He's right. I was struck by how similar we looked. His eyes were blue and mine were hazel, but other than that, the resemblance was uncanny. Jade was handsome in the classical sense, tall with broad shoulders and a strong jaw. Jasper and I, on the other hand, were the sort that people referred to as "cute", always mistaken for being a bit younger than we really were, and we shared the same large eyes and quick smiles. Jasper had always known how to play up his features, using his natural charm to accentuate his boyish looks and attract girls, whereas I'd always been too shy to flirt.

"I brought you something, because I figured this might be an issue," Jasper told me, presenting me with a hat that matched my dress. I nodded and perched it on my head, then glanced in the mirror again. *It'll have to do.*

Satisfied, Jasper went down to the river to wash up, and my eyes widened when he returned, clad in his old Breoch Guard uniform. He glanced at me uncertainly. "I hope it's not too hard for you to see me like this. It's only for a few hours."

We spent the rest of the morning packing up camp, then ate a quick lunch. When we were finished, we climbed atop the horse and began making our way out of the woods.

After about an hour of riding, the gates of Sylvenburgh came into view, and soon we were traversing the crowded city streets. Jasper took the long route across town, avoiding going anywhere near our old home or the Breoch Guard garrison.

It was close to midafternoon when we finally reached the gates that led to the towering stone buildings of Sylvenburgh Academy. Jasper kept his head high as we passed through the gates and down the cobbled path. A stable hand greeted us and asked if he could take our horse; Jasper helped me down and nodded.

"All right," he said to me as the horse was led away, "we need to act confident, just like Mother taught us. Head up, walk tall. I'm Richie Nickelson of the Breoch Guard. And you are not a scared, exhausted krossemage, you're my assistant. Whatever you do, do not call me Jasper."

I gave him a confused look and pointed to my throat.

"Right. I keep forgetting you can't talk." Jasper looked me over. "Maybe keep your right…arm…in your pocket."

I nodded and watched as my brother straightened up to set off towards the school, all confidence and poise. *Just like Mother taught us.* My brothers were always better at this particular lesson than I was; hiding my emotions was never a strength of mine. But I swallowed the lump in my throat anyway and followed my brother, purposely lengthening my stride. Putting the stump of my right hand into my coat pocket, I lifted my chin and followed Jasper into the school.

Sylvenburgh Academy's large foyer was painted with dark tones, and dominated by a sweeping curved staircase made of rich wood and a large chandelier. School had just let out by the looks of it; a throng of students made their way across the foyer and up the stairs, where I imagined the dormitories were. I didn't miss the glances some of them threw at Jasper's uniform. They knew exactly what he was. Or what he used to be.

Jasper stopped a passing teacher and asked her in a crisp voice where the principal's office was located. She threw him a nervous look and pointed down a hallway. Jasper nodded his thanks, and we made our way to the double doors at the end of the hall.

Through the doors was a large office space, also crafted with dark wood. A grey-haired receptionist sat at a massive desk; she looked at us over a pair of spectacles. "May I help you?"

Jasper offered her a nod. "Yes, ma'am. My name is Richie Nickelson of the Breoch Guard, and this is my assistant Ruby. We are looking to speak with Tomlin Jeffries. There's word of magic in the school. Again." He gave her a stern look.

The receptionist looked down at her papers and muttered something, then met his eyes. "He's in his office. I'll see if he has time to speak with you." I didn't miss the sharpness in her tone.

"I should certainly hope he has time," Jasper replied smoothly. The secretary huffed, stood up, and disappeared through a door.

When she returned a moment later, she looked us over. "He'll see you."

I followed Jasper into a room whose entire left wall was covered in books. The man sitting at the desk rose to greet us. He was several inches taller than my brother, with sandy brown hair that was beginning to grey at the temples and an impressive mustache. He looked us over with a pair of deep-set brown eyes. "Officer Nickelson, I assume?"

He nodded and extended a hand. "Mr. Jeffries?"

Tomlin looked him over as they shook, then gestured to a couch and two armchairs stationed by the bookshelves. "Come, sit down. What's this I hear about magic in my school?"

"Close the door, Ruby," Jasper said to me. I nodded, obeyed, then perched on the couch next to my brother.

Jasper looked Tomlin over, squaring his shoulders. "Sir, I'm actually here to ask for your help."

Tomlin raised his eyebrows and sat back in his chair. "My help? With what exactly?"

"I'm not a working Breoch Guard. I was at one time, but some things have happened that changed my views on magic. This being the main one." He gestured at me then. "Show him what they did to you, Ruby."

I took my right arm out of my pocket. "My sister is a magic user. They took her, and, well, you can see what they did."

Tomin looked me over and nodded gravely. "I'm sorry. But I don't understand, why are you coming to me for help?"

"I've heard that you're sympathetic to magic users, sir. It's not actually you I'm looking for though, it's your brother Lachlann. But I have no idea how to find him."

"And what can Lachlann do for you?"

"I heard that he once helped a couple of your students escape Breoch to get to the Isle of Dundere. And I've also heard about a healer in Dundere who might be able to fix my sister up."

"Ah. I see." He sat back in his chair. "You're in luck. Lachlann has been away, but he's meant to come home tonight."

"So you can take Ruby to him, then?"

I turned to Jasper, eyes narrowing. *You're not coming?*

Tomlin frowned. "Don't you want to accompany your sister to Dundere?"

Jasper turned to me. "I'm sorry, Ruby, I wasn't entirely honest with you about this part. I can't come with you."

I gaped at him.

"Why not?" Tomlin asked.

"There's bad blood between myself and some folks in Dundere, and I don't want to run into them," he replied.

My head spun. *He rescued me, and now he's going to abandon me?* I shook my head, tears springing to my eyes.

"I don't think your sister likes this idea much," Tomlin observed.

I shook my head frantically and began to motion for a pen and paper. Tomlin brought me a pen and a small blank notebook, and I glared at Jasper before beginning to write. *I can't believe this! You're going to abandon me? If you don't come with me to Dundere, then I'm not going either.*

I passed the book to Jasper; he read what I wrote and winced. "You don't have much choice, Ruby. You can't stay here. Dundere's the only place that's safe for you."

But you do *have a choice,* I wrote. *And you're choosing to leave me.*

Jasper shook his head. "Ruby, you don't understand, I…"

"Why don't you come back to the farmhouse with us, at the very least," Tomlin suggested. "Lachlann's recently learned to sign; it'll be easier for you two to work this out with him around to translate."

Jasper shook his head. "That's a bad idea."

"Why?"

He sighed. "That's the other reason I can't come along. Lachlann's not likely to want to bring me. He and I have had some skirmishes in the past, too." He pointed at his uniform. "As I say, former Breoch Guard."

Tomlin let out a huff. "So let me see if I understand this correctly, young man," he said, his voice shifting into what I was certain was the tone he used to lecture students. "You were hoping to leave your sister in Lachlann's care, without him having any knowledge of her connection to you, correct? And you were hoping that, thanks to her inability to speak, he wouldn't find out about her familial ties until she'd already been healed?"

Jasper looked down at his hands. "That's about right, sir."

"Well, Ruby's not going anywhere until Lachlann knows the whole truth of the matter. We're all going back to the farm together."

Jasper let out a long sigh of resignation.

"Before that, though, you're going to prove to me that you're not afraid of magic," Tomlin went on. He turned to me, his tone softening. "How do you feel about becoming invisible?"

CHAPTER 3

AN HOUR LATER, we pulled up in front of a large farmhouse outside the city's walls. The air smelled fresh and crisp, rather like the air on the island. I swallowed a lump in my throat as I thought about Kaden. *I hope she's not too worried about me.*

"This is a nice place," Jasper said. He'd been attempting to make small talk with Tomlin the entire ride, clearly trying to calm his nerves about seeing Lachlann.

Tomlin nodded. "My grandfather built it; it's been in the family ever since."

"Who lives here?"

"Right now, just my mother and me, and Lachlann when he's in the area."

"You're not married, then? Never had your own place?"

"Well, aren't you nosy," Tomlin huffed.

"I prefer to say I'm curious."

Tomlin shook his head. "I had my own place at one time, but I moved back home after Father died. Someone needed to help keep the farm running. And no, never got married. Not everyone feels the need for marriage, you know. Are *you* married yet?"

Jasper shook his head. "I'm only twenty-three."

"My mother was married and pregnant with Lachlann and me when she was twenty-three." Tomlin shrugged. "Anyway, let's get you two inside. Lachlann should be home soon enough. Until then, I'm sure my mother will be all too happy to fuss over you."

We followed Tomlin through the main door of the house and into a small entryway. We took off our shoes and followed him down a hall into a large main room that housed both the living and dining areas. The ceilings were high and the walls lined with books, and a fire crackled in a massive stone hearth. The furniture looked to be hand carved from wood, and a pair of large swords sat crossed over top of the hearth. "Take a seat," said Tomlin. "I'll be back shortly with Mother." He disappeared from the room, and we did as he'd asked. I settled down on a couch, admiring the way the afternoon light painted the room in warm hues. This place was not as elegant as my parents' home, but it felt very welcoming.

Tomlin returned a few minutes later with a woman in tow. She was considerably shorter than her son but had the same warm, brown eyes. Her grey hair was pulled back into a braid, and she gave us a wide smile as she looked us over. "Richie, Ruby? I'm Helenne. It's an honour to have you in our home."

I gave the older woman a smile, and Jasper stood up to shake her hand. *Why hasn't he corrected her about his name?*

"Tom needs to go do some farm chores, but I can entertain you until Lachlann shows up," she went on. "I'll make you some tea."

"You're in good hands," Tomlin assured us. "I'll be back in an hour or so. Enjoy your tea."

A little over an hour later, Tomlin returned to the living room, dressed in farm clothes. Jasper had changed out of his Breoch Guard uniform, and he and I had been sipping on tea and eating biscuits for the past hour while Helenne chatted to us about the history of her home; her late husband Duncan who had built most of the furniture in the main room and who was skilled with a blade, pen and paper, and several types of magic; and how proud she was of both her sons, though she did wish that one of them had given her grandchildren. Tomlin returned to the conversation just in time to hear that and chuckled. "You'd best bother Lachlann about that, Mother. My students are all the children I need." Then he cocked his head. "Sounds like Lachlann's here."

Jasper sat up straighter as footsteps sounded down the hall. He turned to Tomlin. "I should probably let you know, my name's not really Richie."

"Oh? What is it then?"

Before he could reply, a voice that sounded very much like Tomlin's spoke from the hallway. "Sounds like we have some visitors."

The man who appeared in the doorway a moment later did look a lot like Tomlin. They were the same height and had the same warm, brown eyes. But this man was wilder looking than his brother. His hair hung to his shoulders, brown but with a touch more blonde than Tomlin's, and instead of a mustache he wore a full beard, also tinged with the first hints of grey. His clothes were less formal too, a tunic and breeches that looked to be hand sewn from rough brown cloth, topped by a simple leather jerkin. An odd-looking stone pendant hung around his neck, its surface engraved with strange whorls. I noticed he was missing his left hand; a hook sat in its place.

He stared at us for a moment, his eyes narrowing in confusion as he looked my brother over. Then he finally spoke. "Jasper?"

My brother stood up and let out a nervous laugh. "Lachlann, how are you?"

Jasper flinched visibly as Lachlann crossed the floor and stopped short in front of him, staring incredulously down at my brother. Lachlann was a good deal more muscular than his twin, I noticed, and looked as if he could easily injure Jasper in a fight. But Lachlann didn't move to harm him; instead, he stood back and shook his head. "What are you doing in my house?" He then whirled around to face Tomlin. "What is *he* doing in our house? Do you know who this fellow is, how much of a danger he could be to Mother? To you, even?"

Tomlin huffed. "Calm down, Lachlann. Obviously I don't know who he is. I only found out minutes ago that he's been lying to us about his name. I know you have a history with him, but that's about all."

"They seem like nice enough kids," Helenne put in, then approached her other son. "Good to see you too, by the way."

Lachlann let out an exasperated chuckle and put an arm around her. "Hello, Mother." I didn't miss how he angled her away from my brother, putting his body between the two of them. Then he turned back to Tomlin. "This is the bastard who shot Kip."

Jasper closed his eyes, letting out a barely audible sigh, and I frowned. *Who's*

Kip?

"Oh." Tomlin's eyes widened. *"That's* why you didn't want to tell me your real name." His eyes flickered to Jasper, then back to his brother. "Regardless, Jasper here says he needs your help."

"My help?" Lachlann snorted. "What makes you think I'd be willing to help *you?"*

"It's not me who needs your help, it's my little sister." Jasper met his eyes and squared his shoulders. "I wouldn't expect you to help me, Lachlann. But from what I saw of you back on the ship, you don't seem like one to turn away a kid in need, and—"

"Oh, enough with the flattery," Lachlann cut in. "This is your sister, I take it?"

Jasper nodded. "This is Ruby. She's a magic user. My older brother caught her and turned her in."

Lachlann's gaze travelled down to the stump of my right hand, and for a moment, I saw pity in his eyes. Then he turned back to Jasper and crossed his arms. *"Your* family has magic in it? You expect me to believe that? How do I know she isn't some poor krossemage you took off the street and are using to deceive me? And even if she is your sister, what do you expect me to do for her? I'm no lifebringer."

"No, but you know one."

Lachlann raised his eyebrows. "You want me to take her to Noelle?"

"Yes." Jasper's voice was tinged with exasperation. "I wouldn't have come here if I knew a better way to get Ruby to Dundere. I know she'll be safe on the Lady Liara, but I have no idea where the ship sails from, or even when. I figure you know that much, and that you and Kirilee might be willing to take her."

Lachlann closed his eyes for a moment. "Kirilee's not with us anymore," he said softly. "We lost her a good four years back, shortly after we last saw you."

"Oh." Jasper shook his head. "I...I'm sorry, I didn't know. What happened?"

"That's a very long story, and not one I feel like telling right now," he replied, his earlier brusqueness returning. He looked at me again. "Your sister— if she *is* your sister— I can likely help. But I'm not bringing you along."

"See?" Jasper said. "I told you it wasn't a good idea for me to come here. It would've been better if Lachlann didn't know I was involved."

"And yet Ruby here refuses to go to Dundere unless Jasper comes along," Tomlin put in.

"Why?" Lachlann turned to me. "Do you sign? I'm not very good, but I've been learning over the past few years." He signed the last sentence as he spoke, his gestures slightly halting.

I raised my eyebrows. *"Yes, I do sign,"* I replied. *"Like Tomlin said, if my brother can't come along, then I'm not going with you."*

Lachlann let out a sigh. "Why not?"

"Jasper is the only family I have left," I explained. *"He rescued me from the place I was being held. My..."*

"Sorry, not sure if I caught that," Lachlann cut in. "Did you say that Jasper *rescued* you?"

I nodded. "That's right," Jasper put in.

"Huh." Lachlann frowned. "All right, Ruby, go on. A bit slower, though, please."

I nodded. *My mother is dead, my oldest brother was the one who turned me in, and my father watched it happen and didn't stop it. I don't want to lose Jasper again.*

Lachlann sighed a second time. "Can I speak with you alone, Ruby?"

I nodded.

He gestured that I should follow him into an adjoining study, where he closed the door and looked me over. "Well," he said, his tone softening, "Jasper of all people has a magikai for a sister." He shook his head. "May I see what they did to you?"

I lifted my right arm hesitantly, and he took my stump in his hand. My skin tingled oddly when he touched me, and I felt a sudden deadening of noise, a loss of some sort of power. I flinched.

"Ah," he mumbled. "Sorry about that." He paused and took a deep breath, and the odd sensation subsided. "It's the anti-magic," he explained. "If I don't keep it in check, it can make magikai uncomfortable." My eyes narrowed as he let go of my arm. *Anti-magic?* "They cut out your tongue too?"

I nodded and opened my mouth to show him.

"Well, you're not lying about being a krossemage. But I want to be sure that Jasper is telling the truth. As I say, you could be some poor krossemage off the street. He could be using you to get to Dundere for, well, who knows why? But now that we're out of earshot, you can be honest with me." He met my eyes. "Are you in any danger from Jasper, Ruby? If you are, I can help you."

I shook my head vigourously.

"And he's actually your brother?"

I nodded. *"I swear it."*

"He rescued you from a prison colony?"

I nodded again.

"I wonder what caused his change of heart," Lachlann mused.

I pointed to myself.

"I don't doubt you were part of it. But the boy I knew four years back was pretty convinced that magic was evil. He wouldn't have gone out of his way to rescue you, sister or not." His eyes narrowed. "Do you know what happened between your brother and me to make me distrust him like this?"

I shook my head.

"Well, before I make my decision, you're going to hear about that." He sighed. "Is there anything else you need me to know?"

I frowned. As uncertain as I was about him, Lachlann seemed to be more willing to listen to me than my brother. I took a deep breath and began signing. *"I need to go back to the island soon. I have a friend there who I was planning to escape with before Jasper showed up. I want to rescue her."* My stomach knotted as I realized that I'd been so caught up in the day's events that I'd hardly thought of Kaden until now. *"I tried to get Jasper to bring her along, but he didn't understand what I was trying to say."* A single tear trailed down my cheek as I signed, and I wiped my eyes with my sleeve. *"I feel awful for abandoning her. She must be so worried about me..."* The tears were coming faster now, and I buried my face in the crook of my elbow, trying not to break down crying in front of this man I'd only just met.

"Hey." He put a hand on my shoulder. "It's hardly your fault that you couldn't communicate with Jasper. I don't know the best way to rescue your friend, but we'll figure something out, all right? Now come on, let's go talk to your brother."

We returned to the living room. It appeared that Helenne and Tomlin had retreated to the kitchen to make dinner, leaving us alone with Lachlann. "It's clear enough that you and your sister aren't lying," Lachlann said to Jasper, "but there are a few things I need to know before I agree to bring you along. It sounds like Ruby needs to hear a few things from you, as well."

Jasper raised an eyebrow. "Such as?"

"You haven't told your sister why I don't trust you, and if she's going to travel with us, I think she deserves to know."

"Right. She knows bits and pieces, but not everything."

"I want to hear your story as well," Lachlann continued. "I want to know what caused that cocky little Breoch Guard I met on a ship four years ago to change his mind so drastically." He was interrupted by Helenne calling us for dinner, and we all headed to the table.

Dinner smelled delicious, and from what little I could sense, it tasted delicious too. I'd learned early on that not having a tongue didn't completely rob me of being able to experience food— when I swallowed, there was a vague suggestion of sweetness or savoury flavour, but it was muted, like trying to hear underwater. Of course, the cooks on Yarel Island never bothered to spice our meals, so eating was a chore. Now, though, I could slightly detect the taste of roasted meat and spiced vegetables, so I ate my dinner slowly, savouring it all.

I noticed that Lachlann had replaced his hook with a fork attachment that screwed directly into a leather base, which allowed him to cut food with it and a knife like a two-handed person. He caught me staring and gave a wry smile. "I have a whole bunch of different attachments; I made them in my forge before I started anti-magic." He gestured at me with his fork. "I'd offer to lend you one, but I don't have another."

"She won't need one after we get to Dundere," Jasper pointed out. "If this healer can actually do what you say she can, that is." He eyed Lachlann skeptically. "Why hasn't she healed you? Didn't you used to have a magical metal arm? You threatened to punch me with it once."

"Right. I decided I wanted to learn anti-magic, and you can't practice anti-magic and have a working magical limb at the same time."

"You're doing anti-magic now?" Jasper stared at Lachlann. "That pendant that looks to be growing into your skin…is that part of it?"

Lachlann touched the small piece of stone. "It is. It's part of being a Bonded anti-mage."

"What's that?"

"It's complicated. I'll tell you about it on our way to Dundere— if I decide to take you, that is. But Noelle can easily heal Ruby's hand and tongue. In the time I've known Noelle, I've seen her restart the heart of a nearly dead fellow, fix a broken back, heal a man who'd managed to catch leprosy, and grow an entire arm from shoulder to fingertips for a girl born without one— not to mention fixing

Trina's eyes, of course." He glanced over at his brother. "Speaking of which, I think it's time for Ruby to hear about how Jasper and I got tangled up with those girls. I believe it starts with you."

I listened intently as Tomlin and Lachlann told the story of Saray and Trina's flight from Sylvenburgh Academy, and how they ended up travelling with Lachlann, Kirilee, and a boy named Kip who seemed rather fearful of magic. And I certainly didn't miss Jasper tensing up when Kip's name was mentioned. *Right. That's the fellow he shot.*

Lachlann explained how they'd ended up at a man named Willem's place, how Lachlann's injury caused them to be delayed there for a couple of months. After they were finished forging his magical metal arm, they embarked on a journey to a different part of the Shrouded Woods— and it was there, Lachlann said, that he first encountered a member of our family. "I only know some of the details of Willem's quarrel with your father," he said, "but it was clear enough that they hated each other, and that Willem was quite concerned by finding members of the Breoch Guard in the middle of the Woods. I didn't think I'd run into your father again, but a few weeks later, the Guard decided to crash my wedding." He raised an eyebrow. "I seem to recall giving your father a bloody nose that night."

"You *broke* it," Jasper corrected, and my eyes widened. I remembered that much clearly, Father coming home with a black eye and a crooked nose. *We're hoping to travel to Dundere with the fellow who did that to him?*

"Did I now?" Lachlann snickered. "Well, he deserved it. Then I think it was the next day that our paths crossed, Jasper." He sat back. "Tell me your side of what happened."

Jasper's shoulders hunched. "Well, I was nineteen at that point and brand new to the Guard. And I wanted to prove myself. Father knew that, so he had me hop on the Lady Liara. I was meant to get close to Saray and her friends, earn your trust, then lead you into a trap." One corner of his mouth turned up. "It worked, too. I was proud of myself for capturing Saray; I was expecting a celebration on the ship that night. But then we got to the docks, and…things changed." He glanced at Lachlann, then at me, his expression growing somber.

Lachlann nodded. "Tell her, Jasper."

"I'd taken Kip hostage to force Saray's cooperation. And when we reached the ship, the captain grabbed hold of Saray, turned to me, and told me to kill Kip." He averted his eyes when he spoke those last few words. "I didn't want to do it, you know. I'd never killed anyone before. And I hesitated. But Father told me I had my orders, and I couldn't see a way out. If I let Kip go, someone else would shoot him, and I might well lose my chance at becoming a respected Guard member. So…I shot him. And then Saray started screaming and threw fire at me." My brother eyed me. "I'm sure you remember me coming home from that, my face and arms all burned up, and my mind a mess."

I nodded slowly. I knew *something* happened to Jasper on that mission, but he'd always refused to talk about it. Then I frowned and turned to Lachlann. *"This Saray girl…is she the one who can cast with her mind?"*

He nodded. "You know of her?"

"There are stories about her on the island," I told him. *"A girl who could*

cast without any words or hand motions, who evaded the Breoch Guard and escaped their ship." I looked at Jasper, astounded. *"My* brother *was involved with all that?"*

Lachlann nodded again. "It sounds like Saray has become a bit of a legend on the island, and you're one of the bad guys," he informed Jasper.

Jasper huffed. "Of course I am."

"So what happened once Saray got taken onto the ship?" I asked.

Lachlann explained to me how Saray escaped her cell and came above deck to a fight between the Breoch Guard and a few members of Gareth's crew, and how Jasper had attempted one last time to keep her from escaping, only to be outwitted again. Jasper averted his eyes as Lachlann told the last part of the story, and when Lachlann was finished, Jasper sighed. "I still don't understand how she did that."

"Did what?"

"Saray managed to set the shrouds on fire from halfway across the ship. I knew she was talented, but I didn't see that coming."

"I don't fully understand it myself," Lachlann admitted. "But what happened after that? What did you do after you returned home from your failed mission?" I didn't miss the smug note in his voice.

Jasper crossed his arms. "Let's just say things got pretty dark for a while."

"If I'm going to trust you, Jasper, I need to know everything. What happened?"

Jasper hesitated, only willing to look at Lachlann out of the corner of his eye. "The moment I pulled the trigger on Kip, it…changed everything. And after I got home, I couldn't stop reliving it. I had nightmares. I started questioning everything I'd believed…" He put his face in his hands for a moment. "I got into some things that were bad for me. I started drinking too much, using teakflower." He eyed me again. "But when they took Ruby, that forced me to snap out of it. It took me longer than I would've liked to stop using the teak, and then to figure out how to rescue her, but here we are." His eyes met Lachlann's. "Is that enough information for you? Do you see now why I've changed?"

Lachlann nodded slowly. "Yes, I believe I do. I can certainly see how Ruby's predicament would have made you question your upbringing." He turned to me then. "So what happened to you, exactly? Tell me about your other brother turning you in."

I nodded and began to sign. *"Our older brother, Jade, is also Breoch Guard. A couple of years back, he married a childhood friend named Gabby, and she and her parents are members of a group called the Witch Slayers, who seem to hate magic users a little more than most folks."*

Lachlann raised his eyebrows as he translated and exchanged a meaningful look with Tomlin. "I haven't heard that name since we were kids," Tomlin said.

I could feel tears welling in my eyes and fought them off as I relayed the rest of my story to Lachlann. When he finished translating for me, Lachlann shook his head. "What sort of fellow just gives up his little sister?"

"One who's been influenced by some very bad people," Tomlin replied. "If Jade is a Witch Slayer like she's saying, then it makes sense." He turned to Jasper. "Was he always this extreme?"

Jasper shook his head. "Jade always tried very hard to fill Father's shoes. I think he felt a lot of pressure, being the eldest. So he's shared Father's views on magic for as long as I can remember. But it's only since he got involved in the Witch Slayers more recently that his beliefs have turned extreme."

"Those views came from his wife?" Helenne asked.

"His wife and her family," Jasper replied. "Gabby's father was a Breoch Guard back when she was very little. But he lost his job because too many magic users outwitted him, and for years after he had an awful job at a factory that paid nowhere near as well. So he hated magic users more than my family did because of all that, and his kids picked up on his views. I'm not sure when Gabby's family joined the Witch Slayers— I'm under the impression it was only in the past few years— but it doesn't seem out of character for them."

"That's sad," Helenne said. She looked over at me. "It must have been hard for you, watching your brother start believing those things."

I shrugged. *"It was scary,"* I signed. *"But I haven't felt close to Jade for years. It's hard to feel close to any of your family when they hunt people like you for a living."*

Lachlann raised his eyebrows and translated, and Jasper averted his eyes for a moment. Then he cleared his throat and looked at Lachlann. "So what about you then? What happened after Saray got back to Dundere?"

"Well, after we got Saray back, Trina's eyes were healed, as we'd hoped," he replied. "And after that, well, we lost Kirilee."

"You still don't want to talk about what happened?"

Lachlann shrugged. "The story involves some sensitive information. If you're coming to Dundere with us, then it might be best if you hear about it there. After that, I went home and then…"

"And then what?" Jasper asked.

"It's not important."

"Oh, come on! You just forced me to tell you how much of a mess I was after I shot Kip. And I was honest with you. You could at least give me the courtesy of doing the same."

"He's right, you know," Helenne put in.

Lachlann sighed. "Fine. I suppose that's fair." He closed his eyes for a moment, gathering the strength to continue. "After I lost Kirilee, I planned to start taking other young magic users over to Dundere so that they could be safe and learn to use their magic properly. But when I got home, I just…crashed. I shut myself in my forge and made swords for six months straight. I talked only to Mother and Tom. They became a little worried about me."

I exchanged a glance with Jasper. "That, uh, that sounds familiar," Jasper said, his voice turning sincere. "Our mother died a year and a half back, and Father reacted the same. Threw himself into his work, wouldn't talk to people much." He took a bite of his meal. "So what got you out of your forge?"

"It was Tomlin, actually. Well, him and a little guy named Frederick."

"One of the students at the Academy," Tomlin explained. "It's funny, right around when we got Saray out, there was an incident where a few older boys were bullying Frederick, accusing him of using magic to steal food. As it turns out, he was doing just that. I caught him doing it myself about a year later, and I took him to my office and told him he had a choice to make. He could stop practicing magic so long as he was in my school, or I could get him out and send him to Dundere. He chose the latter. So I went home and pulled my brother out of his forge and said that I needed him to get himself together, make good on his plans, and take a kid over to Dundere. It worked too."

Lachlann nodded. "Frederick and I set off into the Woods. I ended up running into all my old friends and contacts there, and I realized that they'd missed me. I began to understand that Kirilee wouldn't want me locking myself away from everyone. She'd want me to move on." He sat back in his chair. "So since then, I've been helping young magic users escape to Dundere. I still make swords and armour and sell them in both the Woods and the cities, but I've added a trip to Dundere every few months to my travels."

"Do you help the kids escape without telling their parents?" Jasper asked. "I imagine getting Saray and Trina out would've been simpler, given that they were orphans."

"I ask the student if they're comfortable with their parents knowing the situation," Tomlin explained. "Usually they are. Then I speak to their parents and ask permission to send their child to Dundere, where they'll be safe. The parents almost always say yes. If a student doesn't want their parents to know that they're a magikai, we get the student out, and the official story that we tell the parents is that the child was caught using magic and taken by the Breoch Guard. Those parents react predictably; they tend to disown their child as soon as they hear they're a magikai." He sighed. "It's hard for me to understand how parents can abandon their children so easily."

"Me too, though I don't doubt our parents would have done that exact thing. In fact, I suppose Father did do that, when he refused to help Ruby." Jasper exchanged a glance with me, and I blinked back tears. Then he cleared his throat and turned to Lachlann. "So you've heard what happened to Ruby, and what's caused me to change my mind about magic. Have you figured out yet whether you're willing to take us to Dundere?"

Lachlann nodded. "Well, it's clear enough to me that you've changed, and that Ruby needs our help. So fine, I'll take you both. But I'll be keeping an eye on you."

I grinned at the news. *"Thank you."*

"Most of the magikai I've taken to Dundere have ended up staying there for quite a while," Lachlann continued. "So you may want to figure out what you wish to do with yourself once we get there, Jasper."

"I doubt they'll even let me off the boat, given that the governor likely knows who I am."

"No idea." Lachlann scratched his head with his hook. "There's something else we should discuss, something that Ruby told me about earlier. She wants to go back to the island at some point to rescue a friend she left behind."

Jasper stared at me, bewildered. "Is that what you were going on about when I was trying to get you out? You wanted to go back for your friend?"

I nodded.

"Ah. Not sure if that little boat could've held another person anyway."

"And I doubt Jasper would be able to go fetch her in the same way he got you," Lachlann said to me. "I imagine that security on the island is heightened after your little escape. But once we get to Dundere, we can see if some of the folks there can help you, using their abilities."

I nodded again. As much as I didn't want to delay rescuing Kaden, that seemed reasonable.

"Will we be travelling on Gareth's ship?" Jasper asked.

"Most likely," he replied.

"Why not send them through the portal?" protested Helenne. "I'm sure Ruby here wants to get healed as soon as possible." My eyes narrowed. *A portal?*

"Yes, well, in order to use the portal, I'd have to go through Willem, and I have my suspicions that Willem will want nothing to do with these kids. As I said, he and your father are essentially enemies."

"Willem," Jasper repeated, frowning. "Is that the fellow that took out Father's eye?"

"That sounds right," Lachlann said. "I heard the story once, but it was just after I lost my hand, and I only remember pieces of those first few conversations after I woke up. What I do recall is the way they reacted to each other when we ran into your father and another Breoch Guard in the Woods. There was definitely some history there."

"Willem has to know that none of that is Ruby's fault, though," Helenne insisted. "You could take the kids to Claudi's place at least, get her to summon him, and see what he says."

Lachlann sighed. "Do you remember how I reacted when I saw Jasper within a few feet of you, Mother? I doubt Willem will react any better when his own mother's safety is at risk."

"Except she's not at risk, and neither was I." Helenne huffed. "Jasper seems like a perfectly nice young man, and it would be a shame to make Ruby suffer any longer than she needs to."

"Mother's right," Tomlin put in. "There's no harm in asking Willem if he'll take them, at the very least. The worst he can do is say no. And if he does, you can take the kids to Alexander and Ember instead. They're perhaps a ten minute drive from Claudi's." He eyed Lachlann. "I imagine you might want these two to pay them a visit regardless, to meet a certain fox?"

Lachlann raised an eyebrow. "Good point." He sighed. "Fine. I suppose it won't hurt to ask. We'll head to Claudi's in the morning. It'll be a few days' journey on foot if we go by the road, longer if we go by the Shrouded Woods. But I'm not certain it's safe to travel in the open with you two. I'm sure someone has noticed by now that both of you have run off."

"Could we take the carriage?" I asked.

"We could, except that we don't intend to come back from Flavalan for a while."

"I have a day off school tomorrow, since I worked Banishing Day, so I can take you," Tomlin volunteered. "And if it looks like we're in any danger, I can make you both invisible."

I nodded. *"Good idea."*

"That would be helpful," Lachlann agreed. "We'll need to prepare for the possibility of travelling by ship. Given that it's already May, I doubt I'll make it back here in time for another run to Dundere, so I suppose I'll just stay there for the summer."

"You stay in Dundere?" I asked.

He nodded. "It's where I work on improving my anti-magic."

"Won't Ruby need different clothes for ship travel?" Jasper asked.

"You both will. Don't worry, I have that covered when we get to Flavalan." He eyed us then, considering. "I suppose you two will be staying with us tonight."

Jasper shrugged. "I suppose so."

"Is that all right?" I signed.

"Well, I have half a mind to make your brother sleep in the barn," Lachlann replied.

"Lachlann!" Helenne scolded.

He smirked. "I was kidding, Mother. You can both stay here. Though we only have one spare bedroom, so you'll be sleeping on the couch, Jasper."

Jasper raised an eyebrow. "Do I need to be worried about you killing me in my sleep?"

Lachlann snorted. "Listen, boy, of the two of us, only one has pretended to befriend the other only to lead them into a trap. It's you attacking my family that we should be worried about."

"How about nobody attacks anyone, and we all just get a good night's sleep, hmmm?" Helenne put in.

"Splendid idea," I signed.

A few hours later, Helenne showed me to a small but cozy room with dark wood furniture and a bed covered with a bright patchwork quilt. I put my bag on a small chair and sank down on the bed, my head spinning from the events of the last two days.

"Ruby?" Jasper appeared in the doorway. I eyed him and patted the bed.

He came and sat next to me. "I just wanted to check on you," he said. "I figure today has been pretty intense."

I nodded and retrieved my pen and notebook. *Are you sure we can trust him?* I wrote.

"Who, Lachlann?" He shrugged. "Not entirely. But I don't think we have much choice." He sighed. "Ruby, I, uh, I think I owe you some apologies. Not just for lying to you about planning to come along— which I am sorry about— but I imagine you understand now why I did."

I shrugged. *You're coming with us now, that's what matters,* I wrote. *What else do you need to apologize for?*

"I was listening to you talk about what Jade did, and, well, I figure I wasn't much better than him for a lot of years. I can't imagine what it's been like for you, having to hide your magic from our family, listening to Father and Jade and me swapping stories of turning magic users in, hearing the names we all used to call them." He grimaced. "I feel awful about it. And I'm sorry for that."

I stared at Jasper, not accustomed to this sort of vulnerability from him. He caught my expression and laughed. "I suppose this is strange for you, me being this open. It's strange for me too."

I nodded, then began to write again. *It's not your fault that you were raised to believe what you did. If I wasn't a magic user myself, I might have believed it too.*

Jasper nodded. "I know that. But it doesn't change the fact that I hurt people with my old beliefs, some of them pretty badly. You heard what I did to Lachlann and his friends." His shoulders slumped. "You're my sister. So if I hurt you, that matters, whether it was intentional or not."

I nodded slowly, allowing my mind to wander back to the many dinner conversations spent reminiscing about the magic users Father had captured, and Jade and Jasper laughing and whooping at stories of his more challenging captures. My brothers casually referred to each other as a "hildakin" whenever something seemed to come unnaturally easily to the other, and Mother told her tales of magic being used to kill children, create monsters, and sacrifice people to raise the dead.

You did hurt me, I wrote. *Thank you for apologizing.* I gave him a small smile. *Jade was always worse than you though.*

"Jade was just…obsessed with getting Father's approval." He shook his head. "You know, after what you told us tonight, I have half a mind to head over to Jade's house right now and punch him."

I raised my eyebrows and shook my head.

"Don't worry, I won't. But it's tempting." He sighed. "Was I…always bad to you? We had some good times growing up, right?"

I looked over at my brother, seeing the regret in his eyes, and smiled slightly. *Yes, we did,* I wrote. *I always loved the funny stories you'd tell me when we were kids, and the songs we'd make up together.*

He chuckled. "And the dances. Do you remember the Angry Squirrel Dance?"

I let out a laugh, recalling the boisterous dance routine that we'd invented when I was a child and he an awkward young teen. He'd been trying to come up with his own dance moves to impress the girls at school, and I, at age six, hadn't understood that, so I named the routine after my then-favourite woodland creature. *We had some good times,* I wrote. *But things began to change once I discovered my gift. You were still a decent brother most of the time, but I couldn't stop thinking of what you might do if you knew my secret. So I stopped trusting you and Jade.*

"I don't blame you." He frowned. "I wonder what it'd take to get through to Jade. I mean, I managed to see how wrong I'd gone. Maybe someday he'll get that chance as well." Jasper stifled a yawn and stood. "Anyway, I'd better get some sleep. Have a good night."

He left the room, leaving me to change into my nightclothes and climb into the bed, wondering about all the changes in my brother and what sort of an adventure we were now embarking on.

CHAPTER 4

WE SET OFF in the carriage early the next morning. Tomlin took the reins for the first part of the journey, and Lachlann sat inside with us. He was quiet this morning, and I didn't miss the glances he and Jasper kept throwing at one another.

"What's wrong?" I finally asked.

Lachlann sighed. "Nothing, really."

"I don't believe you. Why are you and Jasper looking at one another like one of you is about to start a fight?"

"What did she say?" Jasper asked.

Lachlann shook his head and translated, eyeing Jasper warily. "Likely because the last time Jasper and I were stuck in a small, covered carriage together, things went very wrong."

"If it makes you feel any better, you're the one with the anti-magic now," Jasper said.

Lachlann huffed. "A lot of good it does on you."

"Why did you decide to practice anti-magic?" I asked, hoping to distract them both.

"Right, you two were asking about that, weren't you?" Lachlann touched the stone pendant below his neck and sat back. "I only first encountered anti-magic when you turned on us, Jasper. I travelled a lot when I was younger, so I've heard many different things, one of them being how anti-magic is used in Dundere and Candesh to keep magic legal but controlled. And I found myself thinking, that seems like a much better idea than the bloody Banishing.

"When your guard friend used it on us, I saw how well it worked, and it made me even more certain that it's a better solution than what Breoch is doing. So when I returned to Dundere, I went to the guard station and asked if they'd be willing to train me. I figured that one day I could come back here and demonstrate how powerful anti-magic is to the authorities, and hopefully help them find a better way to handle magic. The guards made me a deal. They said that if I came to Dundere every summer, I could learn from them on condition that I also work in their force. So now I'm a part-time Dundere guard."

"When are you going to take this to the Breoch authorities?" Jasper asked.

"Not sure yet. I'm waiting for an opportune time. King Edwin is getting quite sick, and I rather think I'd have better luck once his son is on the throne. Kairus is known for being a kind man."

"So what's with the pendant growing into your skin?" I asked.

"Ah, that." Lachlann touched the pendant again. "There are two levels of anti-magic. Most guards use the more basic type. You wear this necklace, which makes you immune to magic, when you're at work and remove it when you're off duty. You can cause another person's magic to fizzle out, but only if you touch them. It's not very powerful, but it still allows you to interact with magic when you need it. If a Dundere guard who uses basic anti-magic got hurt on the job, they could take their pendant off and go see Noelle later in the day.

"But then there's the other type, known as Bonded anti-magic. It's far more powerful, but it's a lifetime commitment. If you decide to become a Bonded anti-mage, you put the necklace on and never take it off. See, aro stone is naturally resistant to magic. I know of magic schools whose practice rooms are lined in the stuff, to keep spells from going awry, and I've heard stories of prisons being built of similar stone. But for some reason, it becomes more powerful the closer it comes to a human heartbeat. So when you wear the necklace for any length of time, it's drawn to your pulse like a magnet and grows into your skin, like a tattoo. After about a year, it fuses to your breastbone. Thankfully, your body stops it from getting any closer to your heart at that point, but once it's fused itself to bone, it can't be removed without killing you."

"Strange," commented Jasper.

Lachlann nodded. "The combination of that stone and your heartbeat makes you far, far more powerful than a basic anti-mage. I have the ability to create a circle of anti-magic around myself now, about 20 feet on each side. I can walk into a room of mages and render them all powerless, if I choose to. It's a heavy responsibility, and in places where it is used for policing, guards who abuse their power are punished harshly."

"I can see why."

"It also renders me completely immune to almost all magic, which isn't always a good thing. Noelle can't heal me, as you already know." He gestured to his hook. "I could, for example, travel in a ship that was built by magical means, but if the mode of travel itself is magical, I can't do it. Willem can't teleport me, nor can I go through portals. It can be a bit inconvenient sometimes."

"Why didn't you just ask Noelle to heal you before you started using the Bonded anti-magic?" I asked.

"If that was an option, I would've. But you see, Bonded anti-magic is powerful enough that it can undo some magical spells, specifically if they were cast on the practitioner's body."

My eyes narrowed. *"How?"*

"Well, for example, if I broke Jasper's arm and Noelle healed it, and later on he decided to become a Bonded anti-mage, he'd be fine, because his body would have healed his arm, under the right conditions. But if it's something that couldn't have happened naturally, it's different. Severed limbs, broken backs, lost sight or hearing— those sorts of things tend to be reversed if someone takes on Bonded anti-magic. Once Ruby's healed up, she could never become an anti-mage without losing her hand and tongue again, or at least the use of them."

"Are there ways for magikai to get around your power?" Jasper asked.

Lachlann eyed him. "Why do you ask?"

"Curiosity." Jasper raised his hands. "As you said yourself, your power doesn't do much on me."

"True." Lachlann sighed. "If they use natural means and trajectory, yes. For example, if Saray were to shoot a bolt of fire at me from a distance, it would extinguish once it hit my anti-magic field. But if she lit a stick on fire and then threw it, the fire would be non-magical by the time it reached me, so I would be injured. Trina could order a dog to attack me, and once it came close, though it wouldn't be able to hear her, it'd still have its orders."

"I forgot about Trina's abilities," Jasper mused. "That dog that used to follow her around, is he still alive?"

"Bailey?" Lachlann shook his head. "He passed on about a year back. He was an old dog when you met him."

"Was he Trina's dog after…everything that happened?" Jasper asked. "I thought he belonged to…"

"He lived with Trina until he died, yes." Lachlann replied.

"That's good. I'm glad he had someone to take care of him." Jasper glanced out the window, clearly ill at ease.

An awkward silence descended on the carriage once again, and I stared out the window. We were far away from Sylvenburgh now; the rolling farmlands had given way to dense forest. Something about the woods seemed familiar to me, and I sat up tall when I realized why. *"Ask Jasper if this is the route we took into Sylvenburgh after he rescued me,"* I signed to Lachlann.

Lachlann repeated this to Jasper, who nodded. "This is the same road. I believe we're pretty close to the ocean now. You'll be able to see the island from the carriage soon."

My heartbeat picked up at his words; I wasn't sure if I *wanted* to see it.

Ten minutes later, the carriage turned, and we were skirting the edge of a cliff high above the ocean. The sea stretched out below us to our left, sunlight glinting on its waves. Jasper peered out the window and pointed. "There. That's Yarel Island."

Lachlann followed his gaze. "Huh. You know, I've seen that island many times but never given it much thought."

I gazed out at what had once been my prison. From here it was just a small patch of green and brown against the ocean's blue. I could make out patches of farmland on it, and the faint outlines of buildings. It looked peaceful, not at all threatening. A lump rose in my throat when I thought of the friends I'd left behind, and a rogue tear trickled down my cheek.

Lachlann caught my expression. "It must be hard for you, seeing that place."

"I'm just thinking of Kaden," I said, trying to ignore the barrage of images seeing the place had conjured up.

He nodded. "I told you, we'll find a way to get her out."

I nodded too and lay my head back against the seat, wiping at my eyes. Jasper reached over and gave my hand a quick squeeze. "What sorts of magic do you think your friends might use to help Ruby get Kaden back?" he asked Lachlann.

Lachlann began talking about the various ways a person could sneak onto the island by magical means, but I found myself only half listening. Seeing the island had left me feeling overwhelmed in a way I could not fully understand, and I fought against the tears that were now trickling down my cheeks. When I looked down at my hand, I saw that it was shaking.

"Tom, stop the carriage," I heard Lachlann call out. Our transport halted, and Lachlann got out to dig through one of the bags in the back.

Jasper took my hand again. "It's going to be fine, Ruby," he said, but his tone was halting; he clearly had no idea how to comfort me.

Lachlann returned with a few blankets. He instructed Jasper to move to the other bench, then had me lie down. Draping one of the blankets over me, he crouched and put a hand on my shoulder. "It's all right, Ruby," he assured me, his voice much more confident than Jasper's had been. "You're safe."

I nodded, squeezing my eyes shut. Lachlann was right, I knew that much, but I still could not stop myself from shaking.

"Here, chew on these." Lachlann offered me a few stalks of a dried plant. "It'll help you feel calmer."

I began to chew as instructed. Lachlann sat back down on the bench next to Jasper, and Tomlin began to drive again. Lachlann and Jasper resumed their conversation about rescuing Kaden, and I felt myself beginning to relax. My eyes drifted shut, and when they opened next, Lachlann and Tomlin had switched places. Jasper was talking animatedly to Tomlin, clearly more at ease with him than with Lachlann.

"So we took every piece of furniture out of Mr. Tafflin's office and put it all in the dining hall— arranged exactly how it had been in his office, down to the inch. The rest of the school thought it was brilliant. But, of course, we all got detention, and our parents were informed." He smirked. "Good thing I was the same size as Father by then; if I'd been any younger, I swear he would have beaten me."

"That was you, huh?" Tomlin grinned, shaking his head. "I heard that story from Malcolm years back. He was actually pretty impressed by your prank, but of course he couldn't tell you that."

"Wait, you and Mr. Tafflin talk to each other?"

Tomlin snorted. "Of course we do. We principals have to help one another out."

"But I thought King's Academy and Sylvenburgh were rivals!"

"That's only the students. We adults are a little more mature than that."

Jasper rolled his eyes, and I laughed. Tomlin looked me over. "Feeling better, Ruby?"

I nodded and rubbed my eyes. The carriage hit a bump, and I sat up, looking outside. We were approaching the gates to Flavalan. I'd only been to Flavalan a handful of times, and I always found it intriguing.

Jasper joined me in surveying our surroundings. "I love this place," he said. "Perhaps one day I'll move here. I feel like I'd fit in better than in Kirstein, or Sylvenburgh for that matter."

I nodded as I took in the bright store fronts, the elegantly designed buildings, and the large open market filled with hawkers selling their wares. The air smelled like the sea mingled with expensive perfumes and spices. Kirstein was crowded and noisy, and Sylvenburgh was a city that relied mostly on factories and farms. Both were pretty in their own way, but Kirstein tended to smell of garbage and human sweat, while the air in Sylvenburgh always smelled a bit like smoke, and a fine black film clung to most things in the downtown area. Flavalan, on the other hand, was a trade port that relied on foreign goods and tourism. It was exotic and colourful, while the other cities were boring, grey, predictable.

Lachlann took a right turn, and we began leaving the downtown area, onto streets lined with lamp posts and cheery little homes. After a few minutes, he stopped in front of one. "Here we are," Tomlin said.

"Who lives here?" Jasper asked.

"Claudi, Willem's mother. We're going to see if we can get you to Dundere the fast way."

"We're meeting Willem at his *mother's* place?" Jasper's eyes narrowed as he got out of the carriage. "This sounds like a terrible idea to me. Do you recall how Lachlann acted yesterday when he found me in your house near your mother?"

"My thoughts exactly," admitted Lachlann. "But Mother and Tom seem to think it's worth a try, so..." He sighed.

We followed Lachlann to the front door of the house. He knocked, and it was answered by a woman who was obviously *very* old. Her skin, about the same colour as Kaden's, was wrinkled and rough, her hair was nearly white, and she stood hunched over with a wooden cane, its head carved into the shape of a bird. When she peered up at Lachlann though, her grin defied her age. "So good to see you boys!" she said, looking from Lachlann to Tomlin.

"Good to see you as well," Lachlann said, stooping to embrace her.

Claudi looked past him to Jasper and me. "Now, who are these two? Have I met them before?"

"No, but you've certainly heard of one of them," Lachlann said. "Can we come in? We were hoping you could summon Willem."

"Of course, my dear!" She stepped aside, and we walked over the threshold.

Claudi seated us in the living room, which looked to me like any other old woman's space. The rug was a rich, plush burgundy with patterns woven into the edges, the furniture was antique and patterned with flowers, and the legs of the dark wooden tables and chairs had been carved into the shapes of swans, trees, and flowers. There were shelves of dusty old books, and a painted portrait of a family of three hung over the fireplace. On the mantle were several brightly coloured vases and jars of shells and rocks, pieces of driftwood and a doll that looked Cherinese in make. I frowned; I'd expected the mother of the infamous Willem to have a living room full of mysterious magical artifacts.

Claudi caught my look and grinned. "You won't find any magic in here, dear. That's all in my study." She winked, then eased herself onto the couch and pulled a pendant out from behind the collar of her dress. She began rubbing the small pink stone in a circular motion.

The man who materialized next to her certainly looked like Claudi's son. He had the same tightly curled hair, and the same mahogany skin. He looked to be older than Tomlin and Lachlann; there were definite laugh lines around his eyes, and his thinning hair and beard were peppered through with grey. "Ah, I see you've brought me more children, Lachlann," Willem said, studying my brother and me. Then his eyes narrowed. "Or are they children? The boy looks a little too old to be one of your Sylvenburgh kids."

"They're not from the Academy," Lachlann told him. "I ended up helping these two out rather unexpectedly." He sighed. "Listen, Willem, you're not going to like this. But they need our assistance."

"More magic-fearers, I assume?" Willem's eyes met mine, and he looked me over. "No, that can't be right. The girl is a krossemage."

"They're both fine with magic," Lachlann assured him. "It's who they're related to that's the issue. Willem, this is Ruby and Jasper Jameson."

"Jameson." Willem frowned for a moment, then his eyes flew wide open, and he turned to Lachlann. "Angus's kids?"

"I'm afraid so," Jasper replied before Lachlann could speak.

"Wait." Willem got to his feet. "Your name's Jasper? *The* Jasper? The one who…"

"Yes, the very same," Jasper replied, exasperation in his tone.

"You brought the children of Angus Jameson into my *mother's* home?" Willem's voice rose as he spoke. "Have you forgotten what Angus *did* to my mother?"

"Oh hush, son," Claudi interjected. "These kids aren't Angus. They didn't commit his crimes."

"No, the older one just shot another man in cold blood! That's not much better, Mother!"

"It wasn't Lachlann's idea, if that makes you feel better," Jasper said. "It was…" He stopped speaking suddenly. His eyes flew open, and he began clawing at his throat frantically.

"You have no right to speak into this after what you did to Kip, boy." Willem's voice was ice.

"By the Fae, Willem." Lachlann touched his pendant, and I cringed as the strange, heavy feeling of anti-magic coursed through the room. Willem recoiled visibly, and Jasper sank to the ground, gasping, as the spell lifted off him.

Willem whirled to face Lachlann. "Did you just *block* me?"

"Yes, I did." Lachlann met Willem's eyes. "You don't have to like these kids, but you have no right to start scaring them with your magic. You're acting just like you did when we brought Kip to you all those years back. I thought you'd learned from that experience!"

"Bringing a kid who's scared of magic to me is one thing. Welcoming a traitor and a criminal who put a bullet in that same kid into my *mother's* home is another. I'm surprised you're willing to travel with them yourself!"

"Trust me, so am I," Lachlann said softly.

"Why *did* you bring them here, anyway?"

Lachlann looked at Tomlin. "You tell him. You were the one who insisted we indulge Mother."

Tomlin carefully explained my situation to Willem. "Lachlann could take them by ship easily enough," he said, "but my mother thinks it best to get poor Ruby here healed up as soon as we can. We were hoping you'd be willing to take them via the shortcut."

Willem's eyes narrowed. "Really? You think I'd be willing to take Angus's children?" He barked out a laugh. "Even if the boy wasn't dangerous, you do realize their father could catch up with them, right? And if he did, he might be able to get information from them."

"Which you could easily wipe from their minds," Tomlin countered.

"Save it," Willem shot back. "I'm not taking them."

"As I figured." Lachlann shot his brother a glare.

"Don't look at me like that," Tomlin retorted. "Blame Mother for this, not me. She was the one who insisted that Ruby needed to get healed as fast as possible. I didn't realize that—"

I let out a frustrated yell and leapt to my feet, causing all the adults to turn and stare at me. "Ruby, what is it?" Jasper asked.

"Would you all just stop?*"* I signed, my gestures exaggerated. Then I turned on my heel and stalked out the front door.

Outside, I let the cool spring air rush over my face as I fought back tears. I wanted to run as far away from the house as I could, but I was well aware that I was in a city I hardly knew, with no way of protecting myself. I sank down on the front steps and buried my face in my arms.

Jasper joined me a few minutes later and sank down next to me. "You all right?"

I shook my head.

He sighed and put his arm around me. "Lachlann shouldn't have listened to his mother," he mumbled. "This was an awful idea."

The conversation inside slowly took on a more civil tone, and several minutes later Lachlann joined us outside. "Sorry about that. We've stopped fighting; you can come back inside now."

Jasper huffed. "Willem clearly doesn't want me in there."

"Yes, well, we won't be here for much longer." He eyed me. "Are you all right, Ruby?"

I sighed and sat upright so I could sign better. *"I'm frustrated."*

"I don't blame you. This whole thing must be quite overwhelming for you."

I shook my head. *"It's not just that. Ever since Jasper took me from the school, everyone's been pulling me this way and that, trying to determine what's best for me, even saying they know what I'm feeling. I'm sure your mother meant well, but she never asked me if I'd rather go by ship or by portal. No one asked me if I was comfortable travelling with you, for that matter, or if I wanted to leave the island in the first place! Everyone here thinks they know what's best for me, and no one bothers to ask me what I want!"*

Lachlann nodded slowly as he took in my words. Then he sighed. "What *do* you want, Ruby? We can't very well take you back to the island. You and Jasper could head back to Kirstein, but you'd be in danger. Do you not want to travel to Dundere and get your hand and tongue restored?"

I shrugged. *"I do want to get healed. But I don't want everyone fighting about what's best for me anymore. At least include me in your conversations."*

"Fair." Lachlann nodded. "It looks like travelling by portal isn't an option, so our best bet is to take the Lady Liara. Willem pointed out that might be good for you anyway."

"Why's that?"

"The best stormbrewer we know is the first mate on the Lady Liara. You might have to wait a couple weeks to get your hand and tongue back, but you could learn a lot from Harvey, and pull your weight on the ship, too." He chuckled.

"And if you're going to travel by sea, not having a tongue might be an advantage. Who wants to endure two weeks of watery porridge and hard tack?"

"I'd love to go back on Gareth's ship," Jasper interjected. "I had quite the adventure last time."

"We'll have to see if Gareth is willing to take you back, given how much trouble you caused," Lachlann said. "But if anyone knows that people can change under the right circumstances, it's him."

"Everything all right?" Claudi appeared on the porch, accompanied by Tomlin and a rather reluctant looking Willem.

Lachlann nodded. "We should get ready to leave."

"What, you're not going to stay for some tea?" she protested.

"I'll come back in a day or two and visit, when I don't have the children of your son's sworn enemy in my care." I didn't miss the edge in Lachlann's voice. "For now, I'm going to take them elsewhere."

"I'll return once I've dropped Lachlann and the kids off," Tomlin said. "Actually, Willem, I was wondering if you wouldn't mind me coming to take a look at your lib—"

"Absolutely. You know you're always welcome in my *home*." Willem shot a nervous glance at Jasper and me.

"Where are we going?" Jasper asked Lachlann.

"The Lady Liara won't be in port for another two weeks, which means I need to bring some of my other contacts into the plan." One corner of his mouth turned up. "It's time to visit Alexander and Ember."

CHAPTER 5

ALEXANDER AND EMBER, I learned on the ride over, were old shipmates of Lachlann's. They'd met on Gareth's ship and married a few years later, and now they owned a clothing store that featured all sorts of exotic fabrics and curious styles. Both of them were a little eccentric, Lachlann told us.

We turned off the main road and onto a small street as Lachlann finished explaining all this. "Here we are," he said. "Prepare to enter the Emporium of Wonder."

"Is that what it's called?" Jasper snickered. "These folks sound quite dramatic."

Lachlann raised an eyebrow. "Oh, you have no idea."

Tomlin deposited us near an alley and bid us farewell. I expected Lachlann to continue down the narrow cobbled street, but he made a sharp turn into the alley instead. My eyes narrowed. *There are shops in an alley?* In Kirstein, alleys were dangerous places, homes to criminals and rats and mountains of garbage. Jasper seemed to mirror my surprise; he stopped a moment and motioned that I should walk between him and Lachlann. His eyes darted every which way as I passed him.

We made our way down the alley, tall red brick walls closing in on each side, and I saw lights twinkling ahead. "I suppose you kids didn't know about this place," Lachlann said, glancing back at us with a smile. His earlier reserve seemed to have faded. "Relax, Jasper. There's nothing dangerous about the Gilded Alley. It's a lovely little spot."

We approached the source of the lights, and my eyes widened as I took in the scene. This alleyway housed perhaps twenty small shop fronts, each of them topped with a golden sign announcing their wares. There was a shop selling exotic spices from southern Cherin, a glassblower whose shop front windows were crafted from stained glass, a combined tea house and bakery, a small pub, and several clothing stores whose windows displayed stately waistcoats, brightly patterned umbrellas, and shoes with impossibly tall heels. We stopped in front of one of the stores and read the golden placard above its doors: *Emporium of Wonder.* The front window showcased a mannequin clad in a green and purple frock coat decked out with jewels and lace and colourful embroidered daisies. Around the base of the coat sat a swath of gauzy pink fabric; nestled within it were several gold bracelets and jewelled combs and pairs of silk slippers. I gazed at the coat. *"It's beautiful,"* I said to Lachlann.

He nodded. "Alexander and Ember are skilled at what they do. You'll have one of those coats yourself soon enough."

"Why?"

"Because you'll need one in Dundere. They're a status symbol there— only magikai get to wear them. Come on inside." He held the heavy wooden door open for Jasper and me.

The inside of the shop was just as gaudy and colourful as the display window. Clothing of all kinds hung from racks and enrobed various mannequins— flowing dresses with embroidered corsets, top hats of all sizes and colours, skirts made of several layers of patterned silk, and long knitted scarves. There were ornate-looking pieces of jewelry displayed on tables throughout the store and a plethora of other curiosities— fantastical creatures carved from wood and stone, whimsical stained-glass window hangings of flowers and boats and fairies, and a collection of small cuckoo clocks decorated with ceramic vines, wooden tiles, or cute animals dressed in human clothes. One table held what appeared to be musical instruments, but none of them were ones I'd seen before. There was what looked like a guitar with gears and a crank handle, a wind instrument carved from stone with holes in all the wrong places, and a collection of small metal bowls that looked like table decorations, each holding a mallet. I was so absorbed with the treasure trove surrounding me that I didn't notice the man sitting by the register. "Lachlann!" he exclaimed, rising to his feet and crossing the room in a few long strides. "I wasn't expecting to see you for another month!"

I looked the man over as he embraced Lachlann. He was quite tall, with olive skin and wavy, jet-black hair that hung nearly to his waist. Black liner accentuated his dark eyes, and his mustache and goatee were waxed into curls. I imagined he was close to Lachlann in age, but even so, I had to admit he was incredibly handsome.

"There's been a change in plans," Lachlann said, grinning as he pulled away from the other man. "It's good to see you, Alexander. Where's Ember?"

Lachlann's words were interrupted by an odd resonant ringing; I looked over and saw that Jasper had picked up one of the strange metal bowls and hit the edge with its mallet. He grinned. "I've heard about these."

Alexander smiled at Jasper amusedly. "Those are Ember's handiwork."

Jasper's eyes widened. "She made these?"

"*They* made them, yes," Alexander corrected.

"Right, sorry, I forgot to explain that to these two," Lachlann said.

"My partner does not quite feel like either a woman or a man," Alexander informed Jasper. "So when we refer to them, we use *they* instead of he or she."

"Ah." Jasper's brow furrowed for a moment, but he nodded.

"Speaking of Ember, I'll go fetch them now," Alexander said. He disappeared behind a beaded curtain, returning shortly after with someone else in tow.

Ember was perhaps a few inches taller and a bit broader than me, and they looked younger than Alexander. Their skin was ivory, and their ice-blue eyes were accentuated with orange and navy and silver makeup, but it was their hair that caught me off guard. Ember's hair rose in several tall, flamelike spikes that made them look taller than they actually were. The spikes had somehow been dyed to look like fire, varying shades of red and orange and yellow worked carefully in. Both Ember and Alexander were clothed in breeches and jewelled frock coats; Alexander's was purple and black with ornate gold patterns stitched in, and Ember's was deep red with a massive fire-breathing embroidered dragon that curled around their shoulders. Ember smiled at us as Lachlann made introductions. "Pleasure to meet you two," they said, "and good to see you again, Lachlann." Then they eyed us. "These two look perhaps a bit older than your usual companions."

"The boy is a little older, yes. They're in a bit of a unique predicament."

"I see that," Ember said, their gaze travelling to my stump. "The girl is a krossemage?"

I nodded.

"And you're headed to Dundere so Noelle can fix you up, I presume?"

"That's right," Lachlann said. "Before all that, though, I was hoping they could meet your fox." My eyes narrowed at his words; I recalled Tomlin saying something about a fox last night at dinner.

Ember and Alexander exchanged a glance, and Alexander nodded. "That's easy enough to arrange; Mischief is sleeping right over there. Shall I wake her?"

Lachlann nodded. "Please do." I followed his gaze to a large, velvety cushion, and only now did I notice the fluffy red fox sleeping on it. Alexander began to stroke her, and the fox made a chirping noise, opened her eyes and shook her head. A pair of black beady eyes met mine, and I let out a small squeal.

"Adorable, isn't she?" Alexander grinned. "Want to hold her?"

I nodded, and he brought Mischief over to me. I peered down at her and stroked her fur, and she made more of her odd chirping noises.

Jasper eyed Mischief. "I've never met a tame fox before."

"She's not exactly tame; she comes and goes a lot, but this is her home," Alexander replied. "I think your sister's smitten."

I grinned at him and shifted the fox so she was nestled in the crook of my right arm, freeing up my hand. *"I'm going to need to find myself a pet fox,"* I signed to Lachlann.

He laughed and translated. "Mischief reminds me a bit of Persius," he said. "Wild, but still oddly attached to some humans."

"Fairy magic will do that to an animal," Ember replied. They glanced at Jasper. "You should hold her too."

Jasper gingerly took Mischief from me. She sniffed at him and chirped a bit more, and he chuckled. "Aren't you the cutest thing ever?"

"Who's Persius?" I asked.

"Kirilee's hawk," Lachlann told me. "Kirilee had a special bond with him that allowed her to talk to him. She passed him on to me, but I don't have that same gift. He mostly lives in the Shrouded Woods now, but occasionally he comes back to the farm to visit. Mother doesn't like him much though; he's always after our chickens."

"She probably wouldn't like this one either then." Jasper grinned. "Can you talk to your fox?"

Alexander nodded. "In a way. Only a few words here and there, but we understand each other. Speaking of which," he turned to Lachlann, "I think you're safe to keep moving forward."

Lachlann nodded, his shoulders relaxing visibly. "I was hoping you'd say that."

"What do you mean?" Jasper asked.

Lachlann exchanged a look with the others, and Ember spoke up. "Mischief has a gift. She can sense the motives of people and tell whether their intentions are good."

"Oh." Jasper raised his eyebrows at Lachlann. "*That's* why you wanted us to meet these folks."

"That's why I wanted you to meet Mischief," Lachlann replied. "I needed to be absolutely sure you were sincere before I was willing to take you any further. Alex and Ember I brought you to for other reasons."

Ember nodded. "Now that their trustworthiness is settled, perhaps we should show these two what else we do for a living." They took Mischief from Jasper and set her down. She scampered around the shop for a brief moment before disappearing out a small door that was clearly created just for her. Then Ember beckoned that we should follow.

Jasper and I followed Ember through a bead curtain into what appeared to be a storage area, and then into a room stocked with large bolts of fabric and baskets containing buttons and lace and other sorts of accessories. A large sewing machine sat in the middle of the room, and several colourful works in progress were spread out on a massive table against the wall, while half a dozen more sat half completed on mannequins. "Alexander and I do specialize in making and selling those clothes you see out front," Ember told us, "but that's not all." They led us to a wooden door at the rear of the sewing room and unlocked it.

My eyes widened as we entered. It was larger than the sewing room and seemed to be split down the middle. On one side was a cauldron, and behind that a shelf full of what appeared to be spices and elixirs and other sorts of ingredients. Several bunches of herbs hung from the ceiling, and a massive leather-bound book sat open on a stand, its pages yellowed with age. The far wall was lined with shelves of small bottles, many of which seemed to glow with an almost ethereal light.

The other side of the room held several long tables cluttered with hammers and anvils and tools that I didn't understand, along with another large book perched on a stand. The far wall of this side boasted dozens of small, glittering pieces on shelves. I went closer to inspect them; they all appeared to be some kind of silver jewelry, many of the pieces inlaid with jewels. Jasper frowned. "You folks make jewelry and…potions?"

"Alexander makes magical potions, I make amulets and magical jewelry," Ember explained. "We can weave any spell that we've learned into our craft. A person can then drink one of Alexander's potions and be able to take on that potion's ability for a time. If you were to drink an invisibility potion, you could become invisible for several hours, so long as you knew the spell's casting words or motions. And if you were to wear one of my invisibility charms, you could be invisible at any time you choose, so long as you were able to touch the charm."

"I suppose your charms are far more powerful than Alexander's potions, then."

Ember nodded and grinned. "That's why mine are considerably more expensive."

"Don't you need a forge for silversmithing?"

"I don't technically need a forge, because I'm a firebrand, in case you haven't figured that out." They pointed to their hair and grinned. "But we have one anyway, through there." They pointed at a small door near the table full of tools. "It's in a small, open-air area. Wouldn't want a forge in here." They wrinkled their nose.

"Very true," Lachlann said as he and Alexander joined us.

I began studying Alexander's side of the room and then pulled out the notebook Tomlin had given me. *Can you show us how you make a potion?* I wrote.

Alexander read my note and grinned. "Absolutely, my dear."

Jasper and I followed him over to his cauldron, where he lit the fire underneath with a mumbled spell and then poured a large pitcher of water in. When he closed his eyes and began to sing, Jasper gasped. I followed his gaze, my eyes widening.

The light fixture above Alexander's work space, which consisted of a treelike wooden structure adorned in several small glowing spheres of varying colours, now released those spheres. They began to float down to Alexander, several landing on him, while a few others circled Jasper and me. "Fairies?" Jasper guessed.

Alexander grinned. "You can't do fairy magic without fairies around, my dear." His gaze then shifted to me. "Let me guess, you didn't know fairies were real?"

I shook my head, eyes still wide. A fairy landed on my right arm, and I held it up to stare at it in awe.

"I've heard about fairies living in the Shrouded Woods, but I didn't think they were here," Jasper said.

"This is about the only place in the cities you'll find them," Alexander replied, plucking a mortar and pestle, a few herbs, and some bottles of liquids I couldn't identify from a shelf. He began dropping herbs into the mortar, the fairies fluttering around him as he worked. "These right here," he said, holding up a jar of dried pink flowers, "are viletta petals, and they are the key to making potions imbued with fairy magic. The magic sticks to them, for lack of a better way of explaining." He put a few of the flowers into the mortar. "Here we have our dried shazar berries to lengthen the effect of the spell, ginger for digestion, yarel seeds for quick absorption into the blood, and chamomile and valerian for sleep—those two are specific to this potion." The cauldron began to boil as he ground the ingredients together. He sniffed the contents of his mortar, and, satisfied, dumped them into the bubbling water. Then he took two small bottles from the shelf. "A dash of honey for sweetness, and just a touch of something special for incredible flavour." He grinned. "This, my dears, is why my potions are so expensive, but also palatable." He poured a few drops of the dark brown liquid into the cauldron.

"What is it?" Jasper asked.

"An extract of vanilla, which is a rare and expensive bean found only in the far south. This particular batch came from Durlann, of all places."

"Durlann? I didn't think Breoch traded with them."

"We don't. That's why they cost so much." Alexander winked.

"Can I try a bit?"

He shook his head. "You probably wouldn't like it in its concentrated form. In potions or cakes, though, it's delicious." He turned to his book and began rifling through it. "Ah, here we are. This is the fun part." I watched as the fairies congregated on the edges of the pot. They began to frolic and twirl in the steam, unbothered by its heat. I saw bits of golden dust falling from their wings into the potion as they danced. Alexander watched them, and then, when enough of their dust had fallen, he straightened up and put his hands into the steam. "By the power of the Fae," he intoned, *"Incantus Sirius Lullabus!"*

There was a startling popping sound, and a massive pink cloud of swirling steam rose from the pot. The fairies twirled within the cloud, dancing and twisting in its vapor. I could hear them singing an otherworldly song and leaned closer to stare at their tiny, delicate forms, the pink droplets clinging to my face. The steam smelled vaguely like candied apples, and I could only imagine that it would taste similar. When the cloud settled, the liquid in the cauldron shone bright pink. "Perfect," Alexander said. "Now that will need to boil down for about ten minutes or so. Perhaps this is the time to talk about your arrangements for the next week or two."

"Yes, we need to discuss that," Lachlann said from across the room. He joined us around the potion, followed by Ember. "I've been bringing young magikai here for the last few years to hide out until the Lady Liara is in port. Alex and Ember aren't able to host young folks in their house, but it's easy enough to have you stay here in the shop."

"Lachlann stays with us," Alexander put in, "but he usually helps Ember with their work while he's here in exchange for us putting up with him— I mean, putting him up." He clapped Lachlann on the shoulder and grinned.

"So we'll just hang around your shop until the ship gets here?" Jasper asked.

"Not exactly," Ember said. "You'll be *asleep* in our shop until the ship gets here. Alex has a sleep potion brewing right now."

"Wait, we're going to sleep for two weeks?"

"That's right. It will be dreamless, and you'll be comfortable. We'll load you two onto the ship in crates, and once you're aboard, you'll be woken up."

"How will we wake up?" I asked.

"That's the captain's job," Lachlann replied. "Gareth knows a song on his pipe that will rouse anyone from a magical sleep."

Jasper frowned. "I don't like it."

"You have little choice, my dear," Alexander said. "It's this or you don't go to Dundere."

His shoulders hunched in protest. "Just the thought of being asleep that long...won't we be vulnerable? What if someone found us and stole us away, or even killed us?" His eyes narrowed. "How do I know *you* won't?"

Alexander and Ember looked at each other and burst into laughter. "Us, kill people?" Alexander snorted. "My dear boy, neither of us would have any idea how. I mean, I suppose I could poison someone with my potions, but other than that..."

"If the person you're trying to kill is asleep, it's easy. Stick a knife in their ribs. Slit their throat. Break their neck."

"But then we'd have to deal with blood, and I faint at the sight of it," said Ember. "And neither of us knows how to break a neck."

"It's pretty easy," Jasper said. "You just have to hold their head like this..." He put one hand on my head, and I shrugged him off.

"You've broken a neck?" Lachlann asked. "I thought you'd only ever killed one person."

"I've never actually done it, except to a few chickens on my uncle's farm. But we were taught how in the Breoch Guard."

"Wait, he's Breoch Guard?" Alexander turned to Lachlann, his eyes narrowing.

"He *was*," Lachlann replied. "Not anymore. That's why I needed Mischief to assess him. Really, Alex, you think I'd bring an active member of the Guard here?"

Alexander nodded slowly. "Well, I certainly hope Mischief was right about you, young man."

"Do you have a memory wiping potion?" Lachlann asked. "It might not be a bad idea to remove the location of your shop from both their minds, given that they have relatives who are still in the Guard."

"Hmmm. Yes, I can arrange for that." Alexander turned back to peer inside his cauldron. "That looks better." He retrieved a pair of small glass vials and a funnel. Then he ladled some of the potion into the vials and corked them. "Two potions of Extended Sleep," he said. "These will knock you two out until you're aboard the Lady Liara." He placed the vials on the table, then glanced at the grandfather clock that loomed in one corner of the room. "Well, it looks like it's time for dinner. Let's head over to the Golden Duck."

CHAPTER 6

THE GOLDEN DUCK, we learned, was a pub just a few buildings down from the Emporium of Wonder. Inside, it was panelled with dark wood and smelled of pipe smoke and liquor and cooking meat. The hostess looked me over and told Alexander and Ember that I was only allowed in so long as they didn't start buying me drinks. We settled at a table near a cheery fireplace, and a chipper woman who looked to be about Jasper's age came by and told us the food specials for the evening. Alexander ordered a round of ales for everyone except me, then turned to me and asked, "What would you like to drink, my dear?"

"Just water," I signed to Lachlann. *"I can't really taste it anyway."* Lachlann relayed my wishes to the server. I didn't miss Jasper's eyes following her as she headed to the bar.

"What sort of ale did you order for us?" Lachlann asked Alexander. "I've not heard of it before."

The two of them quickly got into a discussion about different liquors and their fermentation processes, all of which went right over my head. Jasper was still distracted looking at the bar maid, so I turned to Ember, who gave me a smile. "What do you think of our little shop?" they asked.

I smiled and gave them a thumbs-up, unable to help staring as I took in the variety of shades in their fiery hair. They frowned. "Everything all right?"

I nodded and then tapped Lachlann's arm. *"Ask Ember how they make their hair that colour."*

Lachlann relayed my question, then returned to his conversation with Alexander.

Ember chuckled. "It's all thanks to Alexander's potions."

My eyebrows shot up.

"He has some potions you can put right in your hair that will change its colour. I used a few of them for this." They grinned at me. "I could use one on you if you wanted, make you a brunette or a redhead. Or perhaps you'd rather your hair be a more dramatic colour— blue, for example?"

I laughed and shook my head.

"I could always just add a small streak of blue or green, or whatever you want, if you prefer subtlety," Ember continued.

I shook my head again. The server returned with our drinks then, and we each ordered our dinner. Jasper gave her a grin and complimented her bright blue eyes, earning a smile before she retreated to continue her work.

Lachlann turned to Ember. "Do you folks have any of that colour potion in purple?"

Ember nodded. "Why? Do *you* want purple hair?"

"No, not for me. For someone I know in Dundere. I'm pretty sure she'd enjoy the possibility of a purple streak in her hair."

"Oh, a girlfriend?" Alexander asked.

Lachlann snorted. "I should hope not, given that she's seventeen."

"Are you sure it's not for you?" Alexander's voice took on a more teasing note. "Because you would look absolutely delicious with purple hair, my dear."

Jasper, momentarily distracted from our cute server, asked, "Are you *flirting* with Lachlann?"

"Oh, absolutely." Alexander put an arm around Lachlann, who laughed and elbowed him in the ribs.

"Don't mind him," Lachlann said. "It's all in jest, at this point. Alex here just had a huge crush on me back in our ship days. Unfortunately for him, I don't fancy men."

"A shame," Alexander said. He looked Lachlann over with a scrutinizing eye. "Perhaps we could interest you in a hair potion that, uh, refreshes your natural colour? I do see some grey in that beard of yours."

"A side effect of being forty-one," Lachlann replied. "Also, you forget that your potions don't work on me." He tapped his pendant.

"Right. Well, perhaps we could interest you in some…more colourful clothing?"

Lachlann shook his head. "Stop trying to sell me things, you two. You know me, I'm a simple man with simple tastes."

"You say that," Ember replied, "and yet you pined after Kirilee for all those years. There was nothing simple about her."

"You may have a point." Lachlann sighed and looked away.

Alexander took a sip of his ale. "Still grieving her, are you? Lachlann, you need to move on. Kirilee was a gem, but there's plenty of other gems out there. My sister for one…"

"Enough. I'm not ready, and you know that." Lachlann's voice became irritated, and my shoulders hunched. *Please don't get in a fight. Not now.*

"Yes, stop bothering him." Ember rolled their eyes. "I know you want to set everyone up with someone, but not everyone wants a lover, or is ready for one." They scanned the room. "There are some handsome young men in here, perhaps you should try to set one up with Ruby instead." They eyed me. "Or do you prefer women, my dear? Or folks like myself, who are not quite either?"

I frowned and looked around the table; no one had ever asked me this directly before. *These seem like safe enough people to tell.* Alexander and Ember clearly had no qualms about gender, Lachlann seemed accepting of them, and Jasper, well, he wasn't afraid of my magic, so I doubted my preferences would faze him. I took a deep breath. *"I like both men and women,"* I signed.

"Ah." Lachlann nodded, clearly unbothered by my confession, and translated for me.

"Really?' Jasper's eyes narrowed. "Why didn't I know that?"

"I didn't want Mother and Father to know, so I never told you," I replied.

"You know, I do recall overhearing Mother talking to a friend of hers, wondering if you preferred women. She'd noticed you didn't seem to have much interest in boys, and that you'd never had any boyfriends. Or did you?"

I shook my head. *"I had a girlfriend once, but no boyfriends. I pretended not to be interested in boys. If Mother knew I was at all interested, she'd try to set me up with the nearest noble's son."* Lachlann chuckled at my response before relaying it to Jasper, who smirked. *"What did Mother think of the idea of me liking women?"* I asked.

"If I recall, she didn't like the idea much. She wanted grandchildren, and connections to other noble families, and for Father to give you away at a big fancy wedding." He shrugged. "She probably would have tried to marry you off to some rich noble's son eventually, even if you didn't like men."

"Yes, I know. I suppose I was trying to delay the inevitable." My shoulders slumped. *"Mother had all sorts of ideas of who I should be, and I couldn't live up to any of them."*

Lachlann translated and then turned to give me a sympathetic smile. "If it's any comfort to you, Ruby, folks in Dundere are much more accepting of those who prefer their own gender. The first Dunderi governor lost his wife while he was in office, and a few years later he married a man. The two of them did incredible things for the Isle."

Jasper cocked his head. "You know, I don't think I've ever met someone who likes both men and women before."

"Actually, you have. Kirilee was the same way. She liked men more, but she had a few girlfriends in her younger years."

"And then there's me," Alexander cut in. "I like *people*. I don't particularly care what's in their breeches, or under their skirt." He laughed, and I felt my cheeks redden at his forthrightness.

The server appeared with our food then, and we all dug in. I'd ordered a stew, because I knew I could eat it without having to ask someone to cut my meal up for me. It smelled delicious.

As I took my first bite, a tall, spectacled man stepped onto the stage in the corner of the room and began playing a tune on his lute.

Lachlann secured the fork attachment onto his hook, and Ember studied it as he began to eat. "You've adapted to that thing well, I see."

He shrugged. "I had to. I still miss the old metal arm, but there's not much I can do about it now."

"I'm pretty surprised that you were willing to give it up to learn anti-magic," Jasper said. "I thought you loved that thing."

"I did. It wasn't an easy choice. But I'm pretty committed to bringing anti-magic to Breoch one day. This was the only path I saw to that."

"You know, there is a way to get your hand back," Ember said to him. "Your real hand, not just the metal one. But it would require you to give up your anti-magic at some point in your life."

Lachlann shook his head. "I don't think you understand how Bonded anti-magic works."

"I know that your pendant fuses into your chest and it makes you extremely powerful, and that it's a lifetime commitment," they replied.

"So then you should know that I can't have my hand back, ever."

"You'd think that. But many years back, we ended up helping a couple of anti-mages and a lifebringer. The five of us went out for drinks one night and had a very interesting conversation."

"Why would anti-mages come to you?"

"Because we do have some anti-magic stone in our stash." Ember smiled. "These anti-mages were loyal to their cause, but they were getting rather tired of not being able to heal when they got sick or injured. While we were drinking, the anti-mages and the lifebringer got into a theoretical discussion about how they could get rid of their anti-magic, and they came up with an idea that, while pretty dangerous, might actually work."

Lachlann arched an eyebrow. "All right, tell me."

"You'd need two things to accomplish this. First, a willing lifebringer. And don't even think of asking Noelle, there's no way she'd approve of this. Second, you'd need to find someone who's willing to kill you."

We all gaped at Ember, bewildered. "Kill him?" Jasper repeated. "And then what, have the lifebringer resurrect him? Can they *do* that?"

"That's a complicated question. The answer is, not usually, but there are some exceptions. One of the simpler spells only works on someone who has just died. There's a window of about four minutes between the time a person's heart stops beating and when their brain dies. If a lifebringer can both repair the damage that killed the person and restart the heart in that window, then there's a chance they could bring the person back."

"Right," Lachlann said. "I've heard that before."

"Now, if I understand correctly, the pendant is fused to your breastbone purely through anti-magic?" Ember asked him. "Once the heart stops beating, it detaches, correct?"

He nodded. "So I've been told."

"So someone would have to kill you and then yank the pendant out of your chest, and then the lifebringer would have to repair the damage and restart your heart, all within four minutes."

Jasper whistled. "That does sound risky."

"Very," Lachlann agreed. "I'm assuming the type of death would matter in this case?"

"Absolutely." Alexander nodded. "A bullet would be a terrible idea. Slitting the person's throat would be messy, but it might work. The anti-mages got talking about this, and they figured the best way for everyone involved would be a broken neck."

Jasper laughed. "And we're onto the subject of broken necks again."

"Why would a broken neck be the best way?" I asked.

"Well, it's quick and painless for the poor anti-mage," Alexander explained once Lachlann had translated for me. "It's simple enough if you know the proper technique, and my understanding is that broken bones are one of the easier injuries to heal, so long as the bone is set properly first."

"Actually, that does make some sense," Lachlann said. "I recall hearing from the girls that it was fairly easy for Noelle back when she healed…" He trailed off and glanced over at us. "Never mind."

"What?" Alexander asked.

Lachlann shook his head. "It was something that happened during a rather painful part of my life. I'd rather not get into it now."

"Lachlann, my dear, you know you can talk to me about these things."

"Maybe another time." He turned his attention to Ember. "Your entire proposal is entertaining, but I'm not eager to have my neck broken and risk death just to get my arm back."

"Understandable." Ember smiled.

"You know, there is another option that doesn't involve broken necks," Alexander put in. "Are you aware that fairy magic is somewhat resistant to anti-magic?"

"I've heard that, yes," Lachlann replied. "I know that your potions could be used in a situation where anti-magic is present. Though I still don't think they'd work on me directly."

"Maybe not. But perhaps next time you talk to Hilda, you could see if she would enchant your metal arm with fairy magic. I'd do it myself, but I doubt my connection to the fairies is strong enough."

"Huh." Lachlann frowned. "It's worth asking. I haven't seen Hilda in ages."

"I see her fairly regularly. I'll mention it to her next time we talk."

"Who's Hilda?" Jasper asked.

"One of the few humans that has an immense amount of fairy magic in her."

"What is fairy magic, exactly? How does it work?"

"That's a good question; I wish I could tell you. All I know is that it comes from the fairies, and that the fairies have to choose you to have it."

Jasper pushed his plate away, then finished his ale. "How did you get chosen?" he wondered, gazing down into his empty mug. "Also, can I have another drink?"

Alexander shook his head. "You'd best only have one; if you have too much, it can make you pretty sick when you mix it with the sleeping potion."

"Your sleeping potion is *why* I need another drink," Jasper mumbled. "I'm not sure if I can convince myself to crawl into one of those crates sober."

"I'll teleport you in myself, if needed." Alexander chuckled. "And to answer your other question, my parents were part of the group that protected the fairies within the Shrouded Woods some years ago. The fairies granted many in the group access to some of their magic. Hilda was the group's leader, so the fairies extended her life and made her their protector. My parents didn't expect the magic to be passed on to their children, but my brothers and I have certain abilities that don't come from normal magic."

"What can you do?" I asked.

"Well, aside from using fairy magic to make my potions, I also have the ability to inherently know which of my potions and Ember's amulets will benefit a person in the future. I can't see their future, but when I'm talking to a client, often a particular potion or charm will call to me, so I'll pass that item along to them. Sometimes, very occasionally, I'll feel compelled to offer a potion or charm to a complete stranger."

"So the colour potion to keep my hair from going grey is what called to you when you saw me?" asked Lachlann.

Alexander laughed. "Take it as a compliment. It means you're going to live a long and full life." Then he punched Lachlann in the shoulder. "Don't worry. I actually have a different item in mind for you, but it'll take both Ember and me to make it."

"Fairy magic in a pendant?" Lachlann whistled. "That's potent."

Ember nodded. "It's not normally done. Gives the user too much power. But this one will only be for a very specific use."

As Ember spoke, the musician ceased playing his tune and cleared his throat. "Esteemed guests," he said to the crowd, "I am about to play the song, 'Carry me Home to Verdant Shores,' but unfortunately, my wife has fallen ill and cannot sing the verses. Is there anyone out there who would like to join me?"

Alexander looked around the table. "Any volunteers?"

"I'll do it." Jasper grinned, and his eyes shifted over to the server. *Clearly he's out to impress her.*

"You can sing?" Lachlann asked.

Jasper's grin widened further. "I'm not all trickery and lies, you know. I do have a life outside of being a troublemaker. I'm actually quite talented with a fiddle, as well, and Ruby's skilled on the piano." His eyes flickered to me. "You'll have to show Lachlann once you get your hand back."

I nodded.

Jasper approached the stage, and Alexander eyed him appreciatively. "Handsome young fellow," he mumbled. I rolled my eyes.

"Perhaps, but he's caused my friends and me quite a bit of grief in the past," Lachlann replied. "That's partly why I brought him here."

"Yes, you did say he used to be Breoch Guard."

Lachlann nodded. "I'll tell you the story later."

We watched as the musician chatted with Jasper for a few moments, then began to strum his lute again, though this time his tune was mournful. He started to sing the song's chorus— one I'd heard only a few times before— in a deep baritone. Jasper took over the verses, his voice not as deep as the other man's, but still very smooth and rich. Together they wove a tale of someone who'd spent years lost at sea and was trying to make his way back to the Isles where his lover waited. When they reached the chorus again, Jasper began singing the harmony without being asked to, causing the musician to raise his eyebrows and nod in approval. I grinned; it had been years since I'd heard anyone in my family sing. Yet I could not help but feel a small twinge of jealousy as well. I remembered the days, many years ago, when I'd sung duets with my brother. *I miss being able to do that.*

Beside me, Alexander let out a low whistle. "Quite the jack of all trades, that boy is. Handsome, charming, and skilled in trickery, lies, *and* song!"

"He did terribly in school," I put in, smirking.

"All the smartest people do," Alexander replied. He clapped Lachlann on the shoulder. "This fellow here barely finished school and still isn't the strongest reader, but he's one of the cleverest folks I know."

Lachlann shook his head and laughed, then turned back to watch Jasper some more. "You think he's going to impress that barmaid with his singing?"

"I don't doubt it for a moment," Ember replied. "Unfortunately for him, he's going to be far too asleep soon to do anything about it."

About an hour later, Jasper and I were back in Alexander and Ember's work space, each holding a bottle of the pink sleep potion and staring down at the two long wooden crates where we would spend the next couple of weeks. Mischief had returned, and she was scampering about the room, sniffing things curiously.

Jasper studied the crate nervously. "I don't like it. It looks like a coffin."

"You're not the first person to say that," Lachlann told him. "But so far, none of the kids who took that potion have died."

"You'll be fine," Alexander assured. "Now, Ember and I need to close down the shop, and you should both be asleep by the time we get back." He gave us a sweeping bow. "It was lovely meeting both of you."

"Safe travels," Ember added, giving us a smile.

They turned and left us there. Jasper looked nervously at Lachlann again. "Are you sure this is safe?"

"Absolutely," Lachlann replied. "I know it's hard, Jasper, but you need to trust me. You want to get back on the Lady Liara, right?"

Jasper nodded.

"Well, this is the only way there. Drink up, both of you."

Jasper sighed and climbed into his crate. I followed suit. The straw bedding was a bit scratchy, but it was soft enough. Mischief jumped into Jasper's crate and settled in his lap, seeming to know he was nervous. Smiling, Jasper stroked the fox's fur for a moment. "You'd better not stay in here for long, unless you want to get shipped to Dundere," he murmured. Then he met my eyes. "All right, Ruby, let's do this together."

I nodded and uncapped my vial, my heartbeat picking up as I sniffed the contents. It smelled pleasantly sweet, but also earthy and herbal.

"On three," Jasper said, uncapping his own vial. "One, two, three."

We both drank. "Hmm, that does taste good!"

"You'd best both lie down," Lachlann urged. "It will take a few minutes for the potion to kick in, but once it does, you'll fall asleep fast."

Jasper nodded, then gave me a nervous smile. "See you on the other side, Ruby."

I lay down in the straw, staring up at the candlelight flickering above me. Jasper began to sing to himself, the song from earlier in the evening coming out soft and halting. *Soon,* I thought, *I'll be able to sing along too.*

I closed my eyes and listened to him until sleep overtook me.

CHAPTER 7

I AWOKE TO the smell of salt air. The floor moved beneath me, swaying and rocking gently, its wooden boards creaking with the motion. Their sound, however, was nearly overpowered by a bright, lilting song that seemed to be coming from directly above me. My eyes fluttered open, and I squinted against the daylight that streamed through a nearby window. A tall, grey-haired man stood next to my crate, playing the pipe. I let out a groan.

Lachlann appeared in my field of vision then. "Welcome back. And welcome to the Lady Liara."

I gave him a smile and attempted to sit up, only to flop quickly back down. He laughed and offered me a hand. "You'll be a little weak after sleeping for two weeks. We need to get some food and water into you both."

I nodded and looked around the room. We were in what appeared to be a cabin, vacant except for a couple of bunks and a dresser. Jasper groaned then too, and Lachlann went over to check on him. I stared up at the man who played the pipe. He was clad in a long-tailed coat and a three-cornered hat, and his grey hair curled on his shoulders. *Looks to be the captain,* I decided.

The man stopped playing his song and peered down at me. "You must be Ruby," he said, giving me a wide smile. He looked me over with a pair of blue eyes that, despite his obvious age, seemed merry and youthful. "I'm Gareth, the captain of the Lady Liara. I've been told that you're a stormbrewer."

I nodded.

"My favourite type of magikai to have on my ship. I'll introduce you to Harvey at dinner; you'll be working with him." His gaze travelled from me to Jasper, who was now sitting up. His hair was dishevelled, and his beard had grown fuller in the two weeks he'd been asleep. "And here, we have a scoundrel," Gareth said, his voice turning sober.

Jasper nodded and gave him a nervous smile. "Good to see you again, sir."

"I wish I could say the same." Gareth let out a huff. "You're mighty lucky that Lachlann here seems to like you. If I had it my way, we would have kept you asleep 'til you got to Dundere."

Jasper nodded. "That would have been a shame given how much I enjoyed myself last time."

Gareth frowned. "Aye, I do recall you being a solid worker, when you weren't busy kidnapping and shooting my crew. I s'pose I can give you a chance. But one false move and I'm putting you into the brig, boy. Understood?"

"Understood, sir." Jasper got to his feet a bit unsteadily. "May I show my sister around the ship?"

"Wait 'til after you've eaten. Dinner's nearly ready. Don't need the two of you fainting on my decks for lack of food."

I stood up slowly, then smoothed down my rumpled dress and picked a few pieces of straw out of my hair. Gareth eyed me. "Did you get the girl some proper sailing clothes?"

Lachlann nodded, passing me a bundle. "I had our friends make them up." I peeked inside to see what looked like boys' clothes. "You can't wear dresses when you're working on a ship. I'm not sure if you've worn breeches before, but you will for the next two weeks."

I nodded. *"I've always wanted to try them."*

"Well, this is your lucky day then," Gareth said. I raised my eyebrows, and he grinned. "Harvey and I both know how to sign. We've had a few of your sort on this ship over the years. The rest of my crew isn't the best with it, but you'll be able to talk to the two of us, at least."

"I have more clothes from Alex and Ember for both of you, though you won't need them til we reach Dundere," Lachlann informed Jasper and me. "Dundere's fashion is a bit more colourful than Breoch's"

"What was the gift Alexander said he would give you?" Jasper asked.

"Ah, right. It was this." Lachlann pointed to a ring he wore on his right pinky. "I have another on a pendant. They're made with fairy magic and will apparently allow me to create a connection with another sentient creature, like what Kirilee had with her hawk." He shook his head. "I'm not certain what I'll need this for, but I'm sure I'll find out. They sent something for you two as well." He reached into his shoulder bag and pulled out two smooth green stones. "A summoning stone for each of you, so you can find one another if need be. Alex seems to think you'll need them at some point on your journey."

Jasper nodded. "I'm sure that'll come in handy." I ran my fingers over the smooth, cool stone before pocketing it.

"I made something else for you while I was in Flavalan, Ruby," Lachlann went on. "It won't have much use once you're in Dundere, but I think you'll need it while you're aboard the ship." I opened the small bundle he produced and found myself staring down at a hook, similar to Lachlann's but smaller, with a separate attachment that looked like a knife. "You'll need that hook if you ever have to climb the ropes," he explained. "You don't have to wear it all the time, but it's good for you to have in case."

"What's the knife for?" I asked.

"I thought about making you a fork, but then I realized you likely eat with your left hand anyway. The knife is so you can cut up food. It could also be useful in a fight." He grinned. "Here, try the hook on."

I lifted it gingerly, and Lachlann showed me how to fit the end onto my stump and tighten the straps, which proved difficult to do with one hand. I examined the hook's tip, which was blunted. It was a bit heavier than I expected.

"Do be careful with that around other people," Gareth warned. "It may not be sharp, but you could still take an eye out with it."

"Can I touch it?" Jasper asked me, and I nodded, extending my arm to him. He frowned as he touched the hook's end. "Yes, this could definitely be used as a weapon."

"If Ruby was going to be in this state for longer than a couple more weeks," Lachlann said, "I'd teach her to fight with it. But hopefully there will be no need for that. You might want to bring the knife with you to dinner."

I nodded. *"How do I attach the knife?"*

"Like this." Lachlann showed me how to unscrew the hook and slide the knife attachment into the socket. When he was satisfied I could do it myself, he grinned and stood up. "We need to clear out of this cabin; someone else will be using it once we reach the next port. Ruby, I'll show you where the ladies' bunks are so you can change into these clothes. Jasper, you remember how to get to the men's quarters, I assume?"

Jasper nodded and grinned as he got to his feet. "Happy to be back here," he said to Lachlann and Gareth, picking up his bag and disappearing out the cabin door.

Gareth shook his head. "I hope you're right about him, Lachlann."

"I am. A magical fox told me so, Captain." Lachlann clapped Gareth on the shoulder, then turned to me. "Come along, Ruby, let's get you settled in."

Half an hour later, I sat in the ship's mess deck with Jasper and Lachlann amongst a few dozen other folks. Some were obviously seasoned crew members with sun-weathered skin and salt-matted hair, while others were likely as fresh onto the boat as we were. I noticed a handful of girls, maybe a few years older than me, who wore extravagant hairdos and fancy dresses, and wondered how they'd do at working on a ship.

The breeches Lachlann gave me seemed to fit well enough. They felt odd to me, but I could see how they'd be easy to move around in. Eating with the knife attachment for my hook was taking some getting used to; back on the island, we never ate anything that needed to be cut up, and at Tomlin and Lachlann's home, Helenne had the foresight to cut my food up for me. I glanced around furtively as I struggled with the old motions of slicing into a piece of chicken, hoping no one was watching me.

Thankfully, no one seemed to be paying attention, though I did notice one of the crew members eying Jasper suspiciously. "I remember you," he said, his tone turning threatening. "Isn't this the scallywag who caused trouble on our ship all those years ago?"

Jasper grimaced, but then he met the other man's eyes. "I most certainly caused some trouble, but I don't recall any of it being on your ship."

"Wait, is this the fellow who shot Janice?" a younger man asked from further down the table. He turned to the crew member next to him. "Do you remember, Dirk?"

Dirk shook his head. "No, that wasn't him. This is the one who put a knife to Saray's throat and threatened to kill her if we didn't leave."

"Oh, *him.*" The other young man's eyes narrowed. "What exactly are you doing here, huh?"

"That's enough, boys." A man with a long, dark ponytail who looked about Lachlann's age walked over and clapped the two men on the shoulders. "I could tell stories about where you came from too, Landon. Do you really think Gareth would've let Jasper aboard if he thought he'd be a danger to us?"

Landon crossed his arms. "You've left the Guard, then? Changed your mind about magic?"

Jasper motioned to me. "This is my sister, Ruby. She's a krossemage, and we're taking her to Dundere to get her healed up. I hope that answers your question."

"Huh." Landon frowned and eyed him some more.

"You know what Gareth says, boys," Lachlann put in. "Here on the Lady Liara, your past only matters if you let it. At least, that's what he used to say when I was on the crew."

Dirk raised his eyebrows at Jasper. "If you're really no longer part of the Guard, tell us some stories of the stupidest things you ever saw them do."

"Ah. I do have some of those." Jasper grinned, his shoulders relaxing. "The funniest story I can think of happened to my father. He and another Guard member were sent out to arrest this teleporter, and things went horribly wrong."

While Jasper talked, the man with the ponytail made his way over to me. "Ruby," he said, "I'm Harvey, the first mate of the Lady Liara and a fellow stormbrewer. I hear I'm going to be training you."

I nodded and smiled at him. *Pleased to meet you,* I signed.

"It's exciting to have another stormbrewer aboard," he said, returning my smile. "It's been a good five years since that's happened." He glanced back to where Gareth was eating with a few of the older crew members. "I'd best get back to my meal, but I hope you enjoy your time with us. We'll talk more tomorrow." He returned to Gareth's table, and I went back to my food, half listening to the rest of Jasper's story.

"So, Father finally got a hold of her, but he made the mistake of grabbing onto the sleeve of her dress, not her arm, and this woman somehow managed to teleport right out of her clothes. Next thing you know, Father is standing there holding her dress, and then he and the others see her on the roof of a nearby building in only her hat and her petticoats, smirking at them. From what I heard, a few of the men were so embarrassed they couldn't bring themselves to keep chasing her. And of course, by the time Father got up on the roof, she was gone."

"Did your father tell you this story?" asked Landon.

"Of course not. I was only twelve. But one of my classmates heard about it, and he told me and a few of my friends. It seemed incredibly scandalous, at the time." He smirked. "I'll tell you more stories tomorrow though. I have things I need to do." He turned to me. "You all done your food, Ruby?"

I took the last bite of my meal and nodded.

"Good. Time to take you on the grand tour of the Lady Liara."

It took maybe an hour to see the ship in its entirety. I peeked into the hold, stared in awe at the massive cannons on the gun deck, toured the crew quarters, and was even allowed to take a quick look into Gareth's cabin. Jasper struggled to remember the names of all the sails, but he assured me that Harvey would fill me in.

Here on the Lady Liara, I learned, anyone could sail for free so long as they were willing to do their share of the work. The main crew— those who had been on the ship for over a month— stayed in quarters separate from the passengers, most of whom slept below deck in large dormitory-like quarters. I would be sleeping below too, with at least a dozen other girls. Gareth also kept a few special cabins set aside for passengers of note; Jasper told me that Lachlann and Kirilee had been given one such cabin following their wedding aboard the ship.

Now we sat on the main deck, watching as a small group of crew members pulled flutes and fiddles and drums out of their respective cases. Music and dancing were a near-nightly event on the Lady Liara, and watches were arranged so that everyone got the chance to attend at some point.

Dirk and Landon rejoined us, along with Landon's fiancée Anika, and the three of them began chatting with Jasper about what had happened on the ship since his departure. The earlier tension between them seemed to have disappeared for now.

Meanwhile, a group of younger passengers, including the girls I'd noticed at dinner, huddled nearby, throwing occasional curious glances in our direction. Several of them were engrossed in a story being told by a young man and woman who looked to be siblings, both tall and with delicate features and strawberry blond hair that glinted in the evening sun. The girl met my eyes for a moment and wrinkled her nose.

When the music started up with a merry, lilting tune that sounded similar to some of the music we'd heard at the Gilded Duck, it only took seconds for the deck to fill up with folks clapping and dancing to the rhythm. Landon stood and offered Anika a hand, while Dirk wandered over to the core crew looking for someone to dance with. Lachlann also found a partner easily enough, and I noticed a slender girl with dark hair that fell nearly to her waist approaching us. She smiled shyly at Jasper. "Would you like to dance?"

"Me? Absolutely." He grinned and got to his feet, the girls from the other group letting out a series of whoops as he did. "Enjoy the music, Ruby," he said, glancing back at me, then offering the girl his arm and disappearing into the crowd.

I sat back against the side of the ship, watching the dancers whirl and shake to the rhythm. I could understand easily enough why Jasper liked it here. Whether I would feel as at home here as he did, I wasn't certain, but it was good to see him happy again.

Some time later, I retreated to the bunk. Several of the girls from the other group were there already, chatting and laughing amongst themselves. I'd surmised from things I heard above deck that they were a group of magic users from a university in Kirstein who'd banded together. They preferred returning home for the summer on Gareth's ship, given his lax attitudes about magic use once the ship was away from the port cities. About half of them were from Breoch, but some were from Dundere or other Candeshi islands. When I came into the room, several of them stopped talking and eyed me. I smiled and waved nervously.

The girl who'd asked Jasper to dance looked me over. "Are you Jasper's sister, then?"

I nodded, and a few of the girls began whispering.

"Where are you two heading?"

I motioned for a pen and paper.

"Why do you need a pen?..." The girl's eyes narrowed for a moment until she realized. "Oh, I see. I'm sorry, I didn't know you were a..." Her face turned red.

"Were you a slave?" another girl asked.

I nodded.

"How did you get away?" The first girl's eyes widened. "Did Jasper rescue you?"

I had to force myself not to roll my eyes as I nodded again.

There were gasps from the girls who were clearly now even more smitten with my brother thanks to this new revelation.

"Did it hurt?" another asked. "When they cut off your hand and such?"

Not wanting to relive those memories, I sighed, but before I could respond, another voice cut in, this one authoritative. "Of course it hurt." All eyes turned to the tall girl with the red-gold hair that I'd noticed just before the dancing started. She stood near the door, clearly having just walked in on our discussion. "You can't have your hand cut off painlessly." She snorted. "It's just another example of Breochi cruelty."

The girls nodded their agreement, and the one who'd begun the conversation with me frowned. "If Breoch is such a cruel place, why'd your parents send you and Aidan to school there, Ashlynn?"

Ashlynn rolled her eyes. "It's the only place in the Verdant Isles with a decent university, Violet. The Candeshi mainland is too far away, or so my parents seem to think."

"At least Breoch is a free nation," another protested. "We're not subject to the whims of an empire, unlike you folk from Dundere."

"Yes, but the Candeshi encourage folks to learn to use their magic properly, instead of torturing people for it, like this poor thing here," put in another girl. Several pairs of eyes landed on me, and I felt my cheeks heat up.

"At least she had a cute older brother to rescue her," said Violet.

"Don't go falling for him." Ashlynn warned. "I heard rumours earlier that he used to be with the Breoch Guard. I'm not sure why the captain lets that sort of scum onto his ship."

"He's not *scum!* He *used* to be Breoch Guard, but he's changed," Violet shot back. I nodded my agreement.

The argument quickly turned heated then, Ashlynn denouncing both Breoch and my brother, and I slunk away to my bed. *At least they aren't asking questions about me being a krossemage anymore.* I pulled the covers over myself and closed my eyes.

The ship moved in a slow, steady motion, as if it were trying to rock me to sleep, the creak of the hull a strange, accompanying lullaby. I tried to tune out the bickering of the girls, focusing instead on the rhythmic noises around me, until I was overcome by dreams.

The following morning, I woke up to a pounding headache. I sat up and gasped as a wave of nausea hit me, and a few of the other girls shot me concerned glances. Violet stared at me a little longer, worry apparent in her dark eyes. I dragged myself out of bed, trying hard not to vomit as I pulled on my clothes and stumbled to the mess hall.

The hall was still mostly empty, but Lachlann was there chatting with Harvey at one of the tables. He glanced up when he noticed me approaching. "You don't look so good."

"I feel like I'm going to throw up," I signed.

"Looks like you've got a bit of seasickness," Harvey said. "It's pretty common for newcomers. It'll pass in a few days, but you'd best rest up for now."

"But I thought I was meant to train with you today."

"No point in training until you feel a little better," he replied. "Go back to bed, and take a bucket with you. You might need it."

I nodded, picked a bucket from the stack Harvey pointed me to, and returned to my bunk. Crawling back into bed, I watched the other girls as they got ready for work, donning pants and shirts similar to my own. I needed the bucket within the hour, and for once I was glad to not have a sense of taste. When I thought it was safe, I lay back, trying to ignore the pounding in my head, until the gentle rocking of the ship, nauseating as it was, lulled me back to sleep.

The next few days passed in similar fashion. I drifted in and out of consciousness, my waking hours punctuated by splitting headaches and bouts of vomiting when I did try to keep food down. Kezia, one of the older female crew members, came down to check on me several times, and Lachlann visited too. Jasper came to see me once, glancing nervously around the womens' quarters before entering, clearly concerned that he'd get in trouble for being there. The other girls came and went, a few of them stopping to ask if I was feeling better before returning to their friends. Violet paid more attention to me than the others, often bringing me water or tea that was meant to help with the seasickness. Only Ashlynn seemed to dislike me; she kept her distance and protested whenever Jasper's name came up, which it did several times.

On the fourth day, the headache was gone, and when Kezia came by I requested food. I sat up in my bunk and slowly ate the soup and hardtack she gave me, then gulped down several glasses of water. When I'd managed to keep everything down several hours later, she came back with a heartier meal. "You seem to be on the mend. You should be able to start working with Harvey tomorrow."

That evening I made my way above deck for the first time in several days. We were still skirting the coast of Breoch, but I had no idea where we were specifically. The music and dancing had already started, and Harvey noticed me almost immediately. "Glad to hear you're doing a little better, Ruby. Do you think you'll be ready to work with me tomorrow?"

I nodded and gave him a grin; I still felt a bit weak and unsteady, but I was sure I could at least try to begin my training.

"Good." He smiled. "I need to go speak with a few of the others. But enjoy yourself tonight. There are plenty of folks to dance with." He gestured at the bustling deck and then walked away.

I settled against the side of the ship and watched the dancers. Jasper was, of course, among them; he grinned at me once between dances and then sauntered off to find his next partner. A few songs later, he'd retreated to the other side of the ship, where he regaled a group of the girls from my bunk— all of them clad in their fancy dresses for dancing, as seemed to be their preference— with exciting stories, a tankard of something in his hand. I shook my head.

It was then that I noticed Lachlann was watching Jasper too, and I joined him.

"Has he been like this the whole time I've been sick?"

Lachlann nodded. "I fear this is at least somewhat my fault."

"How?"

"When I told you and Jasper the story of what happened after your brother left Dundere, I left something out." Lachlann turned to face me. "Shortly after Trina's eyes were healed, we learned that Marcus, the governor's husband, is actually Saray's father."

My eyes narrowed. *"Really?"*

"We think the fairies may have been involved in leading them to one another. After that was revealed, Noelle and Marcus ended up adopting the two girls. So accompanying you to Dundere means that Jasper will very likely have to face them again."

"And you decided to tell Jasper this after *he agreed to come with us?"*

"It was part of why I was reluctant to bring him along in the first place. And I wasn't about to tell him Saray or Trina's location until I knew I could trust him, which wasn't until he met Mischief." He eyed me. "I think he would've agreed to accompany you, even if he'd known."

"How did he react when you told him?"

"He wasn't too happy about it when I first let him know, but an hour later he was laughing with his friends and flirting with girls again." Lachlann sighed. "I'm not sure whether to feel good about the way he's acting. He seems genuinely happy, but I imagine at least some of it's an attempt to distract himself. I'm a little worried about him falling back into drinking too much, but beyond that I think it's best to just let him have his fun while he can."

I shrugged. *"I suppose so."*

"You haven't had much fun on this voyage," Lachlann observed. "Though I imagine Dundere will be more pleasant for you."

"It might be easier for me to have fun if I could join in the dancing," I replied.

"Why can't you dance?"

"It's hard to dance with only one hand."

"Is that so? Clearly you just don't know how it's done." Lachlann gestured at his hook. "You don't see this stopping me. Watch." He walked across the deck to where some of the crew were sitting and began conversing with a tall, dark-haired woman. Then he brought her over to me. "Ruby, this is Cerise, one of the crew members. I'm going to have a dance with her, and then she'll dance with you."

"Pleased to meet you, Ruby." Cerise smiled at me.

Lachlann offered her an arm then. "Shall we?"

She grinned and took it, and I watched as they made their way onto the dance floor. Lachlann put his arm around Cerise's waist, and she took his hook in her free hand. I watched as they began to move around the dance floor effortlessly, both of them seeming completely unfazed by Lachlann's appendage. Jasper, I noticed, had returned to the dance floor and was getting very close to the girl he danced with.

When the song ended, Lachlann and Cerise returned. "You see?" Cerise said. "The hook is only as intimidating as you make it out to be."

I glanced down at my stump; I hadn't even thought to bring my hook with me. *"Should I go get mine?"* I signed to Lachlann.

"It's up to you, but for this, it might not be a bad idea."

I went below deck to retrieve my hook, and when I came back, Cerise asked, "Are you ready to try?"

I nodded.

"All right. I'll lead this time." She pulled me into the proper position, taking my hook in her left hand. "Do you know how to dance like this?"

I nodded again.

"Good." Another song had begun to play, this one a bit slower. "Let's go."

I let her lead me onto the floor, and we began a slow waltz. My feet found the old rhythms quickly enough, and I gave Cerise a quick smile. "I can tell you've had practice," she said.

It seemed that others could tell as well; I didn't miss the fact that several folks were watching us as we moved. "I'm not just doing this to show you that it's possible," she continued. "I'm doing this to show them that dancing with someone who's different from them isn't that scary." She smiled. "I hope more folks ask you to dance after this."

Sure enough, after the song ended and Cerise had returned to her friends, a boy from the university group approached me. "Hi," he said. "I'm Cole. You want to dance?"

I smiled as I let him lead me back onto the floor. Perhaps this trip wouldn't be so bad after all.

CHAPTER 8

THE FOLLOWING MORNING after breakfast, I stood with Harvey at the bow of the ship, looking out over the water. The sky was mostly blue today, dotted by a few silvery clouds. "This is perfect weather to practice stormbrewing," Harvey said to me. "Neither completely clear nor overcast." He glanced up at the sky. "I assume you've cast before, given your condition?"

I nodded.

"What did you do?"

I explained to him what had happened while I was sailing with Jade and Gabby, and he nodded gravely when I mentioned that Jade had turned me in. "Your brother sounds like he's deep into some harmful thinking." He sighed. "So you moved clouds using wind, but you didn't stop the rain?"

I shook my head. *"I don't know how to start and stop rain."*

"That will be a good place to start. But first, let's see what you can do with the wind." He gestured to a bank of clouds that sat on the horizon. "Bring those towards us. Gently, though. Keep the wind steady."

I closed my eyes and let my mind drift upwards. Then I made a motion with my hand, touching my thumb to my ring finger while I twisted my wrist counterclockwise. A moment later, I inhaled sharply as my consciousness made the connection; for a second, it felt like I was one with the breeze. There was nothing but me and the wind, my entire existence reduced to cold but playful air currents. A seagull soared above, riding the draft, and I giggled. Then I took a deep breath, regaining my concentration, and willed the wind to blow the bank of clouds in our direction.

"Wind coming from the west!" Harvey shouted back to the crew. "Adjust the sails and prepare for a bit of rain!" I felt the boat begin to shift underneath me as the crew obeyed. The bank of clouds was approaching fast, blocking out the sun. "Excellent, Ruby, you can release control now."

I made the hand motion again, only this time clockwise, and sighed as I felt my connection with the clouds die.

"Was that hard for you?"

I shrugged. *"Not really."*

"Good. Now I'm going to show you how to make it rain. The clouds will break naturally once they get too heavy, but it's possible to make them break prematurely."

"Can I stop them once they've broken?"

Harvey smiled and shook his head. *"I* can, but I've had to learn both waterweaving and telekinesis. If you want to stop the rain, for now it's best to blow the clouds away. As for making the rain come, that requires more concentration than controlling winds. I want you to say your casting words again, but this time try to connect to the clouds instead of the winds."

I nodded and repeated my hand motion. The connection with the wind was instantaneous, unstoppable. I sighed and severed it, then looked at Harvey. *"I don't know how to* not *connect with the wind."*

He nodded. "I figured. I'm going to take control of it, then. When you cast, you won't be able to connect with the wind because my magic will be blocking you. So hopefully you'll be able to divert your concentration to the clouds instead." He smiled. "Ready to try?"

I nodded. Harvey made a hand motion of his own, and I felt the wind shift ever so slightly. "All right," he said, "try again."

I motioned and let my mind drift upwards, only to feel my consciousness slam against a hard wall. The winds were locked away, totally inaccessible to me. An odd shiver went through me, and for a second I swore I could *taste* something. It was sweet and fruity, but I couldn't quite identify what sort of fruit it was. My eyes flew open.

"You're probably sensing my magic," Harvey said. "Try to ignore it. Let your mind attempt to find something else to grab onto, other than the wind."

I nodded and stared up at the cloud bank, willing my magic to connect. It was hard to ignore Harvey's magic, or the odd emptiness I felt without my connection to the wind but I closed my eyes anyway. *Come on, find the clouds.*

The sudden sensation of my mind connecting with something dense and wet and brooding made me jerk back. This was not the easy, playful feel of wind magic; it was heavy and shot through with anticipation, and my entire being was suffused with its dampness, its yearning for release. I gripped the railing, finding it hard to stand under the near-smothering weight of the clouds. "Looks like you got it," I heard Harvey say, and I gritted my teeth and nodded.

"The cloud *wants* to rain, doesn't it?"

I nodded again, my hand tightening on the rail.

"So will the water downwards, similar to how you will the wind in whatever direction you want. This will feel more like letting go than pushing." He chuckled. "Pardon my crassness, but it's rather like, er, using the bathroom. Only be sure not to *actually* piss yourself while you're doing it."

I took a deep breath and attempted what Harvey was asking, relaxing my body as I willed the cloud to release. It was easier than I expected, and I felt myself sighing with relief as the rain began to pour.

"Good job. You can let go of the cloud now."

Severing my connection to the cloud with a gesture, I opened my eyes and grinned at Harvey. "Not bad for day one," he told me. "You still have lots to learn, but this is a good start."

We spent the rest of the morning improving my wind abilities, and by the time lunch came around, I was exhausted but happy. This voyage, it seemed, was slowly beginning to improve.

The following days were much like the first. Mornings were spent working with Harvey, mastering wind and learning the ways I could begin and end rainfalls. I learned that moving clouds upward could help dissipate them. I also learned how to draw moisture from the ocean to form clouds of my own making, a process that often took hours. My first ones were small and not particularly threatening, but I was proud of them nonetheless. Harvey was a good teacher, though not typically talkative. He came across as quiet and withdrawn next to Gareth's endless stories and loud jokes, but I imagined the two men balanced one another out well.

In the afternoons, I began learning other ship duties. Lachlann helped me master the use of my hook so I could help open and close sails. Climbing the rigging and walking across yards was intimidating at first, but once I became accustomed to the rocking of the ship, I found it to be very much like climbing trees.

After dinner, there was always dancing. I was still shy and spent much of my time watching rather than participating, but most nights I was asked to dance by numerous shipmates. Jasper continued his flirting with the girls, and sometimes he would disappear from the dance floor with one of them on his arm.

Late one evening when the dancing was finished, I came below deck to hear raised voices and recognized one of them as Jasper's.

"...you keep your hands off her, you filthy bastard," another male's voice snarled. "She's mine!"

When I rounded the corner, my eyes widened. Aidan had Jasper pinned up against a bulkhead. Jasper's nose was bleeding, and it became clear to me that Aidan had punched him earlier in the encounter. "Yours, huh?" Jasper spat blood at Aidan and glared up at him. "She certainly didn't seem to think that last night!" His words were slightly slurred, and I wondered how much he'd had to drink.

Fire flickered on one of Aidan's hands. "Say that again," he growled. Jasper yelped as his shirt began to smolder.

I let out a wordless cry of protest and lunged forward before I could stop myself. Aiming for Aidan's face, I swung at him with my hook and caught his cheek with the tip. He yelped and turned to me, releasing my brother. "You little bitch," he snarled, taking a step toward me with fire still dancing on his hand. "I should burn off that pretty little face of yours."

A thrill of fear went through me at his words, but I forced myself to stay where I was, hook readied to swing at him a second time. *If I run, he might attack Jasper again.*

Behind him, Jasper tried, and failed, to get to his feet. "You leave my sister alone, you monster!" It was clear enough that he was in no shape to protect me.

Aidan snickered and took another step toward me. Heart pounding in my ears, I was on the verge of turning and running when a female voice interrupted our confrontation. "Really, Aidan? Attacking a helpless little krossemage? That's low, even for you."

I turned to find Ashlynn glaring at her brother, who backed slightly away but kept his gaze on me. "Helpless? Look what she did to my face!"

"I'm guessing it was because you were beating on her brother. Pretty sure I'd do the same if I came across some fellow attacking Alvin, or maybe even you." She put a hand on his shoulder. "Leave these two alone. They aren't worth your time."

The fire on Aidan's hands extinguished. He shot one last glare at me and mumbled something under his breath, then disappeared.

I was left staring at Ashlynn, more than a little surprised by her intervention.

Her eyes narrowed a little as she looked me over. "Are you all right?"

I nodded. Behind her, I watched Jasper climb slowly to his feet. "Uh, thanks for that," he slurred.

Ashlynn turned to face him. "Try not to piss Aidan off again, all right? He's not very fun to deal with when he's angry."

"I noticed." Jasper gave her a lopsided grin and wiped at the blood on his face.

Ashlynn sighed and shook her head. "Watch yourselves, you two." Then she gave me a glance that seemed almost sympathetic and stalked off.

I turned to Jasper, who was steadying himself against a wall. "Well," he said, looking me over, "I didn't know you had it in you to attack a fellow twice your size." He grinned. "Thanks for, uh, coming to my rescue."

"What happened?" I signed, knowing he likely wouldn't understand.

Jasper seemed to catch my meaning well enough though. "Don't worry about it. Girl problems. You're a little young for me to be talking to you about it."

I snorted in response. Then I pointed at his nose and motioned in the direction of the ship's doctor.

"I'll be fine," he assured. "It's not broken. I should get some sleep." Before I could protest, he stumbled off to the men's bunks.

The next night Jasper was back on deck, dancing with the women, but I did notice a subtle change in the girls' cabin dynamics. Ashlynn's moment of kindness toward Jasper and me seemed to have been a lapse in judgement on her part; she began talking about Jasper whenever she got the chance, calling him names and chastising other girls for dancing with him. Violet, meanwhile, became quiet and withdrawn.

One night I awoke to hear her sobbing into her pillow and crept off my bunk to put a hand on her shoulder. "Of course you're the one who comes to comfort me," she said softly.

My eyes narrowed in confusion.

"I don't know what to do about your brother, Ruby," she went on, her voice wavering. "I thought he liked me, but now he won't even talk to me. I'm not sure what I did. Am I just a plaything to him?" She began to cry again, and I settled on the edge of her bunk, trying to comfort her but having no idea how.

Violet departed the ship in Amberline, the final Breochi port before the ship turned northward to Dundere, and the tension amongst the girls seemed to ease slightly after that. Several nights later, I was awakened by a hand gripping my shoulder and shaking it. "Ruby," I heard Jasper's voice cut into my sleep. "Wake up. You're needed on deck."

I stared up at him in confusion.

"It's all men on watch tonight; they figured I was the best one to come get you," he explained. "Come on, Harvey needs you."

A few minutes later, I stumbled above deck, bleary eyed. Harvey stood at the ship's bow speaking in low tones to Gareth; I soon realized exactly why he'd summoned me.

A fork of lightning snaked across the sky, followed very closely by thunder. The air, however, was still and dry. *It doesn't feel like there's a storm coming.*

Harvey turned when he heard us. "Ruby, there you are. We have a problem."

"I see that," I replied, my eyes widening as lightning struck again. *"That storm feels... odd."*

"That's because it's magical," Harvey said. "We're being attacked."

"Pirates," Gareth added. "Pirates with magic." He gestured starboard, and only now did I see the faint outline of an approaching ship.

"It's too clear to easily conjure rain," Harvey explained. "But some stormbrewers can manufacture lightning using only high, sparse clouds. I suspect they also have a firebrand on board, which could be deadly if they get closer."

"What's their plan?" asked Jasper. "Or do you know?"

"My guess is something very similar to what Saray pulled on that Breoch Guard ship, if you recall."

"How could I forget?"

"They likely intend to set our ship aflame using lightning, then gain on us and have their firebrand only put out the fire if we surrender," Harvey explained to me. "Unfortunately, we don't have a firebrand of our own to counter theirs."

I nodded slowly. *"So what do we do?"*

"I have a few ideas. The first should succeed so long as Ruby and I work together. If it doesn't, we'll create a wind to try to send the lightning back their way. And if that fails, we'll call all hands onto the deck and get ready to fight."

"You'd best get back to your station, Jasper," Gareth said. "I'll start giving orders to prepare to run. You tell me when, Harvey."

Harvey nodded. "Understood, sir. Ruby, let's get working."

He took my hand and mumbled a spell to join our magic together, then closed his eyes. *"Arius Dominus Karnium.* Connect with the sea, Ruby."

Immediately, I let my consciousness drift down into the seawater, its presence massive and overwhelming, much more solid than the wispiness of the clouds I was used to working with. Harvey began pulling the water slowly upwards, much like he would if forming clouds. I combined my magic with his own, extending our reach to the stern of the ship. Slowly, a thick fog began to rise from the ocean, enveloping the ship entirely. The lightning crackled above us, directly overhead now, where it licked at our sails but did not catch. Harvey let out a sigh of relief. "The fog has two purposes," he told me. "Yes, it keeps them from seeing us, but it's also better than rain at stopping fires. Move to the starboard side of the ship and back to the stern, and keep the fog spreading. The larger the patch, the better chance we have at escaping. Make sure all the ropes are covered in fog; they catch fire much easier than sails."

I nodded and did as Harvey directed, willing the fog to keep rising as I moved. Harvey, meanwhile, was shaping the fog around the ship to allow just the tip of the bow on the port side to remain clear, thus allowing us sight for sailing. I thickened the fog on the starboard side, drawing it like a large curtain between us and the pirates. Gareth began calling out orders, and the ship picked up speed, turning hard to port. Lightning flashed again, but it was now clearly behind us.

"Keep that fog up, Ruby!" Gareth called back to me.

I nodded, channeling both my magic and Harvey's into the mist. An unexpected *boom* sounded from behind us, and I braced for impact.

There was none.

"They're firing on us, but they have no idea where we are," I heard one of the sailors say, his voice laced with amusement.

Harvey used his reserves of magic to bring in a wind then, leaving the fog patch behind us as the ship picked up even more speed. There were a few more explosions from the other ship's cannons, and lightning flickered one final time above the fog patch. I urged the fog to spread further as we sailed away, hoping to cover our tracks even more.

"We've lost them," Gareth finally announced, and a ripple of relief spread throughout the crew. "Keep moving, though, we don't want them to find us again."

"I think you're good to head back to bed, Ruby," Harvey said, joining me at the ship's stern. "I'll have someone wake you if we need. Thanks for your assistance."

Jasper caught up with me on my way back to the bunks, his eyes wide. "That was amazing! I haven't really watched you work yet, but what you and Harvey just did might have saved us." He shook his head. "I can't believe I used to think magic was evil. It's…incredible." He put a hand on my shoulder. "I'm proud of you."

I grinned at Jasper's words. *"Thank you."*

He squeezed my shoulder and then turned and headed back to his post. I was still grinning as I crawled into my bunk a few minutes later. I knew my talents were useful, but it had never before occurred to me that stormbrewing could be used to help divert magical pirates.

I wonder what else I can do with my gifts, I mused as I drifted off. Whatever the answer, I was sure I'd find out once we reached Dundere.

The next morning found me feeling both tired and triumphant from the previous night's work. After I'd finished breakfast, Jasper sidled up to me while I was working with Harvey, pointed at a tiny mass of land in the distance, and told me that I was looking at Dundere.

The rest of the day was spent busy with the usual tasks, and that night at dinner, Jasper, Lachlann and I were invited to sit with Gareth. "I just wanted you folks to know how well you've done over these past two weeks," he told us. "I've been pleasantly surprised by both of you kids. Ruby, Harvey says that you've improved a lot. And Jasper, you've been a hard worker and haven't caused trouble anywhere other than the dance floor."

Jasper laughed. Clearly Gareth was unaware of his little scuffle with Aidan. "I've had a wonderful time aboard the ship, sir. In fact, I have half a mind to come sail with you for a while once I'm done in Dundere." He eyed me. "Perhaps that's what I'll do once you're settled there, Ruby. I'd like to see the world."

Gareth grinned. "Well, you won't see much beyond the Verdant Isles while you're sailing with me, boy. I don't leave the area too often."

"Why not?"

"Because a good chunk of my crew is magikai, and it seems that much of the magic in the world is centered here," he explained. "The further you get from the Isles, the weaker their abilities become. You didn't know that, huh?"

Jasper shrugged. "Even so, if I were sailing with you, I'd likely see more of the world than I have thus far."

"That you would," Gareth agreed. "Though I must warn you, lad, if you think you're going to spend every night flirting with the ladies like you have been, you're wrong. There are rules about those things if you're part of the crew."

Jasper raised an eyebrow. "Oh? Such as?"

"You're not allowed to get involved with the short term passengers at all, other than dancing with them. No dating or kissing or any of that sort of business. You can date other crew members, but trying to bed the entire female crew is frowned upon."

"Has that been a problem before?"

"There were plenty of shenanigans amongst the younger folk years back, when Lachlann was part of the crew. I felt the need to put some rules in place."

"Wait, was Lachlann responsible for those shenanigans?"

Gareth smirked. "He may have been involved in a few of them."

"Oooh, do tell!" Jasper's smile turned sly. "Were you a scoundrel as a young man too, Lachlann?"

Gareth laughed. "Was he ever!" His gaze shifted to Lachlann, who avoided eye contact, a faint blush colouring his cheeks. "Oh, come on, Lachlann, it's nothing to be ashamed of after all these years! Tell the boy what you were like. It might be good for him to hear that you weren't always the steady fellow you are now."

Lachlann sighed and turned to Jasper. "You know how you told me that shooting Kip messed you up in the head a bit?"

Jasper nodded.

"I was only a couple years older than you when I showed up on this ship. And by that time, I'd killed at least a dozen men, maybe more."

Jasper frowned. "You were military, I'm guessing?"

"Joined up as soon as I finished school. Those years were good for me in a lot of ways. I learned a lot about teamwork, I got stronger and more skilled at fighting, and I made some good friends. But I joined up right in the middle of the war with Ciarlann, after the coup. We were told that the new rulers were harming the people and posed a threat to Breoch."

"Right," Jasper said. "I was a kid when the war happened, and I remember Father saying the same thing."

"And he likely believed it. That's what Breoch wanted. So they sent us in, and we stormed the capital city. It was messy. Many civillians and soldiers died. And right in the middle of it all, I overheard two senior officers talking. Turns out we weren't trying to protect the Ciarlanni folk, or even our own people. We'd only gone to war with the new government because they refused to trade with us. So there I was, on the front lines, killing folks and risking my own life for practically nothing."

"Doing what the government told you to do without looking into it." Jasper nodded. "Sounds familiar."

"So that was enough to make me start questioning why I'd joined. A year later, one of my best friends was killed in battle, and I held him as he died. After that, well, I just couldn't do it anymore." Lachlann looked away again. "I started having nightmares, not thinking clearly, getting angry at people about the smallest things. There were a few times I panicked and nearly ran off in the heat of battle.

In the Breoch military, you're allowed to apply for discharge every seven years. I got out as soon as I could."

"That must've been awful," I put in.

"It was." Lachlann nodded. "After that, I decided to find work on a ship because I liked being at sea. It just so happened the first ship to take me on was the Lady Liara. And by then I was a very troubled young fellow."

"A single-minded swill hound, that's what you were." Gareth chuckled.

Lachlann nodded sheepishly. "I did everything folks do to escape their pain. I drank myself silly, took far too many women to bed, and I got in some terrible scraps over trivial things. I was far worse than you, Jasper." He shook his head. "Then one morning, I showed up to my watch, hardly able to walk because of how much I drank the night before. Gareth sat me down and forced me to explain why I was behaving this way. It took a while, but eventually I broke down and told him everything. He was the one who managed to convince me I wasn't an entirely terrible person for killing folks because I'd been told to. I may have been naive and childish, following orders without thinking about them, but I wasn't evil."

Jasper's shoulders hunched. "So that's why you're willing to give me a chance, then? Because you know what it's like to be ordered to kill and regret it later?"

"Because you remind me far too much of myself at your age," Lachlann said, nodding. "That, and because Ember's fox told me I could trust you."

"So what happened to you after that?" I asked Lachlann.

"Well, I suppose I slowly began getting my wits back. It wasn't easy. But knowing that I had folks on this ship who believed in me, who saw me for who I was and accepted me— that helped. A lot."

"Is it still hard for you to kill?" Jasper said. "I mean, given your reputation with a sword and all, I assume you've done it since?"

"I have, but now I kill only with very good reason, and only when I don't see another way. I never feel good about it, but I think that's for the best."

"I don't know if I could do it again." Jasper shivered.

"I don't doubt you could if it was your own life or the life of a loved one you were fighting for. But I hope you never have to."

The conversation turned to lighter things after that, and when the music began, Jasper excused himself. "I need to go prowl the dance floor one last time," he said, giving us a grin and striding off.

"What about you, Ruby?" Gareth said.

I laughed. *"I don't think I'm as good at prowling as he is."*

"Well, there's only one way to learn. Go, enjoy your last night on the ship. We'll be arriving in Dundere early tomorrow afternoon, and then it's off to see Noelle."

This might be my last night without a hand and a tongue, I found myself thinking as I made my way to the main deck.

One more day, and this part of my life could easily be behind me.

The following morning was spent with Harvey, adjusting the winds to blow us into Dundere Harbour with precision. I gazed out at the green, craggy-topped island as we approached. The small city that surrounded the harbour looked cleaner than most of the Breoch cities, and I couldn't help but admire the glistening metalwork that graced many of the buildings' spires. "I think Ruby had best stay with us from now on," I heard Lachlann say to Harvey as we sailed into the harbour. "The Dundere guards will want to know who my newest charges are."

"Indeed they will." Harvey turned and smiled at me. "Well, I'm glad you were able to sail with us, Ruby. You're more than welcome to come aboard again in the future."

I nodded. *"Thank you for training me."*

"It was my pleasure. I hope the Dundere stormbrewers' guild can pick up where I've left off."

"The who?"

"You'll find out soon enough," Lachlann said. "Come on."

I followed him and Jasper to the middle of the ship, and we watched as the crew began preparing to tie up. Jasper tapped his foot audibly, fiddling with the cuffs of his shirt and generally looking very uncomfortable. *"Is he all right?"* I asked Lachlann.

Lachlann repeated my question, and Jasper huffed. "What do you think? I'm about to go visit some folks who will likely be very unhappy to see me." He frowned. "Do I need to come with you to the governor's? Can't you just drop me off at the market and pick me up once you and Ruby are done?"

"I could," Lachlann replied. "But you're going to run into them eventually, Jasper. You might as well get it over with now. Besides, they're expecting you."

"They are?"

Lachlann nodded and clapped him on the shoulder. "Willem warned them you were coming. It's not going to be an easy day for you, but you'll get through." He turned to me then. "How are you feeling, Ruby? Excited?"

I grinned and nodded. *"Yes, but also a bit nervous."*

"As expected. I have it on good authority that getting healed doesn't hurt, if that helps. Ah, here come the guards now."

I followed Lachlann's gaze to the group of blue-clad fellows who'd just boarded the ship. They began walking around the deck, speaking to all the passengers who were leaving the ship at this port. When one of them approached Lachlann, he grinned. "Good to see you again. Bringing some new magic for us, I take it?"

"New magic and new folks in need of Noelle's healing," he replied.

"I see that," the guard said, his gaze travelling to my stump. "What are their names?"

"Ruby and Jasper Jameson. There may be some notes about the boy; he's caused trouble once here before, but Noelle knows he's coming."

The guard nodded and went to speak to one of the other officers. When he returned, there was a frown on his face. "I'm surprised Noelle's letting this fellow off the boat, but he's been cleared. You folks can go ashore; welcome to Dundere."

We made our way onto the dock, and I followed Lachlann through a throng of bodies. On the shore, a market was set up with merchants selling exotic fabrics and spices and other goods. It reminded me of the market in Flavalan, but somehow even more diverse. "This is a fun place to browse," Lachlann told us. "I'll bring you both back here at some point."

"Lachlann!" I heard a voice call out through the din. "Over here!"

I followed Lachlann's gaze and was surprised to find myself staring at Willem. "Glad to see you folks made it here without trouble," he said, his earlier malice toward Jasper seemingly gone. "Let's get to the carriage. The governor and her husband are expecting you."

A short while later, we'd ascended the winding road that led to the governor's mansion. I heard Jasper's breathing quicken as we passed through the gates. He said nothing, but his eyes darted every which way, looking for threats.

We parked the carriage, and then Lachlann led the way to the front door, rapping on it twice. A tall woman of middling years who exuded elegance answered. Long black hair streaked with the slightest tinges of grey framed her face, and her dark eyes looked back at us kindly. She offered us all a smile, then leaned forward to embrace Lachlann. "Good to have you back," she said, then looked my brother and me over. "This must be Ruby and Jasper. I've heard plenty about both of you." She said the words so mildly that I could hardly tell whether she meant good things or bad. "I'm Noelle, the governor of Dundere."

I nodded hello, and Jasper stepped forward and extended a hand. "Pleasure to meet you, Governor."

Noelle gave him a small smile as they shook, then gestured into the foyer. "Come in. I'll go fetch my husband. The girls should be home soon enough—they'll be thrilled to see you, Lachlann."

Noelle disappeared, and a servant came to take our coats. She was just about to direct us to the parlour when Noelle returned, followed by a tall man whose red hair was streaked with white. The man exchanged handshakes with Lachlann and Jasper, then turned to me and, not batting an eye, extended his left hand. "You must be Ruby. I'm Marcus." I nodded and tentatively extended my hand, which he shook heartily. "I'm excited that you're here." My eyebrows knitted together at his words, and Marcus laughed. "My wife and I are the perfect team to help you out. Noelle can heal you, and me, well, I used to be just like you." He gestured at my stump. "I was a krossemage for over twenty years. So I know the sorts of challenges you'll likely face once you've been healed."

Noelle gestured that we follow her into the parlour, where we seated ourselves on plush couches. Jasper perched on the edge of the seat next to mine, sitting up far too straight. Looking him over, I could see the muscles in his jaw clenching and unclenching.

"Well, then," Noelle began, "why don't you folks tell us how you—" She was interrupted by the sound of the door opening and glanced over at the entryway. "That'll be the girls."

I didn't miss Jasper's sharp intake of breath as two young women appeared. One was perhaps my age and petite, with large brown eyes, and skin a shade darker than Shawnie's. Her hair was loose, falling in black waves around her shoulders, and there was something about her that seemed familiar. The other was older, tall and lean, with red hair that had been pulled back into a braid. She had a narrow face with high cheekbones, bright blue eyes, and a smattering of freckles across the bridge of her nose. Both girls ignored Jasper and me. "Lachlann!" the shorter one squealed.

Lachlann stood, grinning, and both the girls ran to throw their arms around him. "It's good to see you two."

"Are you here for more than just a few days this time?" the redhead asked, pulling away.

"I'm here for the summer. Going to go train with the guards while these two do what they need to." He glanced over at us, and the two girls' gazes followed. The younger one looked more curious than anything, but the redhead's gaze iced over when she looked at my brother.

Jasper stood awkwardly. "Saray, Trina," he said, his voice overly formal. "It's good to see you again."

The older one lurched toward Jasper, and I gasped when I saw fire dancing on her hands. *So this is the girl I've heard stories about.* Jasper stepped in front of me protectively.

Saray ignored me completely, coming right up to Jasper to stare intently into his face. "You healed up better than I expected." Her voice had a frosty edge.

"I recover fast," he replied, eyeing her.

"I see that." Saray's eyes darted to me for a moment, then she turned away from us. "Lachlann," she said, "does Jasper here know about my fiancé?"

Lachlann shook his head. "I made a point of not telling him. I figured I'd let you two decide if you wanted Jasper to know."

"You're engaged?" Jasper said. "Um, congratulations."

Saray ignored him. "In that case, I think I'll invite him over for dinner." She gave Jasper an odd smirk and then turned to Willem. "Would you take me the fast way?"

"Absolutely." Willem got to his feet and took Saray's arm. "*Arius Ravenous Momentus,*" he intoned, and a second later, he and Saray vanished.

Lachlann turned to Marcus. "I still can't believe they're engaged," he said, shaking his head. "Do they have a date?"

"They're planning for next spring, but no solid dates yet," replied Marcus. "There's still that issue to deal with. No solutions thus far."

Lachlann nodded. "I have something for you, from Alexander and Ember," he said to Marcus then, changing the subject as he produced a small leather bag. "I'm not sure what these are for." Marcus peeked in and smiled. "Ah. Heat stones. Take a few for yourself and see what you think."

"What do they do?"

"You drop them in your bath, and they heat up the water using magic. Way more convenient than the stove. We recently had a tub with running water installed here, and I've had one put in your summer rental as well. So you can try it out yourself later on."

"Running water?" Lachlann's eyes narrowed. "How does that work?"

"Well, as of right now, we're using pipes and a bit of water magic to make the system work. Running water is quite the luxury, isn't it Trina?"

She nodded, clearly distracted.

"Stop staring, Trina," Noelle spoke up. "It's rude."

Only now did I realize that she had been staring at Jasper for the entirety of

Marcus and Lachlann's conversation. Jasper met her eyes, and she shook her head. "Sorry," she said. "It's just…well, it's odd seeing someone for the first time and having them look nothing like you imagined."

"What did you imagine me looking like?" Jasper asked.

"Well, I didn't picture you being blond. Or having curly hair. Or…" She trailed off, her cheeks flushing slightly.

"I didn't have curly hair when you first met me. Or rather, I did, but it was too short to tell." He gave her a small smile, seeming to relax a bit. "I'm glad you got your sight back."

"And I'm glad you brought your sister here." Trina turned to smile at me. *She's really pretty,* I decided. "I'm happy you're here, Ruby. Noelle will get you fixed up in no—" She paused as the centre of the room shimmered, and three figures began to materialize. I noticed a shift in the collective mood immediately.

Trina tensed up, her eyes turning to Jasper. Marcus and Noelle stared at him too, and Lachlann wore a look that could be interpreted as a sort of smug amusement.

The three figures had fully materialized now. Willem and Saray were back, along with a tall, slender young man who had short, light brown hair. He surveyed his surroundings with a pair of wide ice-blue eyes, which then landed on my brother.

I didn't miss Jasper's audible gasp as the young man strode towards him. "Hello, Jasper," he said, then punched him in the face.

CHAPTER 9

I LET OUT a cry of protest as my brother stumbled back. Trina gasped at the other young man's behaviour. Marcus and Noelle just looked amused, and I could tell that Lachlann was trying very hard not to laugh. Saray, on the other hand, did nothing to reign in her laughter, fire dancing on her hands.

The man who'd thrown the punch leaned into Jasper, eyes alight with an odd mixture of triumph and disdain. "Bet you didn't think you'd be seeing *me* here, ai?" he crowed. My eyes widened when I saw the flash of steel; the young man had a knife and seemed to be manipulating it using only his mind, letting it hover near Jasper's throat. I leapt up with a wordless cry, ready to shove the young man away if need be.

Jasper's face was white. "*How?*" he finally managed to sputter.

"Magic, obviously." The knife twirled in midair. It was then that the young man seemed to notice me, and he took in my condition. "I can't believe you of all people have a magikai sibling," he said. "What sort of fellow spends his time hunting others like his little sister, ai?"

"I didn't know back then," Jasper protested. "And you're no better than me. You sold Saray out to the Breoch Guard, and now I find out that you can do *that?*" He gestured to the levitating knife.

"I couldn't back then," the other man spat.

"You expect me to believe that you just *became* a magic user?"

"That's exactly what happened," Lachlann cut in. I felt the strange heaviness of anti-magic descend once again when he approached the confrontation. He clapped the other young man on the shoulder, and the knife clattered to the floor. "Enough, Kip. You've made your point."

Kip. My head snapped up, and I gawked openly at him. *That's the name of the boy that Jasper killed.*

Kip's gaze met mine now, and he smiled slightly. "I see your sister has heard of me."

Jasper was too busy glaring at Lachlann to respond. "Why didn't you *tell* me?"

"As I said, I figured it was up to Kip whether he wanted you to know," Lachlann replied. "That, and I wanted to see the look on your face when you saw him."

"It seems we all have some very interesting stories to tell," Noelle cut in. "Perhaps we should do that over dinner."

"Let's take care of Ruby first," Marcus said. "I'm sure Jasper didn't risk travelling all the way to Dundere just because he wanted Kip to deck him."

"Right." Noelle stood. "Can everyone try to get along for a few minutes?" She then held out a hand to me and said, "Ruby, come here."

I approached nervously. Kip took a seat on a couch across the room, as far from Jasper as possible, and Saray looked to Willem. "Can I speak with you?"

Willem nodded, and the two left the room.

Noelle looked me over. "It's only your hand and your tongue that were taken, right? Nothing else to heal?"

I nodded.

"Okay. I'm going to heal your hand first. I've been told that even though the hand is bigger, having your tongue back takes some getting used to." She rolled up the sleeve of my coat and cradled my stump in the palm of her hand. My heart pounded; I wasn't sure why I was afraid of being healed. "Lifebringers cast a bit differently than other magikai," she explained. "I have to sing my spell, and the more complex the healing is, the longer it takes. This might be a few minutes." She closed her eyes and began to sing softly, a mournful song in a language I didn't know. Out of the corner of my eye, I noticed Willem return and motion that Lachlann should join him and Saray in the foyer. As he slipped out, I emitted a small gasp. The scarred skin at the end of my stump, normally devoid of nearly all sensation, was tingling wildly.

As Noelle sang, I could feel the end of it extending and pins and needles where seconds before there had been no feeling at all. I watched in awe as my wrist and then the back of my hand began to regenerate, the veins and tendons visible through my newly formed skin. The beginnings of knuckles began to bulge under my flesh, and Noelle held my wrist steady. With her left hand, she placed her thumb and each of her fingers against my knuckles, one after another, then began to pull her hand back slowly, as if drawing my fingers out. Sure enough, they began to grow, each one tingling with life. I gaped as my fingernails grew back, then the very tips of my fingers. Noelle stopped singing and smiled. Then she let go of my wrist, and I immediately dropped my arm, surprised by the unexpected new weight.

"It'll take time to adjust," Marcus said from the couch. I carefully raised my right forearm, and my hand hung limp.

"Try moving your wrist," Noelle instructed. I did as she asked, and my hand flopped a few times, heavy and clumsy. "Now your fingers."

She led me through several tests to make sure that my hand fully functioned. Saray, Willem and Lachlann had returned, I noticed then. Lachlann grinned when he saw my new hand. "How does it feel, Ruby?"

I attempted to give him a thumbs up but failed. He laughed and sank down on the same couch as Kip. Saray seated herself between them, the fire now gone from her hands.

"All right, now your tongue." Noelle smiled. "I'll be back in a moment. I should wash my hands before I do this."

She left the room, and I turned to Jasper, grinning, to wave my new hand at him. He smiled, clearly happy for me, but his shoulders were hunched and his hands tightly folded.

"Try making a fist," Marcus instructed me. "Good. Now lift each of your fingers. Excellent. Do you play piano, by chance?"

I nodded excitedly.

"Well, playing piano is a great way to get your dexterity back. It might be a good thing for you to try."

Noelle returned with washed hands. "All right, I'm ready. Open your mouth just a bit. This might feel strange."

I did as she instructed, and she put just the tip of her thumb into my mouth, resting it against my lower teeth. Then she cradled my jaw with the remainder of her hand. "This won't take as long, but it'll be far more noticeable than your hand."

She began to sing again, and sure enough, I felt the same strange tingle in my mouth. I could actually feel my tongue growing. At first it was like a tiny piece of flesh near the back of my throat, only just noticeable, but then it began enlarging rapidly, filling my mouth and pressing against the insides of my teeth. Noelle put her finger directly on its tip, drawing it out as she sang. "Good," she finally said. "All done. Let's see it."

No, that can't be right, I thought as I opened my mouth. My tongue felt far too large, overwhelming, like I would not be able to close my lips around it if I tried.

"It feels way too big, doesn't it?" Marcus asked. "Don't worry, that's normal."

"Stick it out for me," Noelle said. "Good. Now, can you try to speak? Just one word. It will be hard."

I moved my tongue against the back of my teeth. "Thank you," I managed to slur.

"You're most welcome." Noelle smiled. "There's just one last thing. Marcus, would you mind fetching the—"

But Marcus was already on his way out of the room. When he returned, he was carrying a bottle and spoon. "It's a simple berry syrup," he said, filling the spoon with a red liquid. "Just want to make sure your taste buds work." I raised the spoon tentatively to my lips.

A rich berry flavour exploded on my tongue, sweeter and more decadent than anything I could ever remember tasting. "Mmmm!" I exclaimed, swallowing.

Marcus let out a knowing laugh. "What's your favourite food, Ruby? We'll have anything you'd like for dinner tonight. Just name it, and we'll make it happen."

"Can I think about it for a few minutes?" I signed.

"Of course. You have a few hours yet before we start making dinner. Perhaps in the meantime, the three of you would like to use the tub with the fancy running water?"

"Is that your polite way of telling us we stink?" Lachlann asked.

"It would be quite an accomplishment to spend two weeks at sea and not stink," Marcus replied. "Trina, why don't you show Ruby how to use the tub, then once she's done, the fellows can take their turns."

Trina nodded and stood. "Come with me, Ruby."

A few hours later, I sat at the massive dining room table, washed and wearing one of the dresses that Alexander and Ember had provided, this one mossy green with leaves embroidered into the bodice. Jasper wore a smart-looking red and purple waistcoat with its own intricate embroidered patterns— a look that would have been considered gaudy back home but seemed to be normal enough here— and Lachlann was clad in his usual dark colours, though I noticed subtle gold stitching running through his navy blue tunic.

I'd ended up choosing roast venison as my meal. Kip nodded his approval and commented on how Marcus and Noelle had plenty of it, thanks to his hunting abilities. The cook served it with several different types of roast vegetables and a rich sauce that made my taste buds dance. My portion was cut up for me, despite my newly formed hand, and I was grateful; I wasn't sure if I had the ability to master both the new hand and the new tongue at once. It took several minutes of eating for me to properly recall how to use my tongue to push food to the back of my mouth, and I nearly caught myself drooling a few times. But the food was heavenly.

As we were eating, Lachlann turned to Jasper. "I believe you have a story to tell these folks."

"Right." Jasper squared his shoulders and gazed across at Saray and Kip. "I suppose I should start by formally apologizing to you two for, uh, everything." He met Saray's eyes specifically. "I'm sorry for betraying you, kidnapping you, threatening you— multiple times, I suppose— all of it."

Saray nodded. "Um…thank you for that."

"And you as well," Jasper said to Kip. "Sorry for…uh, shooting you and all."

Kip huffed, not meeting Jasper's eyes. "At least I didn't feel it," he muttered. "The others you hurt much worse than me. If there's anyone you owe an apology to, it's Lachlann. Kirilee might still be alive if it wasn't for your antics, y'know."

Lachlann shook his head. "Doubtful. Chances are, Trina's eyes would've been healed regardless, and Marcus and Noelle likely would have offered a home to the girls even if Jasper hadn't shot you. And you'd already had a change of heart about magic when all that happened. So the curse likely would have broken anyway." He glanced at Jasper. "You might have cost me a few hours with Kirilee, at the very end. But I can forgive you for that."

Jasper's eyes narrowed. "Wait, how did I cause Kirilee's death? That doesn't make any sense."

"I'll get to that," Lachlann replied. "First, you need to tell them what happened after you got home."

"Right." Jasper sighed, and turned back to Saray and Kip. "I imagine what I did to you two may have messed you up a bit. Truth is, it messed me up too."

Kip snorted. "Are you asking us to try to make you feel better, ai?"

"No," Jasper snapped. "I don't want your pity. But it matters to the story. Before that day, I'd never killed anyone. Haven't done it since, either. And I couldn't stop thinking about it afterwards. If I thought you deserved to die, it might have been different, but I knew you didn't; I knew it was the wrong thing to do. And it got me wondering if the things I'd grown up believing about magic might be wrong, too.

"I spent a good number of years trying to escape it all, and then Ruby was taken, and things changed." I listened to him, blinking back tears, as he told them what Jade had done, how Jasper had planned to rescue me, and how that led us here.

When he was finished speaking, Trina frowned. "So your brother just…gave

Ruby up to the Breoch Guard? No hesitation? I mean, I understand fear of magic, and I know your family is a bit extreme, but giving up your little sister…"

Jasper nodded. "What Jade did was pretty callous. Though what Gabby wanted to do was far worse. From what Ruby told me, Jade gave her up to appease Gabby. I don't like their involvement with the Witch Slayers at all."

"I remember Hilda mentioning the Witch Slayers, but she made it sound like they existed decades ago. Who are they exactly?"

"A group of folks who believe that magic users are basically subhuman and should be killed or tortured," Jasper explained. "I don't know much of their history though."

"I do," Lachlann put in. "Kirilee told me the Witch Slayers have existed since the Banishing, and in the early days, they were the ones who weren't afraid to conduct raids on the Shrouded Woods. They kidnapped and killed plenty of magic users, and the ones who took krossemages as their slaves were very cruel to them. Eventually, their ideas fell out of vogue, and my understanding is that since then, there's only been a handful of them."

"But that's changed recently?" Noelle asked.

Jasper nodded. "From what I hear, yes. The newer Witch Slayers aren't bent on invading the Woods, though. They're trying to get into positions of power. Several of them want to influence the king's court, and others have been working their way up in the ranks of the Breoch Guard. Father finds their views to be a bit extreme, but others within the Guard are quite welcoming." His shoulders hunched. "Breoch is getting more and more dangerous for magic users. I'm glad I got Ruby out when I did."

Marcus nodded and looked at his daughters. "I'm glad these two got out when they did as well. Kip, you'd best be careful on your trips back there."

"I should make sure Willem knows about this too," Kip said.

"Do you know what caused this resurgence?" Saray asked my brother. Her voice still held the standoffish tone from earlier, but it was edged by curiosity.

Jasper sighed. "Honestly, Saray? You did."

"Me?"

"Your ability to cast with your mind has people scared. The Witch Slayers are worried there might be more like you." He averted his eyes. "Also the fact that the Breoch Guard put so much effort into hunting you down, and they— *we*, I guess— still failed. It has the Witch Slayers thinking more drastic measures are needed."

"Wonderful," she muttered. "I leave Breoch, and folks are still being harmed because of me."

"No, folks are being harmed because a handful of people are fearful and unwilling to look beyond their prejudices," Noelle said. "This isn't your fault, Saray."

Saray nodded, but she refused to look at Noelle, and an awkward silence descended on the table. Jasper broke it by clearing his throat and turning to Lachlann. "What were you saying earlier about Kirilee's death somehow being my fault?"

"Right. It wasn't your fault exactly, but you shooting Kip does tie into it. It involves magic and curses though, and those aren't things I understand well." He turned to Trina. "Would you mind explaining this part to Jasper and Ruby?"

Trina nodded and began to tell us about Kirilee's accidental misuse of magic at a young age, which set off a chain of events that had ultimately impacted her, Saray and Kip; and how the curse placed on Kirilee was tied to the three of them. She explained how Kirilee's choice to give up the last few hours of her life was what ultimately brought Kip back and that he was now endowed with Kirilee's magic. Jasper nodded slowly as he took the story in. "So Kirilee was your grandmother, Saray," he concluded. "I would never have guessed that."

"Me neither." Saray gave him a tense smile.

"Lachlann, did you know how old she was?"

"She told me. It was part of why she thought we couldn't be together."

"But it didn't bother you?"

"Not especially. Though it was very strange for me, watching her age so rapidly at the end." He sighed and looked away for a moment. "Do you understand how you shooting Kip was tied into all of that? Kirilee would've died anyway, but there might have been a different timeline if it weren't for the life transfer."

Jasper nodded slowly. "Yes, that does make sense. For what it's worth, I'm sorry." He frowned. "It's hard to imagine that life transfers are real, that they actually *work*. I wouldn't believe a word of it if I didn't know for certain that Kip died that day." He glanced over at me. "Do you remember Mother talking about life transfers?"

I nodded. "She said they use dark magic." My words were slurred, but I was becoming more comfortable talking.

"To be clear," Noelle put in, "life transfers are not normally done in Dundere. The only reason I allowed this one was that Kirilee was dying anyway. They're considered very unethical."

"I can see why," Jasper replied. "So what happened after that?"

"We adopted Saray and Trina," Noelle said. "And Kip went back to Breoch for a time, to train with Willem. He returned here after a few months and began taking classes at the magic school. And, well, life went on."

"Were these the people you said I should talk to about Kaden?" I asked Lachlann.

He nodded. "I'm not certain they can help, but if not, they can likely point you to someone who can."

"Can you explain for me? It's hard to talk too much right now."

"Of course," he said. "Ruby left her friend Kaden on the island. They had plans to escape together, but Jasper didn't understand what Ruby was asking when she tried to signal that there was someone else she wanted to bring along. Ruby wants to go back for Kaden, but we figure it wouldn't be safe to just show up again in a boat. We thought one of the magikai here might have an idea as to how to best go fetch her."

The others all nodded and exchanged thoughtful looks with one another. "You know," Marcus finally said, "I think the best person to talk to would be Willem, given his teleportation abilities."

"When will he be back?" asked Jasper.

"Not for a month at least," Trina said. "I could use my summoning stone to bring him here, though he doesn't like me doing that too often. But Ruby could always go to him."

"I could?" My eyes narrowed. "How?"

"Kip's going to Breoch through the portal to hunt this weekend. You could go with him."

Seeming startled, Kip turned to her, and Jasper cleared his throat. "I don't think that's a good idea."

"You think Kip's going to harm your sister?"

"It's not that," he protested, though I suspected he wasn't being entirely honest. "It's just…Willem didn't want to take us through the portal to get here. He's worried that Father might get the portal's location out of us. So I doubt he'd be happy about Ruby using it."

Saray snorted. "Willem, who once threatened to wipe Kip's memory of his home's location, is worried about people remembering where a portal is?"

"That's what I thought," Lachlann put in. "Though Willem can't really stop Kip from taking Ruby through."

Kip nodded slowly, eyeing me. "I…s'pose I could take you and drop you at Willem's, and then you could head back through the portal once you're done talking to him. Though if he's not home, you'll have to come along with me while I hunt."

I frowned, debating the trustworthiness of the young man who had punched my brother only a couple of hours before. Then I looked to Saray and Trina. "Will either of you be coming along?"

Saray shook her head. "It's not safe for us. I'm wanted in Breoch. If they catch me over there, chances are I'll be executed. At least, that's how someone explained it to me a few years back." I didn't miss the look she shot at Jasper.

"So Saray and Trina can't come, Lachlann can't go through the portal, and I'm *not* bringing your brother along," Kip concluded. "If you're coming, it'll be just you and me."

I sighed, and my eyes flickered to Jasper. He raised his palms. "I don't like it," he mumbled, "but it's up to you."

"If it's what I have to do to get Kaden out…" I turned back to Kip. "Are the Shrouded Woods safe?"

"You'll be safe enough if you're with me," he replied. "I'll be leaving first thing Saturday morning."

The conversation soon turned to other things, but I couldn't ignore the icy tension that emanated from Kip, or the way Saray sat straight and stiff, gripping her utensils just a bit too hard as she ate. Jasper, at least, was trying to play nice; he made conversation with Marcus and Noelle about the trip on Gareth's ship, how much he liked being at sea, and how well I was progressing with my stormbrewing. But I couldn't help noticing how studiously he avoided looking at Kip and Saray when he spoke.

While we were eating dessert— a decadent fruit pie that I ate very slowly, savouring each bite— Lachlann spoke up again. "I think we'd best figure out where these two will be staying." He glanced at Jasper and me. "I rent an apartment when I'm here for the summers, and it has a guest room. I think it'd be best if you stayed with me, Jasper."

I couldn't help but notice Saray's shoulders slumping in relief, or the long, barely audible breath that Kip let out. Jasper nodded, his own posture relaxing slightly. "I think that's a good idea."

"Though I'll warn you, if you stay with me, there will be rules."

Jasper shrugged. "I'm sure I can handle them. What about Ruby? I take it you don't have room for both of us?"

"Not unless you want to sleep on the couch." Lachlann turned to Noelle. "I know Ruby is interested in enrolling at the school of magic. Do you think she could stay in the dorms there?"

She nodded. "I'll have Saray look into enrolling her. Though dorms don't open until the fall. Until then, you're welcome to stay here, Ruby."

I smiled at her. "Thank you."

Noelle turned to Saray. "You'll get her enrolled for us?"

"Of course," she replied, but I saw that her shoulders were hunched again. *Does she not want me staying here?*

"Before Jasper and I head back to my place, I need to go say hello to someone," Lachlann said as he finished his pie. Despite the smile on his face, there was something sad in his eyes when he spoke.

Marcus and Noelle both nodded knowingly.

"Can I come with you?" Saray asked.

"Of course." Lachlann stood, and she followed him towards the back of the house.

I glanced at Trina. "What's he doing?"

"Follow me," she said, getting up from the table. "I'll show you from my room so we can give him some space."

Trina led me back to the foyer and up a long set of sweeping stairs. "You'll be next door to me," she said. "Here, this is my room."

Trina's bedroom was large and airy. Her walls were covered in a purple floral wallpaper, and the bed was swathed in a lacy white bedspread and a variety of coloured pillows. A black cat dozed on an armchair, and a ginger tabby was stretched out on the floor. On a ledge against her window sat a row of plants, and two glassed-in doors led to a patio overlooking the backyard. I followed her through those doors and gasped. The patio was covered in boxes of flowers and hanging bird feeders. Several birds had made nests in the rafters above, and a squirrel perched on the railing, eyeing us. A lone crow swooped down from the roof of the house and landed on Trina's shoulder. She smiled and reached up to rub its feet, then gestured to the garden beyond.

Even in the fading light, the governor's garden was beautiful. Winding cobbled paths meandered through roses, geraniums, and pansies, and I noticed a vegetable patch toward the back. Closer to the house, the yard was dominated by a large tree smattered in pink and purple flowers that glowed in the twilight. Lachlann sat up against it, throwing occasional glances into the branches, and I heard him talking softly. Saray and Kip were there too, but they sat on a bench several feet away.

"What kind of tree is that?" I asked.

"That's a viletta. They grow mainly in the Shrouded Woods. Lachlann likes to visit it because that's where Kirilee is buried."

I listened intently as Trina then told me the story of how Hilda's wife Carmine had worked a complex spell that made the tree grow from a single branch, its roots encasing Kirilee's body. "Lachlann is convinced that she's…still in there. That her spirit is in the tree, somehow. And sometimes I think he might be right. The tree does seem to glow brighter than usual whenever he's here, or when anything exciting happens. Kip proposed to Saray under the tree, and I swear it was shining brighter that night than I've ever seen it."

"I can imagine," I signed. *"I bet she was—"* I stopped, realizing that I could talk now if I wanted to.

Trina laughed. "Don't worry, it's normal to forget you're healed at first. You know, the morning after I got my eyes fixed, I woke up and started shrieking because I'd forgotten I could see!"

"That would be scary." I grinned.

"Oh, it was. It'll take some time, getting used to being healed, but you'll get there."

I nodded. "My tongue still feels too big. I kept worrying that I was drooling during dinner."

"No one would judge you if you did. You're among people who understand these things."

Trina was quiet after that, focused on feeding peanuts to both the squirrel on the ledge and the bird on her shoulder. Enjoying the cool night air and the glow from Kirilee's tree, I relaxed.

After a time, Lachlann got up and left the tree, Saray and Kip following close behind. "I suppose we'd best go inside," Trina said.

We went downstairs to find my brother seated in the parlour with Marcus and Noelle, in deep conversation with them.

Lachlann returned just then, too. "I'm ready to head out if you are, Jasper." He glanced back at Kip. "I'd offer you a ride home, but I feel like that might not go so well."

I saw Kip's jaw clench. "Probably not," he said. "I can walk."

"I'll take you in our carriage," Marcus offered.

Jasper stood and motioned that I should follow Lachlann and him into the foyer. "Are you sure you're comfortable staying here, Ruby?" he asked when we were out of earshot of the others. "I don't mind sleeping on the couch at Lachlann's if you'd rather stay with me."

I shook my head. "I'll be fine." I meant it, too. Trina seemed nice enough, and the governor and Marcus were welcoming. Saray was a bit aloof, but I suspected that had to do with Jasper rather than me.

"All right. Marcus has said that he can give us both a tour of the island tomorrow. So I guess I'll see you in the morning."

I nodded. "Thank you for bringing me here. I…I know it's been a hard day for you."

I watched as Lachlann and Jasper disappeared out the front door. As soon as it latched shut behind them, I heard an audible sigh of relief from Saray. I realized that she was trying very hard not to cry.

Kip saw it as well and put his arms around her. "You sure you're okay with me leaving?" he asked. "I can stay the night if you want."

Saray shook her head and buried it in his shoulder. "I'll be fine," she mumbled. "I know if you stay with me, you won't sleep. You have classes in the morning, and all this has been hard for you as well."

"You're right, I s'pose. I'll come by after class and check on you."

I watched Saray and Kip say goodbye tenderly, then Kip followed Marcus out the door to the carriage. Trina watched Saray cautiously. "Are you all right?"

"Not really. I'll talk to you about it later." She threw a glance at me and forced a smile. "Come, Trina, let's give Ruby a tour of the house."

I had been in houses like the governor's before, but even so, I was delighted by its decadence. I gaped at the full-size ballroom with its massive chandeliers and marvelled at the shelves of books and gadgets in Marcus's study. Back in the parlour, I looked over all the ornaments along the walls: delicate porcelain vases and painted china plates, and wooden decorations that looked to be from somewhere foreign— gifts from dignitaries of other countries, I expected. Returning upstairs, Trina suggested I take a peek into what would be my own room. It was floral themed like Trina's, but featured daisies everywhere— the walls were papered with white daisy print, and the bedspread was a riot of coloured daisies. I chuckled to myself, surprised that the governor of Dundere would allow such bright decor in a guest room. Mother would have never permitted that.

We visited Saray's room last, located high up in a tower. Like her father's study, the room was lined with bookcases. Her walls were panelled in dark wood, but the ceiling was painted a vibrant blue and bore pictures of constellations. Against one wall was a large desk piled with several more books, and a table in the centre of the room held an intricate, coloured glass sculpture of flame. "Wow," I commented, running my fingers over its smoothness. "This is beautiful."

Saray smiled, seeming slightly more at ease around me now. "Father and Noelle had it made for me as a graduation gift." She glanced over at her fireplace, which sparked to life obediently.

"What are all your books about?" I asked.

"Well, I have a few different sorts, but the ones on my desk are all about magic. I'm trying to learn a couple new kinds." She picked one of the books up. "You can look through this one if you want."

I reached out to take it and gasped as I nearly dropped it. "Sorry," I mumbled. "My hand's not working so well yet."

Trina nodded. "You must be tired. I remember feeling pretty exhausted the day I got my eyes healed. Though that was a pretty eventful day in general." She exchanged a glance with Saray, who closed her eyes briefly.

I nodded. "I am tired. Perhaps I should head to bed. I'll take a look at your book another time."

Trina and Saray bid me goodnight, and I heard another sigh of relief from Saray as I shut the door. *Perhaps I should have stayed with Jasper and Lachlann,* I thought. When I'd returned to my room, I changed into my nightclothes and crawled into bed. Only now that I was alone did the weight of everything that happened hit me.

It was hard to believe that I was healed. I moved my hand and fingers in awe, bunched up the soft bed sheets in my fist, ran my tongue— which was beginning to feel less intrusive— along my teeth. *Is this real?*

Despite my elation, it was hard to see Jasper so incredibly uncomfortable. Saray's discomfort was even more obvious, and I had to wonder if Trina, Marcus, and Noelle were entirely at ease with my presence. Would I be a burden to them here in their house? Would my presence be a constant reminder to Saray about the horrors she'd endured at Jasper's hand?

All these questions rattled about in my mind as I drifted off to sleep.

CHAPTER 10

THE FOLLOWING MORNING after breakfast, I went with Noelle and Marcus to Noelle's office, which sat in a wing just off the massive ballroom. A mahogany desk took up a portion of the room, and the walls were lined heavily with books, but the room did not feel at all stuffy, thanks to the picture window behind Noelle's desk. The windowsill was home to a variety of exotic-looking plants, and a pair of fat white couches occupied an entire corner. I perched on the edge of one of the couches at Noelle's invitation; she and Marcus seated themselves on the other.

"Are you ready to learn about how magic works in Dundere?" asked Marcus.

I nodded; speaking was a little more difficult today than it was the night before.

Marcus grinned and looked at his wife. "Take it away, my dear."

"A lot of folks in Breoch believe that magic use in Dundere is a free-for-all," Noelle began, "but nothing could be further from the truth. We have all sorts of rules regarding magic, and not every person with magical abilities is allowed to do whatever they want with them. I assume Lachlann told you our city guard has access to anti-magic if needed?"

I nodded again.

"That's only utilized if absolutely necessary. There are several other things that we do preemptively to ensure magic is being used safely. First and foremost, we have a licensing system for magikai."

Noelle explained the extensive training and licensing system that all magikai in Dundere had to undergo before using their gift freely. The first step, once a child turned twelve, was to attend a class on safety and control. After that, there was work with a magic guild, and then a learner's permit that allowed a magikai to practice basic spells but not advanced ones— in my case, working with wind and rain was allowed with a learner's permit, but I could not yet work with lightning or damaging storms like tornadoes. Magikai were allowed to test for their full license at sixteen, at which point they began learning the more advanced aspects of their craft. "Of course," Noelle said, "if you use those skills in ways that are harmful or illegal, there are consequences."

I nodded. "What sorts of consequences?"

"Well, minor misconduct usually results in fines or occasionally needing to retake certain courses. A second offense is punished with a full revocation of your magic license for a certain time, then a full retake of all the necessary courses. Any offenses beyond that, or any major offenses, can result in prison time. Our jails are made of anti-magic materials."

"You don't ever…make people into krossemages, do you?"

Noelle laughed. "Absolutely not. We seek to control offenders, but we don't mutilate them." She paused for a moment, considering something. "You're sixteen, right?"

I nodded.

"Then you'll need to take the safety courses regardless, but once you're done that, if you can pass all the basic tests, you might be able to get your full license and move on to more advanced training."

"Did Saray and Trina have to take all these courses?" I asked.

"They were tested for each course in order to be fully licensed. Saray had learned enough from Willem that she was fully licensed right away. Trina was only thirteen, so she got her learners' permit, but she had to wait until she was sixteen for her full license, like everybody else."

"What about Kip? Didn't he go back to Breoch to train with Willem? Why not train here?"

Noelle and Marcus exchanged a glance. "Kip was feeling a bit overwhelmed by everything," Marcus said. "Being brought back to life, his new abilities, being in a new place. We figured that if he trained with Willem, he could at least be back in the Shrouded Woods, where he was most comfortable. And he could get a lot of one-on-one attention that he might not have here. Once he settled in Dundere, he had to undergo all of our testing to get his full license."

That made sense. "What happens after you're fully licensed? You can't run a school of magic with just a few courses."

"Well, ever since we opened up dorms, we've begun offering regular classes as well as magic instruction, so students can finish high school and learn magic at the same time," Noelle answered. "We also offer evening classes for adults."

"Once you turn eighteen, that's when the fun really starts," Marcus added, grinning.

"What do you mean?"

"First, you begin your guild work. Magikai here work four days at their regular job and one for their guild. So you'd likely spend that guild day looking for storms and helping ward them off. Also, at eighteen, you're given permission to try new types of magic."

"You mean other people's innate talents?" I asked. "So I could learn to move things with my mind like you do, or heal like Noelle?"

"There are some innate talents that can't be learned," he told me. "Healing is one of them, and the ability to communicate with animals and plants. You could learn telekinesis, though learning a different innate talent takes years of study. However, there are a few easier spells to learn, and most aren't innate talents. The simplest ones are heat and cold spells. Illusion spells are a bit more complex, but they can be really fun once you figure them out. And there are spells to put people to sleep and to hold them in one place, though we are careful who gets to learn those. We also have classes on enchanting items, making potions, and all sorts of other fun things. We recently added a class about fairy magic, but that one is a little—"

"I think you're overwhelming her, dear," Noelle cut in, noticing my wide eyes. "You get the idea, Ruby. Once you're an adult, there are a lot of options when it comes to learning magic." She smiled. "Marcus will take you to the guild hall today to meet the leaders, and I'll have Saray take you to the school to get you enrolled in the safety course on Monday."

"We'll head over to the stormbrewers' guild hall now," Marcus said. "Then after lunch, we'll pick up Jasper, and I'll take the two of you on a tour of the city. Trina's going to join us. Now, we'd best head over to guild hall so Noelle can get to work."

Soon, we were traversing the cobbled roads of Dundere City in Marcus's carriage. I stared out the window, taking in the many food stalls, the merchants selling colourful wares, and the occasional street performers. A chill hung in the air that made me wrap my coat tightly around myself. It had to be early June, but the air here was cooler than I was used to in Breoch, and the mountain peaks to the north were draped with low, ethereal-looking clouds. The air took on a salt tang as we neared the ocean, and I grinned as I realized that this time, I could *taste* it.

We seemed to be heading out of the city, along a road that skirted the rocky coastline. "Where are we going?" I asked.

Marcus craned his neck, then pointed. "Right there."

I followed his gaze and found myself staring at a lighthouse at the very end of a long peninsula. "The stormbrewers' guild hall is a lighthouse?"

He nodded. "It's the best place to see incoming storms that might need redirecting." The road quickly turned rough and bumpy as we made our way along the peninsula, then the trees fell away, and we were bordered on either side by nothing but ocean and a beach made of sharp, dangerous-looking rocks. The lighthouse loomed at the end, and as we neared it, I saw that one side was taken up by what looked to be a small, two-storey home.

Marcus slowed the carriage to a stop. "Come on, I'll introduce you to Chase. He's the lighthouse keeper and the leader of the guild." We climbed out of the carriage, and Marcus strode up to the door and knocked. When it opened, I found myself peering back at a very unusual man.

Chase must have been somewhere between Lachlann and Marcus in age. He had a bushy brown beard, a receding hairline, and a wide smile, but what caught me off guard was his height; the man was several inches shorter than me. He grinned up at us, seemingly oblivious to my bewilderment. "Marcus! I didn't expect to see you today!"

"Good to see you, Chase." Marcus extended a hand. "I've brought someone new for you to work with."

"Is that so?" Chase looked me over. "What's your name, my dear? You must be new to the island; I don't think I've met you."

"I'm Ruby, and I'm from Breoch," I replied.

"Ah. One of Lachlann's runaways, no doubt." He grinned and extended a hand. "Pleasure to meet you, Ruby."

I froze for a moment, uncertain what to do, then I remembered. *Right. I'm healed, aren't I?* I accepted his handshake, heat creeping into my cheeks.

He frowned. "Is everything all right?"

"I'm getting used to having a right hand again," I explained. "I was a krossemage until recently—"

"You were a krossemage?" a female voice cut in. A rosy-cheeked, dark-haired girl of about twelve was suddenly staring at me over Chase's shoulder.

"Sophie, what have I told you about barging in on my conversations?" Chase scolded. "Get back to your lessons!"

"But I want to know what it's like being a krossemage!" she protested, tugging on one of her braids.

I met Sophie's eyes. "Not very fun."

"Well, you don't have to worry about that now that you're here!"

"Yes, and I'm very grateful. Are you a stormbrewer like your father?"

She shook her head. "I don't think I have magic. My mother was the same way."

"Sophie! Lessons!" Chase said sharply.

Sophie darted out of the room, and Chase shook his head with a sigh. "Let's get you upstairs to meet the others, Ruby."

Marcus and I followed Chase through the house, until we found ourselves at the bottom of a massive spiral staircase. Chase began the ascent, and I followed close behind. By the time we reached the top, my legs were burning, and I gasped to catch my breath. "Quite the climb, isn't it?" Chase asked, clearly unbothered by the stairs. "Follow me."

He led us through another door, and I found myself inside a large, circular room. A cheery fire burned in a hearth, which was flanked by several worn-looking couches and armchairs. The walls were covered with maps, and a large work table was set out in a corner, more maps sitting on top, along with several pairs of binoculars. Massive windows let the sun in, and I noticed what looked to be a balcony. "This is where the stormbrewers work from," Chase said, pointing to a young man who looked about Jasper's age standing out on the balcony. "That's Tybalt. He's on watch right now."

We joined Tybalt on the balcony. The wind was fierce up here; I could feel the salt spray of the ocean coating my face. Chase introduced us to the young stormbrewer, then asked what he was seeing. "There's a storm brewing to the southwest, about twenty miles out. Looks to be heading our way. Should I divert it?"

Chase frowned. "Normally I'd say yes, but it might be good for Ruby to see what we can do with storms. Bring it close enough to control it, but keep it north of us, away from the harbour."

Tybalt nodded, then mumbled a now-familiar phrase and closed his eyes, concentrating. Chase turned to Marcus and began chatting, but I kept my eyes glued to Tybalt. He stood perfectly still, breathing deeply. I thought I saw a flash of light in the distance, but it was still very far away. "How is he controlling the storm from this far out?" I asked.

"He's not," Chase explained. "He's just controlling the wind, bringing the storm to us. It'll have to get a bit closer before he can control the storm itself."

"How could he sense the storm from that far away though?"

"That takes practice. You can probably sense incoming weather, right?"

I nodded, remembering the ominous clouds that sat just beyond the horizon that fateful day on Jade's sailboat.

"Well, with practice you can learn to sense exactly where those storms are located." Chase eyed the incoming bank of clouds. "Direct the storm over to our rock, and show Ruby what you can do," he said to Tybalt.

Tybalt nodded, and Chase went back inside. He returned with a pair of binoculars for me. "Look at that little island there." He pointed to a small rocky patch in the sea, barely visible from this vantage point.

I took the binoculars from him, gasping for a moment at their weight in my still-weak hand, then steadied myself. Raising them to my eyes, I peered out at the rocky, barren island as instructed. "Nothing lives there," Chase explained. "Which makes it a good place to practice lightning work. Watch."

I kept my eyes fixed to the island as the storm moved in. The clouds were low and dense, their undersides glowing with occasional flickers of lightning. Tybalt's jaw clenched as he pulled the clouds. "The storm is fighting him," Chase explained. "It wants to move in a different direction. Sometimes that happens. It's not a bad thing, though; it means that he shouldn't have any trouble moving the storm away from the island once we're done practicing."

I nodded.

"See that stack of rocks in the middle?' I moved my binoculars, then nodded again as they settled on the cairn. "Keep your focus there."

Beside me, Tybalt took a deep breath. Lightning flickered for a few seconds within the clouds above the island, and then a bolt of it snaked down across the sky, striking the cairn square on the topmost rock. The cairn crackled with energy, and the ground below glowed white for a brief moment. Thunder roared in my ears, and I gasped and turned to Tybalt. "Wow! That was so precise!"

Tybalt panted from exertion, but he managed a smile. "Thank you."

"That's just a small taste of what stormbrewers are capable of," Chase told me. "Now watch what a master stormbrewer can do."

By the time we left Chase and the lighthouse, my head spun with new information. I had watched Chase clip off the very top of a tree using a tornado while leaving everything else intact, create ball lightning, and chase away the thunderstorm only to create an entirely new one. Tonight, he promised me, he would show off his ability to create sunsets.

I'd learned all sorts of new terms from him, like low pressure system and air mass, and had played a bit with a very eager Sophie before leaving. "What happened to Sophie's mother?" I asked Marcus as we headed back into town.

"That is a very sad story," he told me. "Chase was trained as a stormbrewer, but he was one of the many magic users who wasn't particularly enthusiastic about his ability. He didn't want to control the weather; he wanted to study history at the university in Breoch, and he was frustrated that living here required him to train. But then one evening, when Sophie was just a baby, a tornado blew into town. The stormbrewer keeping watch that night was still pretty new and wasn't paying close attention. The tornado destroyed Chase's home and killed his wife. Sophie survived, though Chase had to dig through the wreckage to find her. Apparently, the fairies showed up and led him to the proper spot; they likely saved her life."

"That's terrible! Poor Chase."

Marcus nodded. "There were several folks harmed by that tornado. Soon after, Chase began studying storms and learning to control them, and just a few years back, he was promoted to the master of the guild." The carriage took an unexpected right turn as he spoke, and I raised an eyebrow questioningly. "Going to pick Trina up before we fetch Jasper. The Academy is a bit out of the way."

"I'm surprised she's joining us. She doesn't seem very afraid of Jasper."

Marcus nodded. "I noticed that too. Trina is quite good at reading people; perhaps she can tell that he's changed."

"Do *you* think he has?"

"Noelle and I had never met him before yesterday. We'd only heard the stories of what he did to Saray and Kip. But he appears genuine enough to me, and Lachlann seems to trust him, which helps. I'm willing to give him a chance, but I understand if others don't feel the same."

Marcus was quiet for the rest of the ride, and pretty soon we were pulling up to a tall, ivy-covered structure. Its windows were inset with coloured glass, and several towers jutted out of its top. Students trickled out of the massive front doors, chatting and laughing with one another. "This looks more like a castle," I said.

"At one time, it was the estate of a very rich man," Marcus explained. "He donated it to the city on the condition that it be used to start a school."

"Is it the only school on the island?"

Marcus shook his head. "There's another in town, larger than this. And there's the school of magic too, of course. This one is smaller, and it charges tuition, but it's been good for Trina and Kip, given that they were both behind in some subjects when they started. Ah, there's Trina." Marcus waved, and I spotted her working her way through the throng of students. She climbed into the carriage and grinned at both of us. "How was your exam?" Marcus asked her.

"All right, I think."

"Nice hair," I said to Trina, pointing at the streak of purple in her black locks. I'd all but forgotten that Alexander had provided the hair-dyeing potion.

"Thanks." She grinned and ran her fingers through it. "I thought about dyeing all of my hair, but Noelle didn't like the idea."

I laughed. "Where are we headed now?"

"To Lachlann's place to pick up Jasper," Marcus replied.

The building where Lachlann lived was in the center of town, directly above the space that Noelle used as an office when she was doing her healing work. Marcus and Noelle owned the building, he explained, and while the bottom was all office space, the upstairs contained several apartments they often let guests who were from out of town stay in. Lachlann used one of them every summer while training with the Dundere guard.

The buildings in this part of town reminded me of parts of downtown Sylvenburgh or Kirstein; they were stacked tall, looming on either side of the narrow, cobbled streets. They were cleaner than the ones in Breoch, though, and when I asked Marcus about it, he chuckled and informed me that most of the fires in Dundere factories were created and sustained by firebrands, and thus created less smoke and soot than regular fire.

Noelle's building was three stories high; the ground floor contained several shops, their storefronts lined up along a raised covered porch. Most of them appeared to be medical in nature. There was a store selling medicines from the Shrouded Woods— most of which, Trina told me, were foraged by Kip on his journeys back to Breoch. There was also an eyeglasses shop, an office for several traditional healers, and a storefront that simply read, "Noelle Westwood, Governor and Lifebringer."

"Why do we need eyeglasses and medicine shops if Noelle is a lifebringer?" I asked.

"Because Noelle is the only lifebringer in the city, and she only does that job part time," Marcus explained. "If we had multiple lifebringers, then they'd be able to attend to everybody. For now, she only takes cases that can't be easily fixed by traditional methods. Our head doctor is named Rayla, and she has a staff of healers who take care of any other medical issues that don't need Noelle."

"Why didn't Noelle decide to be a lifebringer full time?"

Marcus laughed. "This is where we get into one of the frustrating aspects of being a magic user here. Not everyone likes their gift or wants to use their gift as their profession. You already heard about what happened with Chase."

I nodded.

"Noelle wasn't quite as averse to her gift as Chase. She knew from a young age that there was great honour in being a lifebringer. But she was also interested in politics. She knew that she wanted to lead and not spend all her time healing folks. She's found a way to balance both jobs, but it leaves her with very little free time."

"Does she only work here one day a week then?"

"One full day and two evenings. And she's available when there are emergencies, if a person is going to die without her help." He gestured at the shop. "She's not in right now, but you can peek inside if you'd like."

I stepped onto the porch and looked in through the window. There was a large padded slab that looked to be where Noelle's patients would lie down, a few medical tools, and a shelf of what I thought might be medicines or potions. But otherwise, I saw very little equipment.

"She doesn't need much to do what she does," Marcus said. I thought back to the healing I'd undergone yesterday and nodded.

"Let's head upstairs," he continued. "Lachlann and Jasper are likely waiting for us."

Lachlann's apartment was on the third floor. It had a sitting room with high windows overlooking the city, intricate stained-glass light fixtures, and a row of three bedrooms, one of which Lachlann had converted into a leatherworking shop of sorts. The furniture was elegant in a comfortable sort of way; the couches were upholstered with soft, dark material, the tables were made of rough-hewn wood, and a fire burned in the squat, cheerful stone hearth. Jasper was perched on one of the couches drinking tea, his hair a tousled mess. "Did you just wake up?" I asked him.

He nodded. "Yesterday was…a lot for me. I needed sleep." His eyes darted to Trina as he spoke.

But Trina just shrugged. "I think yesterday was a lot for most of us."

"Well, I've been instructed to give Saray some space, so I'll only come to your house if I'm invited from now on. That was one of the rules Lachlann gave me." He glanced over at Lachlann then. "I told you it would've been best if I didn't come to the governor's yesterday."

"You may have been right about that part," Lachlann conceded.

"What other rules were you given?" I asked.

My brother grinned sheepishly. "I'm only allowed to drink two nights a week, and I have to be with Lachlann when I do. There's a pub nearby he likes to go to. And no teakflower, not that I would do that anyway. Oh, and I have to train with him twice a week. He wants me to improve my swordsmanship." He gave a shrug. "Not sure why that's a rule."

"Because people are most likely to turn to drinking too much or smoking teakflower when they're bored or lonely," Lachlann said. "My job is to ensure you are neither of those things."

"And you won't have to worry about teakflower here. The stuff doesn't grow in Dundere, so it's extremely expensive," Marcus said. "But onto more pleasant topics— are you ready to see more of Dundere, Jasper?"

He nodded, his smile becoming more genuine.

"Good. Will you be joining us, Lachlann?"

Lachlann shook his head. "I'm meeting with Desmond this afternoon."

"Who's Desmond?" I asked.

"The chief of the Dundere Guard. And Jasper might be joining me. Depends on how today's meeting goes."

"You're signing up to be a Dundere guardsmen?"

Jasper shrugged. "Hopefully. It'll give me something to do while you get trained. I might learn anti-magic, too."

I nodded slowly; I hadn't expected that, but I'd given little thought to what Jasper would do with himself during my schooling.

Jasper retreated to his room to get himself ready, and then we headed back downstairs and climbed into the carriage. Marcus decided that we were going to tour the market down by the docks first, and on the ride there Trina began asking us about our time on the Lady Liara. Jasper filled her in eagerly, telling her all about the things he'd learned on his journey over and the dance parties at night.

Trina smiled at his enthusiasm. "I'm a little jealous," she admitted. "I've been on the ship, but I was blind at that point, so I didn't get to do much."

"I'm sure Gareth would be happy to have you on board if you want to sail with him for a while. I'm thinking about doing that myself after we're done here."

"Maybe," Trina said. We were approaching the market now, and she sniffed the air and grinned. "I hope you two are hungry."

I nodded; my stomach was just beginning to rumble, and the air was tinged with the aroma of sugar and spices and frying oil. "Smells delicious."

"The market is a smorgasbord of sensory delights," Marcus informed.

I laughed. "Did you make that name up yourself?"

"Absolutely not. It's accurate, though." He grinned. "Come on, I'll show you."

Several hours later, I sat under the glowing viletta tree in the governor's backyard, exhausted from our adventure. The afternoon had been a whirlwind of new sights. We toured the open market, which was alive with noise and crowds. We'd looked at intricate tapestries and garments made from silk shipped from the southernmost tip of the Candeshi empire, visited a young woman selling coats that were almost certainly crafted by Alexander and Ember, and saw some local pottery with what looked like magic runes interwoven into its designs.

And the *food!* Pastries and sweets from all over the world, aromatic spiced tea, delicately seasoned, locally caught prawns…we sampled them all. My newly acquired taste buds were buzzing with delight at the end of our market tour, but the noise began to give me a headache.

After that, Marcus drove us around the rest of the city. We saw the legislative hall where Noelle worked, the large city square where events and gatherings often took place, a theatre, several more shops, and the famous Dundere School of Magic. Unlike the academy, the school of magic was in a squat, modern-looking brick building. Saray would take me on a tour of the school next week, I was told.

We dropped Jasper back at Lachlann's after that and then headed home for dinner. Now I was alone, finally, and the pounding in my head was beginning to subside. I looked up into the branches of the tree above me and sighed. "So, I'm not sure if there's actually a ghost living in this tree, like Lachlann seems to think, but just in case there is, do you mind if I climb you?"

The tree didn't respond, of course, so I shrugged and planted my foot on a large knob on the trunk, hoisting myself upwards.

I haven't been able to climb for quite a while, I realized. For a moment, I was worried that my new hand would fail me, but I found sturdy branches easily enough. I ended up settling in a nice spot on a thick limb about twenty feet up. The glowing flowers surrounded me, and I grinned as I gazed up into them. *Kaden would love this,* I thought, recalling her childlike glee when the island's trees had burst into a showy cloud of pale pink blooms earlier in the spring. The now-familiar ache of missing my friend rose to the surface of my consciousness, and tears pricked at my eyes. *Hold on,* I found myself silently promising her, *I'm coming back for you.*

The next two days passed quickly. I spent the first at the mansion, wandering the halls, trying out my new hand on the piano and doing some of the exercises Marcus had suggested to me, and conversing with whoever was around at the time. The day after that, Marcus took Jasper and me on a tour of the rest of Dundere, driving along bumpy roads high up in the mountains. Both Jasper and I spent much of the ride wide eyed as we took in the strange purple grass that was unlike anything we'd ever seen before, the craggy mountains draped in mist, and the ocean that sparkled in the distance. We also visited a few of the other settlements on the island— a couple of tiny fishing villages situated on the rugged coastline and a mining camp high in the mountains.

That evening, I was invited back to Lachlann's place for dinner. Lachlann was a decent cook, I discovered; the food he made wasn't fancy, but it was delicious nonetheless. He'd recently acquired some venison from Kip and made a stew bursting with flavour. After dinner, he set me up with what I'd need for my journey with Kip the next day. Kip would have a lot of the necessary supplies,

Lachlann told me, but wearing the right clothing for being out in the forest was essential. "The clothes we got you for the ship would probably be best," Lachlann said, "but you'll need another layer to keep warm."

"Even in June?" I asked.

He nodded. "The forest can be chilly in the evenings."

"I thought Kip was just going to drop me at Willem's and go hunt. Why do I need to pack all these extra things?"

"Kip is depending on Willem being home when he shows up tomorrow. But I know how busy Willem's been as of late, so that might not be the case. You may have to spend the day with Kip, or make camp with him, so you'd best be prepared for the possibility." He caught Jasper's expression. "Oh, don't look at me that way. You might not like Kip, but he's not about to harm your sister." Lachlann studied me for a moment. "I think I have something you could wear."

He retreated to his bedroom and returned a few minutes later carrying a colourful patchwork garment. Beside me, I heard Jasper inhale sharply. "I remember that coat. Quite well, actually."

"It must have made Kirilee pretty easy to track, huh?"

Jasper laughed nervously. "Yes. Exactly."

"This was your wife's?" I asked, eyeing the coat. "Why are you giving it to me?"

"I'm lending it to you," Lachlann corrected. "The sleeves are too short for Saray, and Trina is too petite for it. It might fit you a little better, though." He held it out to me. "Try it on. I would tell you to keep it in good condition, but as you can see, it's already a little worn."

I took the garment from him and slipped it on. The sleeves were a bit too long, but it fit well in the shoulders and was only a bit too big around my middle. Lachlann nodded. "Close enough. One of these days, I'll find someone who fits it."

We spent the rest of the evening packing a bag for me with blankets, a bedroll, and a few other things, just in case I had to stay in the Woods overnight. Lachlann also lent me a belt that had belonged to Kirilee, with several pouches and a knife attached to it. Then, satisfied that I was well equipped for my journey, he drove me home.

I felt my stomach knotting as I crawled into bed that evening. I was still uncertain about travelling with Kip, not to mention the Shrouded Woods themselves… I knew the stories I'd heard about them growing up were concocted to keep children out of the Woods, but even so, the thought of spending a couple days wandering around them— especially with someone I hardly knew as my guide— made me a little apprehensive.

It's the only way to reach Kaden, I reminded myself. *And if I manage to get her back, it will be worth whatever is waiting for me.*

CHAPTER 11

KIP ARRIVED AT the house early the following morning, clad in a rough brown tunic and matching trousers and wearing an animal-skin vest and a belt fitted with several knives. His pack was larger than mine, and it had a cooking pot hanging off one side. Attached to his pack was a quiver, and he carried a bow. He looked me over, raising his eyebrows at Kirilee's coat. "Lachlann lent that to you, ai?"

I nodded.

"Huh. Seems to fit you well enough."

"You two leaving right away?" Saray asked, appearing in the doorway.

Kip met her eyes and nodded. "Need to catch Willem early, if we can."

"Can you return this book to Willem for me? I'm not sure if he realizes it's missing from his library."

"Willem has a library?" I asked.

Both of them glanced at me, their expressions suddenly guarded. "He does," Saray said. "He might be willing to show you, but he'll likely have to wipe your memories of it." She undid Kip's pack and slipped the book inside.

"We'd best be off," Kip said once his pack was done up again. He pulled Saray into an embrace. "I'll see you when I get back."

Saray nodded, and Kip pulled away and kissed her. "Enjoy the Shrouded Woods, Ruby," she said to me. "Make sure to stay with Kip."

"I will," I promised. Then I followed Kip out the door into the cool morning air.

We set off walking and arrived at the school of magic about half an hour later. Kip led me to a small brick building around the back. "This used to be a storage shed," he explained as he extracted a set of keys and unlocked the door.

"Why's it locked?"

"To prevent lost children or curious students from accidentally ending up in the Shrouded Woods. And to keep wild animals or curious Woods-folk from wandering through onto our side. Though the Woods side of the portal is well hidden, so folks aren't likely to find it by accident." He pulled open the door and gestured that I should follow.

The inside of the room was taken up almost entirely by a massive circle of swirling light and colour. I couldn't see through to the other side, but it still seemed translucent somehow. I gaped at it in astonishment.

"You've never seen a portal before, ai?"

"No. Are you sure it's safe?"

"I go through it nearly every weekend, and it's not yet harmed me." Kip extended a hand. "Come on, it's not as scary as it looks, y'know."

I glanced at the portal, then at him, and took his hand. It was rough; I could feel calluses on his fingers where he'd pulled at a bowstring likely thousands of times. He gave me a small smile. "Ready?"

I nodded, and Kip took a step into the colourful mist, pulling me with him. I felt a tingle when my fingers touched it, similar to when Noelle had healed my hand, and I heard what sounded like a strain of odd music in my ears. Another step brought on the sensation of cold air across my face, and the smell of dirt and running water. A third step caused the colours to fade, and I found myself in another dark room. *No, a cave.* There was an opening a few feet away, and I could hear a waterfall churning just beyond.

Kip looked back at me and let go of my hand. "Welcome to the Shrouded Woods."

I followed him out of the cave to find that we were tucked behind a small waterfall. A narrow ledge along the side of the rock took us out from behind the falls, and I managed to mostly avoid getting wet as I skirted it and stepped off onto a large, moss-covered rock. We were in the middle of a small clearing, and I gaped up at the massive trees that surrounded us. "This is beautiful."

He nodded. "It always seems I can breathe easier out here, y'know? I—" He was interrupted by a mighty *whoosh*, and I gasped as a massive bird alighted on his shoulder. Kip caught my look and smiled wryly. "Meet Persius. He was Kirilee's hawk."

I nodded. "Lachlann mentioned him."

"She had a magic bond that let her talk to Persius. She gave him to Lachlann before she died, but we pretty quickly found out that Lachlann can't communicate with Persius like she could. I can, though, because of Kirilee's magic. So now Persius lives in these Woods and shows up when I'm in the area." He reached up and stroked the bird's neck. "It's mighty useful having a hawk who can speak to you while you're hunting, y'know."

"I imagine so." I studied the hawk. "Does he travel beyond the Shrouded Woods? I saw a hawk back on Yarel Island who looked a lot like this one, and he was out later at night than normal."

Kip's eyes narrowed. " It might've been him, though most red-tailed hawks look about the same. I can ask him though." He paused, closing his eyes for a moment. "Sounds like he did go there at one point. The fairies sent him." He opened his eyes again. "I s'pose they meant to bring you to us. You must be important to their plans."

"Why would the fairies care about me?"

"No idea. I'm sure you'll find out though." He shrugged. "We'd best get moving. Willem's place isn't far."

A narrow path cut through the dense trees, and Kip followed it easily, dodging roots and slippery rocks with fluid grace. Once or twice he stopped and pulled out a small knife to cut off rogue branches that blocked our path.

The trail began to slope downward, and after about half an hour of hiking, we reached a cliff face. I gaped at the view, the Shrouded Woods spread out below me in a thick blanket of green. I could see a few grassy patches and lakes dotting the landscape, and further off I noticed where the Woods ended and a city began. "That's Flavalan," Kip told me.

"Ah. Where Claudi lives."

"You met Claudi?"

I nodded. "Lachlann took us there to meet up with Willem before we travelled to Dundere. He wanted to see if Willem would take Jasper and me through the portal. Obviously, he refused."

Kip let out a sharp laugh. "How'd Willem react to you and your brother knowing where his mother lives?"

"Not well at all." I shook my head at the memory. "Lachlann said it was similar to when he first met you."

"Ah." Kip nodded knowingly. "That's about what I'd expect."

"Willem's very protective of certain things, isn't he?"

"He is. And he likely won't be too happy when we show up at his house in a few minutes."

"Why? Is it just because of who our father is?"

"No, it's more than that. But it's not my story to tell, y'know? Ask him yourself." Kip gestured at the drop off in front of us. "We're going to have to climb down."

My eyes widened. "All the way down that cliff?"

He shook his head. "Get a little closer to the edge, and you'll see that there's a ledge about fifteen feet down. That's where we're headed."

I did as he told me. "Willem lives there?"

"Yes. Now follow me."

A rope hung from the section of cliff face that we were climbing down. Kip ignored it completely, finding hand and footholds with no difficulty. When it was my turn, I was grateful for the rope. It wasn't a terribly hard climb, but there were a few times I had trouble finding my footing. Kip directed me once or twice from the ground below, and soon enough, I made the final jump and landed on the ledge next to him. The ledge didn't look so narrow now that I was standing on it; there were several small trees growing around a well-established path. One particularly massive tree had branches that grew out over the cliff face, and another smaller one with pink blossoms, much like the tree in the governor's backyard, grew up against the cliff face. Kip parted its branches to reveal a small wooden door tucked into the rock. He knocked.

When there was no answer after several moments, he knocked again, then frowned. "Mustn't be home." He sighed, then glanced over the forest spread out below. "I s'pose you'll be coming with me, then. Hope you can keep up."

I crossed my arms. "You think I can't keep up with you? Is it because I'm a girl?"

"No, it's because I'm fast. " He glanced over at the nearby cliff face. "You afraid of heights?"

"Not especially."

"Good. Because we're about to do something that can be mighty terrifying. You'll have to trust my magic." He walked over to the large tree whose thick branches jutted out over the dropoff, and I followed him. Someone had installed a sort of pulley system there, and I watched as Kip muttered a string of words that caused the system to begin moving. A few moments later, a platform rose so that it was level to where we stood. "Hop on," Kip said.

I stared dubiously at the platform. "Is it safe?"

"I use it every week, and I've yet to injure myself," he told me, stepping onto the platform and grabbing onto one of the large centre ropes.

I put out a foot and tested the platform. It was steady under my weight. Tentatively, I leaned forward to grip one of the ropes, then eased myself onto the platform. "Don't hold that one," Kip told me. "Grab the same one I'm holding. Otherwise you'll burn your hands."

"What happens if I fall off?"

"Don't," he replied, grinning slightly. "If you do, I s'pose I could catch you with my magic. But I make no promises."

"You can move *people* with your magic?"

"As long as they don't fight it. Ready?"

I nodded.

Kip flicked his wrist, and suddenly we were hurtling towards the ground. I stifled a scream as I clung to the rope, the wind whipping at my clothes. *Is he trying to kill me?* The ground was rising to meet us fast. "Kip!" I shrieked. "Stop the—"

Our fall ended as quickly as it started, screeching to a halt just a few inches above the ground. I gaped at Kip, my stomach churning.

He caught my look and smirked. "That's fun, ai?"

"Fun?! Are you trying to kill me?"

Kip alighted from the platform in a single graceful step, then offered me his hand. "Now why would I do that?"

I ignored his gesture and jumped down myself, nearly tripping as I landed. "To get back at my brother for shooting you, maybe?" The words were out before I could stop them, and I glanced at him, shrinking back.

Kip's expression darkened. "If I wanted you dead, you already would be." He shook his head. "We'll stash our bags at camp and then head out to hunt. Let's see if you can keep up."

Hunting with Kip was like chasing a tornado, I decided by the time we broke for lunch. He moved near-silently, sharp and unpredictable but also fluid. Persius flew high above us, and every now and then Kip cocked his head, clearly listening to signals from the bird before pulling an arrow from his quiver and readying it.

He didn't just hunt while he was out here, I quickly realized. He would often stop to pick berries, collect mushrooms, or cut twigs carefully from trees. Occasionally, he would even pull up an entire plant, dusting off its roots before stowing it in his pack. These were the only times he spoke to me; he always explained what he was foraging and what it was good for. Most of the plants he gathered seemed medicinal in nature, and I wondered what use he had for them.

When we finally broke for lunch, he'd shot three birds and a rabbit and had a good number of herbs and roots in a second bag that I assumed was for plants. "You did better than I expected, y'know," he said to me as he pulled the rabbit from his burlap sack. "At keeping up, that is."

I grinned at him. In truth, I'd been left winded several times trying to match pace, and my legs were beginning to ache. But I was proud of the fact that I'd managed.

Kip moved away from the centre of the clearing, rabbit in hand, and pulled out a knife. I looked away while he gutted it. "Not good with blood?" he asked.

"Not particularly," I admitted.

"I s'pose they didn't have you kids doing any of the slaughtering on that farm you lived on, then?"

I shook my head. "That was all the adults."

He nodded, not looking away from his work. "How about you go collect some firewood while I get this rabbit ready to cook, ai?"

I nodded, happy to be given a task that didn't involve blood, and set off to gather some fallen branches.

Halfway through the afternoon, Kip managed to shoot a large buck deer. Unlike the birds and rabbit, the deer didn't die quickly with a single arrow, and I had to look away while Kip slit its throat. "Looks like I've got my work cut out for me for the rest of the afternoon," he said. "This will take some time to butcher. I'm going to bring it back to camp."

Before I could ask how he intended to transport an animal that large, he mumbled his now-familiar casting words, and the deer rose to shoulder height next to him. "Knowing how to teleport would be handy right now," he said to me. "But I don't, so this'll have to do."

I followed Kip back to our camp, surprised at the ease with which he moved the deer carcass through the thick trees. When we arrived, Kip let the deer fall to the ground, slid his bags off his shoulders, and handed me the one that was filled with herbs. "You think you can recognize some of what I gathered earlier?"

"I…think so," I said. "You're not going to send me out there alone, are you? Isn't that dangerous?"

He shrugged. "Doubtful, but I can see how you might be worried. I'll send Persius with you. Unless you'd rather stay here and butcher a deer with me."

I wrinkled my nose and put the bag onto my back, tightening the shoulder straps so it fit me. "I'll go."

"As I thought." He pointed to a padded attachment on the bag, which sat directly on my left shoulder. "Persius can perch there, and it won't hurt you." As if on cue, Persius swooped down from above us and landed on the pad. I tensed involuntarily; the bird was heavier than I'd expected. I could feel his talons dig into the leather, and I glanced up at him. "Hi there," I said, reaching nervously.

"He likes having his neck rubbed," Kip told me. "Don't look him in the eye 'til he knows you a bit better, though. He'll see that as a threat. I've told him you're safe, but he's still a wild bird, y'know?"

I nodded and let my fingers travel up to the back of Persius's neck, burying my hand deep in his feathers.

"That's right," Kip said. "Now go gather. I've got work to do."

Venturing out into the Shrouded Woods alone was both terrifying and exhilarating. I was glad to have Persius close by, but his company did little to stop the childhood stories of bandits and wild animals that played themselves out over and over in my mind.

I nearly tripped on a large root, and glancing down at it, I saw a small patch of mushrooms growing at the tree's base. *Right.* I crouched down to examine them. *These look like the one Kip pulled up earlier.*

Harvesting the mushrooms helped bring me back into the present. I took a deep breath and listened to the sounds of the forest around me— songbirds chirping, small animals scuttling about in the underbrush, and, far above me, the wind rustling the canopy of trees. *This is pretty peaceful, actually.*

I continued my gathering, breathing deeply and enjoying the scent of earth and pine, the freedom that came with being utterly alone. It was then that I realized I hadn't been by myself much in the past several months. The farm didn't really allow it, and ever since arriving in Dundere, I'd spent all my time either at the governor's house or with Jasper at Lachlann's.

It felt like several hours later that Persius landed on my shoulder and let out a squawk. I looked up at him, unsure of what he was trying to communicate. "What is it?"

He squawked again and then took off, glancing back at me over his shoulder. *He wants me to follow him*, I surmised, and took off after him. I could smell food cooking soon enough and realized that Kip had used Persius to call me back for dinner.

At the camp, I found the deer carcass gone, save a small pile of guts that Kip had obviously set aside for Persius. A large chunk of the meat cooked over the fire with some of the tubers we'd gathered earlier, and Kip had already set up the tent. He glanced over at me. "What'd you find?"

"Mostly some mushrooms, yarel blooms, and a few sagie flowers." I looked around then. "Where's the rest of the meat?"

"In a hole underground," Kip replied. "Keeps it cool, and keeps bears away."

"What about the bones and skin?"

"Well, I buried most of the guts— though I'll uncover them later when a friend comes by— but I kept some of the smaller bones and skin for soup and leather making." He gestured at the log he'd moved over by the fire. "Take a seat. Dinner's ready."

We dug into the meal Kip prepared, and as we ate, my mind went to the bag of herbs. "Why are we gathering all this anyway?"

"I sell some here in the Woods," he told me. "The rest I take home. Traditional medicine is good to have on hand in Dundere. Noelle doesn't always have time to heal things like colds and small cuts, and all the guards who use Bonded anti-magic need non-magical cures."

I nodded, recalling the medicine shops I'd seen in the building where Noelle worked. "Right. Where'd you learn about medicine?"

"Kirilee. Learned most of the herbology I know from her too."

"You must have spent a lot of time with her to learn all that."

"Well, not really. It's…complicated." As he leaned forward to take a bite of his food, a pendant slipped out of his shirt and dangled precariously. I noticed a flash of green as it caught the sun, and Kip closed his fist around the medallion with a deft motion.

"That's pretty," I said. "Can I see it?"

He turned to me and opened his hand. The pendant was delicate, crafted of silver in the shape of a leaf. A small emerald in its centre seemed to glow with a light of its own. "Is it magical?"

He nodded and tucked it back inside his shirt. "Not really s'posed to talk about it though."

I crossed my arms. "Well, aren't you full of secrets today?"

"I'm allowed to have my secrets," Kip said defensively. "There are some things I'd rather not share with you."

"Because you think I'll tell Jasper?" Again, I'd spoken before thinking, and I cringed.

Kip put his bowl down. "Not all our interactions revolve around who your brother is, y'know. I know you're not him. But I don't know you very well, and you were raised with the same sorts of beliefs he was."

My eyes narrowed. "But I'm a magic user. Do you think for a moment that I actually agreed with all that?"

He shrugged. "Some magikai do."

"Well, not me. And didn't *you* used to believe that magic was evil? I heard you betrayed Saray over it, but you got past your prejudices against magic. Why couldn't Jasper do the same?"

Kip closed his eyes for a moment. "It's not that I think Jasper's not changed. He brought you to Dundere, after all. But you don't understand what it's like, having someone put a gun to your head. You can't imagine the terror of knowing you're about to die."

"So Jasper shooting you *did* affect you. When he apologized, you acted like it hadn't caused you much harm, other than the obvious."

"Do y'think I want *him* to know what he's done to me?" Kip huffed. "He's not exactly someone I wish to bare my soul to, y'know? Forgive my difficulty trusting the fellow who killed me."

I crossed my arms. "Forgive *my* difficulty trusting the fellow who punched my brother in the face and threatened him with a knife."

Kip opened his mouth to respond, but a rustling in the trees overhead cut him off, and he glanced up. "We have company."

I frowned, following his gaze, then ducked as a large, winged creature swooped down and landed in our clearing. It was perhaps the size of a small horse, with a snout like a lizard's, and it was covered in bright green scales. A pair of delicate, membranous wings that were an almost iridescent green jutted out of its back. I gaped at Kip, who regarded the creature with astonishing nonchalance. "Is that a *dragon?*"

"Of course," an unfamiliar male voice replied. I startled as I noticed for the first time a fellow sliding off the dragon's back. "Good to see you again, Kip," he said, grinning. Then he tilted his head. "How's the new haircut treating you? I'm still not used to it."

Kip shrugged. "Me neither. My head feels very light without all that hair."

"You used to have long hair?" I asked.

"Nearly down to his waist," the other fellow informed me.

"Why'd you cut it?"

"I did it after I proposed to Saray," Kip replied. "None of the noblemen in Dundere have long hair, y'know. I figured that if I'm going to marry the governor's daughter, I should look the part."

"That's…really sweet of you. Though I imagine she liked you just as much with long hair."

"I think Saray liked your long hair *better,* personally," the other fellow said. Then he turned to me. "Sorry, we haven't officially met."

"Right." I extended a hand. "I'm Ruby."

"Ambrose. It's a pleasure to meet you." I looked him over as I shook his hand. He was a bit shorter than Kip, with broad, muscular shoulders, a mop of auburn hair, and a wide grin. He gestured back at the dragon. "And this is Spark. Don't worry, she doesn't bite. Unless I tell her to, of course."

I smiled at him and then stared openly at Spark. "He's massive."

"She," corrected Ambrose. "And actually, no, she's still quite young. She'll be a lot bigger when she's fully grown." He turned to Kip, handed him a large brown pouch, and smirked. "So, you're bringing young women with you into the Woods now, ai? Does Saray know?"

Kip snorted. "Of course she does. Ruby's only with me because she needs to see Willem. He wasn't home when we dropped by earlier."

"Ah. And how do you two know each other?"

Kip and I exchanged a glance. "We don't, really," I told Ambrose. "We just met last week." Spark, I noticed, had moved away from Ambrose and was beginning to paw at the ground, uncovering something that lay buried and slurping at it. "The deer guts?" I asked Kip.

He nodded. "Ambrose and I have a deal. I feed his dragon, and he supplies me with Erill mushrooms." He reached into the bag Ambrose gave him and pulled out a large, brightly coloured mushroom cap. "These only grow in the northernmost wilds of the Shrouded Woods, where Ambrose lives."

"Why do you need those?"

"They're an ingredient in a tea that I've learned to forage for."

"What sort of tea is so important that it has you getting mushrooms from the middle of nowhere to make it?"

I saw Kip and Ambrose exchange a glance. Ambrose grinned, but Kip frowned, and I thought I saw a faint blush colour his cheeks. "My dear," Ambrose finally said, "it's a tea that prevents pregnancy."

"*Oh.*" I felt heat rise in my own cheeks then. "For…uh…you and Saray?"

"No!" Kip replied indignantly.

Ambrose snickered. "Sure, Kip."

"Well, it's not *just* for us. I sell it in Dundere, and here in the Woods sometimes, too. I make nearly as much money with it as I do selling meat. The recipe is a secret, so it's in demand."

"How do you know it, then?"

Kip averted his eyes. "Again, Kirilee."

"And why is the recipe a secret?"

"Because we don't want folks invading the northern reaches of the Woods for mushrooms," Ambrose explained. "That's where the dragons live. Wouldn't be safe for anyone involved."

"But you live out there, alone with the dragons?"

"With my family," he corrected. "We can all speak to animals, but we choose to communicate solely with dragons. We raise them, train them, and keep them out of trouble."

"Huh." I nodded. "That must be a lonely life."

"It can be. That's why I fly out this way pretty regularly, to bother Kip and attend Moon Dances and such. Speaking of which, there's one this Monday if you folks want to join."

Kip shook his head. "We'll be gone by then."

"What's a Moon Dance?" I asked.

Eagerly, Ambrose sat back and began to fill me in. My eyes widened at the description of folks gathering to dance and frolic under the full moon's glow to honour the fairies. It sounded beautiful, enchanting. "That's why you need to come back one day and attend!" Ambrose concluded. "Kip would likely be happy to bring you at some point. Right, Kip?"

"Uh-huh," Kip mumbled, his glancing toward the cliff face.

Ambrose's eyes narrowed. "Everything all right?"

Kip let out a sigh. "It's getting dark. We'd best see if Willem is home yet."

"He won't be home until tomorrow morning," Ambrose said. "He's visiting a friend in Cherin."

"He can teleport all the way to Cherin?" I asked.

"Apparently." Kip frowned. "I wish I'd known that before I brought Ruby with me. I s'pose I'll be sleeping outside tonight."

"It's your tent," I said. "I can sleep outside."

But Kip shook his head. "It's best if I do." I didn't miss the glance that he and Ambrose exchanged.

Ambrose settled in then, and he and Kip began talking about mutual friends in the Woods who I didn't know. I began to drift off, and before I knew it, Kip was shaking my shoulder and telling me to go into the tent. I stumbled inside, crawled under the blankets, and succumbed immediately to sleep.

When I awoke, it was still early; the morning light had only just begun to permeate the tent. I sat up, wondering what had woken me, then winced when I heard something metallic crash into a tree. *Something's out there!* Another crash, then a scuffling sound and some mumbling.

The voice sounded like Kip's, I realized. *Where* is *Kip anyway?* I shuddered at the idea of facing the unknown, but crawled to the entrance of the tent and peeked out.

The camp was a mess. Our cooking pot was flung against the side of a tree, the log we'd been sitting on by the fire had been thrown ten feet, and the rocks from the fire ring were scattered every which way. Kip's quiver was on the other side of the campsite, his arrows strewn across the ground. I scanned the forest frantically, trying to figure out what had caused the chaos. There were no animals that I could see, and no humans other than Kip, who was curled in a swath of blankets, sleeping through it all.

Then I froze.

I suddenly realized Kip's bow was suspended in midair above him. I heard him mumble in his sleep, and my heartbeat accelerated at the now-familiar string of words.

I ducked as the bow came flying at me.

It met the side of the tent instead and clattered to the ground, thankfully unbroken. "Kip!" I hissed. "Kip, wake up!"

When he didn't respond, I gingerly approached him, crawling on my hands and knees to avoid any projectiles. He mumbled the spell again, and one of the rocks from the fire ring rose from its resting place. I seized his shoulder and shook him hard. "Kip!" I shouted. "Wake *up!*"

CHAPTER 12

KIP'S EYES FLEW open, and the rock fell with a mighty *thud* to the ground. "What?" he mumbled, staring at me confusedly. "What happened?"

I moved out of his field of vision so he could see the wreckage of our campsite. "*This.*"

He drew in a sharp breath, then bolted upright, his eyes wild. "Are you all right? I didn't hurt you, did I?"

"I'm fine," I assured him. "You almost hit me in the face with your bow, but I ducked."

"I…I'm sorry."

The meekness in his voice caught me off guard, and I sighed. "No harm done— not to me, at least. Come on, let's get the camp cleaned up, and then you can tell me what's happening here."

When the campsite was restored to some semblance of order, Kip and I sat down on the log, a small fire cracking in the centre of the repositioned rocks. Kip was tense, his shoulders hunched, and he hadn't spoken to me since we began cleaning.

I finally broke the silence. "So you're casting in your sleep."

Kip nodded, not looking at me.

I frowned, recalling the stories I'd heard when I first arrived in Dundere. "Didn't Kirilee have a problem with that?"

He nodded. "She killed someone by sleep casting."

"And you have her magic now."

"Yes, and I also have some of her memories."

My eyes narrowed. "Really?"

"It started after I began training with Willem. Sometimes the memories are helpful. Like I know my way around the entire Shrouded Woods now, and much of my knowledge around herbs and plants only showed up after the life transfer. It's at night that the memories give me trouble."

"What happens at night?"

He began to play absentmindedly with his pendant as he spoke. "I have terrible, vivid nightmares about all the bad things that happened to her. And that's when I start casting." He let out a bitter laugh. "I s'pose it was a mercy that the fairies' curse didn't allow her to sleep, if this is what sleeping did to her."

"Have you told anyone about this? I'd think Willem could help you. Didn't Trina say that Willem's father gave Kirilee a potion for her sleep casting?"

"Most of the folks I'm closest to know," he said. "Willem's tried to help. He gave me the potion for dreamless sleep, which gets rid of my own dreams but does nothing for Kirilee's. He's also tried wiping those memories, which didn't work.

Lachlann gave me an anti-magic pendant and told me to sleep with it next to my bed, and that did nothing as well. I'm not sure why we can't find anything that works." He glanced at me then, shame in his eyes. "You can see why I had you take the tent."

"I can see why you wouldn't want to sleep in the same room as anyone."

"And that's just the problem. I'm meant to marry Saray soon, and then I'll be sharing a bed with her." He shook his head. "She's not worried. She thinks we should just have very little in our bedroom. But I'm still afraid that I'll hurt her somehow. It's why we've yet to pick a date for our wedding. I want to get this sorted before I marry her."

I nodded. "I don't blame you. That's a tough situation to be in, Kip."

"Yes, well, I can thank your brother for it." He huffed. "That's the truth of why I hate him, Ruby. I know he didn't want to shoot me. But if he hadn't shot me, I wouldn't have needed to be brought back, and then I wouldn't be like *this*."

"Is this why you wanted to drop me at Willem's yesterday? So you wouldn't risk me seeing you cast in your sleep?"

"Mostly, yes." He nodded. "I also just…"

"What?"

"It's hard to explain." He poked at the fire with a stick. "When I moved to Dundere, I had a family for the first time since I was a child. But even so, these Woods feel like home to me. I'm not cut out for fancy houses and posh schools. I grew up here, and when I'm here, I feel like I can be myself. I don't have to worry about acting a certain way or saying the right things, y'know? I can get out of my head and just *exist*." He shrugged. "And I s'pose I was worried that having you with me would make me unable to do that. Though, really, it was fine. You kept up well."

"Told you I could." I grinned. "I suppose you and Saray couldn't live in the Shrouded Woods instead of Dundere?"

"Some folks want us to. Willem especially. But Dundere is where she's safest. And she fits in there, even if I don't." He sighed. "But enough about this. We'd best head back to Willem's so you can get what you need from him."

We began packing up, and Kip tried to distract from the heaviness of our previous conversation. "So, you want to go back to the island for your friend," he said. "But only one?"

"It'd be nice to get everyone off the island, but I don't think it's possible. There are a couple of others I'd like to bring along if I could— Shawnie and Alisa. And there's a woman named Starla I got close to, but she seems fairly happy there."

"Starla," Kip repeated. "How old is she?"

I shrugged. "I don't know, late thirties maybe? Do you know her?"

"Possibly. I knew someone with that name once, and it's not exactly common. What does she look like?"

"A bit taller than me, black hair, skin a bit darker than Trina's. And she's all scarred up; she got burned badly at one point in her life."

"Burned?" Kip's eyes narrowed. "That doesn't sound right. Though, if the fairies were involved over on the island…"

"Actually, that makes sense. Starla told me that Persius followed her around specifically."

"Is that so?" Kip glanced up at Persius, who was sitting in a nearby tree. "I wonder if…" He shook his head. "Don't worry about it for now. I'll figure it out."

We packed in silence after that, and an hour later, we were ready to go. We climbed onto the platform once more, and Kip secured the remaining venison in a massive bag. "Ready to fly?" he asked.

I nodded.

Rising up was much different than falling— far less terrifying to be sure— and I found myself gazing around us in wonder as we cleared the tops of the trees. A harsh wind picked up at that height, so I used my own magic to calm it down, just for now. "This is incredible," I whispered.

"I know." Kip grinned. "It's the closest I've ever got to flying."

We made it to the top of the cliff face and stepped off the platform onto solid ground. "Let's see if Willem is home now," Kip said. He strode over to the door and knocked again; this time, someone answered.

Willem peered out at us. "Ah, Kip. I was wondering when you'd be along. Did you bring anything interesting for…" He trailed off when he noticed me there, and his eyes narrowed. "Ruby?"

"She needs to talk to you about something," Kip explained. "If you're worried about her knowing where your home is, you can wipe her memory."

Willem frowned. "You brought her through the portal, I assume." There was a note of disapproval in his voice.

"I did. Again, you can erase her memories if it's a problem. I also have a whole ton of deer meat with me. You can have some for free if you'll put a freezing spell on the rest."

"Done." Willem sighed, then opened the door. "Well, I suppose you'd both best come in, then. Since Ruby already knows where I live, it won't hurt her to see the place."

I glanced over at Kip, thinking of our conversation earlier. "If you want to head back out there, you're welcome to. I can talk to Willem about what I need."

Kip smiled. "Perhaps I'll do that in a bit. I have some business to attend to with Willem first."

"I'll give you a quick tour," Willem said to me. "Would you like to make use of my magical bathing room?"

I raised an eyebrow; I was a bit sore from sleeping on the ground, and I was fairly certain I'd gotten dirt in my hair at least once on the trip. "That sounds lovely."

Not long after, I was clean, though dressed in the same clothes I'd worn the day before. I made my way down the hall toward Willem's parlour but paused when I heard Kip speak louder than I'd expected.

"You don't get to decide this!" he declared. "I never asked for this responsibility."

"Yes, well, it's yours, whether you like it or not," Willem replied flatly. "You're finished school soon enough. You need to come here more in the summer— make a few day trips if need be. The magic is *wrong*, Kip. Hilda, Mother, and I are doing what we can to compensate for you, but folks are struggling to use their gifts, all because *you* won't cooperate!"

Kip let out a huff. "I'll come by on some of the days that Saray's working, fine. But no more evenings out here. I'll be marrying her soon enough, y'know."

"Yes. That's what worries me."

"You know very well that Saray can't live in these Woods. You want me to just abandon love for duty?"

"I did exactly that, once," Willem replied. "Kip, you know the Shrouded Woods are your home. You're more *yourself* when you're here. You've told me that you breathe easier." I raised my eyebrows; Kip had said the same thing to me yesterday. And I had noticed that the odd lilt in Kip's voice seemed stronger than usual over the last few days.

"Yet I'm not about to commit to living here apart from Saray." He sighed. "I'll do what I can. But I'm not you, Willem. I'm not going to leave the woman I love for an obligation that I never asked for."

Kip stormed out of the living room before I saw him coming. He looked me over and frowned. "You weren't supposed to hear that," he mumbled, then turned and stalked out the door, slamming it behind him.

I heard Willem let out an audible sigh. A moment later, he appeared in the hallway. "Eavesdropping, are we?"

I took a step back, startled. "Sorry, I was walking down the hall, and I just heard you two talking; I didn't want to barge in." My eyes narrowed. "What was that *about?*"

"Nothing you need to concern yourself with, my dear." Willem gestured toward the parlour. "Come, sit."

I followed him to the couch and took a cup of tea he offered, stifling my curiosity about the argument. He looked me over, holding his own drink. "So. The daughter of Angus Jameson is sitting in my house, drinking tea."

I eyed him. "I'd apologize, but I can't exactly help who my father is."

"I know. And I apologize if I scared you when you met me at my mother's house. I wish Lachlann had come alone and then only brought you and Jasper if it was needed. But there's not much that can be done about it now." He shook his head. "Is this your first time in the Woods?"

I nodded. "They're lovely. I always heard terrifying stories about them growing up, but there's nothing scary about them."

"Oh, there are plenty of scary things in the Woods. You just haven't met them yet." Willem smirked. "But they are also beautiful. There's both good and bad, like any place."

"So the stories about the bandits are true?"

"Absolutely. Lots of folks move into the Woods because they don't want anyone telling them what to do. Some of them are magikai, and when they use their powers to harm others, it can be a problem. Lachlann lost his arm thanks to some of those folks."

"Right." I nodded. "That's what I was taught about magic growing up, actually. That it had to be illegal not because it was evil, but because people could use it to do evil things."

"And what do you believe about that now?"

"I understand why people would think like that, but I don't believe Breoch handles it right. I like the system in Dundere.”

“And yet there are some in Dundere who find the magic licensing system to be too restrictive.” Willem shrugged. “But enough about that. What brings you here, Ruby?”

Willem listened carefully as I told him all about Kaden. “I want to go back to the island and rescue her,” I explained. “But I have no idea how. Jasper and Lachlann don’t think it’s a good idea to go in by boat again, and I’ve been told that you’re the best person to talk to about doing it magically.”

Willem nodded. “It’s just the one person you want to rescue?” he asked. “You’re not trying to save the whole bunch of them?”

“I do have a couple other friends there. In fact, I’d love to get everyone out, if I could, but I don’t know if that’s possible.”

“It would be extremely difficult, but it could be done. I’m sure I can help you get Kaden out, at least. But it’ll take some time to prepare.”

“What do we need to do?”

“Well, first I’ll need to scout the island out. I can use a ritual that will allow me to see into your memories of the place, so I can determine a good landing spot. That would help me to circumvent the problem of not knowing the island well enough to teleport there. Before that, though, it would be helpful to know exactly where this island is. Do you have any idea?”

I frowned. “When Jasper rescued me, we landed our boat in the woods just southwest of Sylvenburgh. It took us about two hours on horseback to reach Sylvenburgh Academy from where we camped that night.”

Willem nodded. “Let’s take a look at a map, shall we? There should be one in the…” He trailed off for a moment, then sighed. “I suppose this means I’ll be taking you into the school wing.”

I followed Willem back to the entryway, and we began down another hallway that jutted off the foyer. This corridor looked nearly unused; the torches were dusty and the floor less worn. The hall angled sharply to the left, and then we reached what I thought was a dead end. Before I could comment on this, Willem mumbled a spell and placed his hand on the wall, which slowly dissipated into a fine mist and revealed a much longer corridor lined with old, unused classrooms. “The old school of magic,” he told me. “I keep it, as well as my library, hidden.”

“May I ask you a question?”

He nodded.

“Why are you so afraid of my father finding this place? If there were still students here I’d understand, but it’s just a bunch of old classrooms.”

He glanced at me hesitantly. “If I answer that question, I’ll need to wipe the location of my home from your mind.”

“I thought you were going to do that anyway.”

“I suppose you’re right.” He stopped in front of a large pair of double doors. “It’s not the school that’s my concern now. If your father found out where my library was, it would be a disaster.” I followed him through the doors into a large octagonal room lined with books.

I gazed around at the towering bookshelves made from dark wood, many of them lined with very old-looking titles inscribed with gold leaf, though one shelf was filled with scrolls. Couches and worktables in the middle of the room gave things a rather cozy feel, and the floor was tiled with a colourful, whirling mosaic design that glowed ever so slightly. The magic in the room was almost palpable.

"It's impressive," I said. "But…it's just a library."

"It's so much more than that, Ruby." He turned to me with a grim expression on his face. "When the Banishing happened, my father began storing other people's banned books in this library, for a yearly fee. I've inherited his collections and the daunting task of guarding them. It's how I make a living now. This room is full of illegal books brimming with rare knowledge, and the records of ownership could get a lot of people into very serious trouble."

I nodded. "I see why it needs to be kept a secret, then."

"Understand, Ruby, I don't think you'll tell your father anything because you want to. But I worry that if he caught up with you, he might use force to get information. That's what I'm trying to avoid by wiping your mind."

"I suppose that makes sense," I conceded.

"It's for your own good. But I didn't bring you to my library just so I could tell you all the reasons you shouldn't be here. We'd best get what we came for." He directed me to a map on one of the walls. "Sylvenburgh is here," he pointed to a particular spot, "and you're saying you were camped in the woods two hours southwest…" He ran his finger along a section of coastline until he reached a small island sitting just south of Breoch's mainland. "Here, I'm guessing."

Yarel Island, the script next to the island read. "Yes, there!"

"Well, that's a start," he said.

"Now what? You said something about a ritual?"

"Yes, to allow me to look into your memories of the place. If I can see what it physically looks like, it will help me better determine a landing spot."

"Landing spot?"

"Where exactly we want to land when we teleport in. If I have no idea what the terrain looks like, I could easily drop us right in the middle of a lake, or on the roof of a building, or somewhere else inconvenient."

I nodded; that made sense.

"I won't be able to complete the ritual for a few weeks," he went on. "I'll need Hilda for that, and she's preoccupied right now. But when the time comes, she and I will travel to Dundere. Where can I find you?"

"Well, I've been staying at the governor's this past week, but I think they're going to move me into the school dorms at some point. Saray and Trina should know where I am; if you can't find me, look for them." I paused then, considering the timeframe of the plan we formulated. "Are you sure we can't do the ritual sooner? Is there anything I could do to help your friend with her errands?"

He shook his head. "I know it's hard, but you're going to have to wait. Go back to Dundere, get settled in at school. There's plenty of lovely people for you to meet there, Ruby. When the time comes, I'll come get you. I promise."

An hour later, Kip returned to the house. "Feeling better?" Willem asked him when he strode into the kitchen where I was helping make lunch.

Kip shrugged. "My opinions haven't changed, but I don't feel like I want to run back to Dundere and never speak to you again like I did earlier."

"That's an improvement, I suppose," Willem conceded. "Besides, if you never spoke to me again, how could you visit your adopted grandma?"

Kip snorted. "I know where Claudi lives, I could go see her whenever I wanted."

"Yes, but it's much more convenient for you if I bring her here, now isn't it?" Willem smirked and began rubbing his summoning stone. "She'll be in the parlour."

By the time Kip and I reached the parlour, Claudi had materialized on the couch. She grinned when she saw Kip, embraced him, and began asking him about how life in Dundere was treating him. I couldn't help but notice how Kip's posture began to change as he chatted with her. His shoulders relaxed, his voice became more animated, and he smiled and laughed openly, the earlier fight with Willem seemingly forgotten. *I've never seen him at ease like this,* I realized.

I recalled Marcus telling me how Kip had lived with Willem for a time following his resurrection. *Kip's an orphan,* I recalled. *It makes sense that Claudi has become something like a grandmother to him.*

Willem called us to lunch soon after, and we sat down to a decadent meal of venison stew made from yesterday's kill, warm crusty bread, and strange fizzy drinks that changed colour and flavour as we drank them. "These are Kip's favourite," Willem informed me with a wink.

Kip laughed, seeming more at ease around me too. "I like them now," he said. "But the first time I saw one of these, I was terrified. Willem and I got in quite the scrap because of them."

"And then Saray got involved," Willem put in. "The same girl who'd set you on fire only a day before tried to protect you from me."

My eyes grew wide. "Saray set you on fire?"

"She burned my arms pretty badly," he replied. "Look, you can still see scars." When he rolled up his sleeves, I saw his forearms were marked with faint white lines.

"Seems to be a habit of hers," I mused.

Kip's face darkened momentarily. "If you're thinking of your brother, he deserved it."

"So did you, from what I recall," Willem put in. "Didn't you punch her in the face?"

"You punched Saray in the face, and now she's marrying you?" I sat back, smirking. "This sounds like something I need to hear."

Kip grinned. "We'd best head home soon, but I s'pose there's time for one more story."

CHAPTER 13

I RETURNED TO the Dundere School of Magic the next morning, this time accompanied by Saray, and she chatted with me about my time in the Shrouded Woods as we walked. I told her about my impressions of Ambrose and Spark, my time gathering herbs with only Persius as company, and, rather proudly, that I'd been able to keep up with Kip while he was hunting.

The heated conversation between Kip and Willem was still on my mind, and when she asked me what I thought of Willem's place, I found myself blurting out my thoughts before I could stop myself. "Willem thinks Kip shouldn't marry you. I overheard the two of them arguing about it."

Saray frowned but didn't seem surprised. "Ah, yes, that. It's not that Willem thinks we're a bad couple, it's that he believes Kip belongs in the Woods and that I'm keeping him from being there."

"Do you know why?"

"It has something to do with a responsibility to the Woods that Kip inherited from Kirilee. Kip tried to explain it once, but he didn't do a very good job of it; I don't think *he* fully understands it. And Willem won't talk to me about it." She shrugged. "Willem also thinks Kip is much more at home in the Shrouded Woods than he is here. Which, unfortunately, I agree with."

I nodded. I'd noticed the night before that Kip's rigidity seemed to come back following our return to Dundere. He sat more formally, the lilt I'd heard in his voice when we were in the Woods nearly disappeared, and he was far slower to smile.

"I wish there was a way to solve that issue," she went on, "but neither of us sees an easy solution. He's just going to have to keep going back and forth between the two places."

We reached the large front doors of the school as she spoke, and I paused in front of them, staring up in bewildered awe. They were made of a solid, dark wood that seemed to be common here in Dundere, but they were painted with strange golden letters unlike anything else I'd seen since arriving. "What are those?" I asked Saray.

"Magic runes. One of the many ways to keep items enchanted for long periods of time."

"These doors are enchanted?"

She nodded. "They can detect threats to the school, and if they perceive that something or someone is planning to harm the building or the students inside, they'll refuse to open."

I followed Saray with trepidation inside. The same palpable sensation of magic that I'd experienced in Willem's library washed over me when I stepped over the threshold and gazed around the foyer, wide-eyed. It was, in a way, exactly what I'd expected— a towering chamber with a sweeping gilded staircase, a massive stone hearth, and stained-glass windows letting in coloured fractals of light. I was not, however, prepared for the level of astonishing inlaid detail. The banister of the staircase was carved to look like a writhing snake, its lifelike face grinning at us with exposed fangs. One of the metal chandeliers resembled an eight-legged sea creature with lights at the ends of its tentacles, and near the entryway there was a metal receptacle that looked like a shark, its open mouth holding several umbrellas. Intricate statues graced nearly every corner— dragons and fairies and elves, several types of strange, sly looking creatures whose names I didn't know, and majestic beings that appeared to be part horse and part human. Most of these were made of wood or stone, but a few appeared to be carved from gemstones, and most of those were lit up from the inside. I got closer to study them in more detail; there didn't appear to be anywhere for a candle to fit inside.

"It's magic," Saray told me. "Same as all the lights in the school." It was only then that I realized the chandeliers and sconces were not actually lit by candles.

"What about the fire?" I asked, gesturing to the hearth. "Real, or magical?"

"Real. But some of us know how to make it extra magical." She closed her eyes for a moment, and the flames suddenly flared bright blue.

I laughed and went to the fireplace to stare into the blaze, which now eased into a shade of purple. It was there the golden letters carved above the fireplace caught my eye, and I gestured to them. "Are those more runes?"

Saray nodded. "They keep the fire from getting out of control. You'll find them all over the school." She smiled at me then. "Well, come on. Let's get you registered."

Before I knew it, I was signed up for both my summer and fall classes. In the fall, I'd be in a stormbrewing class with a few others in the guild, along with a class on making potions that I'd chosen as an elective, plus the usual slate of academic courses. Saray showed me several classrooms, the massive library that reminded me of Willem's place, the practice room lined in a material that, while resistant to magic effects, was not as powerful as the anti-magic stone that Lachlann wore, and the dorm rooms, where I'd be living once the fall semester began. The entirety of the school surrounded a massive courtyard dotted with wrought-iron benches, which were decorated with intricate scrollwork and garden boxes full of bright flowering plants. Saray told me they had magical properties when used in potions.

The benches sat in clusters around bubbling fountains shaped like dolphins, seahorses and other sea creatures, and one massive fountain in the centre of the square depicted a mermaid rising from the waves. In one corner of the courtyard, a wrought-iron staircase with a locked door at the end of it plunged into a hole in the ground. When I asked about it, Saray told me that an underground river ran directly beneath the school. There was an irrigation system under the courtyard that provided water for the gardens and the fountain, she explained, but only certain school staff were allowed access to it. There were a few staff members around today, and they all seemed pleasant enough. I noticed that they all wore heavily embroidered coats similar to what Alexander and Ember made. "When do I get one of those coats?" I asked Saray. "I heard all magikai own one?"

"You'll get one once you have your full magical license— which might be as early as the fall. You won't want one in the summer, though. It's nearly too warm for me to wear mine." She grinned. "You okay walking home on your own? I have some coursework to do."

I assured her I'd be fine, and Saray left me in the courtyard. I made my way back through the school, an unexpected lump rising in my throat as I walked. *It's hard to believe all of this is real.* A year ago I couldn't have imagined living in a place where magic was legal, but here I was, walking through a school entirely devoted to the craft, with enchanted lights, protection runes and magical fountains, and a library full of knowledge that would likely get a person imprisoned or enslaved back in Breoch. And unlike Willem's school, this place didn't need to be protected by illusions and entrusted to a guardian. It was out in the open, accessible to all. *I can't wait for Kaden to see this place.*

I wiped my eyes and grinned as I left the school grounds, excitement for my upcoming classes overcoming my heavier emotions. *This is certainly going to be an interesting year.*

The week passed quickly, and the following Monday I showed up to the school of magic five minutes early to find my first class, Magic Safety. As soon as I entered the room, I knew I was going to be the odd one out in this course. The entirety of the class, other than me, was made up of kids who couldn't be more than thirteen. They sat in clusters, some of them whispering and giggling over shared inside jokes while others talked loudly about all the things they would do once they were licensed. Several of the kids shot glances at me and whispered even more furtively. The teacher, a petite, pretty, dark-haired woman, who couldn't have been much older than Jasper, sat at her desk in the corner, preparing the day's lesson.

The large clock in the main hall chimed nine, and the teacher stood to look us over. "Good morning, class, I'm Miss Sparks. Welcome to Magic Safety, your first step to becoming a fully licensed magikai." She grinned at the first row of students, and several of the girls giggled again. "Now, let's begin by taking attendance. I think we're missing at least one student…"

The door swung open as she spoke, and a tall, slender young man with messy reddish-gold curls strode into the class. He threw a stack of books unceremoniously onto the desk next to mine, then sat down, his lanky frame barely fitting between the chair and desk.

"Alvin," Miss Sparks scolded. "Late for yet another one of my classes?"

"I'm a creature of consistency, ma'am," he replied. His voice, I noticed, was deep and rich. *Definitely closer to my age than the rest of these kids,* I surmised.

Miss Sparks huffed, then began taking attendance. Alvin raised his eyebrows when my name was called, and he looked me over. He was quite handsome, I decided, returning his gaze. His skin was porcelain with the slightest smattering of freckles over the bridge of his nose, and his eyes were green with flecks of gold dancing in the irises. Something about his appearance seemed oddly familiar, though, as did his name. *Where have I heard someone mention an Alvin recently?*

When everyone was accounted for, the lesson began, and I sat back to take notes. The things we learned were obvious to me, lessons about the ethics of magic and, of course, the cardinal rule— never use magic to harm others, unless in self-defense. Later in the morning, the lesson turned to the *Finita* spell, the quickest way to instantaneously end one's own casting— or, for a very powerful, experienced magikai, a spell cast by someone else. We were given homework to practice using this spell at home. *This is going to be an easy class,* I decided.

Alvin turned to me immediately when we were dismissed. "You're Ruby, right?"

I nodded. "Good to meet you, Alvin."

"I'm glad there's someone else my age here. It's a little odd being in a class with a bunch of twelve-year-olds, don't you think?" He grinned, and I nodded. I recalled learning that Kip was just finishing high school at twenty-one, and wondered if he felt the same.

"So why are you in the kiddie class?" he asked me. "Did you get in trouble?"

"No, I'm new here."

"Ah. One of Lachlann's deliveries from Breoch, I assume? Your accent gives you away."

I nodded. "Sort of. It's complicated. I'm guessing he brings older magikai to this class pretty often?"

Alvin shrugged. "Often enough that we locals are used to it. They don't normally show up in the summer though."

"What about you? If you're a local, why are you in this class? Did *you* get in trouble?"

He smirked. "Actually, yes. I'm a vanisher, and I just got my full license last year. I turned my little cousin invisible so we could play a prank on our parents, and then I lost track of her. Couldn't find her for an hour, poor kid. So I got in trouble and was told by my guild leader that I'd need to come back and retake the safety course."

I laughed, stood up and collected my books. "Well, I'm glad you found her. Invisibility must be handy sometimes."

"It has its benefits," he agreed. "Where are you headed now?"

"Home for lunch."

"Can I walk you? Where do you live?"

"I'll be in a dorm by the fall," I told him. "But right now I'm staying at the governor's."

"The governor's?" His eyes widened. "Well, aren't you fancy."

I laughed. "It's just temporary. Lachlann is friends with their family, and there was nowhere else for me to stay for the summer. It's really nice though. The governor and her family are lovely people."

He rolled his eyes. "If you say so."

"What, you don't like them?" I asked as we exited the school.

"Marcus is pretty cool, but I have no love for Noelle and all her rules. And the girls think they're better than everyone else."

I frowned. "That's not the impression I get from them."

"Well, you weren't in the same class as Trina for the last four years."

I raised an eyebrow. *He has a problem with Trina?* I'd experienced a bit of standoffishness from Saray at first, but Trina had never been anything but welcoming. "What'd Trina do to you?"

"It's a long story. But maybe don't tell the governor's girls that you're hanging out with me." He grinned again and tucked a lock of red-gold hair behind his right ear. "They won't like it."

I thought it might be best to change the subject then, so I asked, "You live with your parents, I assume?"

"Them, and two of my older siblings when they're home from university. The oldest one has moved out, but Ashlynn and Aiden are around for the summer."

"Ashlynn and Aiden?" My eyes narrowed. "You're their *brother?*" As I looked him over more closely this time, the resemblance became obvious. *I knew he seemed familiar. And Ashlynn was the one who mentioned his name, on the ship after Aidan attacked Jasper.*

"Unfortunately, yes." He let out a sigh. "Why? You sound like you're not their biggest fan."

"I was on the same ship as them coming over here," I explained. "They were— I don't know— snobby? Ashlynn seemed to hate me just because she doesn't like my brother."

"Who's your brother?" he asked.

"His name's Jasper. Ashlynn and Aiden don't like him for some reason. I'm not sure what—"

I was interrupted by a sharp laugh from Alvin. "*Jasper* is your brother? Oh, I've heard things about him."

"Such as?" I ground to a halt and turned to face him, arms crossed.

"Well, I was told he had girls falling all over him on the ship. What was it my brother called him— a lecherous tosspot, I think? And also something about him being Breoch Gua— hey, stop looking at me like that. I'm not saying I *believe* all the rumours, only that I've heard them."

I relaxed slightly. "He was a bit of a flirt on the ship, but it wasn't as bad as they made it sound."

Alvin shrugged. "Honestly, Aiden was probably just jealous. He's used to getting all the attention on the journey home. And if Aiden doesn't like someone, Ashlynn will follow suit."

We were nearing the top of the hill where the governor's mansion sat when Alvin stopped walking. "I'd best not come to the door with you." He smiled and gave me a slight bow. "It was lovely meeting you, Ruby. I'll see you tomorrow."

He turned to walk back down the hill, and I stared after him for a moment before heading into the house, happy to have made a new friend.

The next few weeks passed much quicker than I expected; I fell into a routine that was predictable but fun. Mornings were spent in Magic Safety, learning how to better control my casting and how to stop casting quickly when needed. Another required class, Magical Ethics, took place two afternoons a week and was more bookish and less practical. Nonetheless, I found myself enjoying it; it was fascinating to learn about the rules created by early Candeshis in order to make magic safe and accessible for all.

Alvin seemed especially bored in Magical Ethics; he slouched in his chair, tapped his pencil on his knee, and passed me notes. After classes, he was always very talkative, rambling about whatever rumours he'd heard from his older brother and sister, his desire to travel the world one day, and how he hoped to learn teleportation once he turned eighteen because invisibility and teleportation together would make him "impossible to keep up with". He seemed like a decent listener too, though, and soon enough I found myself telling him about my time on the island and my plan to rescue Kaden. He was both fascinated and disgusted by the krossemage system, and he peppered me with questions about what the farm was like and what happened to most krossemages once they'd grown up. He was disappointed when I didn't know the answers.

When I wasn't in afternoon classes, Marcus picked me up from school and took me to the lighthouse, where I learned the finer points of stormbrewing with Chase. A lot of my time there was spent assisting the other stormbrewers with bringing in just the right amount of rain and driving away hazardous storms. Sophie often hung around while I worked, asking me nearly as many questions as Alvin whenever she could get away from her father's scolding. The girl was lonely, I realized very quickly, and I asked Chase if Sophie could come back to the governor's mansion with me on occasion. He reluctantly agreed.

Evenings were spent either with the Westwoods or Jasper and Lachlann. The Westwoods were a busy family, and it wasn't uncommon for one or more of them to not be at home in the evenings, but there was generally still someone to talk to. When Saray was home, she'd often ask about what I'd learned from Chase and give me pointers on refining my technique or regale me with tales of her escape from Sylvenburgh and time in the Shrouded Woods. Trina wasn't nearly as interested in obtaining magical knowledge as Saray or Marcus, I surmised, but she easily chatted about day-to-day life and often asked me about my upbringing and my life before Yarel Island. Trina wasn't the sort of person who needed to talk all the time though; there were many evenings spent reading in her room while she communicated with the animals or read books of her own. She seemed to be Sophie's favourite of the Westwoods; whenever Sophie was with me, she'd ask Trina to call in the birds and squirrels and would spend the evening on Trina's porch petting them.

Marcus and Noelle were often busy in the evenings as well, but when Marcus was free, he occasionally helped me with the process of relearning speech and hand movement. My speech was slowly becoming less slurred, and my new right hand, while certainly not as dexterous as my left, was nearly as strong as it used to be. I spent time playing the piano, as he'd suggested, which seemed to help. Other nights, I would watch Marcus putter around his hobby room, asking questions about his many interests and studies. He and a few of the professors at the magic school were researching the initial origins of magic, I learned, and he enjoyed telling me about his current working theory. Magic was stronger in the Verdant Isles than most places, he explained, and he surmised that since the Isles were formed by a series of volcanic eruptions thousands of years back, perhaps the source of magic lay in the volcanoes themselves, or even the magma inside them. One evening, I jokingly suggested that he take Jasper to the mouth of the island's one known volcano to see if it turned him magical. The following day, he found me in the living room and gleefully informed me that Jasper had agreed to do just that.

I was sitting with Noelle when Marcus showed up. Conversations with her were rare, given her busy schedule, and I treasured the moments we had together. Noelle was powerful, dignified, and yet somehow also gentle. She was beautiful too; she moved with what seemed like a superhuman grace. Every now and then when we talked, I found myself blushing and stumbling over words, as if I had a crush on her— which, of course, was rather silly. Noelle had picked up on my interest in politics and didn't mind explaining the nuances of the Dundere system to me. One day, she told me, she'd take me to work with her to meet Deshi, the deputy governor.

Tonight, Noelle was in the middle of explaining to me how her council helped her make decisions when Marcus interrupted. Noelle and I listened as he told us of his plans with Jasper, and Noelle laughed when he then left for his hobby room. "He keeps me young."

"I can see that."

"I don't think folks have any idea just how much Marcus influences my leadership," she told me. "I wouldn't be half the governor I am without him."

"But weren't you governor for several years before he came along?"

"I was, but I don't think I did nearly as good a job of it. Marcus is the one who encourages me to stand up to the Candeshis when they get too demanding, to try new things, to be open to change. I can be a little too cautious, sometimes. I need someone like him." She smiled. "Do you know how we met?"

I shook my head, and I soon found myself laughing out loud as Noelle told me the story of how Marcus had shown up in her office seeking healing, and, only minutes after he was able to speak again, offered to take her out for dinner the next evening. "I still can't believe that a man who'd been beaten down like he was for twenty years would have the spunk to ask the governor of Dundere on a date."

"I suppose he thought he had nothing to lose."

She nodded. "He's quite the fellow, my Marcus."

Our conversation turned to other things after that, and I resolved to go visit Jasper the next day and find out how his hike had gone.

CHAPTER 14

THE FOLLOWING DAY between classes, Alvin and I sat in the courtyard together. The weather had turned hot and dry recently, and the grass was beginning to brown outside. The plants in the courtyard, though, were still green and flourishing.

"I wonder how the irrigation system for these works," I mused. "Saray mentioned their water comes from an underground river?"

Alvin's eyes twinkled. "Would you like to see it?"

"The river? Isn't the only way in through that little door?" I gestured to the stairs on the edge of the courtyard.

He nodded and gave a quick glance around. "I know how to pick a lock," he whispered.

"What if someone catches you?"

"They won't. Watch." He put a hand on my shoulder. *"Dominae Araknae Invida."*

Alvin's form disappeared in front of me, though I could still feel his hand on my shoulder. *Right.* I had forgotten that Alvin was a vanisher. His hand moved down to my forearm, which I now saw was also invisible, and he grasped my wrist. "Come on!"

We made our way across the courtyard and down the stairs. I couldn't see what Alvin was doing, of course, but after a minute or so, I heard a definite click, and the door swung open. He grabbed my wrist again, and I followed him in.

It was dark in the void beyond, and I heard Alvin mumble the words for another spell. A small ball of light materialized in the air before us, illuminating the cavern. We were standing on a narrow ledge overlooking a massive, churning river. The walls of the cave glittered with embedded minerals, thanks to Alvin's light. "This is beautiful." I looked down at the raging water beneath us then and added, "Dangerous, though. I can see why they don't want students coming down here."

Alvin laughed and mumbled the words to dissipate the invisibility spell.

"How did you make light?" I asked him as he reappeared beside me. "I thought we weren't allowed to learn new spells until we're eighteen."

"In case you hadn't noticed, I don't care much for rules. I found the spell in a textbook and figured out how to use it myself. Light spells are one of the easiest to learn." He sat himself on the ledge and patted the space next to him. I crouched down gingerly, trying not to ruin my clothes.

"Have you come down here many times before?" I asked.

"Usually not during school hours, but yes. I like to come down when I need to think. I tried to hike to the mouth of the river once, but the ledge gets far too narrow in some places. I nearly fell in." He grinned at me. "This is the first time

I've brought someone else here."

"What happens if someone catches us?"

"Then we go invisible again."

"Why didn't you just keep us invisible?"

He looked over at me and grinned. "Because I like looking at you."

"Oh." I felt heat creep into my cheeks. "I…uh, well, I like looking at you too."

"Glad to hear it." He raised an eyebrow. "Would you like to have dinner sometime, Ruby?"

My heart began to race. I found Alvin to be handsome and charming, but I'd been so preoccupied with getting Kaden back that I'd given little thought to romance since I arrived here. "Are you asking me out? We've known each other for less than a month."

"What better way to get to know one another more?" he countered.

"Aren't you worried about how your siblings will react to you taking the sister of the lecherous tosspot out on a date?"

"I don't care what my family thinks of me." He put a hand on mine and tucked a stray lock of hair behind his ear with his other hand. "Come on. Just one date?"

"I…suppose so," I said, my shoulders relaxing as I looked into his face. *Why not?*

"Wonderful. This Friday, perhaps?"

"Sure." I glanced towards the door then, not wanting to tempt our luck much longer. "We should probably get out of here; class is starting soon."

That evening, I headed over to Lachlann's place to find Jasper sitting at the dining room table, looking rather tired. "I hear Marcus took you to the edge of a volcano," I said, joining him.

He nodded. "It was quite the hike."

"And how did the experiment go? Are you magical now?"

"Nope." Jasper crossed his arms. "As I figured."

"You didn't think it would work?"

"Of course not; it's the only reason I agreed to the experiment. You think I *want* to be magical?"

"Well, I'm sure I'll get to hear all about Marcus's disappointment when I get home."

He shrugged. "It was a beautiful view, though. And it was good to get out of here and go somewhere new. I'll take you up there sometime."

"Getting bored already?"

"A little, I suppose."

"I don't blame you," Lachlann put in as he emerged from the kitchen with our dinner. "I'm a pretty boring person to live with. Though you'll be less restless once you're fully trained with the guards."

"I doubt that," Jasper said, ladling a hefty portion of soup into a bowl. "I'll probably just end up walking around town, waiting for the rare disturbance so I can intervene. Dundere isn't exactly a hotbed of crime. You know, that was the thing I liked about working for the Breoch Guard. Breoch isn't short on magic users, so there was always a new lead to follow, a new person to capture. It was…*exciting*." He glanced at me as he took a bite of his food. "I know, it sounds awful."

"If you want some excitement, we can always go outside so I can demonstrate my superior swordsmanship skills again," Lachlann offered.

Jasper snorted. "Sword fighting gets boring too after a while."

"We could switch to live steel and see how bored you are then."

"I said I want excitement, not death." Jasper rolled his eyes.

"Could you teach me to fight?" I asked.

"You?" Lachlann's eyebrows arched. "You want to learn the sword?"

"I already know a bit," I told him. "Mother didn't think it was proper for a young lady, but Jasper taught me a few things in secret when we were younger. I've forgotten most of it though."

Lachlann looked at Jasper, surprised. "You taught her, huh?"

I detected a proud note in Jasper's voice when he replied, "I did."

"Perhaps you and I can teach Ruby together then. That might be something novel for you."

"I suppose we could."

"I feel like this is my fault." I sighed. "That you're cooped up here in Dundere, and you're bored. If I hadn't gotten caught…"

He shook his head. "If you hadn't gotten caught, I might well still be at home, strung out on teakflower and thinking about ending my life. I may be bored, but at least I'm not miserable." His shoulders hunched. "And Dundere might be more fun for me if it wasn't for those bloody twins. They've been spreading rumours, and now none of the younger adults want much to do with me."

"Which twins are these?" Lachlann asked.

"Aidan and Ashlynn Blackwell. They were on the ship. You've probably never heard of them."

"I have, actually. Aidan is a known troublemaker when he's back for the summer. I suppose I'm about to have my hands full."

"What sorts of things does he get in trouble for?" I asked.

"You didn't hear this from me, but he's got quite a temper, and it's worse when he's drunk. He's assaulted several people while I've been a guard here."

Jasper nodded. "He gave me a bloody nose on the ship. Shoved me up against a wall and punched me."

"Over what?" Lachlann asked.

"Something silly." Jasper sighed. "I would have enjoyed my time on the Lady Liara much more if it weren't for Aidan."

"Maybe you should head back to Gareth's ship, then," I suggested. "Aidan's not around to ruin your fun, and it might be a little more exciting than staying in Dundere."

"That it is," Lachlann added. "I spent five years on that ship, and it never stopped feeling like an adventure to me. Being at sea is a lot of work, but it's definitely not boring." He stood then. "Let's get dinner cleaned up and head outside."

We spent the remainder of the evening on the roof, armed with wooden practice swords. Most of my training was spent going over footwork patterns and basic stances that I'd nearly forgotten. Later, Lachlann offered to spar with Jasper, and I sat back and watched the two of them fight. Lachlann was more skilled than my brother, but Jasper had youth on his side. By the end of it, both men were gasping and moaning about how much pain they'd be in the next morning, but grinning despite it.

That was fun, I decided as I got into bed later that evening. I'd come here assuming I'd only learn magic, so the lessons in things like politics and swordsmanship were unexpected. But I was all too happy to be learning them, and I had a good feeling about my future in Dundere.

The following afternoon, I arrived home to find Willem sitting on one of the parlour couches, deep in conversation with Marcus. Accompanying him was a petite woman with white-blond hair pulled into a braid, wearing a colourful dress that reminded me of the creations that Alexander and Ember were known for.

"There she is!" Willem exclaimed when he saw me, climbing to his feet. "Ruby, I'd like to introduce you to Hilda."

Hilda stood as well, and my eyes widened as I looked down at her. Adult women shorter than me were rare, and I had at least three or four inches on her. She extended a delicate hand and smiled up at me. "Pleasure to meet you, Ruby. I've heard good things about you."

"Same to you," I replied. "You're going to help us get to Yarel Island so we can get Kaden out?"

"That's what we're hoping. Do you want me to explain the ritual to you?"

I nodded, and she sank back down onto the couch. I seated myself in a nearby chair and waited expectantly.

"Fairy magic allows me to perform a ritual I call seeing," Hilda began. "You can use it to look into a person's past, which is what we're going to do today. You can also look into their present to try to locate them, and it's even possible to look into their future. The ethics of this are a bit questionable, though, because the future is never set in stone, and a magikai could use the knowledge to harm someone.

"Now, I'm going to warn you, sometimes when I perform this ritual, I come across things that aren't what I'm looking for. I might see bits of your past that I didn't intend to. And I'm pretty good at avoiding it, but I might also see your future." She eyed me. "Are you all right with me doing this and knowing all of that?"

I nodded slowly. "I don't have much to hide about my life. So yes, that's fine. If you see my future though, don't tell me about it."

"I make it a general rule not to reveal any futures I see," Hilda assured. "Let's go out back to Kirilee's tree. That's the place where the fairy magic is strongest, so it's a good spot."

"Where's Carmine today?" Marcus asked as we headed into the garden.

"We had a storm last night, so she had a lot to repair in the garden." Hilda glanced at me then and explained, "My wife talks to plants, like Trina does to animals."

I nodded. "Sounds like you folks need a stormbrewer around."

"It's unfortunate that Firenholme doesn't have many of those; most of them leave Breoch and find work elsewhere." Hilda seated herself under the tree and set out a large stone bowl, a candle, and a dagger in the grass in front of her. She then lit the candle. "Fetch me a jug of water, will you, Ruby?"

I hurried inside, and when I returned with the water, I saw that she and Willem were holding hands, and she was mumbling a spell.

"What was that spell you just cast?" I asked.

"It will let Willem see what I'm seeing," she explained, reaching for the dagger. Upon closer inspection, I saw that it was made of amethyst, and had elaborate silver scrollwork encasing the hilt. "Now, Ruby, I will need a small lock of your hair."

I frowned but allowed her to take it. She held it up to the candle, and I wrinkled my nose as the hair burned, its ash falling into the bowl. Then she filled the bowl up with water. "Are you ready?"

I nodded.

"Sit down then, and we'll begin."

I took a seat facing her and Willem and noticed the fairies were beginning to congregate around us. Hilda closed her eyes and mumbled a spell I didn't recognize, and I saw a plume of purple smoke rise from the bowl. The fairies, meanwhile, began to spin in a circle above it. I could hear them singing in a language I didn't know.

"All right, Ruby, I want you to close your eyes, put your hands on the outside of the bowl, and imagine you are on the island, standing on the shore."

I did so, calling back into detail the beach strewn with coarse sand and rogue driftwood. "Good," Hilda said. "I can see. Can you, Willem?"

"I can," he said. "Ruby, could you look out towards mainland Breoch, to help me determine where we are? Good. Now, I assume that we will be getting your friend at night, correct?"

"Yes."

"I want you to imagine yourself walking from where you are to wherever it is that she sleeps, so I can see the path. Look around you as you go, so there's as much detail as possible."

I did as Willem asked, moving slowly in my mind's eye towards the farmhouse, taking in my surroundings. When I reached the heavy wooden door of the farmhouse, I pulled it open, then walked through the main room and up the stairs to the girls' dorm. "Kaden sleeps here," I told them, locating the cot.

"Excellent," Willem said. "I think you've given me a lot to work with."

"Do I need to go anywhere else?"

"No. You can open your eyes now. The next step will be me visiting the place while invisible and scouting the area out so that I can develop a more complex plan. I should be able to do that this weekend."

I opened my eyes and nodded. "Did you see…anything else while you were looking in there?" I asked Hilda.

"I saw bits of your childhood." She let out a small sigh. "I'm sorry you had to endure the things you did."

"Did you see my future at all?"

"No, but if I did, I wouldn't tell you." She smiled at me, then stood up and began collecting her things. "Well, I think Willem and I will take up Noelle on her offer for tea now; Lachlann should be here soon, and I'm meant to meet with him as well. Do you wish to join us?"

"That sounds lovely," I said and followed them back into the house.

Lachlann showed up about an hour later, wearing his work uniform and carrying a leather case. He greeted Hilda with an embrace, and she smiled up at him. "Ready to get the old arm functioning again?"

He nodded. "Do you really think it'll work?"

"Alexander seemed to think it would. There's only one way to find out. Let's go back out into the garden."

I followed Hilda and Lachlann outside once more, my curiosity piqued. My eyes widened when Lachlann opened the leather case and pulled out a hand and part of a forearm forged of metal.

Lachlann caught my gaze and grinned. "I suppose you've never seen this before. Do you want to take a look?"

I nodded, and he gave it to me to examine. I ran my fingertips over the perfectly formed fingers, then closed the hand into a fist. "I can see how you broke my father's nose with this."

He chuckled. "It can be a pretty vicious weapon when it's wielded correctly."

Hilda took the limb from me then and placed it gently on the grass, and sprinkled a fine purple powder in a circle around it. "I need a drop of your blood," she said to Lachlann.

"Why's blood so important?" he asked. "Willem took blood from me when we were forging it, too."

"Willem put your blood into the alloy to help the arm recognize you as its owner," Hilda replied. "Anti-magic changes your blood ever so slightly, so this will reorient the arm to you."

Lachlann nodded and pricked the end of his thumb with the tip of a knife.

"Now put your thumb on the ashlarite disc inside the socket," Hilda instructed. Lachlann obeyed, and she placed the arm back in the circle. Then she began to sing a long, complex spell.

It sounded nothing like Noelle's casting, which was gentle and melancholy. This song was bright and chirping, with several high-pitched lilting sections. The purple dust began to rise and swirl, obscuring my view of the arm, and the fairies surged in a strange, frenetic dance.

When Hilda stopped singing, the dust dissipated to reveal that the arm was now glowing. The fairies alighted on it as Hilda picked it up and inspected it.

"Well," she said as the glow began to fade, "it looks to have worked." She handed it to Lachlann with a smirk on her face. "Seems like the fairies felt the need to change its appearance a little!"

The arm was no longer a dull silver; now the surface bore a kaleidoscope of muted reds, purples, and blues, with bright gold veins running through it that followed a pattern similar to the blood vessels visible on a human arm. Lachlann asked, "Did Alexander have a hand in this?"

"Well, he supplied some of his own fairies for the job, so there's a good chance he gave them instructions."

"Wouldn't surprise me at all. He has it in his head that I'm too plain in my fashion sense."

"Try it on," I prompted.

Lachlann carefully removed his hook and put the stump of his left arm into the socket of the metal one. He tightened the straps and moved his elbow a few times. "I'm still used to the weight," he mumbled, "which is good." Then I watched as the fingers began to slowly flex and bend.

Lachlann stared down at the hand, seeming fascinated. Then he winced for a moment, and Hilda nodded. "It might cause you pain for the first day or so. Your body is accustomed to anti-magic, so fairy magic will likely feel invasive and uncomfortable."

"Ah." He nodded. Then he looked down at his hand again and grinned. "Well, now, it's good to have you back."

"We have the perfect way for you to test it out," Marcus said, standing on the veranda behind us. "Dinner will be ready soon, and you're all invited."

The following Friday, I told Marcus and Noelle I'd be out with friends for the evening. I met Alvin at the school, wearing a dress that Noelle had recently bought me. It was of the Dundere fashion, dusky blue with a gauzy, flowing skirt and a fitted bodice covered in intricate embroidery and beadwork. It had no sleeves, which would have been scandalous back home but seemed normal here. I brought along a shawl to cover my arms in case I got cold, but the feel of the cool air was still a novelty. Instead, I toyed with the shawl's fringe, trying to ignore the butterflies in my stomach. It had been well over a year since I'd been on anything resembling a date.

When Alvin showed up, I realized that I had overdressed for the occasion. He was wearing a pressed shirt with a simple jade-green waistcoat and dark brown breeches, and he carried a large leather bag. He smiled at me. "You look gorgeous."

"Thank you." I felt heat rise in my cheeks. "So do you." He did look quite handsome, despite the plainness of his clothes. The green of his vest brought out his eyes, and he'd attempted to smooth down his cowlick.

His gaze travelled to my feet, and his smile widened. "I'm glad you wore solid boots. As lovely as you look, I probably should have told you to keep it casual. We're going to be doing some climbing."

"Climbing?" My eyes narrowed.

"You'll see. Come on." He grabbed my wrist and mumbled the words for the invisibility spell, then led me through the doors of the school.

Inside was mostly deserted, save for the cleaner, who was currently mopping the stairs. Or, rather, the cleaner was standing at the bottom of the staircase, whistling a tune as she controlled the mop using telekinesis. *Brilliant,* I thought, watching the mop move smoothly across one step and hop down to the next. *I wonder if this is how Kip cleans his place.*

We snuck past her and down one of the long hallways, heading toward the school's rear stairwell. Alvin laced his fingers casually into mine as we walked. His hands were much bigger than my own, I noticed. My last relationship had been with a girl, whose hands were cute and chubby and smaller than mine; I couldn't help but notice the subtle differences between dating a boy and a girl.

When we arrived at the stairwell, we began climbing the three flights to the top floor. Alvin led me through a maze of corridors until we reached a locked door, where he let go of my hand. I heard him pull something out of his pocket, then he fiddled with the lock, and the door swung open. "Come on," he whispered.

I ventured into the darkness beyond, a bit uncertain as to Alvin's location. Then the door closed behind us. *"Invida finita,"* he mumbled, and a moment later, he stood in front of me, grinning and barely visible. When he spoke the light spell, the room became illuminated— a small, circular space lined with bookshelves and boxes, with a spiral staircase in the middle. He started up the staircase, and I followed. We were inside one of the school's turrets, I realized.

We reached a hatch in the ceiling, and he pushed it open and climbed through. I followed and found myself standing on the roof, overlooking the city and the harbour beyond. The sun was beginning to slide toward the horizon, and the clouds had taken on a red-gold hue. "This is beautiful."

"Isn't it? I figured you'd like it up here. I packed us a picnic."

He began unloading items from the bag he carried. I gaped at the selection of food he'd brought: a loaf of crusty bread, a wheel of cheese, some sort of pastry, and several different kinds of fruit— strawberries, grapes, apples, and berries that looked unfamiliar to me— as well as a bottle of something that was being kept cold by a cooling spell. "You put a lot of thought into this."

"As a fellow should on a first date. Come on, let's eat."

Alvin spread a multicoloured blanket at our feet, uncorked the bottle to pour us drinks, and we began eating. "What are those berries?" I asked.

"Shazer berries. Most folk in Breoch don't eat them, though I hear they're plentiful in the Shrouded Woods. They're delicious."

I tasted one; the berries were incredibly sweet but also had an odd, zesty tang to them. "Mmm."

Alvin grinned and lifted his glass. "To interesting first dates."

I toasted him and took a drink of the sweet, frothy liquid. I wasn't certain if it contained alcohol. "Do you do this on all your first dates?" I asked him. "Invisibility spells and forbidden picnics?"

"I haven't been on many of those, honestly."

"Really? I'm surprised. You seem like quite the charmer."

His eyes widened for a moment, then he relaxed and smiled. "I can be a little charming, yes. But a lot of the girls I was interested in when I was younger just brushed me off."

"Well, their loss. You have a date now."

"That's very true, thanks to you." His smile widened. "I've been wanting to take a girl on a forbidden picnic for a long time." He popped a grape into his mouth.

A silence descended as we ate, and I frowned, searching for a way to fill it. "So, tell me about yourself," I finally said. "You've asked me lots of questions about my life, but I don't know much about yours."

He cocked his head. "What do you want to know?"

"Everything. What was your childhood like? How did you find out about your gift? What else do you like to do for fun?"

He laughed. "I feel like I've had a pretty boring life. Grew up here on this tiny island. All of my older siblings have these strange, unique talents— I'm the only one who's halfway normal."

"What sort of talents?"

"You mean you didn't see what Aiden and Ashlynn could do while you were on the ship?"

"I know Ashlynn can mental-cast illusion, like Saray can with fire. And Aiden, he's…a firebrand?"

"A firebrand and a teleporter," Alvin said. "He was born with two gifts. My eldest brother Arquin is also a teleporter, but he's been able to use his gift since he was five years old and can cross half the world in one jump." He chuckled. "I remember the first time he teleported without meaning to. He was lost for a good three hours. My poor mother."

"Why do your siblings have these special abilities?"

He shrugged. "We're not sure, though my father and Marcus have a theory. My father's father came here from Ciarlann when magic was made punishable by death. So my father is half Cairlanni and half Dunderi. My mother came here from Breoch as a teen. The idea is that the magic in each location is a bit different, so if a person has several different types in their bloodline, that's when they might become a super-mage, as Father calls it. Marcus thinks the same might be true of Saray."

"But he's not sure?"

"Marcus is half Dunderi and half Breochi, but he doesn't know Saray's birth mother's heritage."

"And you've just got one gift."

He nodded. "I'm the boring one in the family. So I have to make up for it by doing crazy things like having picnics on rooftops."

I laughed and took a sip of my drink. The sun had set while we were talking, and some of the clouds that hung low in the sky were becoming luminescent with a warm light. "It must be a full moon tonight," Alvin commented. "Wish we could see it."

I realized this was my chance to show off some of my own talents. I spoke my casting words softly and reached out to the clouds obscuring our view. They slid aside, revealing a large, full moon, its surface tinged pale yellow. I grinned and turned to Alvin. "Is that better?"

He gaped, the moonlight dancing in his green eyes. "You did that?"

"Of course. I'm a stormbrewer." I stared out at the moon and adjusted one cloud ever so slightly so that its wispy edge was bathed in silver. "It's a gorgeous moon, too. Did you know that in the Shrouded Woods, they have a big dance every full moon to…celebrate the fairies, or something like that?"

"Fairies." He chuckled. "Aidan would love that, he's fascinated by fairy magic. Have you been to one of these dances?"

"No. I heard about them when I was in the Woods with Kip though. Maybe sometime I'll sneak back through the portal and go to one."

"Can you bring me with you?"

I laughed. "Sure."

"You know," he said, getting to his feet, "we could always just have ourselves a little Moon Dance right here."

"I…suppose we could."

"Come on." He offered me a hand. "Let's get our picnic cleaned up. I can provide the music." He reached into his pack and pulled out a long wooden box. When he opened it, it began to play a melody.

"You brought a music box to our picnic?"

"Not just any music box. A magical one. This has about ten songs on it, and once it's wound, it can play indefinitely." He grinned. "I think Marcus makes these in his spare time— he may have made this one himself."

I laughed. "You planned for us to dance while we were up here?"

"It was an option. I always come prepared."

We put away the remains of the picnic, then Alvin wound his music box and left the lid propped open. A slow melody began to emanate from it, more complex than anything I'd heard from any normal music box. Alvin offered me a hand. "Shall we?"

I accepted and let him pull me into position. My heartbeat picked up as his hand slid around my waist. I'd danced this way with both men and women on Gareth's ship, but now it felt more intimate, more vulnerable. Alvin kept his eyes on mine as we began to sway together. I was incredibly aware of his touch, the pressure of his fingertips on my waist, the mere inches between our faces.

When the song was finished, he leaned down. "I've wanted to do this for ages," he whispered. "Rooftop dancing."

I grinned in response.

When he pulled me in so that my head was resting on his chest, I didn't fight. I could hear his heart beating in my ear as we swayed together, his arms wrapped around my frame and his chin resting lightly on my head.

When the second song was finished, he pulled back and gazed down at me. "Did you know that when two magikai kiss, they can sense one another's magic?"

I felt my heart jump at his words. "No, I didn't know that."

"Well, I suppose you've never kissed another magikai, then. Would you like to change that?"

I hesitated for just a second. "I've…never kissed someone on the first date."

"Me neither." He pushed his hair behind his ear. "Then again, I've never been on a first date quite this good."

I felt my doubts slip away as I stared up at him. "All right, Alvin. Kiss me."

"My pleasure." He reached down and put his fingertips below my chin, tilting my face toward his.

Alvin was a good kisser, I realized right away. His lips on mine were slow and gentle, not forceful like some new kissers'. And he had no trouble taking the lead. One of his hands slipped into my hair, and the other pressed at the small of my back, pulling me closer. The tip of his tongue met mine, and I shivered. I was becoming aware of his magic. It was light and buoyant, like I'd expected, but I swore I heard a new sound in addition to the music box— a seductive, rich harmony played by an instrument I couldn't identify that left me completely relaxed in his arms, as if this was the most natural thing in the world. He began to move us slowly to the rhythm of the song, his lips not leaving my own.

I'm not sure how long we stayed like that, locked in an embrace with only the music and the full moon as company. When he finally pulled away, I found myself gasping for breath. Night had fallen completely; the moon was higher in the sky and more silvery in colour now. "I…suppose I should get you home," Alvin said. "Don't want the governor worrying about you. We'll do this again, though?"

I gave him a dreamy smile and nodded, and he led me through the hatch and down the spiral staircase, towards home.

CHAPTER 15

A FEW EVENINGS later, Willem showed up at the governor's place we were finishing dinner, a look of concern on his face.

"Is everything all right?" Noelle asked him.

"Not exactly," he replied. "I'm going to need to speak with you and Marcus in private about what I saw on Yarel Island."

Noelle nodded. "We can talk in my office."

"Lachlann is ex-military, correct?" Willem asked.

Kip, who'd returned from the Shrouded Woods only an hour before, nodded. "That's right."

"Well, in that case, I might fetch him too. He likely has a good head on his shoulders for strategy."

"Go get him, we can wait," Noelle agreed.

Willem disappeared from sight, and I exchanged a nervous glance with Trina, feeling my stomach begin to knot up. *What exactly happened on the island that has Willem so concerned?*

Only a few minutes later, he reappeared. "Lachlann and Jasper are on their way. They'll be here shortly."

"Jasper?" Kip echoed. "Why's he coming?" I didn't miss the distaste in his voice.

"Because this is something that you all need to hear. I'll discuss it in private with the older adults first, but I'll fill the rest of you in once we've talked about it."

Kip looked at Saray and then cleared his throat. "I think we're going to head up to Saray's room, then. One of you can fetch us when you folks are ready to talk to everyone."

Willem nodded, and I frowned as they left the room. "They're really uncomfortable around my brother, aren't they?"

I noticed Marcus and Noelle exchanging a glance I didn't quite understand. Trina shrugged. "I mean, do you blame them?"

"Not entirely, but it's strange that they can barely handle being in the same room as him," I replied. "It doesn't seem to bother you that much."

"I know. I'm actually a bit surprised by how little Jasper affects me. But I wasn't there for the worst of what he did. They were. Saray especially."

I nodded. "I suppose so. It still seems a bit excessive though."

Lachlann and Jasper showed up soon after, concern etched on both of their faces. Noelle escorted the older adults to her study right away, leaving me, Trina, and Jasper alone. "Where are Saray and Kip?" Jasper asked.

"They went upstairs," Trina replied.

"Ah. Still avoiding me, huh?"

"Oh, probably." She laughed nervously, then changed the subject. "Tell me, Jasper, how is your guard training going? Are you learning anti-magic?"

Jasper relaxed a bit. Trina's tactic was obvious enough, but he seemed willing to take the bait. "Actually, I don't think anti-magic is for me," he told her. "I tried wearing a pendant, and it was just…uncomfortable. I don't know how Lachlann handles it."

Trina smirked. "Please don't tell me you're secretly a magic user."

"I certainly hope not. If I am, I have no idea what kind. Don't these things normally show up when you're a teenager?"

"Yes, but there are exceptions. I've been able to talk to animals since I was a kid. And your sister is a magikai, which tends to run in families, so it's not impossible. I'll ask Willem about it."

"Please don't. Just…leave it, all right?" Then he frowned, seeming to consider something. "Wait, do you think one of our *parents* is a magic user?"

"I've wondered the same thing," I confessed. "There must be magic in our bloodline somewhere." I shrugged. "Maybe you're reacting to the pendant because Marcus's little experiment actually worked."

Jasper's eyes narrowed. "Doubtful. If I was magical, you'd think I would have some idea what my talent is. All I know is that wearing a pendant makes me feel…sick, almost. Anyway, I'm not learning anti-magic, but I have been training as a guard. I've done a few patrols of the city, and it's been interesting. Lachlann seems to think I'm decent at it."

I heard voices in the hall then, and Willem, Marcus and Noelle returned to the parlour. "We're ready to talk to you now," Noelle said. "Let's head outside."

We gathered in the governor's backyard, under Kirilee's tree. It was the first time, I realized, that we'd all been in one place since Jasper and I arrived. Kip and Saray had joined us and were huddled together on the opposite side of the circle, close to Lachlann and away from Jasper.

Grimly, Willem looked us each of us over. "The situation on Yarel Island is far worse than any of us realized." His eyes fell on me. "First of all, how many krossemages do you assume live there?"

"A few hundred, maybe?"

"There are about five hundred on the adult side, and fifty or so teens," he said. "The teens are purposely sheltered from what adult life is like. There's krossemages packed into dorms, working from dawn till dusk. The jobs you kids have are the easy ones. On the adult side, the work is far harder."

My eyes narrowed. "Strange. They made it sound like the island is a better option than being sold to an owner. They told us that if we behaved, we wouldn't have to worry about being sold off."

"They're likely doing that to get you to cooperate," Lachlann put in. "And chances are, you wouldn't have been sold to an owner regardless."

"What do you mean?"

"Tomlin and I have talked about this a fair bit. The idea of krossemages being sold as slaves to families is nearly a myth nowadays. Back when the Banishing happened, it was popular, but in the last twenty years or so, the idea of owning another human has come to be seen as unethical. People are afraid of magikai and want them off the streets, but they don't want to own them, either."

"So what happens to them?" asked Kip.

"Most are sold to companies to do undesirable work," Lachlann explained. "Factories, mass farms, cleaning, that sort of thing. They're kept mostly out of sight of the public, except for a few who are strategically placed to remind people of what will happen if they fall out of line. Sylvenburgh Academy used to have one of those."

Saray nodded. "Walter, the janitor," she said.

"Do you have any idea what happened to him?" asked Trina.

Lachlann nodded. "Tomlin kept in touch with him. He's living with his aging parents and seems happy enough now that he's back with his family. Tom has tried to convince him to come here for healing, but he refuses." He glanced at Willem then. "But we're getting off topic. Please, continue."

Willem nodded. "I got to the island this morning, while it was still dark, but I was within earshot when the night guards got off their shift and the morning guards began theirs. I overheard several talking about a very important meeting this afternoon. So I decided to stick around, to see what was happening.

"I learned that there has been some trouble since Ruby left. Your little rescue mission sparked something in the krossemages. I suspect that no one had managed to escape the island for several years, and so your disappearance gave them hope that it could be done. There have been at least two dozen attempts since then. But another issue came up as well— and this one is causing the real problem." He looked to Marcus. "I'll let you explain this part."

Marcus nodded. "There's a small fault within the krossemage system. First of all, not every krossemage is right handed, and if they amputate a magikai's non-dominant hand, they'll still be able to cast. You know this all too well, Ruby. However, if a right-handed person has been a krossemage for several years, they will in time become very proficient with their left. You all know that this happened to me.

"Like most krossemages, I had no idea that I could cast with my left hand. I never tried until I arrived in Dundere. But I learned later that it's not uncommon once a person has adapted to using their remaining hand."

Willem nodded. "A few of the adult krossemages on Yarel Island figured all of this out. The guards didn't catch them in time, and word began to spread among the others."

"Are all of them able to cast like this?" Saray asked.

"I don't think so. It takes time to learn. But several have been caught. A few of them used their magic to attempt an escape, and if too many of them learn how to cast this way, then it's only a matter of time before the entire colony becomes unmanageable. Several hundred magikai against a handful of guards? They could easily overthrow them. And the Breoch Guard sees only one possible solution." Willem closed his eyes. "A cull of the entire island."

Mine was not the only gasp. "No," I whispered. "We have to help them."

"Absolutely," Kip chimed in.

Willem nodded. "We're all in agreement here. We can't stand by and let this happen."

"Any idea how long until they act?" asked Jasper.

"In the fall, after this year's food has been harvested. So we have time to prepare. We've come up with a rudimentary plan, but it still needs some refining."

Willem invited Noelle to explain the plan in detail.

"If we do it right, it'll be bloodless," she concluded. "Which is what we want. If we hurt any of the guards, Breoch might take it as an act of war from Dundere. If they manage to connect it to us, that is."

"Can't we get the krossemages to fight, since some of them can cast?" Kip suggested.

"If someone went there undercover for several months to train them, maybe," Willem said. "But that would be incredibly risky. It's safer for us to gather a force to rescue them and not count on the krossemages for their magic. If they're able to help us, then we'll consider that an unexpected advantage."

"What happens after we get them off the island?" asked Trina.

"We're still figuring that part out," Noelle said. "We'd likely have to bring them back here, at least for now. And I'm going to spend a lot of time healing folks."

Willem considered this. "I could create a spell to allow you to share the magical energy of several other magikai, like I did with Kirilee's life transfer. But even so, I'm sure healing them all would take several days. And I don't know where we'd do all this."

"We might be able to house them temporarily at the school. But I doubt our little island would be able to sustain them for any length of time."

"Why do you have to wait 'til they're back here to begin healing them?" Jasper asked.

"Because I won't be coming with those of you who make the trip to the island."

"Why's that?"

"If I was spotted and it was reported that the governor of Dundere was involved in an attack on a Breochi colony, it would almost certainly be interpreted as a political move by Dundere— and thus, Candesh— against Breoch, if not an outright act of war," Noelle explained. "I can't take that risk. So I'll stay here and heal. Lachlann can't make the trip either because it'll involve a portal, so I'll have him coordinate bringing the refugees in once they show up, and Willem and Marcus can oversee the rescue mission."

"Won't the folks up at the Candeshi garrison have an issue with you bringing several hundred Breochi refugees here?" asked Jasper.

Marcus chuckled. "The Candeshi guards care very little about what happens in Dundere. They're just happy to be posted to a place that isn't a war zone. And you underestimate the sway Noelle has over them. She is their healer, after all."

"Will we be going on the rescue mission?" Kip asked.

"Most of you likely will," Lachlann answered. "The folks with the magical talents we need for the rescue are the most essential, but I'd also like to have a good number of magikai present who know how to fight, just in case things go bad. You'd probably be my top pick to go over, Kip, given that you know how to fight both with and without magic."

"What about me?" asked Saray. "I'd like to go, if I can."

"That would be risky," Noelle said to her. "It'd be very beneficial to have you on the island, just in case we need a powerful magikai to fight off the guards. But if they figure out who you are and then connect that to Dundere, they'll probably come here looking for you again. However, you're an adult now, so I'll let you make the call."

"Right." Saray sighed. "I can't keep hiding forever, you know? I'd like to go, but I should try to disguise myself a bit. Cover up my hair and only cast with hand motions. They might not recognize me if I don't cast with my mind."

"And we'd only want you to use your magic if it were absolutely necessary," Willem added. "As Noelle said, we want this to be as bloodless as possible."

"If you folks need some non-magical fighters present, I'll come along," volunteered Jasper.

Lachlann and Noelle exchanged a glance. "You should probably stay here, Jasper," Noelle said.

"Why? I know the island better than most of you. I snuck onto it, remember?"

"That's true," Lachlann agreed. "But if Saray is going, it'd be best if you didn't."

Jasper huffed. "Really? This again?" He turned and looked at Saray. "Listen, I understand that you don't want to be my friend. I know why, and I respect that. But you can't even work in the same vicinity as me? What's it going to take to convince you that I'm sincere?"

"He's right," I chimed in. "In case you haven't heard what he's been saying, Jasper feels awful about what happened. He's not out to hurt you, Saray."

Saray flinched, then took a deep breath and met his eyes. "It's not that I think you're out to hurt me, Jasper," she said. "It's more complicated than either of you realize. Trust me."

"Trust you?" Jasper echoed. "Why should I do that, when you so clearly don't trust me?"

"Because you were the one who betrayed her, kidnapped her, handed her off to folks who planned to kill her, shot me in front of her, and then put a knife to her throat," Kip growled. "You've hurt Saray far worse than she's ever hurt you!"

"How many times must I tell you that I didn't *want* to do any of that? I didn't want to shoot you, or turn Saray over to the Guard, either! But I was in too deep to back out, and if I hadn't gone through with it, Father would have pushed me away further."

"So you were a coward," Kip shot back. "Letting your father control you like that."

"Kip!" I exclaimed indignantly.

Jasper snorted. "You know nothing of family expectations or parents who try to force you into their ideal. And you wouldn't, either— you don't even *have* a family."

Kip leapt to his feet and lunged at Jasper, only to be frozen in place by a muttered spell from Willem. "You sit back down, young man," he said sternly. "We're here to discuss strategy, not get in a fistfight." Willem released Kip, and he slumped for a moment. Saray pulled him toward her and put an arm around him.

"And as for you, that was an incredibly low blow," Willem said to Jasper. "You have no reason to bring Kip's family into this."

Jasper shook his head and crossed his arms. "I don't know what it's going to take for me to prove myself to you folks," he muttered. "Maybe I should stop trying."

"If you want to prove yourself to us, being more careful with your words would be a good start," Noelle said. "Now, if Jasper goes in with the first group, helps direct them around the island, and keeps his distance from Saray once he's finished, would that work for all parties involved?"

"That should be fine," Saray said. Jasper glared at Kip but nodded as well.

"What about me?" Trina asked. "I suppose I'm not much use on the island?"

"Not in a combat role," Lachlann said. "But we were thinking that you could accompany Ruby. You're good at helping calm folks down, and that might be a useful skill."

"That's a good idea," Kip put in.

Trina gave Kip an odd look but then nodded. "I'd like that."

"And Ruby, you know what you're doing," Noelle said.

I met her eyes and nodded slowly. The thought of my task was a bit unnerving, but I knew why it had been assigned to me. "What about Kaden?" I asked Willem. "Are you and I still going to the island soon to get her out?"

Willem shook his head. "I understand why you want to, especially in light of all this, but if we rescue her before everyone else, the guards will see another successful escape, which will make the situation more urgent in their minds. And I worry that might cause them to go through with their plan sooner. I'm sorry, Ruby. Your friend will have to wait like everyone else."

I sighed. Tears pricked at my eyes, and I swiped at them. "How long until we do this?" I asked, trying not to let my voice shake.

"Likely not for a month or two," Noelle replied. "There are going to be a lot of things to organize before we can carry this out. We need to get the rescue itself figured out in more detail but also determine what we're going to do once the krossemages get here. Dundere City isn't particularly large; incorporating five hundred new people will take some work."

The conversation then turned to what would happen after the rescue, and I sat back with a sigh, crestfallen. *How long will I have to wait now?*

That evening, Saray asked to speak to me after dinner. We sat in her room, drinking tea in front of the large fireplace. "I figure I owe you an explanation," she told me. "When you asked earlier why I don't like being around your brother, and I said it's more complicated than you realize, I wasn't just avoiding your question. I'd appreciate it if you didn't repeat this to Jasper though."

I nodded. "I won't tell him. What's going on?"

Saray stared into the fire for a moment, seeming deep in thought. "When I was first learning to work with my gift, I had an issue with losing control," she explained. "I would cast accidentally when I was scared or angry, and shortly after I fled Sylvenburgh, I managed to burn several people over the course of just a few days." She shook her head. "Fire magic without control is dangerous enough. But fire magic without control when you're a mind caster can be catastrophic."

"I can imagine."

"A regular magikai can clamp their mouth shut or sit on their hands to keep themself from casting. But I had to train myself to *decide* not to use my magic, and it was tough. It took a couple of months working with Willem to get my gift under control. He trained me well, though, and after we reached Dundere, I only had one slip-up where I cast fire without thinking. That was at your brother, when he shot Kip."

I frowned. "You didn't mean to burn him?"

Saray shook her head. "He pulled the trigger on that gun, and suddenly I was screaming and had fire spewing out of my hands." She closed her eyes for a moment, then smirked. "I don't exactly regret burning him, though."

"I don't exactly blame you."

She gave me a small smile. "After the Guard left and we got Kip back, I moved on with my life for the most part. I had occasional nightmares about Jasper and the Breoch Guard, but it wasn't something that affected me too terribly. When I found out he was coming back here with you and Lachlann, I was nervous, but I was also a bit excited. I wanted to see how he'd react when he saw Kip; I wanted him to see that I was safe and happy and had a family, and could use my gift without fear. I wanted to show him that I'd *won*." She sighed. "But the moment I actually saw him, something changed. Remember how there was fire on my hands that day?"

"I…think so, yes."

"That wasn't intentional. I lost control. For the first time in years."

"Oh." I eyed her. "That must have been terrifying."

"It was. It *is*. Ever since then, whenever Jasper's around, I have trouble controlling my fire. Seeing him just…brings all the memories back."

"Of him shooting Kip?"

"That, yes, but more so of what happened later that day."

"Which was what?"

"After I escaped my cell on the ship and came above deck," she explained, "Gareth and some of the folks from the Lady Liara had shown up and were fighting the Guard, trying to get me back. Your brother snuck up behind me, put a knife to my neck and threatened to slit my throat if I tried to burn him again." She looked away.

"Oh," I said, my eyes widening. "When Jasper told me that story, he focused more on shooting Kip than threatening you afterward."

"I imagine shooting Kip affected him more, which makes sense if he'd never killed someone." Saray sighed. "When I see Jasper now, my instincts take over. It's hard to think clearly; I get focused on trying to protect myself, and then the fire shows up. I've asked Lachlann to use his anti-magic to keep me from casting, which is why you might have noticed me hanging around him whenever your brother is nearby. I'm avoiding Jasper partly because of how he affects me, but also because I'm trying not to *harm* him."

I nodded slowly as I took in her words. "I'm…sorry, Saray. I'm sorry you had to endure all that, and that it's still affecting you."

She sighed. "I'm not quite sure what to do about it all."

"Well, I imagine it's the last thing you want, but have you considered telling Jasper all this? He's pretty reasonable, I'm sure he'd be willing to listen."

"Lachlann suggested that as well. But I don't know what good it would do for either of us. I would probably spend the entire conversation wanting to run away or trying not to set him on fire, and it would likely make him feel guiltier than he already does."

"Maybe." I frowned. "Perhaps you should just try being around him in small doses, for now at least. Keep a distance, see how close you can get before you start casting, and then work on getting closer."

She nodded. "I suppose I'll have to get used to him eventually, won't I?"

"I suppose so." I sighed. "This is my fault in a way, you know. I insisted that Jasper come to Dundere with Lachlann and me. I didn't want to be abandoned by my family again, and I didn't know Lachlann very well, so I wasn't sure I wanted to travel alone with him."

"I can understand why you'd want Jasper to come along. And I can see that he's changed, too. My mind knows that. But sometimes these things affect you in ways that run deeper than your mind."

"I get that. I had something similar happen to me recently."

"What was that?"

"When we were on our way to Flavalan, I saw Yarel Island from the carriage, and I broke down crying and shaking. It was partly because I missed Kaden, but also, just seeing it made me react in a way I didn't expect."

Saray nodded solemnly. "That makes sense."

My stomach knotted as my thoughts turned from my last glimpse of Yarel Island to the fate of its inhabitants. "I'm so scared, Saray. What if we don't get to the island in time?"

She reached for my hand and gave it a squeeze. "Willem seemed pretty certain nothing would happen until the fall. You'll get Kaden back."

I sighed once more and stared into the fire. "I sure hope you're right."

CHAPTER 16

"**THIS IS GOING** to drive me mad," I said to Alvin the following morning at school.

He nodded gravely, having just spent the last ten minutes listening to me recount the previous day's conversation. "I'm sorry all this is happening. I'd like to help with the rescue, if I can."

"That would be wonderful. But it doesn't fix how I'm feeling right now." I sighed. "How am I supposed to just go on living life, knowing that my friends are in terrible danger and there's nothing I can do for them yet?" My voice wavered as I spoke, and I wiped away a tear.

"Sounds like I have my work cut out for me," Alvin replied.

"What do you mean?"

"Seems to me like you need a distraction." He grinned, tucked his hair behind his ear, and pointed a thumb to his chest. "Hello, my name is Alvin, and I'd like to volunteer to be your distraction."

I laughed, my anxiety dissipating slightly. "And how do you intend to do that?"

"Oh, there are plenty of options. How about another date, for starters?"

"Is this one going to involve picnics in forbidden places?"

"You'll just have to wait and see." He draped an arm around me. "This Friday? Same time, same place?"

I grinned and leaned my head against his shoulder. "All right, Mr. Distraction. You're on."

As it turned out, staying busy wasn't as difficult as I'd anticipated. I threw myself into my usual activities with renewed gusto. At the lighthouse, I began to learn the process of moving air currents to create thunderclouds, something that Chase was happy to teach me despite my technically not being allowed to manipulate lightning yet. He wasn't teaching me to control lightning, he assured me with a wink. He was only teaching me how to create the appropriate conditions for lightning to happen. Once I'd passed my tests and gotten my full license, controlling lightning would be quite easy.

Occasionally, I skipped my time at the lighthouse to attend civic meetings where Noelle and Deshi spoke to the people of Dundere City about the upcoming rescue. Most of the folks weren't willing to participate in the rescue itself, but there were plenty who were willing to donate food and clothing and supplies to make the refugees feel more at home once they arrived. Lachlann and Willem began to organize those who *would* be a part of the rescue, assigning each of them various roles and providing combat training, both magical and mundane. Kip helped with the training too; he seemed very eager to be a part of it.

On the evenings I wasn't with Alvin, I spent my time either at home or at Lachlann's, learning sword with Jasper. Once I had my stances figured out, Lachlann moved me on to different sorts of strikes and counterstrikes, and then to slow sparring with practice swords. Sometimes Jasper and I would spar while Lachlann watched, which was a different experience altogether. Jasper wasn't as sure of himself as Lachlann, but Lachlann played by the rules, while Jasper preferred feints and sneaky moves that left my head spinning. When Lachlann wasn't home, Jasper and I would often wander through the city, sampling food at the market or peering into odd little shops. We even rode to the outskirts and found a new trail to hike. Jasper seemed happy enough on those evenings, and I was glad to help Lachlann achieve his goal of ensuring my brother wasn't bored or lonely.

Nights spent with the Westwoods were equally entertaining. Trina and I occasionally assisted Marcus with his experiments, helping him create potions for better plant life or improved heating stones for the tub, or coming up with new, silly ideas for magical items. One evening, he managed to create a potion that would raise a person's voice by a good octave, and Trina, Sophie and I spent the rest of the evening walking around the mansion scaring people with it. When we weren't helping Marcus, we'd spend hours on Trina's balcony, watching animals come and go and talking about life. Trina currently had a crush on a boy at school named Archie; when she asked me about my own interests, I shrugged and said I hadn't met anyone I was attracted to yet.

Saray and Kip weren't around as often as Trina, but when they were, they joined in on our conversations. I learned that Kip also had an affinity for climbing Kirilee's tree— one evening, he and I had a competition to see who could climb the highest. Kip was more nimble than me, but I was smaller, so I managed to hoist myself onto a high branch that he likely would have broken. The following day, I swore that the tree had grown taller and its highest branches thicker, so naturally, I challenged him again. This time he won. The night after that, Sophie was over, and she climbed higher than either Kip or I had managed.

Saray and I had a contest going as well; on nights when there was sufficient cloud cover, she would create a fireball, and I'd call down the rain to try to extinguish it. Most of the time she won, but every now and then, I'd be able to produce a heavy enough rain to put her fire out. Noelle scolded us for these competitions, saying that it wasn't good manners to affect the local weather for the sake of a game, but we still played when she wasn't around.

Evenings spent with Alvin were the most fun by far. I figured out very quickly that his idea of a good date involved using his invisibility to take us somewhere dangerous or forbidden. We climbed to the top of the clock tower in town, visited the coastline where treacherous rocks and strong waves closed it off, toured the backyards of the town's richer folks, and one evening snuck into the city hall once the cleaner left and had a candlelight dinner in the massive atrium. Most of our adventures ended with us wedged somewhere dark and hidden, kissing fiercely, his body pressed into mine.

"Why don't you want to sneak into my backyard sometime so we can do this?" I suggested after one such session in a dark farmer's field.

He shook his head lazily. "I'd best not, with all that happened with Trina."

"What exactly went on between you and her?"

"Short version of the story is that she was dating this fellow called Frederick, and she cheated on him with me. Then she blamed me for it, and she and Saray ruined my reputation at school."

"Really?" I frowned. It was hard for me to imagine Trina cheating on a boyfriend or her and Saray acting that maliciously.

"It was pretty devastating. I went from being a popular guy to a complete outcast, thanks to them." He sighed, then met my eyes. "But forget Trina and Saray. I have a better idea for our next date."

"Which is what?"

"You'll have to wait and see. I'm…" He trailed off as a few small globes of light began to flit around the two of us. "Well, that's odd."

I stared at them. "Fairies?"

"Yes, but not the type you're accustomed to. The ones at the governor's home are tame fairies from the Shrouded Woods. These are wild fae; they're local to Dundere." One of them landed on my arm as he spoke, and Alvin's eyes widened. "They like you, Ruby. That's rare."

"They don't like humans?"

"They tend to avoid us. It's been said that if a wild fae lands on a person, they've been chosen for something important."

I lifted my arm carefully and studied the tiny creature. Its colours were more muted than the fairies I was used to, and it did not look like a tiny human. This one had an almost triangular face, long pointy ears, and visible canines. It was dressed in tattered clothes, and a long tail protruded from the back of its pants. It met my eyes for a brief moment and then flew away, its companions following. "Well," I murmured, "that was unexpected."

"Indeed," Alvin said. "You're something special, Ruby."

"And you're trying to flatter me." I smirked.

"You like it." He grinned and kissed the tip of my nose, then flopped back and extended an arm. "Come here."

I smiled and lay down against him, savouring his warmth and wondering what exactly our strange encounter with the wild fae of Dundere could mean.

Three days later, we met at our usual spot, and I was surprised when Alvin showed up on horseback. "Hop up," he said, reaching down and extending a hand. "Where we're going is a bit out of the way."

I climbed onto the saddle to sit behind him, and we rode across town, out of the downtown area and into a residential neighbourhood. A good number of the homes were surrounded by sprawling brick walls with iron gates, their facades hidden behind elaborate gardens or towering trees. I could smell salt in the air, and I realized that most of the homes on our right were directly on the water.

Alvin stopped in front of one of them, dismounted, and pushed open a pair of large gates. "Where are we?" I asked as he led the horse inside.

"My house," he told me. I raised an eyebrow; I hadn't expected him to bring me here.

He walked the horse to a stable off the main building and helped me off. "You sneak around back and wait for me there," he instructed.

The beach beyond the Blackwells' home was flat and sandy, unlike the jagged, rocky coastline near the lighthouse. The days grew slightly shorter as August approached, so the sun was already setting, painting the waves a red-gold tone. I grinned and arranged a few of the clouds while I waited for Alvin, adding a touch of purple and scarlet to the sunset. Then I stood back and inhaled the salt air, enjoying the way the breeze ruffled my hair. My curls were at an awkward stage now; they looked shaggy and voluminous but were too short to wear up yet.

"You make lovely sunsets, you know." Alvin's disembodied voice next to me made me jump, and he laughed at my reaction. "Sorry. Couldn't resist." I felt a hand slip into mine.

I looked into the empty space where I knew Alvin would be. "Can you…stop being invisible now?"

"Not quite yet. We both need to be invisible for this next part."

"To sit on a beach?"

"Not quite. Come on." He whispered his spell again, and we began moving.

Alvin led me toward a side door of the house, and we slipped inside. The Blackwells' manor was similar in some ways to the Westwoods' home— large with high ceilings and intricately carved woodwork, its rooms filled with elegant furniture, fine fabrics, and knickknacks that looked to be from faraway places. But Noelle decorated in bright colours and made a point of keeping the curtains open, and the windows as well when the weather allowed it. This home, conversely, had every shade drawn, and the rooms were decorated in dark hues that might have been beautiful if the house didn't feel so stuffy. I clung to Alvin as we navigated, treading quietly until we reached a door at the far end of a long hallway.

We slipped into what I could only assume was Alvin's room. My first impression was that his parents must be like mine in that they didn't allow for much originality in decor. My room back home was all pink and frilly, with shelves of porcelain dolls and books of fairy tales— not because I wanted my room to look like that, but because my mother believed that's how a girl's bedroom *should* look. Alvin's room reminded me of both my brothers' rooms, full of dark wooden furniture, the bed swathed in a blue patterned coverlet, and the shelves lined with expensive books and wooden dragons and soldiers that looked like they'd been carved by hand. On the massive desk next to the shelves was a ship inside a bottle.

The room was elegant but gave little away as to the personality of its inhabitant. Alvin closed the door, mumbled a spell, and we both became visible once more.

"This is your room?" I asked.

He nodded. "It seems like we spend a lot of time kissing on cold rocks or in prickly grass full of bugs. I figured I'd take us somewhere a little more comfortable."

I bit my lip. "We're, uh, just going to kiss, right? Because I don't think I'm ready for…"

"If that's what you want, just kissing is fine." He smiled and tucked his hair behind his ear. "You don't need to worry about things getting out of hand." Then he sank down on the bed and lay back, stretching his lanky form across it. "Come here."

I hesitated for only a moment, then joined him on the bed. He wrapped an arm around me, pulling me close. "See? Much more comfortable than most of the places we end up."

"You're the one who takes us to those places," I pointed out with a smirk.

"You seem to like it too. But I figured I'd try something a little different today." He turned his body so he was leaning over me, then lowered his head to press his lips against mine, tenderly at first, then with more deliberation. I felt myself relaxing. Alvin traced my jawline with his fingertips as he kissed me; I reached up and wound my hand into his hair. *He's right, this is much more comfortable than our usual spots.*

Alvin shifted himself even further so that he was now mostly on top of me. I felt my heartbeat pick up as his lips met mine with renewed vigour, the sensuous song of his magic playing in my mind like an echo. For a moment, I found myself thinking that perhaps I *could* handle more than just kissing. I wanted him closer than he already was; I wanted more of him, however that might look. So when he sat up, unbuttoned his shirt, and slipped it off, I didn't complain.

I let my hands wander over the smooth, muscular planes of his back when he returned to kissing me. I held him close, savouring the feeling of him under my bare arms. This sensation of skin against skin was new.

His own heart beat against mine. His lips moved to kiss my jawline, then my neck, then my collarbones. I let out a small, involuntary moan.

When his lips wandered an inch or so lower and met the fabric of my dress, he pulled away and stared down at me. "You should take this off."

My eyes widened at his suggestion, the earlier feelings of hesitation returning. "Alvin, I don't know if…"

He grinned and attempted to smooth down his tousled hair. "You don't know if what?" he asked, tucking a lock behind his ear. Then he leaned down and kissed my nose.

I giggled, relaxing a little. "I might be able to take this off. But it's a bit of work; you'll have to help…"

I was interrupted by the bedroom door as it flew open. "Alvin, I need to borrow—" The voice caught, and I turned and saw Aidan staring down at us.

"Ever heard of knocking?" Alvin replied, sitting up. "I'm busy."

Aidan's look of shock turned to disgust when he studied me. "I remember you. By the Fae, Alvin, I'd expect you to have some standards."

"What's that supposed to mean?" Alvin demanded, climbing off me to glare at his brother.

"It means if you're going to take a woman to bed, it should be one who isn't Breochi trash." He looked beyond Alvin then and sneered at me. "You led him into this, didn't you? Convinced him to show you his room, then started taking his clothes off, right? I should have known that the little sister of that bottle-sucking skirt-chaser would act just like him."

"That's not true!" I protested, sitting up. "And don't talk about my brother that way!"

"I'll leave your brother alone when you leave mine alone," Aidan replied, his voice turning soft, menacing. "Consider yourself warned. Have fun with your filthy little friend, Alvin." Then he turned on his heel and slammed the door.

I looked at Alvin with wide eyes. He stared back at me and then swore under his breath. "Well, that complicates things."

I nodded, lost for words. The euphoria that accompanied our earlier activities was fading fast, and I felt my cheeks flush. "I, uh…I think I should leave."

To my surprise, he agreed. "Let's get you home. Don't want you to be here if Aidan tells my parents." He reached for his shirt and began to button it up, and I attempted to straighten out my rumpled dress. Finally, when we were ready, Alvin cast the invisibility spell on us both, and we slipped out the door.

I woke up the next morning feeling uneasy. The previous night's events played over in my mind, and something about it all felt…*off.* It wasn't Aidan's intrusion that bothered me, or the fact that Alvin had snuck me into his room in the first place. It was the direction my mind had gone in the heat of the moment— how badly I'd wanted to be closer to Alvin, and how easily I'd ignored my earlier convictions about not being ready for anything beyond kissing.

How close I'd gotten to taking off my dress.

I mulled this over while eating breakfast, paying little attention to Saray and Trina's banter as they ate their eggs and toast. I only looked up from my food when a knock at the front door startled us all.

Marcus went to answer it and returned with a worried look on his face. "Jasper's here for you, Ruby. And by the looks of it, he needs to see you too, Noelle."

I got up from the table. Noelle followed me to the entryway, and my eyes widened at what I saw.

Jasper's face was badly bruised. One of his eyes was swollen nearly shut, there was a gash on his cheek, and his forearms were blistered with burns. "Jasper! What happened?"

"I'll explain later," he told me. "I'm here because I need to talk to you, Ruby."

"I think you need to see Noelle first."

Jasper shrugged. "I'll heal up. I've had worse things done to me. Come on, Ruby, let's go for a walk."

"Oh no you don't." Noelle's voice was firm. "You do not walk into my house looking like this and leave unhealed, young man." Her eyes narrowed as she studied his face. "Your nose is broken, isn't it?"

He nodded. "Lachlann snapped it back into place last night, so it shouldn't heal crooked."

"It won't heal crooked because I'm going to deal with it right now. Take your shoes off, come inside, and have a seat."

Jasper sighed and cast a wary glance at the hall beyond. "Fine."

Trina poked her head into the parlour as Jasper sat down. "You look terrible," she said.

Jasper gave her a half smile. "Thanks, Trina. You really know how to make a fellow feel great about himself."

She rolled her eyes and ventured further into the room. "You're not even going to tell us what happened?"

"A fellow who had a grudge against me from our ship days decided to come into the pub last night with a friend and attack me for an absolutely ridiculous reason. He was very drunk, and he tried to use magic on me. Hence the burns." His eyes flickered to the hall beyond, where Saray stood at a distance, watching.

My eyes widened at Jasper's story. *So that's where Aiden went.*

"You don't feel like naming this fellow by chance?" Noelle asked. "I could have him charged."

He shook his head. "I don't feel the need to bring you into this. The guard already knows about it; they'll be keeping an eye on him."

Noelle nodded, then went to work healing Jasper's injuries. "Are there any more?" she asked when she'd tended to all she could see. "Bruised ribs or anything?"

"Right, I nearly forgot." He frowned and began to unbutton his shirt.

I gasped at the bloodied bandage plastered to his left side, close to the bottom of his ribcage. "He tried to stab me. He was clumsy, though, and hit a rib. I don't think much damage was done."

"How do you *forget* that someone stabbed you?" I demanded.

"I heal fast, and as I say, I could tell it wasn't very deep." He shrugged off his shirt and attempted to peel off the bandage himself.

"I'll do that," Noelle cut in. It was hard to judge the seriousness of the wound once the dressings were removed; everything was bloodied. "Why didn't you have Lachlann bring you here last night? This could have been serious."

"He wanted to, but I wouldn't let him." Jasper exhaled deeply as Noelle began to sing her spell to heal the wound. "That does feel better. Thank you."

"Why won't you tell us who did this?" Trina asked. "Whoever it was tried to kill you, Jasper."

"I'm not sure if he was actually trying to kill me or just very drunk and wanting to cause me harm."

"How'd you get away?" Saray wondered, still standing at a distance with her arms crossed.

"Well, Lachlann came in with his anti-magic to stop the fellow from trying to set me on fire. And then the guard arrived to break up the fight. They didn't arrest anyone though, just sent them home with warnings."

I gaped. "They sent them home after someone tried to *stab* you?"

"They didn't see that part." He shrugged.

"Was Lachlann injured as well?" Noelle asked.

"One of the guys decked Lachlann when he tried to pull him off me, so he's got a black eye but nothing else. I know you can't do much for Lachlann though."

Noelle nodded. "Tell him to put ice on it. In the meantime, you're all healed up." She looked Jasper over to make sure nothing was missed. "You'll just need to wash the blood off yourself, then you'll be good as new. You and Ruby can go have your talk now."

Jasper and I settled in the backyard, where I studied him. Despite being newly healed, he looked tired. His shoulders were slumped, and a frown creased his face. "Aidan did this to you," I said.

He met my eyes and nodded.

"Why?"

"That's what I want to talk to you about. Apparently, he caught you in bed with his little brother. He came at me claiming that you seduced Alvin, and that my flirtatious ways were rubbing off on you."

I sat back and crossed my arms. "First of all, I didn't seduce Alvin. If anything, he's been the one seducing me. Second, we weren't 'in bed', we were kissing *on* the bed, but we both had our clothes on. Well, most of them." I shivered, remembering how close Alvin had come to convincing me to take off my dress. "And third, why was Aidan attacking *you* over something that *I* supposedly did?"

He nodded. "It didn't make a lot of sense, really."

"Even if I had seduced Alvin, and even if we were in bed together, it would still be on me. I'm my own person." An unexpected wave of anger surged through me, and my hands balled into fists. "How dare he attack you like that! I should go over there and—"

"Don't." Jasper raised a hand. "You'll make things worse, Ruby."

"But he tried to kill you, and the guards just sent him home!" I huffed. "I'm glad they got to you in time to save you, but that still seems suspicious."

Jasper chuckled. "Actually, I wasn't completely honest about that part. Lachlann and I had the situation under control by the time the guards showed up. Once Lachlann got Aidan's friend off me, my training kicked in, and I was able to handle Aidan on my own."

"Your training? You mean what you're doing with Lachlann?"

He shook his head. "My Breoch Guard training. I didn't want to get into that in front of Saray and Trina, though."

"What did you do to him?"

"In the Guard, you're taught to look for a weakness when dealing with a person more powerful than you, and then use that against them. An injury, a thought pattern, another person, even." He shrugged. "I try not to think that way anymore, but if I see someone as a threat, it's hard for me not to look for weaknesses, just in case they try to harm me."

I nodded.

"I noticed Aidan has a bad knee," Jasper continued. "So last night, I kicked him there, hard. It worked; he let me go and started screaming about how I'd assaulted him. When the guard showed up, Lachlann explained everything to them, and they let us all go with a warning." He gave me a tight smile. "It's the main reason I don't have smoke coming out of my ears right now. Yes, I got beat up pretty bad, but in the end, I *won.*"

"Ah." My shoulders hunched. "That much makes sense. But I still can't believe he went after you for something you didn't even do. Why didn't you tell Noelle who it was?"

He raised an eyebrow. "Because I was trying to protect you."

"From what?"

"Getting into trouble." He shrugged. "I know Marcus and Noelle aren't our parents, but I'm not sure how they'd react to whatever was going on between you and Alvin last night."

I shrugged. "Hard to say. I mean, I'm pretty sure Saray and Kip are sleeping together. Kip and another fellow in the Shrouded Woods were talking about this tea that prevents pregnancy."

"Saray and Kip are a little older, though, and they've been together for years. There might be different opinions about someone your age and a fellow you only met in the past couple of months." He frowned. "You and Alvin are…dating, then?"

"I suppose so."

"And you said he's been seducing you?"

I bit my lip. "He can be persuasive. He convinced me to go into his room last night."

"He's not pressuring you, is he? Making you do things that you're not comfortable with?"

"Not exactly, but…" My shoulders hunched. "Well, last night it did feel like things were moving very fast. It's complicated."

"Sounds like it." He was silent for a moment, then ventured awkwardly, "If, uh, if you need any of that tea, I have some."

I glared. "I told you, we're not sleeping together."

"I know. But I have some in case that changes."

"How did you get a hold of it anyway? You convinced Kip to sell to *you?*"

He shook his head and laughed. "Gareth had a stash of it on the ship because some of his crew members are dating each other. Lachlann passed me some when he worried I was getting out of control."

I snickered. "I'm surprised you have any left."

"What, you think I took every woman on the ship to bed?"

"You had a bit of a reputation as a flirt. Or, as Aidan called you last night, a bottle-sucking skirt-chaser."

"He said that?" Jasper snorted. "If I wasn't so angry at him, I'd think that a pretty great insult." He shook his head then. "I know what people thought of me on the ship, but a lot of it was assumptions. I was a flirt, yes, but most of the women just wanted to kiss and cuddle. I only took one of them to bed, and that was because she specifically told me she wanted to. One can be a flirt and still respect others' limits, you know. Unfortunately, that one encounter is the main reason Aidan hates me so much."

"That was Violet, I'm guessing?"

"Right, you were there when Aidan decked me, weren't you? I hardly remember, I was so drunk that night."

"What happened that made Aidan so upset? It sounded like the two of them were together, and she had a fling with you?"

Jasper shook his head. "She and Aidan were never together. But he had his eye on her, which I didn't know. She didn't have much interest in him at all, but he was trying very hard to change that. So anyway, one evening while everyone was dancing, Violet and I snuck into the girls' dorm and had ourselves a good time. But afterwards, when we were lying there cuddling, Ashlynn came in and caught us. She took one look and ran off. Then I suppose she told Aidan, and when he found out Violet had been with someone else, he was furious. The next night was when you saw him beat on me." He sighed. "I really liked Violet, to the point where I could see myself dating her. But I had to ignore her for the rest of the trip and flirt with other girls just to keep Aidan off my back. Poor girl, she looked so hurt every time she saw me."

I nodded, recalling Violet crying late at night shortly after the incident. "Why didn't you tell her what happened?"

"I did, right before she left. But I waited because I didn't want to make things worse. She might have confronted Aidan, and I'm not sure how that would have gone." He sighed. "Aidan and Ashlynn seem to be accustomed to getting whatever they want, and I have the impression they throw tantrums when things don't go their way. So be careful with Alvin, all right? There's a chance he's like that too."

I shook my head. "He's nothing like them."

"Either way, his family is crazy. I don't want you getting hurt. And if you feel like things are moving too fast, you need to tell Alvin that. He can't read your mind— if he's making you uncomfortable, you need to be direct with him, even if it's not easy for you. And if he doesn't listen when you tell him to back off, then get someone else to intervene. You can tell me, if you want. I'll talk to him."

"And risk having Aidan beat you up again?" I sighed. "No way."

"Well, then find someone else you trust to talk to, all right?"

I hesitated for a moment, then forced a smile. "Sure."

"Promise?"

I nodded, having no idea how I was going to fulfill my word. "I promise."

CHAPTER 17

I FELT MY earlier confusion fade after Jasper left, and a new emotion took its place— rage over what had been done to him. Even more confusing was the city guard's choice to simply send Aidan home with a warning. *I need to do something about this,* I decided.

I let Marcus know that I was going to be borrowing one of the horses. Trina was out in the stables tending to a few of them, and she raised her eyebrows when I approached. "Going somewhere?"

I nodded. "I have an errand to run."

"Which horse are you going to take?"

"Which horse wants to go for a ride?"

She laughed, paused for a moment, then gestured to a speckled black and white horse. "Benny here will take you. He's already been groomed."

"Thanks." I gave Benny a pat and began tacking him up.

"Is your brother all right?" Trina asked me as I worked.

I sighed. "Physically, he's fine now that Noelle's healed him up. And he's acting like what happened is no big deal. But that could be him putting on a tough face."

"What did the other fellow attack him over?"

I gently fastened Benny's saddle in place. Alvin had told me not to talk to Trina about him, so I decided I'd better not say much. "It was something they fought about on the ship. It came back up last night, and the fellow decided to take his anger out on Jasper."

"Huh." Trina shook her head. "Do you know who it is?"

"Jasper told me his name, but I can't put a face to it," I lied.

I worked in silence after that, then bid Trina farewell and mounted Benny.

When I reached the gates of Blackwell manor, I dismounted and let myself in. My heart pounded in my ears as I led Benny up the path to the house. *Will I actually have the courage to knock on that door?*

As it turned out, I didn't need to. I was met in front by a tall, formally dressed man with strawberry blond hair that was beginning to grey. *This must be Alvin's father.*

He stared down at me through a pair of spectacles. "What can I do for you, miss?"

"I'm here to see Aidan," I told him, lifting my chin.

"Is that so?" The man frowned. "Who may I tell him is wishing to visit?"

"My name is Ruby."

The man squinted at me for a moment, then turned on his heel and disappeared into the house. I stood nervously in the front yard, wondering if I should follow him.

A moment later, a form materialized on the front porch. Aidan was seated on a chair that he'd teleported outside with him, his leg bound in bandages. He sneered at me. "What do *you* want?"

I took a deep breath and joined him on the porch. "I want to know why you took your anger at Alvin and me out on Jasper."

Aidan rolled his eyes. "Your brother is a bad influence on you, you little trollop. He got what he deserved."

"What happened between your brother and me last night had nothing to do with Jasper. If you want to get angry at someone about it, talk to one of *us,* not him. And even if Jasper was somehow responsible, he didn't deserve to get beaten up the way he did."

"*He* didn't deserve it? Look what he did to me! I'll likely never walk normally again!"

"So go to Noelle and get healed." I snorted. "I saw what you did to him. I saw the wound on his chest. You tried to kill him!"

I hadn't noticed Mr. Blackwell eavesdropping on our conversation from the front door; now I heard him inhale sharply. "Is that true?" he demanded of Aidan.

"It is," I told him. "He stabbed Jasper in the chest. Thankfully, the knife hit a rib."

Mr. Blackwell eyed Aidan. "You didn't tell me about that part, son."

"Leave my brother alone from now on," I said to Aidan. "If you hurt him again, I'll bring Noelle into it."

Aidan's eyes glittered with hate. "I already told you my terms. Leave *my* brother alone, and I'll leave yours alone."

"Ruby?" A familiar voice cut into our conversation, and Alvin appeared in the doorway behind his father. "What are you doing?"

"Your brother attacked Jasper after he found us last night and nearly killed him. I'm making sure he doesn't try that again." The words caught in my throat a little, and I stared at Alvin for a few long seconds, my stomach knotting as unease about what had happened between us last night returned. I forced myself to turn away and walked toward Benny. "I should go."

"Ruby, stop." Alvin brushed past his father onto the porch. "We should talk about this."

"I...I'm not ready to talk about it with you. Not yet. I need to think." I mounted Benny, turned us around, and began to walk down the path.

"Come on, Ruby, talk to me," Alvin insisted, following me. "We can work this out."

I blinked back tears, refusing to let myself look at him, trying to ignore his words. *If I acknowledge him, he'll talk me into staying and doing whatever it is he wants from this, just like he tried to last night.*

He continued to follow, pleading with me to stop, and when I reached the gate, I spun around and glared at him. "I *said* I'm not ready to talk about it!" I snapped. Then I took off at a trot, leaving Alvin staring, bewildered, after me.

"You did *what?*" Jasper demanded.

I'd gone to Lachlann's rather than home after confronting Aidan; I didn't have to worry about Alvin trying to follow me here. Like many other members of the Dundere guard, Lachlann had small pieces of anti-magic stone in various corners of his apartment that would prevent Alvin from sneaking up on me cloaked in invisibility. Normally, the stones made me feel slightly off-balance, but today they were comforting.

"He needed to be told off, after what he did to you," I replied.

"He didn't try to attack you, did he?"

I shook my head. "He called me names and threatened me, but that's about it."

"I wouldn't do that again, Ruby. I get that you were angry. I'm angry too. But those Blackwells, they're vindictive." He sighed. "So what, you're just going to camp out here so Alvin doesn't find you?"

"I need some time to think about last night before I talk to him."

"Well, you don't have to tell me what happened, but you're not going to shock me if you do. I've admitted plenty of my own mistakes to you."

I sighed and met his eyes. "I told Alvin I wasn't comfortable with more than kissing. But in the moment, when it was starting to get intense, I...I felt like I *could* have gone further." The words were coming out fast now. "Half an hour before, I was convinced that I wasn't ready, but something changed. I feel like if Aidan hadn't burst in, I might have ended up sleeping with Alvin." I looked at my brother out of the corner of my eye. "Is that...bad? Wanting those things so much?"

Jasper chuckled. "You're asking the bottle-sucking skirt-chaser for moral advice, now?"

I rolled my eyes at him.

"You know," he said, "I think *wanting* to be intimate with someone is pretty natural. Whether you decide to do it may or may not be a good choice, depending on the situation. Like with most things in life."

"Do you think it would have been a good choice for me?"

"Well, if you didn't have any of the tea handy, it would've been risky physically. Whether you'd feel good about it afterwards, well, I can't say for certain." He frowned. "You seem a bit unsure whether you actually *wanted* to sleep with Alvin, so I figure it's good that you didn't. From my own experience, it's best to only be intimate with someone if you absolutely know you want to. Otherwise you end up with regrets."

I eyed him. "Do you have those sorts of regrets?"

Jasper nodded, not meeting my eyes. "I regret some of my...encounters. Not all, but definitely a few of them." He frowned and stared toward the window for a moment, and I thought I saw his cheeks redden slightly.

"Does talking about all this with me make you uncomfortable?"

"It's a little strange. But I'm your brother, so I suppose if you're going to talk to a fellow about all this, I'm a good choice. I doubt Mother was very forthcoming with you about these sorts of things. Father certainly wasn't with me."

I nodded. Mother had rarely spoken to me about the intimacies that came with growing up.

Jasper cleared his throat a bit awkwardly then, seeming to want to lighten the mood a bit. "You up for a game of chess while you're hiding here?"

"You'll beat me, like you always do."

He chuckled. "Well, it'd be nice to win for a change. I've been getting soundly beaten by Lachlann every time we play."

"Really? He doesn't strike me as the chess-playing sort."

"Me neither. Lachlann isn't an intellectual, but he is definitely a strategist. He and Tomlin used to get into board-throwing matches when they were younger, they were so competitive. It's one of the only things they're both good at."

Jasper set up the board, and soon we were engrossed in our game. We had been playing for quite some time when we heard a knock.

"Huh. Wonder who that is," Jasper said.

"I'll go find out." When I answered, I found myself staring back at Alvin, who didn't look a whole lot better than Jasper had that morning; he had a black eye, and his lower lip was cut open. "Alvin! What happened to you?"

He shook his head. "Don't worry about it. Can I come in?"

"Um, sure, I suppose so." I let Alvin into the apartment, and he followed me to the living room. "How'd you find me?"

"I decided to wander for a bit, and I came across your horse, so I asked around and found out Lachlann lived up here. I figured that's where you'd gone."

Jasper raised an eyebrow when we came into the room. "Well, now, you must be the infamous Alvin."

"And I suppose you're that fellow my brother keeps ranting about."

"The local bottle-sucking skirt-chaser, at your service." Jasper gave Alvin a mock salute. "You don't look so good."

"And you look better than I expected."

"Rumour has it that the governor in this town is a healer. Maybe you should pay her a visit."

Alvin raised his eyebrows as he sat down. "I would, but then I'd likely just get beaten up again."

Jasper frowned. "Did Aidan feel the need to beat someone else up after Ruby confronted him?"

"No. It wasn't Aidan."

"Who, then?" I asked.

Alvin shifted from one foot to the other. "It was my father," he admitted, not meeting my eyes.

"Your *father* did this to you?" I repeated incredulously. "Why?"

"He wasn't too happy about what happened between us last night." He sighed. "Don't tell anyone else."

"It happens to the best of us," Jasper said, reaching over and clapping Alvin on the shoulder. "Our father did the same thing to me, once, for about the same reasons."

I frowned. "Father beat you up?"

"Not quite like that," he gestured to Alvin, "but he belted me pretty good. I was twelve, and he caught me kissing a girl behind the school." He chuckled, obviously trying to lighten the mood.

"I'm surprised it only happened once, knowing you and all your skirt-chasing," I teased.

"I learned at a young age to be sneaky about my escapades. Though it seems

I haven't been sneaky enough as of late, which is why your brother hates me." He eyed Alvin.

Alvin frowned. "What happened between you and Aidan exactly?"

"Short version of the story is that while we were on the Lady Liara, I slept with a girl that Aidan was into."

"Ah." Alvin's eyebrows lifted. "Yes, that would do it. I remember when I was about eleven, I got a bit of a crush on his then-girlfriend, and when he figured it out, he pushed me up against a wall and told me to leave his girl alone. As if his kid brother was a threat to his relationship." He sighed. "If it makes you feel any better, Father beat on Aidan worse than me after finding out what he tried to do to you last night."

Jasper snorted. "Serves him right."

"Maybe, but he's just made Aidan even angrier. I'm not sure who he hates more right now— you or Ruby. You'd both better watch yourselves."

Jasper considered this. "I've never met your father, but Aidan's gotta be about my age, and he's bigger than me. You'd think he could take out an old guy."

"Or use his fire," I chimed in.

"He could," Alvin admitted. "But then Father would disown him, and he'd lose everything. His money, his school tuition, all of it. So he sticks around, tolerates Father during the summers when he's not in classes, and hopes he can find himself a wife soon so he can be out on his own."

"Ah." Jasper nodded. "Hence his dislike for my skirt-chasing ways."

Alvin sighed. "Yes, exactly. Listen, Ruby, can we go for a walk? I want to talk to you in private." He regarded Jasper then. "No offense."

"None taken." Jasper raised his hands. "You two can stay here. I've had a rough day, and I could use a nap."

When Jasper left the room, I sighed and looked Alvin over. "I've made this all worse, haven't I?"

"I know you meant well, but yes, you have." He closed his eyes. "I think Aidan was actually trying to protect me, by pinning what happened last night on Jasper."

"How so?"

"I've gotten into some trouble with girls here and there, and Aidan knew my father wouldn't take kindly to him finding us in my room. He had to make it someone else's fault."

"So he tried to kill my brother in an attempt to protect you?" I shook my head. "I think he just wanted an excuse to hurt Jasper, and this gave him one."

"Maybe."

"Look…" I took a deep breath. During my match with Jasper, I'd been pondering much more than the chess game, and I had a better idea of what I wanted to say now. "I think I need some space."

Alvin's eyebrows knitted as he went over my words. "You're breaking up with me?"

"I…don't know. Were we even together in the first place?"

"Well, I certainly thought so, after last night."

"Last night is a part of it." I bit my lip. "It was strange for me, Alvin. I enjoyed myself a lot, but I also felt like you were pressuring me."

"How?"

"I said I didn't want to go all the way, but you just kept doing things that were getting us closer and closer to that, and…" I sighed, unable to find words. "It all felt *off*."

"Well, why didn't you say so?" He frowned. "If you'd told me to stop, I would have."

"I…I just couldn't, for some reason. I don't know. It doesn't make much sense to me either. But that's not the only reason I need some distance." I met his eyes. "Your brother said that he'd only leave Jasper alone if I left you alone. And I like being with you, but it's not worth my brother getting beaten up and almost killed."

Alvin's eyes narrowed. "Jasper's an adult, and he seems like he's a decent fighter. He can handle himself."

"Against a magikai with two deadly gifts and a grudge? I don't think so."

"Ruby, relax. Aidan will get over his grudge. I'm sure we can make our relationship work— we'll just need to keep away from my house and be a little more sneaky about it. Which is easy enough to do when you can turn invisible." He grinned and tucked a curl behind his ear. "Come on, give me another chance."

I closed my eyes and shook my head. "I'm sorry, Alvin. Maybe in a few months or so we can try again. And I'd like to be your friend regardless. But for now, I need some space."

Alvin huffed a frustrated sigh, and I thought I heard him mumble something under his breath. "Ruby, why don't we go for a walk? You'll feel better if we get some fresh air."

"What part of 'I need some space' don't you understand?" I said, firmer this time. "Leave me alone, Alvin."

He recoiled at my conviction. "Fine. I'll leave you alone. I'll just go back home, where my father is likely to beat me up again."

"Alvin, I didn't mean it like—"

"Oh, stop," he snapped, standing. "Do you understand how awful a day I've had? I came here to hide, and now you're telling me to go away? I don't need this." Before I could protest further, he stomped down the hall and slammed the door, leaving me staring after him.

Luckily, I didn't have much time to worry about what had happened between Alvin and me, because the next morning, Noelle informed me that we would be ready to execute the rescue plan the weekend after next.

I spent the following week helping collect food and used clothing from the citizens of Dundere, making the dorms ready for the krossemages to live in, and going over the strategy as many times as possible with the older adults. I knew exactly what my part in it all would be, but it still made me nervous.

At school, Alvin avoided me, sitting on the opposite side of the classroom and leaving me to eat my lunch alone. It was hard not to feel an ache in my chest when I watched him take his seat at a faraway desk, refusing to look at me, but I told myself it was for the best. I was the one who said I needed space, and that's what he was giving me. But even so, I found myself missing him, longing for the feel of his arms around me, his laugh, the way he always fiddled with his hair when he was nervous.

By the time the day of the rescue arrived, I was beginning to regret my actions. *Maybe he and I could make a relationship work, so long as we kept it a secret.*

I was a little surprised when he showed up with the rest of the volunteers at the school of magic that night. I was one of the people responsible for signing folks in to make sure everyone was accounted for, so when he arrived at my table, I stared up at him dumbfounded, my stomach in knots. "You're here."

"Of course I am. I said I would help, didn't I?"

I gave him a small smile. "Thank you."

He nodded and made his way into the school.

Thankfully, the next two people to arrive brought me out of my rumination. "Ruby!" Sophie exclaimed as she strode up to my table, her father in tow. "Are you excited to go rescue your friends?"

I gave her a grin. "I am. You two are part of the welcome team, right?"

She nodded. "I wanted to help with the rescue, but Father won't let me."

I chuckled, and Chase said, "There's not much I can accomplish over there other than hit people with lightning, so I'm not sure what Sophie here thinks she would do."

"I could talk to the younger girls and make sure they know we're safe."

"I have Trina taking care of that, but you can definitely help reassure the younger teens once they get over to this side."

Sophie nodded, satisfied, and headed into the gymnasium with Chase. I continued signing folks in, trying to ignore the knot in my stomach that refused to release. I would have been nervous tonight regardless, but having Alvin around certainly didn't help.

When everyone was accounted for, I made my way to the gymnasium, where Willem was just calling us to order.

"Let's go over the plan once more," he began. "Team one— that's all you teleporters and vanishers, and the ones who know the sleep spell— are going in first. Jasper will lead this team initially, as he knows his way around the island, and these four," here he gestured at some strong-looking young men, "will accompany you, in case anything goes wrong and you need non-magical backup. The vanishers are going to deal with the guards on the teens' side, and the teleporters will take those on the adult side." He pointed to a few spots on the map that Jasper and I had helped him mark. "To our knowledge, the guards will be stationed in these locations, but they could be anywhere." He then began assigning pairs of volunteers to various guard stations and posts throughout the island. "Once your assigned guards are under a sleep spell, take them to the main barn where we'll be tying them all up. Once that's dealt with, Ruby and Marcus's teams will go in." He explained to our group in detail all that we'd be doing. I knew the plan by heart already, but the refresher was good, even if my role still left me anxious.

"Lachlann, you've got your welcome team ready to go?"

Lachlann nodded. "I'll be waiting at the portal to bring people through and direct them up to the school. Once we have everyone through the portal, I'll address them here in the gymnasium."

"Wonderful," Willem said. "It sounds like we're ready to head in. It's close to midnight— I'll teleport over first and do a quick look-around to make sure everything is as we expect. I should be back very soon." He nodded at all of us, then promptly disappeared from the room. When he returned about five minutes later, he was grinning. "Everything is exactly as I hoped," he said. "This should be easy. Let's move."

CHAPTER 18

THE FIRST TEAM filed out the side door of the gymnasium, destined for the portal that Willem had created. Alvin was a part of that team, and I felt my shoulders relaxing slightly as he followed the others out of the room.. "It'll likely take a little while for them to finish their part of the task," Lachlann told us. "The rest of you might as well get comfortable."

I sat along one of the gym walls, and Trina slid down next to me. "How are you doing with all this? Are you scared to go back?"

I shrugged. "I'm more scared about being the one to give a speech."

"You must be excited to see Kaden again."

"Oh, I am, but…I'm a little nervous as well." I sighed. "I know it doesn't really make sense."

"Sometimes exciting things are also a bit scary," she replied. "Were you nervous when Noelle healed you? I know I was."

I nodded. "That's a good point. I was too."

"You'll do fine with addressing everyone," she assured me. "Think of it less like giving a speech and more like giving directions to a group."

Saray came over to join us then, her bright hair tied up in a scarf. She was trailed by Sophie. "You two ready to head over?"

Trina and I both nodded.

"This is exciting. I wish I could do more than stand around and be ready to set things on fire if I have to."

"Is going back to Breoch scary for you?" I asked.

"Going back to some little island where I'm not likely to be recognized isn't so bad. Sometimes I miss Breoch, you know. The Shrouded Woods especially."

"Maybe you could go back to the Woods if you kept your hair tied up like that," I suggested.

She shook her head. "It's too risky, or so Noelle thinks anyway."

"Will you be all right over there without Lachlann?" Trina asked her.

Saray frowned. "I should be fine so long as there's distance. I was in the same room as him tonight, and I've managed to keep my gift in check." She glanced at Sophie as she spoke, clearly not wanting to explain herself to the younger girl.

"I'd love to see the Woods," Sophie put in. "Is it true that there are dragons?"

Saray turned to her, clearly relieved at the change in subject, and began filling Sophie in on all the strange things she'd seen during her time in the Shrouded Woods.

Some time later, Willem reappeared. "The guards have all been put to sleep and restrained," he told us. "We're ready to go in."

I felt my heartbeat pick up as I followed Saray and Trina outside. We made our way across the darkened lawn towards the familiar storage shed. Willem had temporarily closed the portal to the Shrouded Woods, creating a new portal against a different wall that would take us to Yarel Island. I stared into the swirling, luminescent hole as we approached it.

"I've never gone through a portal before," Trina said to Saray.

"Me neither." Saray glanced back at me. "Is it strange?"

"Very," I told her. "It's not scary though. Just odd."

The folks in front of us stepped through, and I looked at Trina and Saray, squaring my shoulders. "Ready?"

Trina nodded. "Maybe you should go through first."

I grinned. "Do you want to hold my hand?"

"Sure." She smiled, interlocking our fingers, and I noticed her hand was cold. I gripped it tightly in mine, trying to calm my own nerves. I was not at all afraid of the portal, but what lay beyond was definitely more intimidating.

We stood in front of the bright, whirling mass for a moment. Then I took a step into the mist, pulling Trina with me. There was the familiar tingle and the odd strain of music, then my foot sank into sand.

The first thing I noticed was the smell. The ocean's scent was obvious in Dundere at certain times of day, especially if you were close to the coast, but on Yarel Island, the aroma was constant. A wave of emotion swept through me as I inhaled the familiar aroma of ocean, seaweed, and damp rocks, and for a moment, I was afraid that I would break down and cry like I did in the carriage on the way to Flavalan all those months ago. I swallowed the lump in my throat as I stepped the rest of the way through the portal, and found that we'd emerged under a large tree just off the beach that bordered the teen section of the island. I raised my eyebrows. *I think this is where Jasper hid his rowboat.*

"Come on through," Willem urged us from beyond the veil of branches. I pulled Trina forward, her eyes widening as she took in the long, sandy beach.

All was quiet on the island save for the murmurs of the magikai who were already assembled. Jasper caught my eye from across the beach and waved but kept his distance. Kip strode over to us and put his arm around Saray.

When the last of the team made it through the portal, Willem looked us over. "All right, we're ready for the second phase of the mission," he said, keeping his voice low so as to not wake the sleeping prisoners. "Marcus, you take your team to where the adult magikai are."

Marcus nodded and headed off with several others in the direction of the hole in the fence that someone from the first team had already created.

"Ruby, you and your folks head up to the farmhouse. Those of you who are reinforcements, stay back here. We'll reconvene on this beach as soon as we've gathered all the krossemages."

I nodded. The others who were coming with me to the farmhouse began to assemble. Jasper and another young man named Kona both made their way over. I took a deep breath. "Are we ready?"

They all nodded.

"Then let's head in."

My heart thundered in my ears as we crept towards the familiar farmhouse. I opened the door as quietly as possible, and we filed inside, sneaking down the darkened hallway past the main room. At the bottom of the staircase, I paused. "You folks stay here unless I say otherwise."

I ascended the rickety staircase alone, eased the door to the girls' dorm open and slipped in. A lump rose in my throat as I looked over the familiar forms of the girls sleeping on their cots. It seemed like just yesterday that I was one of them.

Starla's bed was in a corner, separate from the rest, and I crept over to gently shake her by the shoulder. "Starla, wake up," I whispered.

She stirred in her sleep, then bolted awake, eyes wide, seizing my arm with surprising force. "Shhh," I said. "It's Ruby. I've been healed, and I'm here to rescue you."

She blinked up at me a few times, then shook her head and let go of my arm. *"How?"* she signed.

"I'll explain soon enough. Everyone on the island is in danger, but my friends and I are here to help. Can you go upstairs and wake Matt, then come down to the living room? We'll explain what's happening there."

Starla nodded slowly and then swung her legs over the side of her cot. She followed me out into the hall, where the moon shone through a window on the landing, and paused, looking me over in awe. I grinned and waved my right hand at her. "I know it's hard to believe," I said. "But I'm here. Now go get Matt."

Minutes later, I stood in the living room with Trina, Jasper and Kona. I heard two sets of footsteps descending the creaky staircase, and Starla appeared, trailed by a very confused-looking Matt.

"Hi, Matt," I greeted him, waving. "Bet you didn't expect to see me again."

He shook his head. *"Why would you come back here?"*

"Because you folks are in trouble. But before I go into all that, Starla and Matt, meet my brother Jasper and my friends Kona and Trina."

Beside me, Trina let out something between a squeak and a gasp, gawking excitedly at Starla. Starla clapped her hand over her mouth, her eyes going wide. When Trina spoke, her voice shook. "Is it…really you?"

Before I could ask what was going on, Trina had crossed the floor. She took Starla's hand in her own and looked her over incredulously. "By the Fae, what have they *done* to you?"

Starla let go of Trina's hand and began to sign frantically. *"How can you see?"* She glanced at me, waiting for me to interpret, but Trina answered before I could.

"I went to the governor of Dundere to get my eyes healed, just like you told me I should." Her voice was beginning to tremble with raw emotion. "And we're going to get you fixed up too. I can't believe you're *here* of all places. I thought about trying to find you one day but…" Her voice broke, and Starla pulled her into an embrace.

I stared at them, dumbfounded. "How do you two know each other?"

Trina looked back at me, her face streaked with tears. "This is my mother."

"Your *mother?*" I had no idea Starla even *was* a mother.

Trina nodded. "I…I can't believe…" She trailed off and buried her face in Starla's shoulder.

Jasper looked them over, then sighed regretfully. "I'm really happy for both of you. But we need to keep moving, all right? You two can spend as much time as you need together once we get you out."

"Right." Trina reluctantly pulled away from her mother but kept an arm around her. "Sorry, it's just…I wasn't expecting this." She swiped at her eyes.

Starla nodded. *"What do you need to tell us?"* she asked.

I began explaining everything that Willem had discovered in his investigation. Starla's face fell when I mentioned the planned cull, and she and Matt exchanged a terrified glance. "So we're here to get you all out," I concluded. "I have a few friends who are rounding up the adults, and we're here for the teens. We've dealt with the guards for now, but we only have a few hours."

"How are you getting us out?" Matt asked. *"And where are we going?"*

"To Dundere," I told him. "I know it sounds impossible, but you'll need to trust me. I'll tell you more once we've assembled everyone. The plan is to get all the krossemages onto the beach. I'll explain the rest from there."

Matt nodded slowly.

"Starla, can you help Trina and me wake up the girls? Jasper and Kona will go with you, Matt."

Matt signaled that Jasper and Kona should follow him, and they began to make their way up the staircase to the boys' dorm on the third floor. I followed.

Trina clung to her mother while they trailed behind me, and I fought off an unexpected pang of jealousy. I didn't miss my parents, not at all, but I suspected that if I ever did reunite with Father, it would not be all tears and hugs.

We reached the girls' dorm, and Starla moved to light the lamps. The girls began to stir as the room was illuminated.

I took a deep breath. "Hi, everyone," I said to them. "It's Ruby. I've come to get you all out."

At the sound of my voice, several of the girls sat up, regarding me with wide eyes. I offered them a nervous smile and waved my right hand.

Alisa sprang from her cot, lurching at me, and I grunted as she collided with me in a firm embrace. I had to laugh; Alisa was normally more reserved than this.

"Hi," I greeted her, smiling.

Kaden was on her feet now as well, and I pulled away from Alisa to stand face to face with my friend. She stared at me, eyes narrowed, as if she were trying to figure something out. *"You came back?"* she finally signed, cocking her head.

"Of course I did," I replied, taking her into my arms. It took a moment for her to hug me back, and when she did, her body was stiff against me. *Something's wrong.*

"How did you get healed?" she asked when I pulled away.

"You'll hear about it soon. And you can get healed as well, if you want to. You can have your hand and tongue back!" Tears pricked at my eyes as I stared into her face; I couldn't believe this was finally happening. "I've missed you so much."

She stared back at me, and I thought I saw tears in her eyes too for a moment. Then she sighed. *"I think Starla needs you."*

I turned to where Starla was indicating to the other girls that I was to be trusted and that we were here to rescue them all. *Whatever is wrong with Kaden will have to wait,* I decided. "We don't have much time," I told the girls.

"Everyone is going to meet on the main beach, so I'll explain more then. Grab a change of clothes, and get ready to move."

It only took about ten minutes for the girls to reach the main beach. The boys hadn't shown up yet, but a good number of adults had begun to trickle in. Alisa busied herself trying to organize some of the younger, obviously terrified girls. A few of the others surrounded me, examining my new hand and asking where I'd gone, and I couldn't help noticing the ones who hung back instead, glaring at me. Kaden kept her distance, shooting me the occasional glance but not getting too close.

At the sound of Kip's voice, Trina's head snapped up; he had returned with a few more adults in tow. "Kip!" she called. "Come over here, I need you to meet someone."

Starla's eyebrows shot up. *"Is this your cousin?"* she signed.

Trina nodded. "We found each other."

"What about Kelvin?"

"He died the winter after he and Kip fled. Got sick when they were living in the Woods. I'm sorry."

Starla nodded, her face falling.

Kip made a beeline for us and stopped to look down at Starla, then Trina. His eyes went wide, and he clapped a hand over his mouth for a moment. "I was right!"

"You *knew?*" Trina asked.

"I suspected. Ruby mentioned a woman named Starla. I didn't say anything to you because I didn't want to get your hopes up, y'know?" I heard his voice tremble slightly as he spoke.

Starla stared up at him warmly. *"He's gotten tall. Does he know how to sign?"*

Kip laughed. "Yes, I do. And I s'pose I have. It's good to see you again, Aunt Starla." He reached to embrace her, then frowned. "How'd you end up here?"

"I'll explain everything later."

"That's a good idea. We'll catch up when we get to where we're going. Still lots more to do right now." He glanced towards the farmhouse. "Here come the boys."

I watched the trail of young men approaching, led by Jasper and Kona. Shawnie broke from the group and came to us, grinning when he saw me. To my surprise, he pulled me into a hug. *"It's good to see you,"* he signed when he pulled away.

I grinned and introduced him to the others. When Shawnie noticed my right hand, he grabbed hold of it, then began peppering me with questions. Out of the corner of my eye, I noticed Willem beckoning me over, so I squeezed Shawnie's hand and promised him he'd find out all about the healing process soon. Then I headed over to Willem.

"We're ready for you to make your speech, Ruby," he told me. "Everyone is here."

I nodded, my heartbeat accelerating as my gaze swept over the crowd. I had never met the majority of the adults on the island, and several of them eyed me suspiciously, signing amongst themselves.

"Stand up here," Willem suggested, gesturing to a rock nearby. "It'll be easier for the crowd to see you." He touched my shoulder and mumbled a spell. "Now they'll be able to hear you as well."

I climbed up and cleared my throat. My voice was much louder than I was used to, and the chatter between the speaking folks died down as all eyes settled on me. "Hi, everyone," I began. "Some of you know me, and I'm under the impression that most of you who don't have at least heard of me. My name's Ruby, and I escaped from here a few months back. I had my hand and tongue restored, and now I'm here to get all of you out."

The krossemages listened as I explained how I'd escaped and how I'd learned about the planned cull. There was a chorus of gasps, and then some began signing rapidly to each other, but I couldn't help noticing the small group of adults who stood off to one side, arms crossed, their expressions skeptical.

"We've made a magical portal to take you to Dundere, where you'll be safe and can receive healing from the governor, if you want," I concluded. "Our plan is to leave now."

One of the adults let out a noise, and my eyes darted to him. He came closer so I could see him better when he asked, *"How do we know we can trust you?"*

"I used to be one of you," I replied, signing to him as I spoke.

"But you abandoned us. You ran off and left us at the mercy of the guards." I saw a few others from his group nodding.

"What do you mean?" I asked.

Before he could respond, I heard shouts coming from beyond the beach, and I stared as about a dozen figures charged down the winding path towards us. "By the Fae," Marcus muttered.

A gunshot sounded, and my eyes narrowed. *Since when do the guards here have guns?* "Stop!" one of them demanded. "Nobody move, or we'll start shooting!" Most of the assembled krossemages shrank back in fear.

"You and Trina get everyone through the portal," Marcus told me. "We'll take care of the guards."

"I'll go to the barn and see if the folks watching the other guards need help," Willem said. "Don't wait for me. When everyone is through the portal, send this off." He handed something to Marcus and teleported away before any of us could protest.

"Magikai, on me!" Kip yelled. "Like we practiced."

Another shot sounded, and Kip sent the guard's gun flying with a wave of his hand. Saray mumbled a spell, and a wall of fire sprang up between our group and the guards. "Try shooting us through *that*," she said.

A fellow whose name I didn't know touched Kip's shoulder and rendered him invisible. Seconds later, arrows flew from high in a nearby tree, over the fire and into the cluster of guards.

I watched as several bats flew out of another tree then, and dove viciously at the guards. A pair of owls joined the fray too, gliding in from a different direction, talons poised. A few of the guards began screaming.

"Nice work." I grinned at Trina. "Now let's get these folks out of here."

"This way, everyone!" I called out and hurried for the portal, Shawnie and

Alisa trailing after me. Trina and Starla followed close behind, and Starla turned to sign to the rest of the teenagers, encouraging them to follow.

The teens came more readily than the adults, staring into the portal with wide eyes. Many of the grownups hung back, huddled together, signing frantically among themselves, while several others joined in the fight, using their talents to assist our team. "You go first," I said to Trina. "I'll make sure everyone gets through."

Trina nodded and led her mother into the portal. Shawnie poked the colourful mist with his finger before venturing in, and Alisa followed immediately after. Kaden went next, giving me a long glance before disappearing into the mist. The rest of the teens followed hesitantly, some glancing back at the fighting before they disappeared.

"The guards are all down," Jasper reported. "There were only a dozen or so of them; no signs of anyone else coming."

"Wonderful," I said. "Let's get the rest of these folks to Dundere."

The last of the krossemages made their way through the portal, and Marcus and I were left on the other side, staring at one another. "Well," he said, "I'd call this a success, even if some of the adults were uncertain about it."

I nodded. The ones who had called me a traitor were the last to go through the portal, but even they'd acquiesced when they realized what their alternatives were. "Is that everyone?"

"I haven't seen Willem or the fellows watching the barn yet," Marcus said. "But Willem did say to go ahead without him."

"Right." I knew Alvin was among the folks in the barn and couldn't help but wonder how he'd fared.

Marcus produced the item that Willem had given him, which I now saw was a flare. He lit it and plunged it into the ground, then I followed Marcus through the portal's strange, swirling mist.

Lachlann was waiting for us when we reached the other side. "Welcome back," he said to us. "Who's left over there?"

"Just Willem and a few others who are keeping an eye on the guards," Marcus told him. "They'll be along shortly."

"I'll wait for them. You folks head up to the school."

I found Shawnie, Alisa and Kaden huddled together in the dining hall, drinking the tea that was provided to them. The room was packed with rescued krossemages; most of them signed excitedly amongst themselves or nervously studied the Dundere folks who circulated with drinks and blankets. Sophie was one of the blanket distributors, but I noticed she was moving mechanically, stifling yawns and clearly trying to stay awake. Starla sat near my friends, her arm around Trina, and Saray and Kip leaned against the wall next to them, both looking exhausted.

I sat down next to my friends, grinning. "I can't believe you're here! Just wait 'til you meet Noelle tomorrow. She'll get you all healed up, and we'll have so much fun together!"

They all smiled and nodded, but their smiles were bland, confused. My mind went back to the night Jasper had rescued me so many months ago. "Sorry, I'm a little excited. You must all be really overwhelmed."

Alisa nodded and rested her head on Shawnie's shoulder; Shawnie looked like he was about to pass out from exhaustion. Kaden glanced around the room and frowned. *"Are you sure these people are safe?"*

I nodded. "Absolutely. They've done nothing but help me. You can trust them." I noticed Jasper walking across the floor to us and waved him over, then began making introductions. I didn't miss the way Kip eyed him as he spoke to my friends. Saray, it seemed, had fallen asleep on Kip's shoulder and was unbothered by Jasper's presence for once.

"How did your brother get you off the island?" Shawnie asked me. *"Did he use a portal as well?"*

I laughed. "No, Jasper doesn't use magic." I glanced at my brother then. "Why don't you explain?"

As Jasper began talking, Lachlann came into the room and waved Marcus over. I noticed the concerned look on Lachlann's face as they spoke. When they were finished, Marcus headed outside, and Lachlann walked up to the podium. "Welcome to Dundere, folks," he addressed the room. "I'm Lachlann. Tomorrow, the governor will be here to talk to you about your stay in Dundere. I'm just going to let you know what's happening tonight."

He filled everyone in on the dorm arrangement and tomorrow's breakfast, as well as their meeting with Noelle. "You're safe here," he concluded. "Now, go get some rest."

"You can come stay with me, Mother," Trina said as we got to our feet.

Starla frowned and turned to Alisa. *"Are you all right with watching the younger girls tonight?"*

"Absolutely. Go stay with your daughter." Alisa gave me a smile then. *"We'd best get some sleep."*

I nodded. "Do you want me to stay with you girls tonight?"

"I think we're all right. Not sure how much room there is anyway." She reached forward and embraced me. *"I've missed you, Ruby. We'll see you tomorrow."*

I watched as she, Kaden and Shawnie followed the others down the long hall that led to the dorms. Marcus returned to the room and was talking with Lachlann again; only now did I realize what they were likely concerned about. "Where's Willem?"

Both Kip and Saray, who'd since woken up but looked incredibly sleepy, frowned at my question. "Maybe he went home from the island," Saray suggested. "He doesn't live in Dundere, why would he come back here?"

"There were a few others with him. Alvin and another vanisher whose name I don't know. Willem went to check on them at the barn."

Saray's nose wrinkled. "Alvin? Good riddance."

I ignored her comment and went to join Marcus and Lachlann where they were talking. I repeated my question there, and Lachlann sighed. "We aren't sure what's happened to Willem, or the others who were with him. The portal closed before they got back. Marcus and I can't figure out why."

"It could be that Willem closed it from his side, or that the spell failed,"

Marcus put in. "Either way, he and the others aren't coming back to Dundere tonight."

"Do you think they'll be all right?" I asked. "What if they were attacked by the guards?"

"If anyone can handle themselves in a fight, it's Willem. I'm fairly certain that the guards on Yarel Island don't have anti-magic, so I don't know what they could do to overpower him. I wouldn't worry too much, Ruby."

It was Alvin, not Willem, who I was worried about, but I shrugged. "If you say so."

"We should head home," Marcus said. "Looks like Starla will be coming with us. I'm so happy for Trina."

Lachlann nodded. "Me too. Of all the places for her mother to be…" He glanced across the room and smiled. "I wonder what happened to her?"

"I'm sure we'll find out soon enough. Let's close this place up for the night and go home. Tomorrow's going to be busy."

CHAPTER 19

THE FOLLOWING MORNING, I came downstairs to excited chatter. When I reached the parlour, I discovered that Noelle had already begun healing. Starla's missing hand and foot were completely restored, and Noelle's hands were currently placed on Starla's face, thumbs positioned under her jaw and fingertips pressed into her forehead. Trina hovered nearby holding a small mirror, her eyes wide.

"All right, I'm done," Noelle declared. "Are you ready to see the results?"

Starla nodded and opened her eyes, and Trina let out a squeal of delight. Now that her burns were healed, I could immediately see the resemblance between Starla and Trina. I'd already noticed that they shared the same wide brown eyes and heart-shaped face, but now I also noticed similarities in their noses and eyebrows.

Starla looked into Trina's mirror for a few long seconds. She ran her fingertips over her now-smooth cheek and gave her reflection a smile— the first smile I'd seen from her that wasn't lopsided— then swiped at her eyes. "Thank you," she said to Noelle. Her speech was slurred but coherent, and her voice was perhaps a bit deeper than I'd expected. Her gaze shifted to Marcus and then back to Noelle. "Thank you both. For taking care of my girl. I can't believe she was here of all places…" Her voice broke, and Trina put an arm around her.

"Do you want me to heal up any of your other scars?" Noelle asked, gesturing to what was still visible on Starla's neck and left forearm.

She shook her head. "I'll keep those. As a reminder of what I've overcome."

"Which is what, exactly?" I asked.

She met my eyes. "It's a very long story, but it's one that some of you need to hear. Perhaps I can tell you tomorrow, once I'm more used to speaking."

"All right," replied Noelle. "I should get over to the school. I have a long day ahead of me."

Starla looked up to meet my eyes, smiling and waving her newly formed hand at me. "It feels strange, doesn't it?" I said.

She nodded.

"Have you tried the raspberry syrup yet?"

Her eyes narrowed, and Trina clapped her hands. Marcus stood, grinning. "I'll be right back," he said. "Starla, you're going to enjoy this."

About an hour later, I arrived at the school of magic with Trina and Starla. We passed by a classroom full of magikai engaged in a spell that had them all in a circle. I noticed Saray, Kip, and Chase among them. Noelle was in the centre, and she appeared to be glowing slightly.

The gymnasium was full of krossemages again, most of them sitting in small clusters or finishing up breakfast. Several young people gasped when they saw Starla, and moments later, she was being flocked by rapidly signing teenagers. A younger girl named Hazel grabbed Starla's hand and began examining it; Alisa shyly touched Starla's cheek, marvelling at the now-smooth skin. Shawnie sidled up next to me. *"This is incredible,"* he signed.

I nodded. "Soon it'll be your turn."

"Were you nervous when you got healed?"

"I was," I assured. "It's normal." I spotted Kaden on the other side of the room, caught her eye and waved. She looked immediately away and began talking to another girl. *What's gotten into her?*

"I'll be right back," I said to Shawnie, weaving my way over to tug on Kaden's sleeve. "Can we talk outside for a moment?"

Her eyes narrowed, but she nodded.

Kaden followed me out, and we sat down nearby on some steps. "Are you all right?" I asked.

She shrugged. *"As all right as I can be. Why?"*

"You don't seem like yourself. I thought you'd be thrilled to see me, Kaden, but it feels like you're avoiding me. I know you're probably a little overwhelmed right now, but aren't you happy?"

She stared off into the distance for a moment before turning to me and beginning to sign. *"I'm happy that you're safe. I'm glad you brought me here and that I'm going to get healed. But I'm angry at you."*

"Why?"

"Because you left.*"* She let out a huff. *"We had a plan to run off together, and you abandoned that plan to go with your brother. You abandoned* me.*"*

I felt the blood drain from my face. *She really is mad.* "Kaden, I wasn't trying to abandon you. I wanted to bring you along. But Jasper dragged me out of the farmhouse before I could explain."

"You could've just told him you wouldn't go," she countered.

"And not take my one chance at freedom?"

"So you'd choose your freedom over me, then."

I shook my head. "I can't believe this. I understand why you're mad that I didn't bring you along, but to suggest I should have just stayed? If I had, we might all be dead in a few months!"

"Forget it." Kaden stood. *"I need some space. Just leave me alone for now, all right?"* She stalked off towards the main hall, leaving me staring after her in a daze.

I didn't return to the gymnasium for a good ten minutes. All I could do was sit against the side of the school, trying to wrap my head around Kaden's reaction.

When I heard Noelle begin to address the krossemages, I came inside to listen to her announce that the teens would all be healed today. She dismissed us soon after, and the adults dispersed, some of them heading back to the dorms and others signing to one another about going out to explore the city.

I sat in a corner, blinking back tears, and watched as the teens formed a long, nervous line against the wall next to an adjoining office where the healings would take place. Starla and Trina moved amongst them, reassuring them that the healings would be quick and painless. Trina shot a concerned look my way, and I knew I should join them, but I was too busy trying not to cry.

Skye, a girl I didn't know very well, was the first to enter the office, and she soon emerged, grinning and showing off her new hand. The rest of the lineup burst into throaty cheers, and I couldn't help but grin.

I didn't see Kaden when she got healed; she left the gymnasium for the dorms immediately. Alisa and Shawnie came to find me after their own healings, eager to show off their new hands and give talking a try. "My tongue feels huge," Alisa slurred, her voice high and a bit reedy.

I pushed down my sadness and laughed. "Trust me, your tongue is completely normal. Did they give you the raspberry syrup?"

She nodded and grinned again. "It was amazing."

Shawnie frowned. "Are you all right, Ruby?" he asked, his own words coming out equally slurred. His voice was deep and rich and had a slight melodic lilt to it.

"Kaden and I had a bit of a fight. I didn't realize how mad she was at me for leaving."

They exchanged a knowing glance. "I'll go talk to her," Alisa said.

She wandered off in search of Kaden, and Shawnie and I began walking through the gymnasium to check on the others. Sophie had been given the task of distributing the raspberry syrup; she gave it out eagerly while admiring the hands of the newly healed teens and telling them how wonderful their lives here would be. Marcus was busy showing several young people how to increase the strength in their hands. I saw that Hilda and Carmine, who had also made the journey out, were talking and signing with several of the former krossemages.

Lachlann showed up just as lunch was being served, and Trina dragged Starla over to him so she could show off Noelle's handiwork. Seeing Lachlann brought my concerns about Alvin back to the forefront of my mind, and I wandered over to him, Shawnie in tow.

Starla brightened when she saw us, and she took Shawnie's new hand in hers to examine it. "How does it feel?"

"A bit strange," Shawnie slurred. He then looked Lachlann over. "Why hasn't Noelle healed you?"

"Oh." Lachlann glanced down at his metal hand. "That's a bit of a story."

"Any idea yet what's happened to Willem and the others?" I asked.

"Unfortunately, no." Lachlann shook his head. "If we don't hear from them by tomorrow, I'll have Kip go to Willem's place through the portal and see if he's there." He gave me a reassuring smile. "I'm sure they're fine, Ruby. You just need to be patient. They'll show up eventually."

The cooks made a massive meal for the teens' dinner. Noelle, Marcus, Trina and Starla all headed back to the house, but I decided to stick around and watch my friends' reactions to the food. Alisa ate hers slowly, savouring each bite before commenting how delicious it was. Shawnie ate quicker, sampling small portions of nearly everything on the table. Kaden had returned to us, but she sat on the other side of Alisa and ignored me.

In the middle of dessert, one of the side doors to the gymnasium swung open, and I let out a gasp as Willem walked through, followed by Alvin and the other vanisher whose name I'd forgotten. Lachlann went immediately over to them, clapped Willem on the shoulder, and began chatting with him. I hastily finished my pie, ran over to Alvin, and threw my arms around him.

He gasped, then chuckled and returned my embrace. "Hi," he said, his tone uncertain.

"I was so worried about you."

"You…were?"

I nodded, my voice wavering as I spoke. "I thought you might be dead."

He pulled back and looked me over. "Well, I assure you, I am very much alive."

"What happened?"

"That's quite a tale. Do you want to go for a walk and chat about it?"

I hesitated for just a second, then nodded. "Sure. But shouldn't you be getting home to let your folks know you're alive?"

"They can wait." He eyed the table. "I wouldn't mind some dinner before we go. Is there enough left over?"

"Should be," I said to him. "Come on, I'll introduce you to my friends."

When he finished eating, Alvin and I sat up on the roof of the school in the same spot where we'd had our first date. Dark clouds sat on the horizon, and the air was heavy with the promise of coming rain. The silence between us felt heavy too. For once, Alvin was not rushing to fill it with his words. When he spoke, his voice was hesitant. "I was a little surprised at your reaction to seeing me."

"So was I," I admitted. "I was so scared that something awful had happened to you. Lachlann assured me I didn't need to worry because you were with Willem, but Willem's just one man. Things could have gone horribly wrong."

Alvin nodded. "They did go wrong. That's why we got stuck behind."

"What happened? Did the guards wake up?"

"Not at first. Those guards who attacked your group by the portal were working in an underground food storage area that Willem didn't know about. Everyone else was still contained and asleep in the barn at that point. By the time Willem got to us, though, a few of the guards in the barn were beginning to wake. Willem, Jackson and I incapacitated them, but we'd only just gotten them back to sleep when more began to wake up. Willem realized we were in over our heads, so we did everything we could to just hold the guards off. When Willem saw the flare, he left Jackson and me to fight while he closed the portal. Then he grabbed us and teleported away, to the outskirts of the Shrouded Woods. I think he meant to send us all the way to the portal near his house, but we didn't make it that far." He frowned. "Willem…ran out of magic."

My eyebrows arched. "What? I didn't think that could happen to someone like Willem."

"Me neither. Apparently, holding the portal open for that long took a lot more magic than we thought, and then having to fight those guards and teleport us out— it was all too much. So the three of us ended up stopping to rest for a few hours. Even after that, Willem was very tired and grumpy. He seemed to think it was Kip's fault that he ran out of magic, though I'm not sure why." He shrugged. "So

Willem blew on this whistle, and about ten minutes later, a fellow named Ambrose showed up on a *dragon*."

"Ah." I grinned. "I met Ambrose and Spark when I was in the Shrouded Woods with Kip."

Alvin nodded. "Apparently, he and Spark have a sort of taxi service in the Woods that folks can access with these special whistles. I have one now, too." He pulled a small wooden whistle out of his pocket and showed it to me. "The ride was pretty terrifying at first."

"Why? You're obviously not afraid of heights." I gestured at the drop-off below us.

"It wasn't the heights that scared me, it was the fact that I was riding a *dragon*. My brother used to tell me that the dragons in the Shrouded Woods sometimes eat people. I asked Ambrose about it, and he told us he'd heard stories of folks being fed to dragons as punishment hundreds of years ago. But he said that he has very good control of Spark." Alvin grinned. "Did you know that there are actually about two dozen dragons living in the Shrouded Woods, but they all live in a region to the north where there aren't many humans?"

I nodded. "Ambrose told me all that."

"Anyway, there were a few scary moments when Ambrose lost contact with Spark, and she started to go the wrong way. But eventually they flew us to this ridge, and soon enough we were at Willem's place. It's odd though, I can't quite remember how to get there anymore."

"Me neither. He likes to keep the location of his home a secret."

"Too bad, because it was incredible! Jackson and I got to use his bathing pool while he cooked us something to eat, and we had an amazing lunch. Then Willem said that he desperately needed a nap before we could go any further. We all ended up sleeping for a few hours."

I snorted. "Here we were, worried about you folks, and you were bathing and napping?"

"That's right." Alvin smirked. "So after all that, we left his house and went through the portal, and here we are!" He raised an eyebrow. "You were really worried about me, huh?"

"Yes." I glanced at him out of the corner of my eye, my cheeks beginning to burn. "I was."

He sighed. "You know, Ruby, I think I may have overreacted last week. I understand why you were scared to be with me after what happened to your brother." He gave me a small smile. "I'd love to be friends with you, if you think we can make that work."

My eyes narrowed. "Funny, because I've been thinking that *I* overreacted."

"Really?"

I nodded. "I'm still a bit worried about Aidan and his grudge toward Jasper. But I realized that if I let those fears control my relationship with you, then I'm letting him *win*."

Alvin's lips parted, and he began to fiddle with his hair nervously. "So…you'd be willing to give us another chance?"

"I think so. We'd have to be careful to keep it secret though. And I want to take it slow this time. Like I said, I felt like things were moving too fast when we were in your bedroom. I like kissing and all, but I'm not quite ready for anything beyond that."

Alvin nodded, his green-gold eyes sparkling. "I think we can make that work."

"One more thing," I said to him. "I might not be able to go on as many dates with you over the next few weeks as you'd like. I need to spend some time with my friends from the island. I've missed them."

He nodded. "Your friends seem nice. Can I spend time with them as well?"

"That'd be lovely!" Then I frowned. "Though things are a little tense between Kaden and me right now."

"Why?"

I explained to Alvin what had transpired between us earlier, and he shook his head. "Sounds like she's being a touch unreasonable. Maybe I should talk to her."

"Why would she listen to you?"

"I can be persuasive." He slipped an arm around me and gave me a little squeeze. "So, question for you."

"Yes?"

"You said you like kissing, but you don't want to go further." He grinned and tucked his hair behind his ear. "May I kiss you now?"

I felt my heart begin to race, and I smiled up at him. "By all means."

Alvin leaned down and trailed a finger across my jawline, then he tilted my chin up slightly. His lips on mine were gentle this time; there was none of the earlier ferocity. I leaned into him, feeling all the tension of the last few days beginning to dissipate. After about a minute, he pulled away and pressed his forehead against mine. "It's good to have you back, Ruby," he murmured.

I couldn't agree more.

CHAPTER 20

THE FOLLOWING MORNING, I wandered downstairs to discover that the family was eating breakfast in the garden. Kip had forgone his usual weekend excursion to the Shrouded Woods because of the rescue, and he and Saray were lying back in the grass, both of them still obviously tired from the weekend's events. Starla was eating her breakfast slowly, savouring each bite, while chatting with Marcus about ways to strengthen her hand. Trina waved me over.

Noelle had finished eating and was examining a patch of petunias that appeared to be going brown. "Not sure what these need."

"I can help," Starla offered.

"With the garden?"

She nodded. "Watch."

Rising from where she'd sat eating, Starla walked over to the flowers, closed her eyes and mumbled a spell. We all looked on as the flowers began to straighten themselves. Their horn-like blooms opened, petals turning vibrant shades of pink, red, and purple once again, and their leaves became green and plump. "Just need more water," Starla said. "This has been a dry summer."

"You can talk to plants!" Trina exclaimed. "Like Carmine."

"Carmine?" Starla frowned. "Oh, yes, Hilda's wife. I met her yesterday. Lovely woman. I didn't realize we shared the same talent. Do you want to see more of what I can do?"

We all nodded, and Starla gestured to a long, trailing vine that crawled up a nearby lattice. The vine detached itself and bent toward her, wrapping snugly around her legs and hips. A second flick of the wrist caused the vines to retract from her body and return to where they'd originally rested. "You see how I could use this to fight people. It can be handy in a…" She paused and tilted her head, then we watched as she made her way over to Kirilee's tree. "Now this," she said, "is unique."

"What do you mean?" asked Trina.

"Most plants can think and feel more than people realize," Starla explained. "But it's fairly basic intelligence. They can talk to me about the weather or what they might need. And trees are especially smart; they can communicate with one another through their root systems." She stared up at the viletta in front of her. "But this tree is different. It seems to have…a human soul."

Trina and Saray both gasped, and Saray sat up. "Can you…talk to the soul? Does it have a name?"

Starla nodded. "Does the name Kirilee mean something to you?"

Trina let out a shriek.

"I knew it!" Saray squealed. "I knew she was in there! I was right, and so was…" She clapped her hands over her mouth for a moment before removing them to whisper, "By the Fae. Someone needs to go get Lachlann!"

Kip's eyes narrowed; he seemed less excited by this news than the girls. "She's not trapped in there, is she?"

Starla inclined her head again for a moment, then shook it. "No. She struck a deal with Hilda before she died. She and Carmine cast a spell that allows her soul ten years in the tree before moving to the next world, since she was concerned about all of you and wanted to keep an eye on things for a bit. Though she can leave earlier if she wants."

"Hilda and Carmine *knew?*" Marcus exclaimed. "And they didn't *tell* us?"

"Kirilee didn't want you folks to know at first. She wanted you to be able to grieve and move on. Though she hoped you'd figure it out eventually."

Marcus chuckled. "Sounds like something she'd do." He approached the tree, put a hand on the trunk, and smiled fondly up at it. "Hello, Mother. Back to your old tricks, I see?"

Starla frowned. "Kirilee is your mother?"

"My mother, Saray's grandmother, and, well, she has connections to all of us here. You included, actually."

"What are they?"

"Ask her yourself."

"Right." She stared up into the tree's boughs for a couple of minutes, occasionally frowning and nodding. Then she sighed. "I never thought I'd say this after everything she did to me, but poor Maeva. No wonder she was so fearful."

Kip's eyes narrowed. "What did she do to you?"

"That's a story for another time."

He frowned then. "Can I talk to Kirilee? I've some things I need to ask."

Starla nodded. "Go ahead."

"Can she hear what I'm saying, or do you need to speak to her for me?"

"She can hear you if you're close to the trunk."

Kip placed a tentative hand on the tree. "Hi, uh, Kirilee," he said, somewhat awkwardly. "First of all, thank you for…for saving my life back there. And second, well, I'm having some problems with your magic."

We all listened carefully as Kip recounted the issues with sleep casting that he'd been having and the damage he found done to things when he woke up. "I have no idea what to do," he concluded. "And no one else seems to either. I'm not sure if you'd have any ideas, but if you do…" His shoulders sagged. "Please help."

Starla studied Kip for a moment, then inclined her head again. "She's not completely sure," she said finally, "but she thinks that it might be because your magic is now connected to the fairies. She says that you should talk to Hilda and see if she can help you out."

"Hilda." Kip nodded. "I hadn't thought of that."

"Also," Starla went on, "she's incredibly proud of you for adapting to your magic like you have, and she's thrilled for you and Saray to get married." She glanced over at Saray and then at Trina too. "She's proud of all of you, and she has things to say to each of you. As well as to…Lachlann, was it? I spoke with him yesterday, right?"

Trina nodded. "That's right." She turned to me. "Could you go fetch him, Ruby? He should be at home. Don't tell him what's happening— I want it to be a surprise."

I nodded, understanding that the family wanted some time alone with their old friend. "Sure." Then I stood, stared at the tree one last time, and headed out of the backyard.

When I returned later, it was with a rather confused Lachlann in tow. On my way over to his place, it had occurred to me that perhaps Alexander's gift for him had been meant for this very encounter, so I asked him to bring it along.

Saray and Trina's faces both lit up at the sight of him. "Hello, girls," he said. "What's going on? I hear there's an animal of some sort I might need to talk to?" He fingered the ring he wore.

"Not an animal," Trina said. "You remember my mother, right?"

Lachlann smiled. "Of course. Good to see you again, Starla."

"Mother, tell him what you can do."

Lachlann listened as Starla explained her gift to him. "What Trina wants me to tell you," she concluded, "is that there is a human spirit living in that tree. A spirit named Kirilee. She's been talking to me, giving me messages to pass on to the girls and to Kip, and...now she wants to speak to you."

He stared at her for a moment, dumbfounded, his eyes wide. Then he turned to Trina. "You swear this is real?"

She nodded eagerly. "Mother didn't even know Kirilee's name when she approached the tree. She doesn't know why we're so excited for you to talk to her, either."

"And she gave me advice on how to deal with my sleep casting," Kip put in. "Advice that Aunt Starla couldn't have known on her own. This is real, Lachlann."

Lachlann nodded slowly, eyes still wide. Then he walked over to the tree and put a hand on its trunk. "Well, now," he finally said, "I knew you were in there."

"She was very fond of you, wasn't she?" Starla said from behind him. Then she drew in a breath. "Wait. Were you...married to Kirilee?"

He turned to her and nodded. "I was."

"Well, what she's asking me to tell you makes a bit more sense then."

"Wait," I said. "Don't tell him anything yet. Let's see if Alexander's charm works."

"Ah, yes." Lachlann produced the amulet from his pocket. "I think you might be right about what it was meant for, Ruby."

"What's that?" Starla asked.

Lachlann explained Alexander's gift to her. Then he unclasped the pendant's chain and fastened it around one of the tree's limbs.

The effect was instantaneous. I felt the jolt of magic reverberate off the tree; it appeared, just for a moment, to be engulfed by lightning, and its blossoms flared a luminescent pink-white. Lachlann gasped, his eyes widening, and I saw the same pink-white brilliance flash in them for just a moment. Then he stared at the tree, his mouth agape. "I can...I can hear her," he whispered.

"What's she saying?" Trina asked.

Lachlann paused, closing his eyes as he listened, then he took a deep, shuddering breath. "She says that she loves me dearly, but that I can't stay married to a tree. She says I need to move on, to stop grieving her."

Starla nodded. "As someone who also lost my spouse many years ago, I know it can be hard to let go."

"I…" Lachlann pressed his forehead to the trunk of the tree. "She's right," he finally said, his voice catching. "*You're* right, Kirilee." He stared up into the tangled branches, then turned back to Starla. "She can hear me?"

"If you're close by, yes. Though with that pendant of yours, I imagine you won't need to speak out loud to communicate with her unless you want to."

He nodded. "I still love you," he said softly to the tree. "But you're right. I know you wouldn't want me to spend my life mourning. You told me that much the night you died."

Noelle cleared her throat softly and ushered us aside. "Let's give Lachlann some time alone with Kirilee, shall we? I need to head back to the school."

"All right." Starla nodded. "I owe you folks a story anyway; perhaps I'll tell it when we all gather for lunch." She cocked her head again one more time, listening to something she heard from within the tree. "Ah," she said. "Kip, Kirilee would like to speak with you alone later on. She says to borrow Lachlann's ring."

Kip nodded. "Will do." Then we all followed Noelle into the house, leaving Lachlann and Kirilee alone.

True to her word, Starla informed us at lunch that she was ready to explain everything that had happened to her. "This story is painful," she began. "It will be very hard for you to hear, Trina, but it will be harder for Kip." She met his eyes. "I suspect you may want nothing to do with me after I tell you this. And if that's the case, I'll accept it." She sighed. "You two aren't full cousins. Your fathers were half brothers, born fifteen years apart. And I'm seven years younger than Trina's father. So when I married Daryn, it always felt like Kailann and Maeva— Kip's parents— were like an aunt and uncle rather than siblings. I liked Kailann; he seemed like a strong and kind man. However, I didn't know what to make of Maeva. She was usually polite and kind, but she was very fearful. And any mention of magic made her panic and become irrational— Daryn eventually told me what happened to Maeva's sister, and after that, her fears made sense. Anyway, the two of them didn't have children until well into their thirties; I think they'd had some trouble conceiving. But when we had Trina, I was thrilled that her cousins were only a little older than her.

"Our families spent a lot of time together, so the pox hit us all at once. This particular strain didn't hurt children much, but we adults were sick for weeks. Maeva and I survived; our husbands did not. And losing Kailann left Maeva unhinged. It was my idea to sell the house that Daryn and I owned and move in with her, partly for my own security, but also to ensure that you and Kelvin were cared for." She glanced at Kip.

"A few months later, I noticed Maeva coming and going from the house at odd hours, leaving the children with me. Her views on magic became even more stringent; she'd rave about how magic users were animals to be hunted down for sport. Of course, I kept my own talent well hidden." She eyed Trina. "Unfortunately, Maeva noticed your gift before I did, when she caught you talking to Bailey." She looked around the table. "I assume you folks know what happened after this?"

We all nodded.

"All right then, I'll spare you the details. But after Trina was attacked, I took her and ran to the only doctor I knew. He cared for her for a month, and neither of us was sure she'd even survive at first. We were both relieved when we realized she'd only lost her sight."

She turned to Trina. "It was the doctor's idea to send you to Sylvenburgh Academy. He had contacts there. It seemed like the best option. I couldn't take you back to Maeva's, and I didn't know where else we'd live. So I gave you up to the Academy. It broke my heart, but I couldn't see another way to protect you."

Trina nodded and slipped her hand into her mother's.

"Between the doctor's bill and the tuition for the Academy, though, I found myself nearly broke," Starla continued. "So now I was truly trapped. I went back to Maeva's and settled into life there.

"About a year passed, and during that time I learned why Maeva had been sneaking out at night. Seems she'd gotten involved with a group of people called the Witch Slayers, who took their hatred of magic users to an extreme. They saw us as animals to be used and tormented and eventually killed. They wanted to make us hurt. Maeva occasionally held meetings at our house. I doubt that she would've attacked Trina if it wasn't for their influence."

Kip let out a breath. "That explains a few things. We've heard about these Witch Slayers recently. They sound truly evil."

"They were," Starla replied. "And Maeva eventually became suspicious; she assumed, rightly, that Trina got her magic from me. And while I was normally very diligent about hiding my gift, I'd been using my magic very subtly to keep the garden thriving, since I knew Maeva was very proud of her plants. One evening, she walked outside just as I spoke to a drooping sunflower, and it straightened right up. That's how she found out. I ran from the house, and she alerted the Breoch Guard. They caught me, and, well, we all know what happened next."

We nodded, and my eyes closed against the memories of waking up without my hand and tongue.

"But things didn't go as I expected. The Guard allowed Maeva to buy me back as a krossemage. She got rid of the other servants and put me to work. And she was cruel to me, of course. She barely fed me, made me do the most disgusting chores, called me names and beat me. Worse still, she began bringing me to her Witch Slayer meetings, to be a plaything for the others." She stared down at her food. "I won't get into all the things that happened, but they were horrific. And after nearly a year, I...snapped." She sighed. "I was outside tending to the rose bushes late one spring evening with a torch nearby for light. Maeva came to get me for a meeting, and I shrunk back and began to cry. I didn't realize it, but I called out for help inside my head." She looked at Trina. "Now, you may have realized that folks who talk to plants and animals have our own sort of mind casting. We don't have to say special words to talk to them, it just happens."

Trina nodded.

"When I called for help, the plants heard me, and they decided by their own will to respond. The rose bushes grew around me in a massive, thorny tangle, so Maeva couldn't get to me. She began screaming and cursing, and then she grabbed the torch, threw it at the rose bushes and set them ablaze." Starla shuddered. "I hacked at them and screamed and, somehow, made it out alive with my clothes and hair on fire. And then I ran. Maeva caught up to me near the front of the house and tackled me. I called out to the plants again, and the ivy growing on the side of the house reached out and wrapped around her. It began to strangle her, and it didn't stop even after she fell unconscious. That's how she died." She met Kip's eyes as she spoke. He stared back at her for a moment, sighed deeply, and put his head in his hands.

An awkward silence descended as we all waited for him to respond; when he didn't say anything, Trina took Starla's hand. "What happened after that?"

"I don't remember all of it. I blacked out from pain soon after Maeva died. When I awoke next, I was in a prison cell being tended to by doctors. After I'd healed up a bit, I was asked to write down my account of what happened that night, then I was taken before a judge. I thought I'd be executed— not only for killing Maeva, but for my ability to cast despite being a krossemage. But the judge took pity on me. He said I'd suffered a lot already and sentenced me to spend the rest of my life on the farm.

"I don't think the folks at the farm knew what to do with me. My one foot was so badly burned that they'd amputated it, so I was learning to walk with a peg leg, and I was all scarred up. So they put me in charge of the girls, and that was one of the best things that happened to me in those days." She turned to me. "It was healing for me, taking care of you all. I feel like I was robbed of being a mother. I dreamed of having a big family, but I only had one child, and I didn't even see most of Trina's childhood. So taking care of others helped fill that void."

"I'm glad we were able to help you heal." I smiled.

"Me too. My life on the farm was not so terrible. But I endured awful things to get there, and I did awful things, too." She sighed. "I've tried to tell myself that it was the plant who killed Maeva, not me. I summoned it, though, and I likely could have called it off. But I was in too much shock and pain to think about that." She turned toward Kip. "As I said before, Kip, if you want nothing to do with me, I understand."

Kip finally met her eyes. He was holding back tears, but when he spoke, his voice was firm. "You acted in self-defense. I can't begrudge you that. I likely would've done the same thing." He shook his head. "In honesty, the thing that hurts me most isn't that Mother is dead, or that you killed her, it's knowing that she became so cruel and hateful in the end."

Starla nodded. "Maeva's paranoia about magic made sense, given what happened to her. But she let that fear take her to evil people who twisted it into something terrible. There are good and bad ways to handle fear, and she chose the latter."

"It's a good thing I met Saray and Trina when I did. I can see myself having gone down a similar path without them. I hated magic users once too, you know."

"I'm glad you didn't go that direction." She gave him a small smile. "I would like to have a good relationship with you, Kip. You and Kelvin were like sons to me at one point. But I know that can't happen unless you're willing to forgive me, and that's your choice to make, not mine."

"Well, given that I managed to forgive the person who killed my aunt in a magic accident, perhaps I can also find it in myself to forgive the person who killed my mother in self-defense." He gave her a tense smile and then sighed. "Right now, though, I think I need some time alone. Between this and my earlier talk with Kirilee, I've got a lot to think about." He stood and left without further comment.

Starla sighed. "I suppose that was the best reaction I could hope for."

"He'll come around," Saray assured her. "He always does. I think you're incredibly brave, personally."

"And I think the same of you, after hearing your story earlier." Starla smiled at her. "Though you'll have to forgive me if I act a bit skittish around you. I'm quite afraid of fire, you know."

"That makes sense. I'll keep my gift as far from you as I can."

We all went our separate ways after that, but my mind stayed on Starla's story for several hours. Next to what she'd been through, my present conflicts with my friends seemed miniscule. *If Starla had the strength to endure all that she did, then certainly I can handle a bit of aloofness from Kaden,* I decided.

Nonetheless, I hoped that she would be willing to talk to me soon enough.

CHAPTER 21

AN UNEXPECTED WEATHER system blew in that afternoon. I spent the remainder of the day and a few days afterwards helping the stormbrewers at the lighthouse. I ended up sleeping in quite late the day after all that was done, so I didn't get a chance to return to the school of magic until late that afternoon. Most of the adults had been healed by that point, and the halls were filled with excited folk trying out their new hands and alternating between signing and slurred speech. A few of the adults were showing off their gifts as well; I saw a woman who had to be at least sixty laughing like a child as she blinked in and out of teleportation, a younger man shapeshifting into various animals while his friends watched, and a fellow who scared a woman while he was invisible, only to reappear, burst into laughter, and kiss her. I grinned as I watched them; I'd only been without my hand, tongue, and magic for a handful of months. I could only imagine the glee that would come with having those things restored after years or even decades.

There was also a group of adults who had decided not to be healed, and they sat together watching the others, signing among themselves and tentatively trying to cast with their left hands.

Alisa, Kaden and Shawnie were seated in the courtyard, enjoying the sun. Kaden stood when she saw me, and my stomach knotted. *Is she going to run off again?* Instead, she gave me a tentative smile. "Can we go somewhere and talk?"

"Uh, sure," I stammered. "We could take a walk down to the beach."

She nodded, and we set off walking.

Kaden was silent for a while, looking around with wide eyes as she followed me through busy streets and then down a rocky, winding path. We reached the beach and seated ourselves on a large, fallen piece of driftwood.

I looked at her expectantly, my heart beginning to pound, and she peered out at the ocean. "This place is beautiful," she murmured.

I nodded. "I love it here."

"I see why you do." She fell silent for a few moments more, seeming to be caught in contemplation, before turning back to me and clearing her throat. "So, anyway, I should probably tell you why I wanted to chat. Your friend Alvin came to see me yesterday."

"Did he? What'd he say to you?"

"He wanted me to give you a chance. He explained to me how your brother dragged you away from the island without giving you much time to protest."

"I told you the same thing."

"I know." She shrugged. "Alvin was…persuasive."

I chuckled. "That sounds like him. Did he tell you why it took so long for me to come back?"

She shook her head.

I explained how Lachlann suggested that we make a rescue plan once we reached Dundere, how Willem needed time to scout out the place, and then how, upon learning about the proposed cull, he and the others insisted that I wait until we were ready to execute a full rescue before coming back for Kaden. "Believe me, I wanted to come for you much sooner than we did," I concluded. "But it seemed like everything was working against me. I'm sorry."

She nodded, her shoulders hunched. "Things changed a lot after you left, you know."

"What do you mean?"

"Well, word spread about you like wildfire. No one had escaped the island in years, and they couldn't figure out how you'd done it. It was a little scary. But it was also…inspiring. It showed the rest of us it could be done. And so others began trying to escape. Some of them got away, some didn't. And the ones who didn't were…dealt with." She sighed. "The rules changed too. We weren't allowed to wander around in the evenings anymore, and the guards were grumpy. They'd punish us over the smallest things. I remember them getting mad at the teens because the strawberry patch wasn't bearing enough fruit. As if we could control that."

I nodded, taking in her words. "I'm sorry I put you in that position."

"There's another thing you should know," she continued, "about what happened when I was taken. It might help you understand why I was so angry at you." She sighed. "I can't believe I've never told you this story."

"I think most of us didn't like talking about our pasts on the island," I said. "It hurt too much."

"That's true." She glanced at me. "Do you mind if I switch to signing? I'm not used to speaking for this long; it's getting tiring."

"Go ahead. I understand completely."

She nodded and began. *"I think my upbringing was happier than yours. I was part of a big family, and there was lots of laughter and singing and love. But there was also a very deep fear of magic. I didn't even know I had magic until last year, and my family caught me the very first time I cast. It was by accident, like it often is. We were on a hike, and my gift…just happened. They all saw it. My entire family turned around on their hike, went back to the carriage, told me that I couldn't come with them, and drove off. They left me alone in the woods."*

"Oh, Kaden. That's horrible!"

"I walked until I found my way back into the city, and I lived on the streets for about a week. Then some thugs tried to rob me, and I accidentally cast again to get away. That's when the Breoch Guard took me. My ability is hard to ignore, so everyone saw it."

"What is your ability?"

Kaden smiled at me, almost shyly. "I can fly."

"You can *fly?*"

"It's pretty rare. I think I can make other people fly, too, though I haven't tried it yet."

"You're welcome to try on me," I volunteered.

She nodded, her smile becoming more genuine. "I usually only fly around at night because I don't want to scare people. I've been trying it out since we got here."

"So, you accidentally flew in front of your family?"

She nodded. "I've heard stories about people losing control of their gifts when they're scared or angry. But the first time it happened to me, it was because I was *happy*. I was daydreaming, actually."

"What about?"

Looking sheepish now, she explained, *"Last year, a new girl arrived in my class. She was absolutely gorgeous. I'd had crushes before, but nothing like this.*

"On the day my gift showed up, I got bored with hiking, and I found my mind wandering to her. I was imagining asking her out and kissing her. And I think you can guess what happened."

I raised an eyebrow. "You…floated up into the sky?"

She nodded. *"Then my family abandoned me. Which brings me back to why I was mad at you. When you left, I wondered if you'd done something similar. Does that make sense?"*

"It does. My family abandoned me too, in a way. So I get it."

"What happened to you?"

I told her the story of how Jade turned me in and how Father stood by and watched as I was taken away. Kaden sighed when I was finished explaining it all. "It's amazing how the people we think love us the most can just turn on us like that when they find out we're different."

I nodded in agreement. "I'm sorry I brought those feelings back up for you."

"I should probably apologize too, for assuming the worst about you. And for the way I acted back on the farm."

"What do you mean?"

"I was just…angry. I'm not even sure why you hung out with me." She gave me a slight grin.

I shrugged. "There were plenty of things on that island to be angry about."

"Some of it was a choice, though," she signed. *"I was afraid that if I ever felt happy and ended up daydreaming, I might cast again by accident."*

I frowned. "Wouldn't you *want* to do that? You could've flown away from the island."

"When I cast by accident, I didn't have much control over when it stopped. If I tried to fly away, the spell could break when I was over the water. Anyway, I figured that if I stayed angry, I wouldn't give myself away. If I kept myself from being calm and happy, then I'd be safe."

I bit my lip. "That's…sad."

"It was." She sighed. "I'm naturally a pretty silly person. My parents used to say that I was always bouncing off the walls." Her shoulders hunched. "I probably owe Alisa and Shawnie apologies for being angry as well. They don't know my story."

I eyed her. "It's strange how little we know about one another. For example, I had no idea you liked women," I grinned. "I do too."

"Really?"

"Both men and women, actually. Though right now I'm dating Alvin."

"I wondered if you two were together. I only like women. Boys are gross."

She gave me a wry grin.

"I'm going to tell Shawnie you said that," I teased.

"I wonder if we should tell these stories to him and Alisa."

"That's a good idea. Perhaps they'll share what happened to them as well."

"Maybe." Kaden grinned, stood up and offered me a hand. "Let's go find out."

Later, I sat on a bench in the courtyard with Shawnie, Alisa and Kaden. The sun streamed down on us, and butterflies flitted between brightly coloured flowers. Kaden and I had both told our stories, and now Shawnie and Alisa told us theirs, both of which, interestingly enough, involved using their gifts to handle bear attacks.

Alisa was a teleporter and had run into a bear on the way home from her friend's house one evening. She teleported away, but in her panic forgot to set her destination before casting and ended up teleporting right into a celebration in the town square.

Shawnie had the ability to shapeshift into a cougar and was at the beach with friends when they'd gotten between a mother bear and her cubs. He defended his friends using his gift, only to be turned in by some other folks on the beach.

Shawnie and Alisa, we learned, both grew up in the same farming town of Amberline, and they knew each other casually before all this happened. "Alisa was popular, and I was a nerd, so we never hung out," Shawnie explained. "But I was at the town square the night that she teleported, and I heard about her getting taken away. So when I ended up on the farm myself a few months later, I looked for her."

"Can we see your cougar form?" Kaden asked.

He hesitated for a moment. "I suppose so. We'll have to go outside, though, somewhere with bushes nearby for privacy. I have to take my clothes off before I shift, or I'll ruin them."

We went out to the yard where the storage shed-turned-portal sat, and I gestured to a nearby grove of trees. "You can probably get undressed in there," I said.

He nodded and disappeared into the bushes, and a few minutes later, a huge, majestic cat stepped out. Alisa squealed, and Kaden took a startled step back.

Shawnie's cougar was svelte and tawny coloured, with amber eyes and a white muzzle. I faced him, forcing myself to ignore the urge to run as he approached us. Alisa took a step forward, and he nuzzled her arm.

She ran her fingers through his fur. "Come on," she said. "He doesn't bite."

I tentatively reached out and stroked his fur. It was sleek and velvety, but far coarser than that of a housecat. "Trina needs to see this."

Kaden hung back, clearly still uncertain, and I eyed her. "I want to see your gift too."

"Right." She gave me a shy smile and mumbled a few words, then began to rise into the air. She hovered just a few feet above us, then flew carefully in our direction, where she reached out a hand to stroke Shawnie's fur while still hanging there. "Now if you attack, I can fly away," she explained, grinning.

I felt a few drops of rain on my forehead as she spoke. "Well, I suppose it's my turn to show off." I mumbled my casting words, finding the wind with my mind, and blew the clouds away.

Alisa grinned as the sunlight returned. Then she muttered a phrase of her own and suddenly reappeared on the other side of the yard. Shawnie let out a playful growl and darted after her. "Oh, you want to play, do you?" She stood her ground, grinning, only to teleport away seconds before he reached her.

I was in the midst of pondering how I could use my gifts to liven things up when a pair of hands gripped my shoulders, and a voice said, "Boo!"

I startled, then grinned when I realized who the voice belonged to. "Try to catch Alisa," I whispered.

"That's the plan," Alvin replied, his hands leaving my shoulders.

A few seconds later, Alisa squealed. "Hey, what's going on?"

"Come get her, Shawnie!" Alvin's disembodied voice called out.

"That's not how this works!" Alisa teleported again, and when she reappeared, Alvin was visible, his hand latched around her wrist. She recoiled for a second but then relaxed and grinned. "I didn't know who you were for a moment there."

Alvin let go of Alisa's hand and gave her a mock bow. "You and I should play tag sometime."

"Try catching *me*," Kaden said. She grinned, rising higher into the air before landing next to me.

Alvin eyed her. "Did you and Ruby end up..."

"We're good now. Thank you for encouraging me."

"It's what I do." Alvin slung an arm around me.

Alisa looked him over. "You got left behind with Willem, right? How'd you escape?"

He took a seat on the grass and began to recount the story of what happened.

"I can't believe you rode a dragon," Alisa said when he was finished. "I'm jealous." Shawnie, who'd changed back into human form while Alvin was telling his tale, nodded in agreement.

"I can hardly believe it myself," Alvin replied.

"I'd like to fly next to a dragon, but I'm not sure about riding one," Kaden put in.

Shawnie nodded. "I want to meet this Willem fellow. He sounds fascinating."

"You folks sound like you need an excuse to visit the Shrouded Woods." Alvin glanced at me. "Remember how you told me about the Moon Dance that happens every month? Maybe we could all go to the next one together. It'd be easy enough to get a ride." He pulled out his whistle and grinned.

"That sounds incredible!" Kaden said.

"The full moon was last week," I put in. "So that gives us three more weeks to plan."

"Wonderful!" Alvin said. "Let's make this happen."

When I got home that evening, Saray was absent from the dinner table. Kip showed up halfway through the meal, and Marcus frowned. "I wasn't sure if you were still here. Where's Saray?"

"In her room. She doesn't feel like eating right now."

"Is everything all right?" Noelle asked.

"No." Kip sat down at the table. "Saray's going to need some support from all of you for the next little while." His eyes, I noticed, were red, and his voice wobbled ever so slightly as he spoke.

"What's happened?" Trina said.

He let out a long, shuddering sigh. "I just broke up with her."

CHAPTER 22

ALL HEADS TURNED towards Kip, mouths agape.

Noelle frowned. "By the Fae, why would you do that?"

Kip sat back in his chair and took a deep breath. "It's not that I don't love her, y'know? But Kirilee and I had a talk the other day, when I borrowed Lachlann's ring, and she helped me understand why Willem's been so intent on me living in the Shrouded Woods. He's always talked about responsibility and duty, y'know, but he never explained what would happen if I didn't go back. Kirilee did, and now I see why I need to live there permanently. My absence is…affecting the magic of the Woods."

"What do you mean?" Marcus asked.

Kip's shoulders hunched. "Kirilee said after the Witch Slayers set fire to the Shrouded Woods, the magic that was always within the forest got far, far stronger, and it needed a focal point, someone to flow through. Otherwise it'd just turn into chaos. People's gifts would appear and disappear at random, or they'd flare and become very powerful for a short time. So a few magikai were chosen to be those focal points; they're known as the Bearers, and they're all tied to the Woods. Kirilee was one of them." He produced the leaf pendant from inside his shirt. "Kirilee slipped this onto me while everyone else was getting ready to do the life transfer, because she knew that the spell would also transfer her responsibility to me. She assumed I'd go back to the Shrouded Woods after I was resurrected, so she didn't have a problem with that."

"How did my mother manage to come to Dundere, then?" Marcus asked.

"She asked one of the other Bearers to take on her load of the magic as well as their own, but it's not something that can be done for long." He sighed. "I figured that going back every weekend would be enough. But the magic is starting to degrade. When I'm present in the Woods, it works, but when I'm not…" He frowned. "Willem ran out of magic during our rescue because of this, and I've had Ambrose tell me stories of suddenly losing his connection to Spark. Kirilee said that if I don't commit to living there, the magic of the Shrouded Woods itself will weaken, and it'll leave the woods-folk more vulnerable to attacks. With the Witch Slayers rising up again, that could mean disaster."

Marcus nodded and sat back pensively. "Did she tell you that you need to break up with Saray in order to return?"

Kip shook his head. "That was my own choice. I know we could stay together, and I could come visit here every now and then. But there's no point thinking about marriage with that sort of arrangement."

"And there's no chance she could live in the Woods with you?" I asked.

"She suggested that. But it'd only be a matter of time before word got back to the Breoch Guard. And if they managed to catch her, well, we all know what'd happen. Living with me could get her killed, and I'm not willing to take that risk. Saray has a future here. She deserves to be with someone she can make a life with."

Marcus reached out and put a hand on his shoulder. "I hope you and Saray are able to make things work in time," he said. "But I understand. Are you leaving for the Woods right away, then?"

"Tomorrow," Kip said.

"Will you come back and visit?" Trina asked.

"I hope so. I'll be making trips through the portal to supply sellers with meat and herbs and such. But I think I need to give Saray some space, y'know?"

We all nodded solemnly.

Kip finished his dinner in silence and stood. "Well, I'd best head home; I have lots of packing to do."

Trina, Marcus and Noelle followed him into the foyer to say goodbye. The moment the door shut, the house went silent. Then Marcus sighed. "That was unexpected."

"Is he…gone?" a voice came from above.

"He is," Noelle said. "Come down, Saray. We need to get some food into you."

When she joined us in the dining room, Saray's face was nearly white, and she moved mechanically, letting Noelle lead her to a seat. Her eyes were red and her mouth drawn into a grim line. "I…I'm so sorry," I offered.

She nodded. Trina sat next to her and took her hand while Noelle fetched her some dinner.

"Did he tell you what happened?" Saray asked when Noelle returned.

"He did," Noelle said.

"I…I understand why he needs to go. It'd be selfish to want him to stay here if it'll endanger the Shrouded Woods. But there has to be a way for me to live there too. There has to be a way for us to stay together…" Her voice broke, and she wiped at her eyes.

"Couldn't you just stay at Willem's?" I suggested.

"Kip thinks if I did, I wouldn't be able to leave Willem's place at all, that I'd have to spend my entire life trapped inside. And he doesn't want that for me."

Marcus put a hand on her shoulder. "You're a smart young woman, Saray. And Kip has a good head on his shoulders. If there's a way to make this work, one of you will think of it."

"I hope so. But it feels like he's already given up. He doesn't want to raise my hopes, so he's just resigned himself to…" She trailed off and began to sob, and the family all moved to comfort her. I waited for a moment, then backed quietly out of the room. It was obvious that the Westwoods needed some time alone.

I spent as little time at the house as I could in the weeks that followed in order to give the family space. It wasn't hard to keep away; I had plenty to occupy me outside of home. My classes resumed, and I still spent time training at the lighthouse with Chase, but now I also spent much of my free time with Shawnie, Alisa and Kaden, often accompanied by Alvin and occasionally Sophie. Chase seemed to be a little more relaxed than he was at first about letting Sophie hang out with the newcomers.

Alvin and I took my friends on a whirlwind tour of the island. I showed them the lighthouse, and I had them over to my place for dinner a few times. Shawnie changed into his cougar form one night and took Trina and Alisa on a ride through a nearby park on his back. We spent several evenings with Lachlann and Jasper as well; Kaden was very eager to learn the sword from Lachlann, and she and I spent a few hot nights sparring well past sunset, both of us tired and happy by the end of it. Lachlann was impressed by her ability to pick up sword fighting so easily, and he began teaching her how to utilize her ability to fly in conjunction with the sword.

My time alone with Alvin was less frequent than before the rescue, but we managed to go on several dates. He was more cautious now, less reckless about both the locations of our dates and the kissing sessions that inevitably accompanied them. We spent an evening climbing the rocks near the lighthouse, had dinner on the beach, and one Saturday, we spent most of the day wandering around the market. When he kissed me, he was more gentle now. Part of me missed his earlier ferocity, but I told myself that this was for the best. For now, at least.

As the days became shorter, and summer began its inevitable slide into fall, both Alvin and I grew busier with preparing for our exams and upcoming licensing. When I could, I practiced magic safety with Saray, who seemed to be dealing with her loss by pouring herself into study of both magic and work. She led me through numerous drills to ensure that I could rein in my gift as needed.

On the night before my test, Kaden asked if she could come over for the evening, as Alisa and Shawie had a special date planned. Trina was out with her own friends that night, and Saray was teaching a class at school, so we climbed up into Kirilee's tree and seated ourselves on a sturdy branch. Kaden gazed up at the stars and sighed. "This place is so magical. Sometimes I wonder if I'm in a dream, being in this place where magic is allowed, having my hand and tongue back. Having you back."

"Me?"

"I missed you when you were gone. I spent a lot of time with Alisa and Shawnie, but of course they wanted time to themselves as well."

"Is it strange for you that I'm dating Alvin, and Alisa and Shawnie are still together? Do you feel like the odd one out?"

"A little." She looked away for a moment. "I look at how cuddly you all are with each other, and I get a bit jealous. I want someone to cuddle."

"Well, there's nothing saying that friends can't cuddle. Though it'd be a little awkward up in this tree. Come on." I clambered down the branches and hit the ground with a thump, then gaped as I watched Kaden float lazily down. "Right. I forgot you could do that."

When I settled against the trunk of the tree and put an arm out, Kaden hesitated for a moment before lowering herself to the ground beside me and leaning her head against mine. She was a few inches taller, but she was also thinner, so my arm fit around her shoulders easily. "Don't worry," I said. "I'm sure there's a lovely lady out there just for you."

She shrugged.

"Do you like anyone right now?"

She eyed me for a moment, then nodded.

"Who?"

"I'm not telling." I felt her shoulders tense.

"Oh, come on, why not?"

"Because if I actually tried to date this person, it'd mess a whole bunch of things up." Her eyes flickered to mine. "It's best if I keep it to myself."

With a frown, I went through a list of names in my head. "It's not Trina, is it? I don't know if she's into girls, but I could be wrong."

She laughed. "No, not Trina. Trina's really pretty, but she's not my type, I don't think."

"How do you know?" My voice turned teasing. "You hardly know her. Maybe you should give her a chance, hmm?"

Kaden snorted, then burst into giggles. "First you tell me that you don't know if Trina likes women, and now you're trying to set me up with her?"

I laughed; she had a point.

"Look, forget I said anything. Finding a girlfriend isn't that important to me anyway."

"Then what is?"

"I want to be somewhere where I can feel free to be myself. And where I have good friends around me. And…"

"And what?"

"I want to…make a difference in the world, you know? I want to do something that makes life better for people."

"I know what you mean," I said. "I look at Noelle, at all the things she's accomplished and how much she's helped the people of Dundere, and I'm…in awe. I'd love to be able to help people like that one day."

"In awe, huh?" Her eyes narrowed. "Wait, you don't have a crush on *Noelle*, do you? She's a little too old for you."

"And a little too married," I added. "I wondered if I had a crush on her a while back, but I've realized I just admire her a lot. And I think she's pretty."

"That much I agree with you on," Kaden said.

We were quiet after that, gazing up at the glowing viletta leaves in companionable silence. *Kaden's right,* I found myself thinking. *This is all very much like a dream.*

I could only hope that it would last.

CHAPTER 23

ALVIN AND I both passed our exams easily, and the following afternoon we stood with the majority of the younger students in our class, reciting the pledge to use magic safely and only for good. I went home carrying a small card that identified me as a fully licensed magikai and my very own coat, handmade for me by Alexander and Ember. Mine was a dusky blue, embroidered with soft grey clouds and lightning made of shiny white material, and raindrops fashioned from small blue jewels. I was excited about my license, of course, and even more excited about my coat, but all of that paled next to tomorrow's trip to the Shrouded Woods.

I told Noelle that I planned to stay at the school with Kaden and Alisa that night, and in the afternoon I went to meet them, a blanket and a change of clothing stowed away in my pack. Alvin beat me there, and he was chatting with the others. He waved me over and put an arm around me when I approached. "Ready for an adventure?"

"Absolutely. Did you bring the tent?"

He nodded. "It's going to be tight, fitting all of us in there. We're going to have to cuddle." He winked. "I figure you won't mind that."

"I'm sure it'll be fine," Alisa said. "Let's get out of here."

We soon emerged from the cave on the other side of the portal, and I watched as my friends took in their first glimpses of the Shrouded Woods. Kaden paused and closed her eyes, inhaling the aroma of bark and mud and greenery, while Shawnie bent down to examine a glistening patch of mushrooms at his feet. Alisa stared up at the massive trees that rose on all sides, her eyes wide. "This is gorgeous."

"Indeed it is," Alvin replied. "And this is only the beginning."
He led us down the rope ladder and onto the ledge, where we could see the Shrouded Woods spread out below us. "Willem lives around here somewhere," I mused, "but I can't remember where, exactly. It's a shame— he has an incredible heated bathing pool in his house and a secret library, and he makes magical milkshakes!"

"A secret library?" Shawnie's eyebrows shot up. "I'd like to see that."
"Maybe we can talk someone into taking us there tomorrow," Alvin suggested. Then he pulled out his whistle and blew it. At first, it seemed like nothing happened. "Humans can't hear the dragon whistles," he said.

While we waited for the dragon to arrive, there came the mighty screech of a raptor, and Kip's hawk Persius appeared. He looked me over with his black, beady eyes. "Oh, hey there," I said, grinning. "I forgot about you."

"You know that bird?" Alisa asked.

"This is Persius. He used to be Kirilee's hawk, but now he spends most of his time with Kip." I wrapped my cloak around my forearm and held it out tentatively, and Persius immediately came to land.

"He likes you!" Kaden exclaimed.

"He remembers me, at least," I replied, reaching up my free hand to cautiously stroke his feathers.

"Can I try?" Alisa asked.

I shrugged. "I don't see why not. Just don't look him in the eye."

Alisa and Kaden both took turns stroking Persius's feathers. Then Persius let out a sudden squawk and swooped into a nearby tree. Spark had arrived.

Alvin jumped to his feet and waved at Ambrose.

"Good to see you folks," Ambrose said. "Are you looking for a ride?"

Alvin nodded. "This is my girlfriend Ruby, and my friends Shawnie, Kaden and Alisa."

"I remember Ruby. Is this everyone else's first time in the Shrouded Woods?"

"Yes," Kaden responded. "We want to go to the Moon Dance."

"Ahhh." Ambrose frowned. "I'd love to take you all, but Spark here would have trouble carrying more than four of us. I'd have to take some of you now, then come back for the others."

"That shouldn't be a problem," Kaden said. "I can fly, so I won't need a ride."

"That still leaves us with one too many."

"True." Kaden eyed me. "Though I've been told I can use my ability on another person, just like a vanisher can make other people invisible. I haven't attempted it yet, but Ruby said a while back she'd let me try it on her."

"Right. Perhaps we should test it out before we go flying over that." I gestured at the drop.

"Of course. Here, let's give it a try." She put a hand on my shoulder.

"Wait," Alvin interrupted. He frowned and pushed his hair out of his face. "Don't you want to ride with *me,* Ruby?"

I looked from him to Kaden, momentarily conflicted. Then I sighed. "I…suppose so. You can take me another time, Kaden."

I didn't miss the hurt expression on her face, but she quickly turned to Alisa. "Will you fly with me? Or do you want to be with Shawnie?"

"Sure, I'll fly with you."

Kaden gave her a small smile and put a hand on her shoulder. *"Incantus Momentus Gravita,"* she intoned, and I watched her and Alisa rise slowly into the air.

Alisa's eyes widened, and she clung to Kaden's arm. "This is incredible!"

"I'll say," Ambrose agreed. "Come on, everyone, climb aboard, and let's get to the Moon Dance!"

Moments later, we were all airborne, and I straddled the massive leather saddle that Spark wore. Ambrose sat at the front, gripping a pair of handholds, and I was wedged up against Alvin, whose arms were wrapped around my waist. Shawnie sat at the rear.

Ambrose instructed us on how to use the thin leather ties that were part of the saddle to tie ourselves in so that no one would fall off.

Now Spark hovered about five feet above the ground, wings flapping, waiting for instruction. Alisa and Kaden floated next to us, Alisa still firmly clasping Kaden's hand. Ambrose glanced back at us and grinned. "Are you all ready?"

We nodded. I gripped the handhold in front of me, and Alvin's arms tightened around my waist.

Ambrose paused, seeming to give Spark a command, and we began to slowly move forward. I gasped as the ledge dropped out from under us, trying to decide whether this was more or less terrifying than my ride with Kip. I heard Alisa let out a small shriek as she and Kaden cleared the edge.

"I'm going to go slow for now," Ambrose called out to Kaden. "When I speed up, yell if I'm going too fast for you."

"Will do," Kaden called back. The dragon banked right and picked up speed slightly, then we dropped lower, skirting the side of the mountain. Next to us, Alisa was becoming braver; she had let go of Kaden's hand and was laughing and whooping as she flew. Kaden did a somersault in the sky, then dared Alisa to do the same. I watched them, trying to ignore the pangs of jealousy I felt. *That could have been me.*

The sun dipped below the horizon as we flew, and soon enough, the moon was rising on our other side, large and luminescent and pale yellow. I saw the fire and heard the music before we approached the glade.

Spark let out a puff of fire and a loud braying noise, and the music below ceased. "Show-off," mumbled Ambrose as we descended. "Could never work as a spy with this one."

"I could've turned him invisible," Alvin said. "He still would have given himself away, but it would've been a lot funnier."

Kaden led Alisa into a long dive, and the two of them were on the ground long before we landed. Ambrose hopped off of Spark and bowed to the group. "I bring newcomers," he announced.

"I see that," a tall, bearded man replied, standing. "And where are these folks from? They don't look quite like the city folk we've seen before."

"That's because they're from Dundere."

"Dundere?" The man cocked his head. "And how did a bunch of children from Dundere end up over here?"

"Through the portal Kip used to visit on the weekends, before he moved here."

"I forgot about that. I s'pose we don't have to worry about these ones running off to the Breoch Guard, then." He gave us a smile, picked up his fiddle, and began to play a new song. Alvin slid off of Spark and offered me a hand. "Shall we?"

I looked over the dancers and took in the lilting music. *This reminds me of Gareth's ship,* I realized. *Jasper would love this; I should have invited him.* Then I turned to Alvin and grinned. "Let's."

We joined the dancing easily. I wasn't sure if Alvin knew how to dance to this sort of music, but if not, he figured it out very easily. I took in the dress and mannerisms of the woods-folk as we moved among them. Saray and Trina had told stories about the scant clothing, inked skin, and wild hairstyles of the Shrouded Woods, but none of it seemed too abnormal to me. I'd worn pants on a ship, drank a sleep potion from a fellow who wore eyeliner and fancy jewelry, and seen all sorts of exotic styles worn in Dundere. So the ways of the woods-folk were just another interesting thing to learn.

After several dances, I felt Alisa's hand on my arm. "Alvin, may I dance with you?"

Alvin gave her a puzzled look but nodded, and Alisa looked at me. "Go dance with Kaden."

I nodded and glanced around, finding Kaden sitting on a log, watching the scene that unfolded around her. I grinned and held out a hand. "Want to dance?"

She frowned for a moment, then took my hand.

"Are you all right?" I asked as I pulled her into the throng of dancing couples.

She shrugged. "I don't see why you and Alvin invited the rest of us if you were just going to spend the whole time ignoring us."

Her words stung a little, and I closed my eyes. "I'm sorry. I didn't realize it would be like this. Then again, I haven't gone to a dance with all of you before."

"It's not just that." Her eyes narrowed. "I…wanted you to be the first one I flew with. I was looking forward to it. I think you would've enjoyed it too."

I nodded slowly. "Honestly? I wanted to fly with you more than to stay on Spark."

"Then why didn't you tell Alvin that?"

"I…I don't quite know. He was just very convincing. He does that sometimes. It's…hard to explain." I smiled and held her hands tighter in mine. "But I'll fly with you another time. I promise."

"All right." She gave me a smile then that seemed almost shy.

"Right now isn't flying time, though," I went on. "Right now is dancing time." I dipped her back without warning, and she startled, then burst out laughing.

In retaliation, she gave me an impish grin and began twirling me around, fast. When she stopped, I was gasping for breath. "You're…a good dancer," I panted.

"I took lessons as a kid," she told me. "I love to dance. I like it more than playing the piano, honestly."

The music slowed considerably, and I grinned at her. "Well, since you're clearly the better dancer of the two of us, why don't you take the lead for this one?"

She nodded and slipped an arm around my waist, and we began to move together to the song's rhythm. I hadn't danced with a woman since Cerise on Gareth's ship, and the difference caught me off guard for a moment. Kaden and I were likely about equal in weight, but she felt wispy and delicate after dancing with Alvin for so many months. Her bicep under my left hand was slim but well developed, and her hand in my own, while likely no smaller than mine, felt tiny. "I should dance with women more often," I murmured to her.

"If you ever want one to dance with, come find me," she replied.

Several dances later, I felt a tap on my shoulder. "May I cut in?" Alvin asked.

I smiled at Kaden and gave her a small bow, then turned to Alvin. *He's been drinking.* I hadn't seen any alcohol at the party, but I also hadn't spent any time sitting on the logs where the food and drink were being handed out. The smell of liquor was immediately obvious on his breath, and his gait felt uneven as we began to dance. I'd seen my brother like this enough times to recognize the signs. "What were you drinking?" .

"I'm not sure, but it was delicious," he told me. "Here, try some." He leaned down and kissed me, and I tasted something sweet and berry flavoured on his lips. "We can go find you some if you want," he offered.

I shook my head. "Thanks, but I'd rather just dance."

"As you wish." He pulled me into position, and I leaned my head against his chest as we began to sway together. "I missed you," he mumbled to me.

"Missed me? I was dancing with Kaden for maybe twenty-five minutes."

"And I missed you during all of them." He kissed the top of my head.

I laughed. "You're insatiable."

"Oh, you have no idea." His embrace around me tightened. "The Woods are amazing, don't you think?"

"I do."

"If I asked you to run away and live here with me, would you do it?"

I chuckled and shook my head. "Why would I want to run away from Dundere?"

"Because then you'd get to stay with me."

"You've had too much to drink, Alvin. We can talk about this when you're sober."

"Are you telling me to stop talking? Because I can do that easily enough." He grinned and leaned down again, letting go of my hand to pull me in close. Hungrily, ferociously, his lips pressed against mine, and his hands raked through my hair as we swayed to the music. My heart began to pound with excitement, yet at the same time, I was painfully aware of how exposed we were. I managed to pull my lips away from his for a moment. "Alvin," I whispered, "we're in public."

He let go of me for a moment and pushed his hair behind his ear. "Let's go somewhere not-so-public then."

I was about to accept his offer when the song died and a new one began. I felt a hand on my shoulder once more. "May I cut in?" I heard a familiar voice ask.

I turned and felt the blood drain from my face.

It was Kip.

CHAPTER 24

ALVIN GLARED AT Kip. "I don't think you should be dancing with my girlfriend," he said, pushing his hair out of his face as he spoke.

"I think that's for her to decide." Kip raised an eyebrow, giving Alvin an expression that I didn't understand. Then he turned to me. "Ruby, will you dance with me, ai?"

I met his eyes. "I…suppose so."

"All right then." Kip pulled me into position, leaving Alvin gaping at us, and we moved into the throng of people.

Dancing with Kip was quite different from dancing with Alvin. Kip was only a bit taller than Alvin, and, while still slender for an adult, he was considerably more muscular than my usual dance partner. His hand in mine was callused from life outdoors, and he moved with a sure grace that made Alvin's dancing seem more cocky than confident. Kip, of course, did not pull me in when dancing; he kept a decent amount of space between our bodies. "Didn't expect to see me, did you?" he asked as we moved to the music.

I shook my head. "Did Persius tell you we were here?"

"He did. Though I was coming tonight anyway, and I wouldn't have been able to miss you and Alvin sucking each other's faces off." He frowned. "Do Marcus and Noelle know you're here?"

I sighed and shook my head. "They think I'm sleeping at the school with Alisa and Kaden."

"And the folks at the school think Alisa and Kaden are sleeping over at your place, ai?"

I nodded, blushing, and he chuckled. "Saray and I did that sort of thing too, when we were younger. She told Marcus and Noelle that I was taking her with me to Willem's for the weekend, and I told Willem that I was staying home to work on schoolwork. Truth was, we were back at my place the whole time, fooling around." His grin faded abruptly, and he let out a sigh. "How is Saray?"

"I haven't seen much of her. I think she's been trying to keep busy with work, and I've been busy with my friends. But she's…quiet."

He nodded, then squared his shoulders. "So you and Alvin are dating, ai?"

"Yes."

"Where are you staying tonight?"

"Alvin brought a tent. We're planning to all sleep in it together."

"I wish you'd told me that you folks wanted to come to the Moon Dance. I could've had you make camp with me, where you'd be safe."

"Last time I camped with you, you nearly destroyed our campsite. I thought you didn't want people to know about your sleep casting."

"Ah, that. I went to see Hilda after I moved back here, and she's given me a potion of faebane. It blocks the fairy magic that was making me sleep cast. So you'd be safer with me than out here. There are dangers that you and your friends likely don't know about." His eyes flickered to where Alvin was sitting. "Including young men who've had too much to drink."

I snorted. "I'm not worried. I've seen my brother far more drunk than Alvin dozens of times, and he's never tried to hurt me."

"Yes, but drink does different things to different folks, y'know? Just be careful." He let go of my hand for a moment and reached into his pocket. When he took my hand again, there was something smooth and round in it. "That's a summoning stone. If things go wrong tonight in any way, you can call me."

I nodded, and then my eyebrows arched as a thought occurred to me. "Are you going to see Willem tomorrow?"

He nodded.

"Can we come with you? My friend Shawnie really wants to meet Willem. But neither Alvin nor I can remember where he lives."

"Good. You're not meant to remember." Kip smiled. "I s'pose I can take you. Rub the summoning stone in the morning. I'll come to you folks and get you there using magic." The music was beginning to die off, and Kip frowned. "And you and I will need to have a chat about Alvin later. There's some things you should know about him."

"Like what?"

"I'll tell you when we have our…" Kip trailed off, staring beyond me. "Is that *Sophie?*"

I let go of him and turned around just in time to see a girl with familiar brown pigtails dart into the forest. "Oh, no you don't," Kip muttered and took off running after her. I quickly followed.

I doubt I would have been able to track Sophie through the darkened forest alone, but Kip seemed to have no problem spotting her. He gained on her easily enough, and when she looked back, I caught her expression for a second. I put a hand on Kip's arm. "She's terrified," I whispered to him. "Let me handle this."

"Sophie," I called out into the darkness, "stop running! You're going to get lost. Please come back."

There was a pause as the sound of footsteps ahead of us ceased. Then came a whisper. "Please don't tell my father."

I sighed. "Sophie, come back here."

Kip spoke a light spell, and a few seconds later, she approached the glow, her eyes wide with fear. "What are you doing out here?" I asked.

"I…I followed you and the others," she confessed, her voice shaking. "I heard you talking about the Moon Dance, and it sounded fun, so I convinced one of the vanishers at the school to make me invisible. I told them it was for a prank. Then I followed you through the portal."

"How did you get to the Moon Dance, though?"

Her shoulders hunched. "I climbed onto the dragon behind Shawnie. There was a bit of room left on the saddle."

"Sophie, you could've fallen off and been killed."

"I…I know. It's just that…Father never lets me do anything." Tears began to trickle down her cheeks. "I spend all my time in the stupid lighthouse with no friends. Father makes me do my lessons at home, he's worried about the other kids being a bad influence. I hear all about the adventures everyone else has, and I just want to have some fun…" She swiped at her eyes. "If you tell Father about this, he'll never let me out of sight."

I sighed. "Sophie, do you think your father would react any better if you showed back up at home tomorrow and never told him where you went? He'll be angry at you whether or not he knows you came here. He's probably sick with worry right now."

She nodded, a tear trickling down her face. "Yes, but if he knows I followed you here, he likely won't let me spend time with you anymore. He'll think you're a bad influence too." She began to toy with one of her braids. "There has to be another way."

"Tell you what, Sophie," Kip said. "I'll take you back to your home, and I'll tell your father that I came to Dundere to drop off wares and you followed me back into the Woods. I won't say anything about Ruby or her friends. He'll still be upset with you, but he's not likely to see them as a bad influence that way."

Sophie paused for a moment, then nodded.

"Let's head back to the dance and see if Ambrose can fly us to the portal," Kip suggested.

We made our way back, and Kip and Sophie wandered off in search of Ambrose. A moment later, there was a hand on my shoulder, and I startled as Alvin materialized next to me. "So you won't wander off into the forest with me, but you'll go off with *Kip?*" I didn't miss the disgust in his tone.

"What?" I gaped at him.

"Nasty fellow, he is," Alvin muttered. "Going after girls as young as you. I'm going to tell Saray." He frowned. "No, she wouldn't believe me. I'm going to tell your *brother.*"

My eyes widened as I realized what he was implying, and I burst into laughter. "You think Kip was trying to…" I snorted. "Of course not! Kip would never do something that inappropriate! We ran off because we realized that Sophie followed us here." I gestured at where Kip and Sophie were now talking to Ambrose. "See?"

Alvin stared at them and shook his head. "Are you sure you're not falling for him?"

"Kip is way too old for me. You really think I'd be interested in him? I think you have a jealousy problem when you're drunk."

"I'm not drunk," he protested, swaying as he spoke.

"You most certainly are. My older brother is a bottle-sucking skirt-chaser, remember? I know a drunk fellow when I see one." I put my arm around him. "Come on, I'm putting you to bed."

I felt a twinge of resentment as I led him back to where our bags were. There had been a few times over the last four years when I'd come across Jasper passed out in the parlour or mumbling incoherently to himself in the halls late at night, and I'd had to be the one to put him to bed. *Why do I keep getting stuck taking care of boys who drink too much?*

Arriving where we'd stashed our belongings, I was surprised to see that our tent was already set up. I heard a giggle as I opened the flap and saw that Alisa and Shawnie had beaten us inside and were lying against each other, Shawnie's hands tangled in Alisa's hair. "Sorry to break up your party," I whispered as I pulled Alvin inside. "Someone's had too much to drink."

Alvin flopped down on his bedroll. "Maybe we should join the party," he mumbled. "Separate from them, of course."

I put my hands on my hips. "I don't know if you deserve that after what you suggested about me and Kip." I heard Alisa let out a gasp.

"Oh, come on." Alvin grinned up at me and brushed his hair out of his face.

I sighed. "Fine, but no more nonsense about me cheating on you, all right?"

I lay down next to him, and he pulled me in. His lips pressed against mine, tasting of berries and alcohol. I heard Alisa giggle, then a moment later the noise from the other side of the tent suggested that she and Shawnie had returned to their previous activities. When Alvin pulled away to remove his shirt, I frowned, wondering for a brief moment if he was going to pressure me again. *He's not going to try to get us completely naked with Alisa and Shawnie in the tent,* I decided. When he leaned down and kissed me again, his lips pressed hungrily into my own, and I relaxed, enjoying the feeling of his skin on mine. I pressed my fingers into the hard muscles of his back, savouring his warmth. *I've missed this,* I realized. Alvin had been gentle with me as of late, and for good reason, but a part of me longed for the ferocity of our earlier kissing sessions.

When I heard Kaden crawl into the tent some time later, I pulled away from Alvin and rolled over, pressing my back against his chest. He enfolded me in his arms, nibbled on my ear, and mumbled something again about us running away. Moments after that, his breathing evened out, and I closed my eyes, hoping sleep would come quickly.

The following morning, I woke to birds singing outside. The hard ground pressed into me, and a warm hand gripped mine tightly.

My eyes flew open when I realized it wasn't Alvin's.

Alvin was in the far corner of the tent, still sound asleep, his breathing heavy. Alisa and Shawnie were cuddled together, Shawnie snoring lightly. I had somehow moved into the center of the tent and ended up with my arm slung over Kaden. She was still asleep as well— I could feel her ribcage expanding and contracting under my arm. But her grip on my hand was strong, and it was giving me pins and needles.

I gently pulled my hand out of hers, shaking it out, and sat up. *How did I end up over here?* I thought over what happened after Alvin fell asleep, trying to piece it all together.

Last night was my first time sleeping next to a love interest, let alone enfolded in his arms, and I hadn't realized how *warm* I'd get. Alvin radiated heat, and several minutes after his breathing evened out, I found myself gently extracting myself from his embrace, happy to lie next to— but not tangled up with— him.

How I'd gotten tangled up with Kaden instead, I was uncertain. She was definitely not as warm as Alvin, though.

I looked Alvin over, smiling at his dishevelled red-gold hair, his peaceful expression, the way the morning light made his freckles stand out. *He really is something.* And yet, I felt a sense of foreboding at Kip's concerns from last night, at whatever it was he wanted to tell me.

Whatever Kip wanted to say might not be true, I realized. He could have genuine concerns about Alvin and yet be wrong about him. *He's wrong in how he sees Jasper, so the same could be true here.*

Kaden rolled over, and her eyes fluttered open. "Morning," she greeted me.

I smiled at her. "How'd you sleep?"

"Better once you were cuddled up to me." She grinned.

I frowned and glanced at Alvin; thankfully he was still asleep. "How did that happen anyway?"

She shrugged. "I woke up in the night, and you were pressed up against me. I didn't mind— I was too cold anyway." She yawned and sat up. "What's the plan for today?"

"Well, Kip said that he would take us back to Willem's so that Shawnie could see the library. I'm supposed to use the summoning stone he gave me when we're all packed up."

"We're not in trouble, are we? I saw Kip dancing with you last night, and I wondered if he was going to tell the teachers where we are."

"He says he's not going to. But he was a bit worried about our safety out here."

Alisa murmured something and pulled Shawnie's arms around her. Kaden chuckled. "Someone doesn't want to get up."

"Two someones." I glanced over at Alvin, then I tentatively reached out and shook his shoulder.

He groaned and flung an arm over his eyes. "My head," he mumbled.

"He's got a hangover," Kaden said.

I nodded. "I suppose I should go find some water for him."

"I'll come with you."

I nodded, pulled on my cloak, and crawled out of the tent in search of water, Kaden in tow.

CHAPTER 25

A LITTLE OVER an hour later, we stood in front of Willem's home. We'd packed up without incident, and Kip used a trick with the summoning stones to get us all back to his camp before giving us a ride up his strange rope contraption. Kaden opted to hang on with the rest of us rather than fly because she thought it looked fun, and now we watched as Willem opened the door, his eyes widening. "You brought friends, I see."

"That I did." Kip gestured at each of us. "You likely remember both Ruby and Alvin." Willem nodded and smiled. "And this is Kaden, Alisa, and Shawnie. Shawnie's the one we're really here for; he wants to meet you and see your library."

Willem frowned for a moment, then nodded and let us all in. Kip turned to me. "Why don't you show the girls where the bathing room is, Ruby? Shawnie, Alvin, and I can go look at the library with Willem, and then we'll take a turn."

I was not expecting Kip to take charge like this, but I shrugged. "Sounds good. This way, ladies."

I led Alisa and Kaden down the long hall into the bathing room, and we all shed our clothes and eased into the warm water. "This is lovely," said Alisa, leaning back and closing her eyes.

"I agree." Kaden smirked. "It's nice not to have the boys around for once." Alisa laughed, then opened her eyes and cleared her throat. "Speaking of which— Ruby, I think this is a good time for us to talk to you."

"About what?"

"About the way Alvin's been acting." She shook her head. "Normally, I like Alvin, but this weekend he's been…almost possessive of you."

I nodded. "I noticed the same thing. Though last night he was drunk, so perhaps he wasn't quite himself. I think he gets jealous when he's drinking, especially given that nonsense he was spouting about Kip."

"What did he say?" Kaden asked.

"Kip and I ran off into the woods because we realized Sophie had followed us to the Moon Dance. When I got back, Alvin seemed to think I'd run off with Kip for…other reasons." I rolled my eyes. "As if I'd be interested in him, or Kip would be indecent enough to come after me."

Alisa snorted. "Yeah, that *is* ridiculous. I was thinking about what happened before that though, when Alvin convinced you to ride on the dragon instead of flying with Kaden— that was odd. Kaden told me you said you didn't really want to ride with him, but you sort of felt like you couldn't resist?"

"Something like that."

"Something is up with him. I have a suspicion, but it's not something I want to go accusing him of unless I know I'm right." She sighed. "Just be careful with him, okay?"

I raised my eyebrows. "You sound like Kip last night."

"So Kip has an issue with him too?"

"Well, he was worried about what Alvin might try, given that he was drunk. Alvin didn't do anything to hurt me last night, though. He was just…affectionate." I eyed Alisa. "And I get the impression you and Shawnie were being the same way."

"Trust me, they were," Kaden muttered, rolling her eyes.

"There was something else Kip wanted to tell me about Alvin, but he hasn't said what it is yet. I'm guessing it's related to what happened between Alvin and Trina back in the day."

"What *did* happen?"

"Well, according to Alvin, he and Trina dated several years back, and she cheated on him and destroyed his reputation." I shrugged. "I don't know the details, and I'm not sure what Alvin told me is even true. Trina doesn't seem like the type to cheat on someone or intentionally hurt them."

We washed up and towelled off, put our clothes back on, and headed through the corridors to find the others in the library. Shawnie was poring over a book with Willem, Alvin sat on a couch, clearly still nursing a hangover, and Kip was pacing back and forth near the entrance to the library. His head snapped up when we entered. "You girls all cleaned up?"

We nodded.

"Wonderful. Alvin, Shawnie, your turn."

"You're not joining us?" Shawnie asked.

He shook his head. "I'll bathe when I get home. I need to talk to Willem privately."

Shawnie nodded, then closed the book he'd been looking at and disappeared down the hall, Alvin in tow. Once they were out of earshot, Kip turned to us. "All right, I need to talk to you girls." He gestured at the couches. "Take a seat."

We complied, and my heart pounded as I stared up at Kip. *What is this about?*

He took a deep breath. "You girls don't know me that well, and it's not up to me to tell you who you should spend time with or date. But there are some things you need to know." He eyed me. "What'd Alvin tell you about his magic?"

"He said he's a vanisher and that everyone in his family has special abilities but him."

"That's what I figured. And it's a lie. Alvin has a special ability too, and I think he's been using it on you. Possibly you two as well." He nodded at Alisa and Kaden.

"What do you mean?" Kaden asked.

"Alvin has two gifts, like Aidan, but he didn't want to tell you about the second one. Alvin is a vanisher, but he's also a charmer."

Alisa sucked in a breath. "I knew it."

"You did?"

"I suspected it, after some things I saw yesterday. My aunt was a charmer."

I frowned. "I've never heard of this before."

"Charmers are almost as rare as lifebringers," Kip explained. "They use their magic to persuade other people to do what they want."

Kaden's eyebrows knitted. "That sounds dangerous."

"It's the only innate talent that most magikai consider to be inherently bad," Willem put in. "It's not, of course— like all magic, it can be used for good or for ill. But there's a lot of fear around what a charmer could do, so most keep their gift a secret."

"How was he charming me if he didn't use words? Can he cast with his mind, too?"

Kip shook his head. "Doubtful. I can't see someone having two gifts *and* mental casting. I figure he might've found a way to disguise his hand motions, to make them look like a nervous habit or just part of how he moves."

"Huh." I shook my head. "That's…quite the claim."

"Not really," Alisa countered. "I've seen what charmers can do."

"Did your aunt use it to harm people?"

"I don't think so. My cousins lived just a few blocks down the road, so we were always at each other's houses, along with lots of other kids from the neighbourhood. If we ever got rowdy or started fighting, she would mutter things, and we'd all just calm down. Everything felt so…light and safe when she did that. Eventually, one of the neighbourhood kids realized something was off though, and they told their parents, who told the Breoch Guard." Alisa's shoulders slumped. "I haven't seen my aunt since they took her."

Kip nodded gravely. "I'm sorry."

"Light and safe," I mused. "I've felt like that around Alvin before."

"So he has charmed you then." Kaden frowned.

"But aren't those feelings normal when you're dating? I know I felt similarly around my ex when we were together."

"They can be, but he probably amplified them," Alisa put in.

"Do you think Alvin's used his abilities to harm people?"

"He has," Kip informed me. "Trina was one of them."

I nodded slowly. "Alvin said that Trina cheated on another fellow with him, and that she and Saray destroyed his reputation."

Kip snorted. "She didn't cheat on anybody. And I s'pose the girls did destroy his reputation, but they didn't do it just to be mean."

"What exactly happened, then?"

"That's her story to tell, not mine. I think you should ask her about it." Kip sighed. "Anyway, Alvin won't be able to charm any of you very easily now."

"Why not?" Kaden asked.

"Charming doesn't work as well on people who know about the caster's abilities," Willem interjected from where he stood nearby, thumbing through a book. "Once you know a person is a charmer, it's not too difficult to determine when they're using their power on you."

"Ah." My shoulders relaxed a bit. "We should tell Shawnie as well, then."

"You're not going to keep dating him, are you?" Kaden's eyebrows furrowed. "He sounds dangerous."

"She's right," Alisa put in. "Just because he can't charm you easily doesn't mean he's a safe person."

"Please don't keep dating him." Kaden took my hand.

Why does everyone feel the need to tell me who they think I should date? I glanced around the circle at my friends, unable to ignore the seriousness of their expressions. "Fine." I sighed. "I'll break up with him. But not today, when he's feeling so sick."

Kaden nodded, seeming satisfied. Willem began putting books away, then gestured to the door. "We'd best get back to the main house if I'm going to give you kids some lunch before you head home."

We followed him to the kitchen, and Shawnie and Alvin joined us soon after. Lunch was delicious, as expected, but I barely tasted my food. My stomach was in knots, and I kept throwing glances at Alvin, uncertain what to do with him now.

Thankfully, he was ill enough that he didn't notice my own unease. He picked at his food and drank several glasses of water at Willem's prompting. When we were finished eating, I stood. "I think we need to get this fellow home." I put a hand on Alvin's shoulder.

Willem nodded. "I agree."

"Can I stay with you for a while?" Shawnie asked Willem. "I want to talk magic a bit more, then go for a run in the forest in my other form."

Willem chuckled. "Absolutely. You're a shapeshifter, huh? You'll have to tell me more about that."

I bid Willem and the others farewell soon after and made my way up the rope ladder and towards the portal, Alvin following me almost mechanically. Alisa hung back, looking up into the trees with wide eyes. "I hope we can come back here."

"I'm sure you'll get the chance," I assured her. "Shawnie would be thrilled to come back with you anytime."

We reached the portal and made it safely to the other side, where I turned to Alisa and Kaden. "I'd best get Alvin home. I'll see you sometime this week."

They disappeared into the school, and Alvin and I walked out to the main road to look for a carriage to take him home. We settled on a bench, and he put an arm around me, resting his head against mine. I tried to ignore the knot in my stomach and took his hand. "Just go home, drink lots of water, and sleep. You'll feel better tomorrow."

He nodded. "Last night was a lot of fun, even if I feel like death now."

"It was," I agreed. "You don't really believe that nonsense about Kip, I take it?"

"Oh." He shook his head. "That was the drink talking. I don't think anything actually happened between you two, don't worry. Apparently, drinking makes me jealous." He laughed. "Are you free next Friday night? I have another date idea."

I closed my eyes. *How do I do this?* I knew I had to break up with him at some point, but when? And how? *Maybe he hasn't used his abilities to hurt me,* I found myself reasoning. If anything, he'd likely used them to make my life better. I recalled Kaden telling me that Alvin had persuaded her to give our friendship another chance. *So maybe this charm thing isn't as dangerous as the others think.* And really, who was I to judge another person for a talent they happened to have been born with? If I left him simply because of his magic, I was no better than most of the people of Breoch.

I sighed. "I can do Friday," I said to him.

He grinned. "Excellent."

I'll give him one more chance, I decided. Now that I knew of his abilities, I'd go on one last date with him and see how it went. If I caught him trying to charm me into something I didn't want, I'd end it right there.

But like every other magikai, he deserved a chance to do the right thing with his gifts.

The week that followed was miserable. I found myself avoiding both Alvin and my friends. Seeing Alisa and Kaden would undoubtedly result in them questioning me about Alvin, and if I told them I was planning to go on one more date with him, I was sure they'd try to talk me out of it.

My feelings about Alvin were even more conflicted. I found myself replaying many of our dates and conversations, trying to figure if and when I'd been charmed by him. *Did he really charm me so that I'd ride on the dragon with him instead of flying with Kaden? Or am I just confused about who I'm most loyal to?*

I spent the majority of my time at the lighthouse with Chase and at home in the evenings. Now that I was fully licensed, Chase began teaching me how to create thunderclouds and generate lightning from them at will. I spent an entire afternoon trying to hit the stack of rocks on that nearby island with a lightning bolt, only succeeding after several hours of practice. In a few weeks, Chase promised me, he'd begin teaching me how to create a hurricane.

Sophie followed me around and watched me work, but she was subdued and never once asked to go see her friends at the school. She must have been told she wasn't allowed to leave the house anymore as a punishment for sneaking off.

The night before my date with Alvin, I went over to Lachlann's and spent the evening training with him and Jasper, working off some of my nervous energy. After training, we headed over to the pub. Jasper had recently bought himself a fiddle, and tonight, instead of drinking, he joined the musicians on stage. Lachlann sat back and sipped his ale, listening. "He's really talented."

I nodded. "When we were kids, we used to perform duets; he'd play fiddle, and I'd play piano. Maybe one of these days I'll convince him to come over to the governor's place, and we can do that again." I smiled and rested my chin in my hand. "I'm proud of him, you know. He's come a long way from where he was a year ago."

"Me too," Lachlann agreed. "I think getting him out of your family home probably helped a lot."

"And you being willing to give him another chance likely helped too."

Lachlann nodded.

"Do you think everyone deserves a second chance?" I asked.

"Everyone?" He frowned. "Not really, no. I think it depends on a lot of things. How badly the person hurt you, whether they're likely to do it again. Whether they're sincere in wanting to change. I gave Jasper another chance because he took a huge risk by coming to me, and because it was obvious enough that he was sincere. Though you recall, I still needed Alex and Ember's fox to confirm that for me before I really started trusting him."

I nodded.

"I was also able to give him another chance because I wasn't the person he hurt the most. I completely understand why Saray avoids him and why Kip despises him. I can't expect them to be willing to forgive him, because he hurt them far worse than me. However, I think that Kip and Jasper would likely accomplish some pretty incredible things working as a team, and I've told Jasper as much." He eyed me. "Why do you ask? Are you planning on giving someone a second chance?"

"Kind of."

"Well, be cautious, and don't trust them fully right away. These things take time."

I nodded. "Thanks. I'll keep that in mind."

I sat back, listened to the music, and tried not to think too hard about the second chance I'd be giving Alvin tomorrow night.

CHAPTER 26

I MET ALVIN in front of the school the next evening, and he greeted me with a long embrace. "Where've you been this week?" he asked. "I've missed you."

"I've been pretty busy at the lighthouse." I pulled back and grinned at him. "It's good to see you though. Where are we off to tonight?"

His green-gold eyes sparkled. "Somewhere fancy for dinner. Have you ever been to the Emerald Room?"

"You mean that posh restaurant at the Grand Emerald Hotel? No, I haven't."

"Well, we just so happen to have a five-course meal lined up."

My eyes widened. I'd gotten used to fancy food living at the governor's place, but this sounded even more luxurious than what I was accustomed to.

Alvin offered me an arm. "Shall we?"

I grinned and took it, my earlier worries fading for the time being. "Let's."

A while later, I found myself sitting on the roof of the Grand Emerald Hotel, my legs hanging off the side and Alvin's arm around me. The restaurant fed us marvelously, as expected; we'd dined on a delicious roasted vegetable salad topped with goat cheese and pecans, delicately spiced grilled prawns, duck legs glazed with honey, roast lamb stuffed with savoury vegetables, and a large fruit trifle for dessert. Now we were both full and happy.

I grinned as I looked out over the nightlife of Dundere City. "You always find the best rooftops to sit on."

"I have to do something with my spare time. I get bored pretty easily—Dundere City is so *small*." His arm around me tightened. "In fact, I'm thinking about running away from here."

"You said something about that the other night. You wanted me to run away to the Shrouded Woods with you."

He laughed. "That was the drink talking. The Woods are lovely, but I wouldn't actually want to live there."

"Where then?"

He shrugged. "Maybe somewhere on mainland Candesh. Somewhere with lots of tall buildings for me to sit on."

"Why do you want to run away?"

"I'm just…tired of this place. I've lived in the same city my whole life. And a lot of folks here don't like me, thanks to Trina and Saray. I want a fresh start." He grinned. "You could always come with me."

I froze, wondering if he was about to try charming me into following him. "Come with you?" I let out a nervous laugh. "I mean, maybe if we wait a couple of years. But I want to finish school first."

"Of course." He toyed with my hair, and I relaxed slightly. "I'll stick around for a while at least."

"Good." I grinned up at him, and he ran a finger softly along my cheekbone. Then he leaned in.

Kissing Alvin tonight didn't feel any different than usual. As always, my heartbeat picked up, and I felt myself melting into his embrace. He wound his fingers into my hair and kissed me harder. Then I gasped as he pulled me into his lap. A little giggle escaped me as his lips left mine and brushed against my eyes, then my cheek, then my neck. I buried my face in his hair and breathed in the scent of him. *He hasn't tried to charm me once tonight,* I decided. *Everything is going to be fine.*

Then he pulled away and looked up at me. "Happy?"

I gave him a grin and nodded.

"I have another surprise for you." He pulled me off his lap, stood, and offered me a hand. "I rented us a hotel room for tonight."

My eyes widened as I got to my feet. "You...did?"

"I bet you've never stayed in a hotel before."

"I...I haven't, but why?"

"Why did I rent us a room? Because all of this," he leaned down and kissed me again, "is a lot more comfortable when we're not outside, don't you think? And things got a little complicated last time we were indoors."

I stared up at him, my heartbeat thundering now. "That sounds lovely, Alvin. But I'm not sure if I'm ready for that."

"For spending a night with me? You did it back in the Shrouded Woods."

"Yes, but we were in a tent with three other people. If we're in a hotel room, we'll probably end up sleeping together."

He grinned. "I'd expect so, seeing as the room only has one bed."

"That's not what I mean."

"I know." His grin faded, and he gazed down at me. "We don't have to go all the way, Ruby. We can just kiss and cuddle and all that." One corner of his mouth turned up. "But I did steal some of my brother's tea, just in case."

I shook my head. "I'm not ready for that, Alvin. With you or with anyone."

"All right then, so we won't go quite that far. But the hotel room will still be fun." He grinned and tucked his hair behind his ear. "Come on."

I felt myself beginning to relax. "All right. I suppose we could—" I froze mid-sentence. *Wait a minute.*

"What's wrong?" He took my hand in his. "Ruby, is everything okay?"

He just tried to charm me when he tucked his hair behind his ear. My head spun as I recalled all the times he'd performed that tiny action.

When he asked me out.

When he kissed me.

When we were alone in his bedroom.

When he convinced me to get back together with him...

I slowly pulled my hands away from his and took a step back. "You've...been charming me all this time."

His eyes narrowed. "What do you mean?"

"When you do this," I tucked one of my own curls behind my ear, "you're casting a spell. To persuade me to do what you want."

"And what makes you think I could cast a spell like that?"

"Well, you're a charmer, so—"

"Who told you that?" he interrupted, his face darkening.

"Does it matter? The point is that you've been—"

"Who *told* you?" he demanded once more, lunging at me and grabbing me by the shoulders. "Was it Trina? Or Saray? I warned you not to tell them about us!"

"It was Kip. He saw us together at the Moon Dance and was worried about me. And rightfully so, it seems!" I shrugged out of his grip, shaking. "Don't you dare grab me like that again!"

"So what now?" His eyes blazed. "Are you going to leave me, like everyone else? Run off, destroy everything we had? I thought I mattered to you, Ruby. I thought—"

"What is going *on* here?"

The voice from above startled us both. When I took a step away from Alvin and looked up, I felt the blood drain from my face.

"Kaden?" I said. "What are you *doing* up here?"

Kaden hovered over the hotel, fury etched into her features. "What are *you* doing up here with *him?* I thought you said you were going to break up with him!"

"Oh, really?" Alvin crossed his arms.

"I…I was…and I told Kaden that I would, but then I thought I'd give you one more chance, and…I'm sorry." I wasn't sure if I was apologizing to Alvin or Kaden.

"You lied to me. And to Alisa and Shawnie too!" I didn't miss the hurt in Kaden's voice.

"All right, that's enough, you two," Alvin cut in. "Let's get you home, Ruby."

"How do you intend to do that?" Kaden asked. "There's no way Ruby can get down from here herself. How did you two get up here anyway?"

"What do you care?" he snapped. "Come on, Ruby, let's go home."

"Don't go with him." Kaden's voice was pleading. "I'll fly you home. He's just gonna hurt you if you go with him."

"How do I know *you* won't hurt me?" I demanded. "You're mad at me too!"

"I'm mad because I *care!*" Kaden hovered closer and extended a hand. "Please, Ruby, come with me," she begged, her tone softening slightly.

I looked from her to Alvin. *Kaden hasn't spent months trying to charm me into doing what she wants,* I reasoned. I sighed and took Kaden's hand.

"I can't believe you," Alvin snarled. "Do I mean nothing to you, Ruby?"

"Shut up!" Kaden snapped at him, and before I knew it, we were hurtling away, Kaden's hand locked around my wrist. I gazed down at the city lights and floundered in midair for a moment, suddenly terrified that Kaden would drop me. She looked straight ahead, her jaw clenched, refusing to speak to me or meet my eyes. Her grip on my wrist was like iron as she pulled us towards the governor's house and deposited me in the driveway. "I can't believe you lied to us."

"Kaden, I'm sorry." I shook my head. "I just wanted to give him one more chance…"

"And where did that get you?" She huffed. "He looked like he wanted to push you over the edge. Next time you go on a date with someone dangerous, at least let your friends know!" She turned away from me and flew off before I could answer her.

I let myself into the house, shed my shoes, and practically ran up to my room, Shutting the door behind me not too quietly, I collapsed onto the bed and burst into tears.

CHAPTER 27

A few minutes later, I heard a knock on my door. "Ruby? You okay in there?" The door cracked open a bit, and Trina's head popped in. "What happened?" She came to perch on the edge of my bed, putting a hand on my shoulder.

"I...I made a terrible decision," I blurted. "I don't know what to do." My voice broke, and I began sobbing again.

"Tell me what's going on." She climbed onto my bed and leaned back against the pillows, gesturing that I should join her.

Between sobs, I told Trina everything that had happened between Alvin and me over the past several months. "I'm just so confused," I finished, gasping for breath as I spoke. "Am I an idiot for giving him another chance? I think Kaden hates me now, and I don't know how Shawnie and Alisa are going to react. Have I just ruined my friendships with everyone?"

Trina was silent for a few minutes, rubbing my back while I cried. Once my sobs had subsided, she spoke. "I wish I'd known Alvin was bothering you. I would've warned you about him."

I frowned. "What exactly happened between the two of you? He said something about it a while back, but Kip told me it was mostly a lie. He didn't explain what really happened though; he said that was your story to tell."

"What did Alvin say about me?"

"He told me you dated that Frederick fellow, cheated on Frederick with him, blamed him for it, and then you and Saray destroyed his reputation."

Trina shook her head. "I suppose that's how he'd see it. It's definitely not all true, but parts of it aren't exactly a lie, either. Alvin and I were in the same grade at the Academy, and he, well, he targeted me, I guess. I was brand new and just getting used to being able to see, so he sidled up to me on my first day and tried to be my friend. And it was fine at first. The other girls were a bit cliquey when I showed up, and they ignored me, so it was nice to have a friend. But then, same as you, he started to try to get me to kiss him. I was thirteen, I wasn't even thinking about a boyfriend at that point!" She laughed. "But he...succeeded. He used his charm ability to convince me to kiss him. And after that, he had it in his head that I was his girlfriend, even though I'd never agreed to that.

"About six months later, Frederick came along, from my old school in Sylvenburgh, and it was just so nice to have someone familiar around, other than Saray. So he and I started hanging out a lot, and I spent less time with Alvin. I wasn't trying to be unkind to him, but he'd been making me uncomfortable for months by then, and Frederick was better at, well, being decent. Frederick and I actually did end up dating a few months later, and Alvin was furious at me. He felt like I'd ditched him for Frederick. So he charmed me into kissing him again, but he did it in the front hall of the Academy, in front of dozens of people. Of course, word got back to Frederick, and he was very hurt and angry. He broke up with me."

My eyes widened. "Wow. I'm sorry."

"The whole thing was so strange," Trina went on. "So I didn't say much about it to anyone. I was furious with myself; I was convinced that I'd chosen to kiss Alvin, and that this was all my fault. I started having trouble in school and trouble eating. Noelle noticed and asked me what had happened, and I finally told her everything. She was the one who realized there might be something magical involved. So she spoke to Alvin's parents. They didn't want to talk to her at first, but she persisted, and eventually they admitted that he was a charmer. They'd been trying to figure out what to do about his gift, but they were lost. No one knew how to train a charmer, or wanted to. So they'd been ignoring his talent, hoping it would go away. They begged Noelle not to tell anyone. Noelle agreed to only tell our family. So she talked to Saray and me about what she'd learned, and Saray was furious. I was shocked, and hurt. And afraid that he might do it again.

"Noelle told us not to tell anyone, but both Saray and I thought that was a terrible idea. If no one knew about Alvin's ability, he could continue to get away with hurting girls. So we went against Noelle's wishes and told our friends. Word got around the school, and suddenly Alvin went from being a fairly popular fellow to being a complete outcast." She frowned. "Saray and I didn't realize how much damage we'd do to Alvin's reputation by telling people. We wanted to warn other girls, but we didn't think beyond that. Suddenly everyone was suspicious of him. No one could have a conversation with him without wondering if he was trying to charm them. Even the teachers started acting wary around him. Most of the students just stopped talking to him altogether. I feel bad about that part. Saray and I weren't trying to turn everyone against him." She sighed. "Things got better for him after a couple of years; the kids in my grade started accepting him, and he began approaching the girls again, this time just using his natural charisma instead of magic. I don't think he got anywhere with most of them, though, likely because there was always some concern that he might be trying to charm them. So when you showed up— a new girl who didn't know his history or his secret— he must have been thrilled."

"Right." I nodded. "So did Frederick take you back?"

Trina shook her head. "He had it in his head that I could've resisted Alvin. And maybe he was right, I'm not sure. But Frederick left the island a year ago to go to university, so it doesn't really matter anymore." She sighed. "Can I tell Noelle about this? I think she should know."

"I suppose so."

"And you're going to need to confront him at some point, Ruby. Tell him that the way he acted tonight wasn't acceptable. Otherwise he'll just keep doing it."

"But you said he can't charm me easily now."

"It's true. But with or without his magic, he can still be persuasive. Manipulative, even. He needs to know that you're not going to put up with it." Trina stifled a yawn then. "I'm getting tired here. You all right if I go to bed?"

"Yeah, that's fine."

Trina gave my shoulder a squeeze and left me to get ready for bed. I changed into my nightclothes and crawled under the covers. The tears returned as soon as my head hit the pillow, and I cried myself to sleep.

I woke up the following morning with a pounding headache, but managed to drag myself out of bed and downstairs, where I ate breakfast mechanically. I knew what I needed to do today, and I wasn't looking forward to it.

About an hour later, I walked into the courtyard of the school of magic and found Alisa, Shawnie and Kaden sitting in their usual spot. Kaden saw me coming and glared. "What are *you* doing here?"

"I'm here to apologize." I sat down on the bench across from them. "I'm sure you're all mad at me for lying to you, and I don't blame you. I wanted to break up with Alvin, but…I just couldn't. I felt like he needed one more chance to prove himself. If I had a partner who broke up with me because they were scared of storms and found out I was a stormbrewer, that would be unfair, right?"

"I suppose so," Alisa conceded.

"So it didn't seem fair for me to break up with him just because he has a talent that isn't his fault." I sighed. "But last night I talked to Trina, and she told me what happened between her and Alvin. Now I understand why Kip warned me about him. Now I wouldn't go back to him."

"What *did* happen between Trina and Alvin?" Shawnie asked.

I told them the story. "You all were right. He is dangerous."

"As we figured." Kaden's tone was flat, and she only looked at me out of the corner of her eye.

"How did you know where we were last night?" I asked her.

She huffed. "I saw you two leave. You met outside the school, and I was up on top of the roof. So I decided to follow."

"You *followed* us?"

The words came out like an accusation, and she snorted. "Aren't you glad?"

"I…yes, I suppose so. Why didn't you confront me earlier?"

"Because I didn't want to make a scene in the restaurant, that's why." She shook her head. "I just wish you'd told us what you were doing. Can you imagine how much danger you might have…" She trailed off suddenly, and her eyes went wide as she looked past me. I turned and found myself staring right at Alvin.

He strode up to me, smiled, and put a hand on my shoulder, as if last night had never happened. "Hey, can we talk?"

I looked up at him, my heart pounding, then nodded.

"Let's go for a walk, all right?"

"No." I stood and pointed to an empty bench out of earshot of my friends. "We can talk there."

Alvin frowned, but he followed me over to the bench and sank down next to me. "I need to apologize about last night, Ruby," he said. "Remember how I said that Saray and Trina nearly ruined my reputation once? Well, it was after they learned about my gift. They went and told everyone in school about it and spread a bunch of rumours about me too. So I'm a little sensitive about people knowing, which is why I overreacted when I found out that you knew." He gave me a lopsided grin. "Will you give me another chance?"

I sighed and met his eyes. "I already did, Alvin. I went out with you last night knowing full well that you were a charmer. My friends tried to convince me not to, but I figured that you deserved one last chance. But you tried to use your charm on me to get me to spend a night with you. Once we were there in the hotel room, who knows what you might have charmed me into doing."

"I told you, I wasn't going to pressure you to sleep with me."

"You said that, but how do I know whether that was true? You charmed me into so many other things..." My voice broke, and I shook my head. "I can't do this. I can't be with you knowing how many times you've tricked me."

"You don't mean that." Alvin grabbed my hand. "Ruby, think of all the good times we've had. Dancing under the full moon, running off to the Woods. Our picnics, our dinner last night. You can't think I charmed you into *all* of that?"

I stood. "I don't know anymore. Now let me go."

"Ruby, please." He stood too, not letting go of my hand, and leaned his face down to my ear. "Run away with me, Ruby," he whispered. "We could have such a wonderful life together. We could—"

"Oh, cut it out, Alvin." I hadn't seen Alisa approach, but now she stood next to us, Kaden by her side. She shoved Alvin away from me, and he stumbled back. "I know exactly what game you're playing. You don't get to manipulate people into loving you."

"We know your secret too," Kaden put in. "Kip told Alisa and me about your charming little ability. And Alisa told Shawnie. We're going to make sure that all the Yarel Island girls know about it, so you can't use it on any of them, either."

Alvin recoiled, and his face went pale. "You wouldn't dare." His voice took on a dangerous note.

"What, do you think you're going to be able to charm us out of doing it?" Kaden shot back.

Alvin stared at her for a moment. "Well, I happen to know your little secret as well," he finally sneered. "You're in love with Ruby, and that's why you were so angry when you saw her with me last night."

I gaped at him, then turned to Kaden, bewildered. "Oh, don't act so surprised," Alvin said to her. "I saw the way you were looking at Ruby at the Moon Dance. You want her for yourself. That's what's really motivating you."

Kaden glared at him. Her eyes flickered to me, then she looked away.

"You're wrong about that much, Alvin," Alisa said. "I don't know how Kaden feels about Ruby, but whatever she may feel, she's mad at you— *we're* mad at you— because you tried to hurt Ruby. Don't you go turning this on us!"

Alvin huffed, then turned to me once more. "Do you really think they're telling the truth, Ruby? That I'm a manipulator who's out to hurt everyone? I would have hoped you'd know me better than—" He froze suddenly, his eyes going wide and looking beyond me. Shawnie had taken on his other form. He let out a low growl at Alvin, and several nearby students recoiled.

Alvin glared. "You wouldn't dare."

Shawnie growled again and lunged, stopping just short of attacking Alvin, who stumbled backward, tripping and nearly hitting the tile. He recovered and looked at Shawnie, then me, his eyes wild with fear and anger. "You know what? Forget this. Forget all of you." He spun on his heel and stormed off.

The rest of us were left staring at one another, except Kaden, who wouldn't look at me. "I should go," she muttered, nearly running back to the dorms. Shawnie retreated to the side of the building to change back into his human form.

I eyed Alisa. "Was Alvin right? Does Kaden have a crush on me?"

"I think that's something you'd have to ask her yourself," Alisa replied. "Not today though. Maybe once she's calmer." She reached out and squeezed my hand. "You've both had a tough few days."

I nodded. "I should probably head home. Thanks for standing up for me." I stood and made my way out of the school, feeling both relieved and defeated.

I had done what I needed and broken up with Alvin. So why did I feel like this was far from over?

CHAPTER 28

I BEGAN TO slowly feel lighter as the next two weeks passed. My friends didn't seem angry at me anymore, and we spent our days wandering the market or walking the beach, taking in the late summer heat. Noelle was busy making arrangements for the Yarel Island adults to move out of the dorms once September rolled around. Several of them would move into newly built apartments around town; others had plans to return to Breoch or venture to other lands. Most of those staying were committed to learning a new job and joining a guild, and magic safety classes for everyone living in dorms were taking place. When my friends were in class, I would train at the lighthouse. As promised, Chase began to show me the basics of forming a hurricane.

Kaden was a bit more reserved around me than she'd been before Alvin's accusation, and I spent many nights trying to figure out how to talk to her about this strange gulf that had been forged between us.

One hot evening in August, there was a large party at the governor's mansion celebrating Saray's twenty-first birthday. Kaden, Alisa, and Shawnie had a big test the next morning, so they weren't attending, but the mansion was packed with young folks I'd never met before, teachers from the school I'd only seen in passing, and magikai of all different sorts. One of the teachers from the school of magic challenged anyone who was willing to a magic duel in the backyard, and I spent a good few hours watching magikai attempt to outwit the others with their talents. Then there was dancing in the ballroom and a buffet dinner in the grand dining hall, and soon I was being passed from dance partner to dance partner, thoroughly enjoying myself. I wondered if Kip was going to show up for the party, but he did not. Saray seemed happy enough, but I didn't miss the moments when her eyes shifted to the door, clearly wondering if anyone else was going to join us tonight.

My head was still spinning when Lachlann, the last guest to leave, bid us farewell around midnight. Noelle ordered everyone to bed once the food was cleaned up, saying that the rest of the tidying could take place the next morning. I made my way up to my room, closed the door, and had just removed my shawl when a familiar voice spoke out of nowhere. "Hello, Ruby."

My entire body tensed, and I began backing towards the door. A hand grabbed my wrist before I could make it all the way there, and Alvin materialized in front of me.

"What are you doing in my room?" I hissed.

"Oh, I've been following you around all night." He moved so he was between me and the door, his arms folded. "I've been waiting to catch you alone so we could talk without your friends hovering around."

I put my hands on my hips and glared up at him. "All right. What do you want to say to me?"

"Do you really believe what they're telling you, Ruby? Do you really think I'm a manipulator?" He snorted. "I was a friend to Trina when she was brand new and didn't know anyone, just like I was a friend to you. And I keep getting vilified for that, over and over."

"It's not your friendship we don't like, Alvin," I replied. "It's the fact that you don't seem to be able to take no for an answer. Just because you were kind to me when I was new and lonely doesn't mean that I owe you a date, or a kiss, or anything of that sort. Did you befriend me because you wanted to be a friend, or because you saw me as a potential girlfriend?"

"Both, I suppose." He shook his head, and I noticed a small glint of gold in his left ear. "Do you know what it's been like for me, Ruby? I spent my whole childhood thinking that when I got older, I'd get some sort of special talent like the ones my siblings have, only to learn that one of my talents is more a curse than a gift. My parents were ashamed of me, they hid my abilities instead of celebrating them. And then, once Trina and Saray told everyone about my gift, the whole school began treating me like an outcast as well. Do you have any idea what it's like to have people hate you for something that's not your fault?"

"My father is a high-ranking Breoch Guard, so yes, I do know what that's like." My heart thumped wildly in my chest, but I forced myself to lift my chin and glare at him. "I'm sorry that you've had it rough. I really am. But that's no excuse to follow me into my room. That is an absolute misuse of magic, and when Noelle finds out, she'll likely revoke your license."

"You wouldn't dare tell her," he growled, grabbing me by the shoulders and shoving me against the wall. His eyes narrowed, and for a moment, I thought I saw them flash golden.

"Don't you touch me!" My voice rose as I met his gaze and tried to shake him off.

Alvin's eyes widened, and the gold disappeared. "I...I'm sorry," he whispered. "I wasn't trying to scare you." He buried his face in my shoulder for a moment, and I squirmed, trying to get away from him. When he looked up again, his eyes were wet with tears. "I was going to take you tonight," he mumbled. "Aidan and I had plans to take you and Jasper, but...I just can't force you to come with me. I love you too much." A tear trickled down his cheek. "Run away with me, Ruby. Start a new life with me. Please."

I stared up at him, my heart sinking. *What are they planning to do to Jasper?* When I finally found my voice, it shook terribly. "This isn't love, Alvin. Charming someone into doing what you want isn't love. Sneaking into my room isn't love. And whatever you were planning on doing to me and Jasper, that certainly isn't love, either. Now go home, and don't come back."

"How are you going to stop me?" His eyes were golden once more, and his hands were on my shoulders, nails digging into my skin. "I could sneak back in here whenever I wanted, you know. I could stab you in your sleep if I felt like it."

"Let go of me!" I shot back. "You think you're the only one here who can use magic? I could hit you with lightning the moment you walked out that door." As if on cue, I heard thunder rumbling outside. A gust of wind blew in through the window and tore at his clothes. "I am not a weak little girl to be threatened,

Alvin. I am just as powerful as you are. And if you don't get out of my house *right this moment,* I swear I'm going to—"

I was interrupted by my bedroom door flying open. *"Nalalae Eroknae Sangnatae,"* I heard a male voice shout, and Alvin froze in place, unable to speak or move. I turned back to see Marcus standing there, his face contorted with fury. "You do *not* threaten my houseguests, young man," he snarled, then turned back towards the hall. "Noelle!"

A moment later, Noelle appeared in the doorway, glancing between Alvin and me. "What was this fellow trying to do to you, Ruby?"

It took me a moment to find my voice; when I did speak, my words rushed out, nearly incoherent. "He went invisible and followed me into the house, and then he started threatening me and…" I trailed off, fighting the tears that pricked at my eyes.

Noelle stared coldly at Alvin. "I know all about you, young man. I remember what you did to Trina, and I looked into your records after I heard you were harassing Ruby. Seems like you were in that safety class for a similar offense, hmm? Stalking girls who weren't interested in you?" She sighed. "Whoever sentenced you last should have done this." She met his eyes with gravity. "Alvin Blackwell, as governor of the Isle of Dundere, I hereby strip you of all your magic licenses for three years. If you are caught using magic during that time, you will face imprisonment, and once you've regained your privileges, you will have to start your training from the beginning." She glanced at Marcus. "Now, my husband will take you home and inform your parents of what you've been up to."

Marcus nodded, took Alvin by the arm, then muttered another string of words. Alvin sagged as the spell holding him in place broke. He let Marcus drag him out of the room but turned back to me as he was being taken away. "Don't think I'm done with you," he hissed.

The moment I heard the front door slam, I sank to the ground, shaking. Noelle crouched down and put an arm around me. "Come on," she said gently, "let's go downstairs."

I let her lead me down to the parlour. She put a blanket around my shoulders, then ducked out of the room, returning a few minutes later with a glass of water. I drank it mechanically, my head spinning. "Are you injured at all?" I heard her ask me. Her voice sounded distant, detached.

I shook my head. "He…he grabbed my shoulders and pinned me against the wall, but that was all."

"Well, if you start to bruise at all, let me know." She sat down next to me. "Breathe deep, Ruby. I don't want you fainting."

"Is everything all right?" Saray appeared in the doorway, a concerned look in her eyes.

"It's fine. Your father and I have things under control," Noelle assured.

"We need to get to Jasper," I found myself saying. "Right now."

Noelle nodded. "I can see how being around your brother might be helpful."

"It's not that. Alvin said that he and Aidan had plans to take Jasper and me somewhere. I think they were going to kidnap us. We need to make sure he's all right."

Noelle let out a long breath. "All right. Once Marcus is back, we'll head to

Lachlann's place."

Saray, Trina and Starla all crept into the room and gathered around me. I sat with them, my head spinning, as Noelle explained to them what had happened. Finally, we heard the front door slam.

"Noelle? Ruby?" I heard Marcus call out.

"In here," Noelle replied.

He appeared in the doorway a moment later, his face grim. "Alvin shouldn't be bothering you anymore," he told me. "His parents were absolutely livid when I told them what he'd done. If I heard correctly when I was leaving, he'll be grounded for a good month or two." I flinched at his words; I imagined Alvin would be in for a good beating from his father along with the grounding.

"Ruby and I need to head to Lachlann's now," Noelle told him. "Apparently there was a plan to kidnap Ruby and Jasper, and she wants to check on him."

Marcus's eyebrows shot up. "Let's go then. I'll come along."

Soon, we were standing in front of Lachlann's front door. Noelle knocked, and a moment later Lachlann answered. He was still in the clothes he'd worn to the party, but his hair was dishevelled, his face pale. "Lachlann?" Noelle asked. "Are you all right?"

He shook his head. "Not exactly. It's a good thing you showed up; I was about to fetch either you or the police chief."

"What happened?"

Lachlann sighed and looked away for a moment. Then he met Noelle's eyes. "I just killed Aiden Blackwell."

CHAPTER 29

I GAPED AT Lachlann.

"You…killed him?" Noelle repeated.

He nodded. "I got home, and Aidan was here, and he was—"

Noelle raised her hand. "First, tell me how recently he died."

"Maybe five, ten minutes ago?"

"And what did you kill him with?"

"I shot him."

"In the head?"

Lachlann nodded, and Noelle let out a sigh. "Well, so much for bringing him back."

"You don't want to bring him back." Jasper appeared in the doorway behind Lachlann. "He was trying to kill me."

I looked Jasper over. There was blood on his nightclothes, his hair was a dishevelled mess, and there were scratches all over his face. I couldn't miss the red marks on his neck, either, which were slowly beginning to darken into purple bruises. "Again?" I asked.

Noelle's eyebrows shot up. "He's tried to kill you before?"

"He was the one who beat me up at the pub that day."

Noelle let out a long sigh. "Where's the body?"

Lachlann beckoned that she should follow, and he led the way into Jasper's room. The window was flung wide open, and the room was an absolute mess. The bedside lamp had been knocked to the ground, a chair was tipped over and broken, and the contents of a bookcase were strewn across the floor. In the middle of it all lay Aidan Blackwell's unmoving body, face down, his hair stained with blood.

Noelle knelt gingerly next to him and pulled back his hair to reveal a bloodied wound where the bullet had entered. She put her hand over it, mumbled a spell, and began to hum softly. Jasper watched her with curiosity. "What are you doing? You said you couldn't heal him."

Noelle ignored his question until she had finished her song, then met his eyes. "I can't heal him. But most lifebringers can see what caused the wounds. By looking into it while it's still fresh, I can verify whether the stories you and Lachlann will tell me are valid." She glanced at Marcus. "Can you go fetch Desmond? I'm going to talk to these two."

Marcus nodded and left, and Noelle led the rest of us into the living room. I followed, my own encounter with Alvin temporarily forgotten. Noelle asked for a pen and paper and then looked Lachlann and Jasper over. "All right," she said when we were seated, "I want to hear Jasper's account first."

Jasper nodded, smoothed down his hair, and began to speak. "I was just about to get into bed when I heard a scraping sound. It seemed to come from the window.

I went over to investigate and was shoved backwards onto the ground. Then Aidan jumped through the window and tackled me. Someone must've made him invisible, and the spell broke when he came through the window, because he seemed surprised for a moment that he wasn't invisible anymore."

"Probably Alvin put an invisibility spell on him," I put in.

"And the spell broke because I have anti-magic stones all over this place," added Lachlann.

"That must be it," Jasper continued. "He jumped on me, and I tried to fight him off. I did all the things you do when you're fighting dirty, but nothing worked. It was like he was…stronger than normal." Jasper frowned. "He got his hands around my neck eventually, and he kept muttering this spell over and over, but it obviously wasn't working. I thought, this is it, I'm going to die. And then Lachlann came into the room, started yelling at Aidan and trying to pry him off me, but he couldn't for some reason, even though Lachlann's gotta be way stronger than Aidan. Then there was a big boom, and Aidan collapsed on top of me. I got out from underneath him, and there was Lachlann with his gun."

"Do you remember the words to the spell Aidan was trying to use?" Noelle asked.

Jasper frowned. "Something momentous, I think?"

"Teleport spell. He was trying to take you somewhere."

"That makes sense after what Alvin said to me," I put in.

Jasper's eyebrows arched. "Wait, what did Alvin do?"

"We'll fill you in after we're finished with this," Noelle said, turning to Lachlann. "All right. Your turn."

Lachlann's shoulders hunched. "My version is pretty similar to Jasper's. I came home after the party and heard a scuffle in Jasper's room. My gun is stored with my work uniform in the hall closet, so it was closer at hand than any blades. I grabbed it and went to see what was happening, and I found Jasper tackled by someone who was clearly trying to choke him. It took me a moment to figure out who it was.

"So I followed my training. First I yelled at Aidan to let go of Jasper. He ignored me, so I tried to pry him off. Like Jasper said, though, Aidan was stronger than I anticipated, unnaturally so. I tried flaring my anti-magic, and it seemed to weaken him just a bit, but he was still too strong. Then he kicked me in the stomach, and I went down. I realized I really couldn't fight him. I wasn't sure if shooting to injure would work, given that he was clearly on something, so I shot to kill." He sighed and averted his eyes.

"You think he was on something?" Noelle said. "A drug?"

"A magic potion. Likely something using fairy magic, given that it worked in my house. I'm pretty sure my friend Alexander makes strength potions; it was probably something similar to that."

Noelle nodded and wrote a few things down. "Well, everything both of you said matches what I saw, so that's good." She sighed, then reached over to where Lachlann sat on the couch and put a hand on his arm. "You did everything by the book. And you did what you had to. I can see that."

Lachlann nodded and gave her a tight smile.

"But that doesn't change the fact that this might get messy. The Blackwells are an influential family. They'll almost certainly try to have you charged with murder— not that the charge will stick, with what you've shown me. But whether or not you can be charged with anything, they'll want revenge. It might not be safe for you to stay here."

"What happened with Alvin?" Jasper cut in. "Did he attack you, Ruby?"

"Not in the same way," I replied. "He didn't try to knock me out. He snuck into my room and cornered me."

Jasper and Lachlann both listened as I told my own story. I noticed Jasper's fingers tightening against the arms of his chair as I spoke, and his mouth drew into a grim line. "That bastard," he muttered when I was done speaking. "I should hunt him down."

"Please don't. We have enough dead people on our hands here," Noelle said.

"Are you…all right?" Jasper asked me.

I blinked hard, trying to control the tears that threatened yet again.

"It's all right. You're allowed to cry." He got up from his chair, settled beside me on the couch, and put an arm around me.

I sniffled and swiped at my eyes. "Why are you the one comforting me here? You and Lachlann both had a far worse night than me, by the sounds of it."

"That's probably true. But Alvin must have scared you pretty badly regardless."

"I'm afraid to sleep in my room now," I told him. "What if Alvin comes back?"

"I can give you some of my anti-magic rocks if you like," Lachlann offered.

"I'm thinking it'd be best if the two of you stay at our place tonight," Noelle said. "Jasper, I imagine you don't want to sleep in your room while it's in that condition, and I don't want anyone coming here seeking retribution."

Marcus returned as Noelle was speaking, accompanied by Desmond and another guard I didn't know. Lachlann stood when the captain approached, his earlier nerves clearly returning. "Sir."

Desmond nodded at him. "I hear we have a body to deal with." His eyes flickered to Noelle. "Governor, I assume you've already corroborated their stories?"

"I have. They're telling the truth."

"Let me take a look at the body first, then we'll chat. Randall here is a teleporter; he'll move the body once I'm done."

Desmond and Randall disappeared, and Marcus settled down in the chair that Jasper had been sitting in. When Desmond reappeared a few minutes later, he said, "All right. Let's hear what happened."

Lachlann and Jasper both filled the captain in, and then Desmond asked me about my earlier encounter with Alvin. "I'm going to have to go to the Blackwells' place in the morning to let them know about Aidan," he said when we were finished. "I suppose I'll be doing an investigation while I'm there, trying to figure out what the boys were up to." He turned to Lachlann. "As Noelle said, you did everything by the book, but things tend to get complicated whenever there's a death. It's probably best that you stay at the governor's for now, and keep your head down. Don't go out unless you have to. I'm going to have to ask you to step down from the guard until the investigation is complete."

Lachlann nodded. "Understood, sir."

"Now, you folks had best get moving. It's late, and we may need to investigate further tomorrow."

Later on, I lay on my bed, trying to calm my nerves. As soon as we'd arrived back at the mansion, Saray, Trina and Starla began peppering us with questions about what happened. Jasper excused himself abruptly and asked to use the tub, clearly trying to avoid Saray. Lachlann headed to the backyard to talk to Kirilee, and I retreated to my room while Noelle filled the others in on the night's events. My head spun with all that had happened in the past few hours; I doubted sleep would come to me anytime soon.

I soon heard a knock on my door. "Come in."

Saray and Trina entered, their eyes wide. Both of them carried steaming cups of something. "How are you doing?" Trina asked.

I shook my head. "I wish I knew. Tonight was just…" I trailed off, the lump returning to my throat.

"I can imagine." Saray put her mug on the bedside table and sat down next to me.

"Who's the other mug for?"

"Jasper. I'm going to check on him in a few minutes," Trina told me.

"What is it?"

"Sleeping tea. It's from the Shrouded Woods, and it'll knock you out. My mom took some out to Lachlann."

I nodded. "He seemed pretty shaken up by the whole thing."

"Well, my mom will be a good person for him to talk to. She understands what it's like to have to kill to defend another."

In the hall, we heard someone approach and then a knock. "You all right in there, Ruby?" I heard Jasper ask.

"I should go give this to him," Trina said, gesturing to the tea.

"Make sure he's doing okay," I said. "He's not really talking to me about it because I had a bad night as well."

"I will," Trina promised, then slipped out the door.

Alone with Saray, I sipped my tea. "Do you think Alvin will come back here?"

"Not for a while, at least," she replied. "I know his parents were pretty angry at him."

"I'm just glad we're not in class together anymore." I shook my head. "I feel like the next time I see him, even if he's civil to me, it's just going to…bring everything back."

Saray nodded. "Trust me, I understand. It's hard to face someone who's attacked you like that."

"Have you ever been attacked that way?"

"Once. It wasn't over the same sort of thing, not at all, but…" She glanced at the door nervously.

"Oh." I nodded, realizing what she was referring to. "Well, I'm sorry Jasper has to stay here for a few days. Are you more comfortable around him now than you used to be?"

"Yes, but it's still not easy. I think you and Lachlann might be right, though. I need to talk things out with him." She put a hand on mine. "Are you all right to stay here alone tonight? We can switch rooms with you if you want."

"Thanks, but I think I'll be okay. Lachlann gave me some anti-magic rocks to protect myself." I sighed. "I should try to sleep. I hope the tea works."

Saray bid me goodnight, then took my empty cup and left me alone.

The following morning was quiet and tense. Marcus and Noelle both had work, Starla was in town running errands, and Saray had holed herself up in her room, reading and clearly avoiding Jasper. Lachlann went back to his place early to fetch several things, and he now had a leather project spread out on the deck, an obvious attempt to distract himself from the events of the night before. Jasper left for work shortly after I woke up, only to return an hour later saying that he'd been given the day off and that Desmond would be coming by the house shortly. Desmond arrived after lunch, accompanied by Noelle, and we all gathered in the parlour. "I have some news," he began. "I went by the Blackwells' this morning to tell them about Aidan's death and investigate what he and Alvin might have been up to. While I was there, I learned that Alvin fled the house sometime last night. He wasn't around when his parents woke up."

My eyes widened. "Do you think he's gone invisible? Despite what Noelle said?"

"It wouldn't surprise me. We have guards scouring the island for him, but he hasn't turned up as of yet."

"How'd they react to the news about Aidan?" Lachlann asked.

Desmond sighed. "They were heartbroken, of course. But they let me investigate regardless. And I did find some things of interest on their property. There was an abandoned outbuilding that contained a lot of rope, some pretty nasty-looking knives, and a few other implements."

I felt my stomach turn. "You think they were going to *torture* us?"

"That's what I thought, initially. But a few hours later, Ashlynn Blackwell showed up at the station and asked to speak with me. She told me that she could fill me in on her brothers' plans, so long as the rest of the family was left out of the investigation and none of this was made public." He glanced around at each of us. "What I'm going to tell you doesn't leave this room."

We all nodded.

"It seems the boys planned to kidnap both Ruby and Jasper, and bring them back to that outbuilding. Aidan wanted to torture and kill Jasper. Alvin had been trying to talk him down, but after Ruby rejected him, he decided to go along with the plan. He wasn't intending to torture you, though, Ruby. He planned to run away with you somewhere and start a new life."

I shuddered, remembering him saying those exact words to me the night before.

"The Blackwells do want a more thorough investigation into Aidan's death. And they know that they can't charge you with murder, Lachlann, but they will likely try to get you banished from Dundere."

Noelle nodded. "I figured that might be what they'd push for. Perhaps I can make a deal with them allowing Lachlann to visit us on occasion but remain on my property while in Dundere."

"That might work." Desmond stood. "I'd best be off. I'll come by and check on everyone in a few days."

Noelle showed Desmond out, and people began to drift from the parlour. Saray stayed sitting, though, and when Lachlann got up to leave, she stopped him. "Stay, Lachlann. And you as well, Ruby. And...you." Her eyes flickered to Jasper.

"Me?" He frowned. "What is this?"

"I need to talk to you about something. Ruby, you can stay for this as well. And Lachlann, you know why I need you." Lachlann nodded.

"Why's that?" Jasper asked.

"Because Lachlann has anti-magic. And I need anti-magic whenever I'm around you. There are some things I haven't told you." She gave him a nervous smile and began to explain to him how his presence was making it difficult for her to maintain control of her magic. "I've asked Lachlann to use his anti-magic to keep me from casting, which is likely why I don't have fire dancing on my hands right now," she concluded

Jasper nodded. "That's...difficult. I'm sorry I made you like this."

Saray's shoulders hunched. "I'm not telling you this just to make you feel bad. I think I know how to fix it."

Jasper cocked his head. "Tell me."

"Last night, after my parents and Ruby left to go check on you, Trina got Starla and me talking about her fear of fire and how she might be able to overcome it. I suggested that learning fire magic might help her with her fears. Then she'd be able to extinguish fire if it came too close to her. But I also suggested it because I figure that getting to understand the thing that scares her might help her be less afraid of it. And that made me think about my own fears. About you. Maybe I just need to get to know you better as a person, so that way I see you as more of a human and less of a threat, you know?"

Jasper frowned. "I suppose. So you want to...know more about me?"

She nodded. "I mean, it wouldn't hurt to try. Perhaps you and Lachlann and I could go for a walk? Maybe a hike in the woods or something. And we could just...talk. About our lives and our childhoods. About what made you join the Breoch Guard. And maybe even about what happened on that ship. I don't think it'll be easy for either of us, but I figure it might help me. And maybe it'll help you as well."

Jasper raised his eyebrows. "You might be right."

Saray turned to Lachlann then. "Would you be willing to help with this?"

"Well, I would, but it seems I'm under house arrest right now. Though if Jasper wears his stone pendant, then he should be safe from your fire." He smiled at Saray. "I'm proud of you for trying to work through this."

"Thanks." Saray smiled. Then she glanced at me. "Could you come along?"

"Me? I suppose so. But what would I do?"

Saray shrugged. "Talking to your brother is a big first step. I'm not sure if I'm quite ready to go hiking in the woods alone with him."

I smiled. "That's fair. When do you want to go?"

"I was thinking about the weekend. I'll be pretty busy once the school year starts up." She looked to Jasper. "Does that work for you?"

"It should. I can take you up to the volcano that your father showed me, if you'd like. And if you still think I'm a terrible person by the time we reach it, you can push me off the edge."

Saray laughed. "I probably won't take you up on that. But I suppose we'll see."

CHAPTER 30

THE FOLLOWING DAY, Alisa, Shawnie and Kaden showed up, all of them concerned about me after hearing what had happened with Alvin and Aidan. While we sat and visited, Kaden noticed Jasper's fiddle case in the living room, and she asked him if he played. The afternoon turned into one of dance and music, with Jasper accompanying either Kaden or me on the piano in the ballroom. Trina showed up part way through with her flute, and Marcus and Noelle came to dance. Trina convinced Starla to drag Lachlann inside to dance with her, and Shawnie waltzed with Alisa. At the end of a song, Shawnie approached me. "My turn," he said.

"You play?"

"I'm not as good as you or Kaden, but yes. Go dance and enjoy yourself." His eyes slid to Kaden as he spoke, and I quickly understood exactly why he was offering to play.

Shawnie traded off with me, and I joined Kaden as the music began. "You, uh, want to dance?"

Her eyes widened. "Yes," she squeaked.

I laughed and took her hands in mine. "Well, I assume you're not mad at me now."

She shook her head. "I wasn't really that mad in the first place. It's complicated."

"Sounds like you and I need to have a talk sometime." I raised my eyebrows as a thought occurred to me. "Are you busy this coming Saturday evening?"

"Not that I know of."

"I'm hiking to the top of a volcano with Jasper and Saray, and I wouldn't mind some company. The two of them have finally decided to talk out their issues."

"So you're there as a buffer?"

"Yes. My plan is to hang back and let them talk. I'd enjoy myself more if I had someone to chat with, though."

"Right. Sure, I'll go with you."

"Excellent," I smiled, then dipped her low as the song ended.

The week went on, many days ending with dancing in the ballroom or sword fighting in the backyard. Kaden came over most evenings, and I found myself looking forward to our upcoming chat on Saturday. When we danced, I couldn't help but notice her proximity to me, the grace of her steps and the way she wound her fingers into mine. Sword fighting brought out another side of her— a fierce, competitive streak that I found both entertaining and very appealing. *Am I getting a crush on Kaden?* It was odd suddenly seeing a friend, who I'd known for nearly a year, in this new and different light.

When Saturday arrived, Kaden showed up just after dinner, as planned. Marcus agreed to drive the four of us out to the mountain, and the ride was tense. It seemed like neither Kaden nor I wanted to begin our talk until we were out of the city. Saray was sitting with her eyes screwed shut, her breathing deep and deliberate. "What are you doing?" Jasper asked her.

"Trying not to cast," she replied. "Last time you and I were in a carriage going into the woods together, things didn't go so well."

"Right." Jasper glanced at me. "Ruby, why don't we switch seats?"

I swapped with him so that Saray and Jasper were no longer on the same bench, and I saw Saray's shoulders relax and her jaw unclench. She kept her eyes closed until we reached the base of the mountain, though, where Marcus gave us detailed instructions on how to reach the volcano. We thanked him, then began our ascent up a wooded path. Jasper and Saray walked in front, while Kaden and I hung back. For the first few minutes, we were both silent, tense.

Eventually, Jasper began to talk to Saray, his voice too low for us to hear. Kaden glanced around as the trees closed in above us, the noise of the city fading away. "This is beautiful," she said softly.

"It is," I agreed. "Dundere is really growing on me."

She nodded, and then the awkward silence descended once again until I cleared my throat. "So, uh, about the night where you found me on a date with Alvin. You say that you weren't really angry with me?"

Kaden nodded slowly. "I *was* angry, I guess, but more than that, I was scared," she admitted. "I was scared he was going to hurt you. Scared that you wouldn't come with me. Scared that you still loved him."

"I don't know if I ever quite loved him. I liked him a whole lot, and I liked going on dates and kissing and all that. But I don't know if that's what love is."

"There's one other reason I was upset with you." Kaden gave me a quick, nervous smile. "Alvin was right about my little secret. In case you hadn't figured that out yet."

My eyes widened. "You're…in love with me?"

Kaden's smile turned shy. "I'm not sure about love, exactly. But I do like you, Ruby. I've had a bit of a crush on you ever since you showed up on the island."

"I had no idea. At least not until Alvin said something."

"I kept it to myself because I didn't know that you also liked women. After you told me you did, I couldn't stop thinking about you." She sighed. "I was glad when you ended things with Alvin because he was obviously dangerous. But I was also glad because I thought that maybe I'd have a chance with you." She looked away for a moment. "If you're not interested, I understand. I value your friendship too much to force anything to happen."

"Kaden, I…" I trailed off, struggling for words. "I think it could work. Over this last week or so, I've started to feel things for you that weren't there before. I'll need to give it a bit of thought." I gave her my own nervous smile. "It's so strange to me that you've liked me all this time, though. You always seemed mad at me back on the island."

"I wasn't. Remember what I said about trying to make myself angry so I wouldn't lose control?"

I frowned. "It sure didn't seem that way. I remember the day I ran off, you were mad at me for going to watch the fireworks."

"I just didn't see how you could enjoy them. If anything, I was jealous of you."

"Jealous? Why?"

"Because you always seemed so…content. Being a prisoner, losing your hand and tongue, it didn't seem to bother you. I remember you saying once that you thought the island was peaceful." Her shoulders hunched. "I'm not sure how you did that. I couldn't get over what had been taken from me. I *was* angry, but not at anyone in particular. And I focused on my anger to make sure I didn't lose control of my magic again."

"That makes sense," I replied. "But I think you had more taken from you than I did. You had a happy family and a good upbringing. I was angry about losing my hand and tongue, but the island was the first place where I didn't feel like I was being forced into a mold. So being stuck there didn't bother me as much as some people."

Kaden nodded. "I'm sorry your family wasn't kind to you. Though Jasper seems decent."

"He's gotten better." I glanced up the path, then frowned. "Looks like we've lost him and Saray. We're going to have to start walking fast."

"I have a better idea." Kaden grinned at me. "Want to fly with me again? I promise it'll be more fun this time."

"I…uh…sure," I agreed. My heartbeat picked up again, though I was fairly certain it wasn't the thought of flying that caused it.

Kaden offered her hand to me, and I took it, her fingers winding between mine. "Ready?"

I nodded.

She spoke the flying spell, and we began to rise slowly off the ground. We cleared the tops of the trees but stayed relatively low. I spotted Jasper and Saray quickly, and Kaden took us down so we hovered above them. "Look up!" I called.

They both lifted their heads, startled. "By the Fae!" Saray exclaimed. "Which one of you can fly?"

"Me, obviously," Kaden said. "Would you two mind if I took Ruby for a little adventure in the sky?"

They exchanged a glance. "Go ahead," Saray said. "We'll meet you at the top."

We nodded, and Kaden lifted us again. The tops of the trees fell away as we rose, and I gaped at the view. Rolling hills covered in tall grasses or populated by lush trees spread out in every direction. Some low-lying sections were draped in fog, and I spotted several rocky outcroppings that looked like they would also be good hikes. The ocean mirrored the sky in the distance, its waves dancing with the oranges and pinks of the setting sun. "This is amazing," I whispered.

"I know," Kaden replied. "It's beautiful."

"Do you want to go faster?" I asked. "Because I can make that happen."

"How?"

I flicked my wrist, and the wind picked up behind us, sending us hurtling forward. Kaden let out a whoop of delight. "We really work well as a team," she exclaimed.

"I think so too." I gave her a shy smile and felt myself relaxing. Being up here in the clouds with Kaden felt…natural to me. *Perhaps I never noticed her because I thought romance was all about intensity*, I realized. My relationship with Alvin had been full of extravagant gestures, stolen kisses and midnight escapades, picnic dinners on the rooftop of the school. Being with him was fun, but not exactly relaxing.

Whereas Kaden, she felt like home.

I turned to her. "Want to have a picnic sometime? I know a lovely spot."

"Sure." She laughed and turned us toward Dundere City. It sprawled out beneath us, the setting sun glinting off metal roofs. I could see the governor's house from here, high atop its hill, and beyond it, the school of magic. I grinned, realizing that I'd be moving my belongings into the dorms tomorrow morning. *This is going to be a great school year.*

Kaden noticed the smoke the same time I did and drew in a sharp breath. "I think…I think the school's on fire!"

Sure enough, a column of black smoke was beginning to curl into the sky from the front of the school. I saw a hint of orange flame, just barely visible from this distance.

"Let's go take a look." Kaden directed us towards the flames. I began trying to summon clouds as we flew, but the sky held nothing but fading sunlight. "There's men down there," Kaden mumbled. "An army of some sort? Looks like an attack."

"But who would…" I squinted at them, and then my heart plummeted into my stomach. "They look like…Breoch Guard?"

"Come on," Kaden said. "We have to tell the others."

She turned us around, and we began flying back to the mountain. As we neared, we could see that Saray and Jasper had made it to the top, where the peak dipped into a large, mossy crater. It looked like they, too, had noticed the fire.

Kaden pointed her feet towards the ground again, and I followed suit. We landed next to the others, and Saray turned to us. "What's going on down there?"

"It's some sort of attack," Kaden said. "A bunch of uniformed men. And I hope I'm wrong, but if Ruby and I recognize the uniforms correctly, they look like Breoch Guard."

"That's impossible," Jasper said. "How would Breoch Guard manage to get…" He trailed off, and he and Saray exchanged a glance.

"The portal," Saray whispered. "They've breached the portal. We need to get down there." She turned towards the path that led back down the mountain.

"Wait," Kaden said. "It'll be quicker if we fly. You saw what I did with Ruby."

Saray nodded. "You're probably right."

"Are you sure it's safe?" Jasper frowned. "You can make three of us fly at once?"

"I can lend Kaden some of my magic," Saray said. She put a hand on Kaden's shoulder and mumbled a spell.

Kaden cast the flying spell on each of us, and Jasper let out a laugh as he rose from the ground. "This is incredible!"

"I agree." Saray gave him a tense smile. "I've never done this before."

"We should move," Kaden urged. "Ruby, give us some wind."

I closed my eyes and summoned the wind to our aid, and we took off towards the city, flying faster than before. Saray exchanged a grin with me, then let out a whoop. I couldn't help but smile back. As grim as the situation in front of us was, it was impossible to deny that flying like this was fun.

We soared over top of the trees and towards the column of black smoke that rose from the school. My eyes widened as we approached, and Jasper let out a groan. "This is bad."

What looked like several hundred Breoch Guard had poured into Dundere. The majority of the fighting took place close to the burning school; the local guards had assembled and were working to push the Breoch Guard back. But several of the Guard had split from the larger group and were running through the streets, shooting at civilians and setting fire to other buildings. I saw one Guard attempt to pin a screaming woman down, and bile rose in my throat. Just as I debated whether I could hit that particular man with lightning, a bullet whizzed past me, narrowly missing my arm.

Jasper swore. "They've seen us. Kaden, do you know which building is Lachlann's from up here? I should get my weapons."

Kaden nodded. "I think so."

"Get us onto the roof, as fast as you can. We're not safe up here."

"Hold on, everyone," Kaden said. "Ruby, more wind."

I called the wind to gust, and we hurtled toward the rooftop, a few more bullets whizzing by. "Get ready to land," Kaden yelled.

We all hit the flat rooftop running, driven by the wind's momentum. "Get close to the ground, everyone," Jasper called as he landed, dropping into a crouch. We followed suit. "I'm going to open the hatch to the building, and we'll all head into Lachlann's apartment."

I peeked over the side of the roof out of sheer curiosity. Several of the civilians had begun fighting back against the Breoch Guard, some of them using weapons of their own, others using their magic. I saw one woman fling a guard's gun away from him using telekinesis; another man appeared behind one of the guards and slit his throat. A teenager even encased a guard in ice, a power I'd never seen before.

"Ruby, come on," Jasper said. "We need to get inside where it's safe."

I gave the battle below one last look, then followed the others down the hatch.

When we reached the apartment, we were surprised to find Lachlann inside, working to strap on a suit of black leather armour. "I thought you were under house arrest," Saray said.

"I was, but then this happened. Noelle told me to come back here, suit up, and meet her downstairs."

"Do you know what's going on?" Jasper asked.

"The Breoch Guard breached the portal and set the school on fire. We don't know how they found the portal though. I hope Trina's thought to summon Willem; we'll need him for this fight." He sighed. "Can you folks help me strap this armour on?"

We assisted Lachlann with his breastplate and greaves, and then Jasper changed into his police uniform. Both of them armed themselves with swords and guns. "Do you have any extra blades?" Kaden asked Lachlann.

"Have you used live steel before?"

"No. But you've seen what I can do with blunted metal. I can handle this."

Lachlann frowned, considering, and then sighed. "I suppose I can arm you. I don't have any armour that would fit you, but I still have Kirilee's old belt; we can put one of my smaller swords onto that." He disappeared into another room and returned carrying the belt I'd worn into the Shrouded Woods and a short sword. "All right," he said once Kaden had strapped herself in, "let's head downstairs."

CHAPTER 31

WHEN WE GOT downstairs, we found Noelle standing outside her office, surrounded by the rest of her family. Several magikai waited nearby for their orders— guild leaders I realized.

Noelle saw us approach and let out an audible sigh. "Glad to see you kids are safe." She turned to Lachlann. "I need someone to take charge. The police are doing a wonderful job dealing with the main group of Guards, but we need more help. As you can see, a good number have broken out into the streets, and then there's all the mages trapped in the school."

I felt the blood drain from my face. "What?"

Noelle glanced over at me. "They made a point of setting the school on fire once everyone had settled down for the night. Most of the Yarel Island folk are still inside. My guess is they've flocked to the interior courtyard. I already have most of the firebrands down at the school trying to control the flames, but they're massive."

Lachlann nodded. "And you want me to take over?"

"Yes. I'm sure you know that Dundere doesn't have an army of its own. We're too small. And the magikai, they're powerful, but they're fractured. I need someone with a military background to take command. You're our best option right now."

Lachlann frowned. "Wouldn't it be best to have a magikai take charge? What about Willem?"

"Willem isn't responding," Noelle said. "Trina's tried summoning him three times, and he still hasn't come." I didn't miss the concern in her voice. "They need *you,* Lachlann. You have both military and police experience, you know how to think tactically, and you're a natural leader." She smiled. "I wouldn't pick you if I didn't think you could do the job."

"You think they'll listen to an anti-mage telling them how to best use their magic?"

"They'll listen to you if I tell them to. And you'll listen to me, too." She raised her chin. "You are living here and serving in the Dundere guard, which means that, as of right now, I'm your governor. And I'm giving you an order."

Lachlann's eyes widened; clearly Noelle didn't pull rank on him often. "Well, in that case," he replied, "yes ma'am." He gave her a firm salute.

Noelle chuckled and clapped him on the shoulder. "You'll do just fine. Come on, let's give these folks some orders."

"Gather the guild leaders, and I'll see what I can come up with."

Noelle began calling the guild leaders in, and Saray turned to Lachlann. "If you need people to fight the fire from the inside, I don't mind being one of them. Kaden can make me fly again, and I'll drop into the courtyard."

Lachlann frowned. "That could work, but I'm worried about smoke. Are you able to command the direction of the smoke as well as the flames?"

"I might be able to help with that," I put in. "I could make a small storm inside the courtyard and pull everyone into the eye of it. Though that might make the fire worse."

"If you and I work together, we might be able to control that," Saray said.

"And I can fly people out of the courtyard," Kaden put in. "I can only put the spell on a few at a time, but if I can get some volunteers, we'll start pulling people out."

"I can help with that if you make me fly again," Jasper said.

"That's a good idea." Lachlann nodded. "If we can get a few teleporters to help as well, that would be ideal. Though, of course, it'd be best if we could get those folks out of there more than a few at a—" Lachlann stopped talking abruptly and turned at the sound of quickly approaching footsteps.

Saray's eyes went wide. *"Kip?"*

Kip skidded to a stop next to Lachlann, gasping for breath. He was clad in a green suit of armour and armed with several blades and a bow. "Uh, hi," he greeted Saray, giving her a nervous smile. "Sorry I'm late for the battle."

"How did you know that we were…"

"Willem and I heard the guards moving through the Shrouded Woods. They beat us to the portal, but Willem and Hilda are fending off a good number of them from their side. I got through just before they got the portal closed."

"Well, I'm glad you're here," Saray finally said, giving him a small smile.

"So am I," Lachlann said. "We could really use you."

The guild leaders had all arrived by now, and they huddled around us, eager for instructions. Lachlann took a deep breath. "All right, folks. You can see that the Breoch Guard had the advantage of surprise, but we have the numbers and the home turf. We just need to organize. Do we have eyes on the portal to make sure there's no one else coming through?"

"We do, the police are covering that," Noelle said. "It's been about half an hour since the initial surge, and we haven't seen anyone new."

"Willem's closed it from the other side," Kip put in.

"Good. So it seems like the police have the main battle pretty well in hand, but some of the guards have broken away and are attacking civillians in the streets."

"Those aren't normal Breoch Guard," Noelle said.

"Oh?" Lachlann turned to her.

"They don't have the same uniforms, and they're certainly not following orders. Starla thinks the Breoch Guard brought in a contingent of Witch Slayers, likely because they're less fearful of the Shrouded Woods."

I shuddered at her words, and Lachlann's eyes went wide. "Well, we'd best work on eliminating them, then. And even more urgent than that, we have the issue of the mages trapped in the school. Here's what we're going to do."

Lachlann began explaining his plan, assigning a different task to each guild. When he got to the stormbrewers and asked them to create a localized rainstorm over the school to help quench the fire, Saray spoke up. "I have an idea."

Lachlann turned to her. "What's that?"

"Have the stormbrewers create a more widespread rainstorm. When I was on the Breoch Guard ship, we were saved in part by Harvey bringing in rain. I know the guns they're using don't fire well when they're wet, so that'll force the Breoch Guard to switch to blades, which will give the common folk a fair chance against them."

Lachlann raised his eyebrows and nodded. "That's a good idea. Of course, it'll mean that our police can't use guns either, but we're all skilled with swords. Thanks for that, Saray."

"One problem," Chase put in. "We've had so little rain as of late that forming clouds will take a bit of time. We'll work as fast as we can, but I can't promise we'll be fast enough to put out the fire."

Lachlann nodded. "You can only do what you can. Get started."

"All right, I'll fetch the—"

"Father!" A young voice interrupted, and my eyes widened as Sophie collided with Chase.

"Sophie! What are you doing here?"

"I was scared someone might've shot you!" she cried, clinging to him.

"Well, I'm here, and I'm unharmed, all right?" Chase put an arm around his daughter. "Lachlann, can I get a teleporter to take Sophie home?"

"I want to stay and help!" she protested.

"Absolutely not. You're in a lot of danger right now, Sophie. And what would you do?"

She shrugged. "I need to do *something*. I can't just hide at home while the city is being attacked!"

"Sophie, listen to me, we don't have time for—"

"Stop!" She pulled abruptly away from Chase. "Stop trying to protect me from anything that could go wrong! I'm tired of hiding at home because you think the world is too dangerous for me!" She began playing with one of her braids. "There has to be something I can do." I frowned, noticing the familiar pattern her hand was moving in. *Wait a minute.*

"Chase?" Noelle cut in. "Would you be comfortable with Sophie assisting the doctors inside the medical centre?"

Chase let out a sigh. "Fine." My eyes widened, and I stared at Sophie, recalling her telling me when we'd first met that she didn't have any magical abilities. *Does she have any idea what she just did?*

"All right, there you go, Sophie," Lachlann said. "You'd best head inside and see what kind of work they can find you."

Sophie nodded and hurried to assist however she could. Chase shook his head. "Sorry about that," he mumbled and went off to round up the stormbrewers.

Lachlann turned to Kaden, Saray, Jasper and me and went over our plan to get the mages out of the school. Then he looked to Noelle. "I'm sure you know what to do."

"Of course." Noelle nodded. "Though I'm thinking it might be best for the doctors and me to set up at city hall. There's more room there for healing work, and it's more central. Get me a teleporter, and I can move my entire office over there."

"We're going to need guards for you, as well. I'm willing to be one myself, as city hall is a good place to give orders from."

"Some folks will probably try to use their guns despite the rain," Marcus added, "and if we do have to deal with bullet wounds, Noelle and I will need to work together. I can also help with arrow wounds in the same way. So I can be the second guard."

Lachlann nodded. "All right, let's get to work."

The faintest wisps of clouds began to form above the ocean soon after we'd parted ways. I added my own power to the storm, calling the clouds to thicken. Then Kaden, Saray, Jasper and I rose into the air. "Get close to me," I told them. "I'll try to keep the smoke away from us as we fly over."

I took control of the wind, causing it to blow in a circle around us to keep the smoke out of our faces. It didn't work perfectly; all of us were coughing as we made our way through the massive plumes of grey that billowed from the school. Through the haze, I noticed that a fair number of the Yarel Island folk had gotten safely out; most of them were huddled together a good ways from the fighting, many of them coughing and struggling to breathe. I saw Alisa and Shawnie among them and breathed a sigh of relief. "Those folks need medical attention," Saray said.

Kaden nodded. "I'll go back to the medical centre after the first run and see if Lachlann can find a teleporter who can get them all back to Noelle."

The smoke cleared somewhat directly above the courtyard, and amidst the sounds of crackling flame and falling wood, I began to hear a new sound.

Screams.

They were muffled and mingled with coughing and gasping. We flew lower, and I realized I could make out faces through the haze. Although several of the mages had managed to escape, those who remained—still a few hundred— huddled together. "We're here to help!" Kaden shouted down to them. A few weak cheers went up in response.

We plummeted to the courtyard, landing in soft piles of ash. My heartbeat picked up as I looked around; we were surrounded by fire.

It licked at the building on all four sides of us, blackening the stone and consuming everything it could burn within. I felt someone collide with me and saw that a younger girl whose name I didn't know had latched onto me, shaking and crying. "Get us out of here," she sobbed.

"We will," I promised. Then I gazed around at the terrified, ash-covered faces. "Who here is the most hurt?"

A few were brought forward, and Kaden and Jasper each took to the sky again, carrying the injured with them. I noticed both of them beginning to cough and gasp as they took flight. *This is bad.* "Everyone get close to me," I shouted as I began to call the wind to circle us and keep the smoke at bay.

As I worked, I noticed clouds forming above us, and I glanced up at them anxiously. *They're not ready.* The clouds were still weak, too wispy to put out a fire of this size. I began to move the wind in a circle, but it only provided a small amount of relief from the smoke, and if anything, it seemed to make the flames leap higher. Saray stood near the building, eyes closed as she fought against the flames, but she could only do so much. A few others, obviously firebrands themselves, joined her.

A group of teleporters appeared then and began to pull people out. Alisa was among them; she gave Kaden and me a quick hug before disappearing with the young girl who'd clung to me. I kept my attention on the wind, and I could tell that it wasn't enough. The clouds above were beginning to thicken, but I knew that they would only be able to produce a weak rain at best. We were all coughing again, and out of the corner of my eye, I saw an older man catch someone as she collapsed. "Get those two out next!" I called to Jasper as he and Kaden reappeared. Both of them had torn pieces of their shirts wrapped around their noses and mouths to try to control how much smoke they were breathing in. My eyes stung fiercely, and I noticed one of the younger mages hunched over the fountain in the center of the courtyard, trying to wash the smoke out of his eyes.

Wait a minute.

An idea came to mind, one that I hadn't thought about since my time on the Lady Liara. I turned to the remaining mages. "Are any of you telekinetics?"

Only one put up his hand. "What do you need?"

I led him to the corner of the courtyard, where the small staircase led down to the locked door. "Can you pull that door off its hinges?"

He frowned. "Should be easy enough. Why?"

"I need access to the river. I have an idea."

He nodded, closed his eyes, and flicked his wrist. I saw his jaw clench as he fought against the locks and hinges, but a moment later, the door broke free.

I thanked him, then mumbled my casting words and reached into the cavern with my mind, calling on the river below. A few moments later, mist began to snake its way up to us. I put my face into it, feeling instant relief as the smoke around me cleared. "Everyone come over here!" I called out to the remaining mages.

We huddled around the doorway as the mist rose and filled the courtyard. The violent coughing all but ceased, and I heard several folks let out gasps of relief. I made the mist rise higher and fan outward, slowly enveloping the remains of the building. I saw the fire on the outer edges of the courtyard begin to sputter. The clouds above us broke right then, their rain adding to the effort. Turning my face up, I breathed in the sweet, life-giving air.

Kaden and Jasper continued lifting people out of the courtyard, and I kept the mist rolling in, my head spinning as I focused all my energy on keeping it rising. It felt like a good hour later that Saray let out a whoop. "I think the fire's out!" she exclaimed.

"That it is," Kaden called down as she landed, followed by Jasper.

I let out a sigh of relief, and the world began to spin around me as he spoke. I keeled over and hit the ground, gasping.

"Ruby, you all right?" I heard Jasper ask.

"She's probably exhausted from having to hold a spell for that long," Saray shouted over to him. "Why don't you get Ruby out of here so she can recover? Kaden, go let the telekinetics know they can punch that hole in the wall now that the fire's out, and then come back for me. I'll be more use outside now."

Jasper nodded and helped me to my feet. Then he wrapped his arms around my waist, and a moment later we were airborne, soaring over the plumes of smoke and into the fighting beyond. A few men fired at us as we flew, but their guns fizzled out. I saw the telekinetic guild leader gathering all the other telekinetics below, preparing them to punch a hole in the school wall to get the remaining mages out. Kip looked up and made eye contact with me.

"I'm going to get you to Noelle," Jasper told me as we flew over them. "Just in case you've inhaled too much—"

His words were cut short by a scream. A moment later, I realized it was my own, and then all I could think about was *pain*.

CHAPTER 32

MY GUT WAS on fire, my breath coming in gasps. The world spun violently, and I realized I was falling. I tried to think of the words to summon the wind, tried to convince it to catch me, but I couldn't speak, could hardly breathe. The ground hurtled up towards me. *I'm going to die.*

Then, barely a foot off the ground, something caught me.

"Got you." I heard Kip's voice nearby and realized through my haze of pain that he'd seen what was happening and caught me using his telekinesis. Glancing down, I saw the source of my agony— a crossbow bolt buried in my gut, just below my ribcage.

"Oh, thank the Fae," I heard Jasper exclaim from just above us, his voice disembodied and strange. "I thought I'd lost you, Ruby, I…"

The rest of Jasper's words were lost to me as I was tackled. The cushion of telekinesis was gone now, and I was on the ground, a hooded figure pinning me down. I heard Kip let out a yelp nearby and then there came a thud. I blinked, the face above me— and the quiver on the person's back— coming into focus. My heart dropped when I realized who held me down and who had almost certainly shot me. *What is* she *doing here?*

"G…Gabby?" I gasped. "Let me up!"

Gabrielle's face was contorted with hatred. "I don't think so," she growled. "I should've killed you back on the boat."

I turned my head. "Help," I managed to squeak. But Kip, it seemed, had also been tackled by one of the other Breoch Guards and was caught in a fight.

One of Gabrielle's hands closed around my neck, and I felt her begin to press down. *She's going to kill me.* "Gabby…no…st—" I gasped.

"Gabrielle!" I heard Jasper's voice now as he landed next to us. "Gabby, stop it!" He reached down to pull her off me; she responded by elbowing him hard in the stomach with her free arm. Jasper doubled over, and my vision began to swim. *No, please. Not like this.*

Then, through a haze of pain and encroaching darkness, I heard a softly mumbled string of words. A spell.

Gabrielle let out a shriek, and her hands slackened around my neck. I gasped for breath, my vision slowly returning.

A moment later, I realized Gabrielle was suspended above me by magic, and only then did I see the point of a crossbow bolt— from the very quiver that Gabrielle had been carrying— protruding from her chest. A boot entered my field of vision, and Kip kicked Gabrielle off of me. He pulled open my tunic and assessed the damage.

Next to me, I could hear Gabby coughing and gurgling. Through a haze of pain, I saw Jasper hovering in the background, his eyes darting between Gabby and myself. Gabby let out a laboured, choking breath, blood bubbling on her lips. Kip's eyes flickered to her, and he flinched visibly. Drawing his knife, he came to stand over her.

Jasper's eyes widened. "Wait, Kip, you don't have to *kill* her!"

"Would you rather she die slowly and painfully?" Kip's voice was flat. "She can't survive this, Jasper. Neither can Ruby, unless we get her some help."

Jasper shook his head. "You don't understand, now Jade will never—"

"We don't have time for this." I didn't see Kip open Gabby's throat, but a second later, I heard a long, gasping sigh, and Jasper squeezed his eyes shut. Then Kip gathered me up, and I screamed involuntarily as the pain in my stomach flared.

Then he was running, and all I could think about was the pain, worsened by each jostling step he took. It seemed like he ran for hours.

I eventually heard more voices, first Kaden and Saray asking what happened, and then Trina, who'd clearly seen Kip running with me from her vantage point. Then, finally, Marcus. "Well, that doesn't look good."

"Do you want me to assist Noelle?" Kip asked.

"No, I'll do it. You get back out on the field. Lachlann, can you cover for me?"

"On it," I heard Lachlann reply.

Then I was inside city hall, being lowered onto a hard surface, and I heard Kip describing my condition to Marcus and Noelle. My vision was beginning to darken again. "Ruby?" I heard Noelle's voice, soft and concerned. "Stay with us, Ruby, we're going to get you healed up."

I felt a hand take mine. "I'm here," Kaden said. "Hold on, Ruby."

A moment later, I heard footsteps and then Jasper's voice. "Is she…going to be all right?"

"She will if we can get this bolt out quickly," Noelle told him.

I gritted my teeth against the pain and fought to stay conscious. Marcus hovered above me, concern etched into his face. "All right, Ruby, I'm going to pull the bolt out. It's buried pretty deep, so this is going to hurt. But once I'm done, Noelle will heal you, and then you won't be in pain."

I attempted a nod.

"Are you two willing to hold her down for us?" Marcus asked Kaden and Jasper. "It'll make it easier for Noelle and me."

"I'll take her legs," Kaden said. "I don't think I can watch this."

I felt a pair of hands grip my calves and another my shoulders. I looked up and saw Jasper staring down at me, his eyes wide with concern. I noticed that his forearm was bloodied and realized that the crossbow bolt must have grazed him before it hit me, causing him to let go. Then Marcus came into view, holding a piece of leather. "Bite down."

I gripped the leather between my teeth. "Go," I heard Noelle say, and then I was screaming into the leather as my insides turned to fire. I tried to thrash, but Jasper and Kaden held me securely. Noelle, I realized, was singing, just as she had when she'd healed my hand and tongue. I heard Lachlann in the background telling Saray, Kip, and Trina to leave me be, to get back out there and fight. It sounded like they were arguing with him.

"It's out," Marcus said. "Your turn, Noelle."

Her singing grew louder now, and I shuddered as the pain decreased, then faded altogether. Soon I was gasping for breath, and Marcus and Noelle grinned at one another. He walked over to her side of the bed and put his arm around her. "Always a pleasure being your teammate."

Then there was the blast of a gunshot, and Noelle keeled forward.

She landed on me, and a second later Jasper was pulling me off the slab where I'd been lying. "Get down!" he hissed, ducking. I stared at him, then at Kaden on my other side, who'd followed Jasper's lead. *What's happening?*

"Noelle?" Marcus stared down at her, a dazed expression on his face.

"Marcus, I…" Noelle's voice was hoarse. She tried to push herself up into a standing position, and failed.

Marcus swept her into his arms and put her on the slab. "What happened?" Then his eyes travelled down to her blouse, where a dark stain was spreading on her left side. He took a deep breath. "Don't worry, Noelle, we'll get it out. Hold still, all right? I'll get the bullet out and then you can heal yourself, it won't be too—" He was interrupted by the sound of another gunshot, and then he let out a cry of pain and sank down.

I heard more screams and cries from outside, and saw Saray, Kip, and Trina running back towards the hall. Lachlann stepped in front of the entryway, blocking them. "Stay back!" he hissed. He had his own gun out of the holster and was looking around furtively. "There's someone out there with a gun, and I can't…I can't see where they are." For the first time since I'd met him, I heard fear in Lachlann's voice. A third gunshot sounded, and a bullet whizzed over my head.

"Lachlann!" Noelle's voice was surprisingly strong, and he turned to face her.

I saw her signing something to him. I couldn't make out what she was saying from my angle, but I saw his response. *"I can't. You'll die."*

Noelle spoke again, her voice raspy. "That's…an order."

Lachlann closed his eyes, his shoulders slumping. Then he gripped his pendant, and a moment later, I cringed as a wave of anti-magic blasted through me. I saw the other magikai recoil.

Not ten feet in front of Lachlann, right next to Saray, a figure appeared on the covered portico, his gun trained on Lachlann. The blood drained from my face as I took in the familiar strawberry-blond hair, the lanky build, the smug grin.

Saray let out a gasp. "Alvin!" she cried. "You traitor!"

CHAPTER 33

ALVIN RESPONDED BY seizing Saray and jamming his gun into her temple. "Put your weapon down, Lachlann, or I shoot her."

I watched, wide eyed, as Lachlann lowered his gun. "Put it on the ground," Alvin said. "And then your sword belt." He glanced over at Kip. "You. Same thing. Sword belt on the ground." Both men complied.

Beside me, Jasper let out a soft laugh. "You missed one." I glanced over at him to see him pulling his gun from its holster. He ducked behind the slab and crawled around me. Kaden moved in where Jasper had been and grabbed my hand. I noticed hers was ice cold.

Both Lachlann and Kip were disarmed now, and Lachlann stood, hands raised. Alvin grinned at him. "Now, you're going to take a walk with Saray and me, and you'll keep that anti-magic going so I can hand her off to the Breoch Guard."

"I knew that you were a creep who has no respect for women," Saray snarled. "But a *traitor?* You'd turn on your own people?"

"*You're* not my people. You're one of *them.* Or have you forgotten? A helpless orphan from Breoch who thinks she can just show up here and get the royal treatment." He smirked at her. "You're the real reason they're here, you know. They wanted to burn those mages to a crisp in their sleep, of course, but more importantly, it gave them an excuse to come look for you. Their captain told me as much when I went to the Guard hall in Sylvenburgh to report what I'd seen here." My mouth fell open at his words. *Alvin was the one who led the Guard to the portal?*

On my left, Jasper shifted, and I heard the click of him moving a bullet into place. He aimed the gun towards Alvin, who hadn't noticed him yet. Saray had, however, and her eyes went wide when she saw what he was doing. "Tell Saray to keep him talking," Jasper hissed to me. "This is trickier than I thought."

I met Saray's eyes and signed to her. She gave me a slight nod, then let out a sharp laugh, much to Alvin's surprise. "Really? Again? You folks are lacking in creativity." Her voice was higher than normal, but she managed a smirk.

Alvin raised an eyebrow. "What do you mean?"

"Putting a gun to someone's head to force another's cooperation. Using anti-magic to rein me in. This has all happened before. And in case you weren't aware, I *won* last time."

Alvin snickered. "You won't get away so easily now. The Breoch Guard knows your tricks. They have ways to contain you."

"Only, just like last time, your plan is full of holes," she countered. "First of all, you're not going to actually kill me."

"And what makes you think that? I'm not afraid to put a bullet in someone, in case you hadn't noticed." He nodded at Noelle.

Saray went pale for a moment. Then she squared her shoulders. "That may be true. But that doesn't change the fact that you won't shoot *me*." She smirked again, but it was obviously forced; I could see her smug facade beginning to crumble. "After you ran away, you went to the Breoch Guard, gave away the location of the portal, and told them I was in Dundere. Am I right?"

He huffed. "Mostly."

"Well, if you're in it for the money, then you'd best keep me alive, because I have a few contacts in Breoch, and I know from talking to them that the price on my head is five times higher that way. The Breoch Guard wants to execute me publicly to make an example out of me. So you're not going to shoot me."

Beside me, Jasper sighed. "I don't think I can make the shot without hitting Saray," he whispered. "If she was shorter, maybe, but Alvin's got her between him and us like a shield."

"And if your plan is to take me to the Breoch Guard," Saray was saying now, "once we're off this porch, you wouldn't be able to shoot me, with the rain being the way it is. So you'd be unarmed, and even if Lachlann came along to keep the anti-magic going, don't think for a moment that he wouldn't attack you as soon as he was able. Kip too. So you'd be facing off against them, and me, and likely some of these other folks. So again, your plan is full of holes. Now, are you going to let me go?"

Alvin chuckled softly. "Absolutely not," he said. "You misunderstand one thing, Saray. Sure, I'd like to get some money for handing you in, but this is about revenge."

Her eyes went wide, and I saw them dart to Jasper. "Revenge?" she repeated.

"Your quarrel is with me, Alvin, not Saray," Lachlann spoke up. "If this is about your brother, take it out on me, not her."

"I am taking it out on you," Alvin said. "The best way to hurt you isn't to cause physical pain. It's to hurt someone you care about."

Beside me, Jasper swore. "Alvin's right," he mumbled.

Alvin figured out Lachlann's weakness, I realized, thinking back to my conversation with Jasper after Aidan's first attack. *But I wonder what Alvin's weakness is?*

"This isn't *just* about you," Alvin went on. "It's about Saray and Trina, and Marcus using that spell on me the other night, then ratting me out to my parents. It's about Noelle and her ideas about what I should be allowed to do with my magic, and about Ruby." He met my eyes for a moment, and Jasper ducked. "She knows what she did."

Wait a minute. I do know his weakness!

I noticed him tug at a strand of Saray's hair as he spoke, his hand moving in a familiar, almost obsessive motion, and a thought occurred to me. "I have a plan," I whispered to Jasper. "But you'll have to trust me. Shoot as soon as you have the chance."

"So I have no problem killing you right here, Saray, in front of everyone," Alvin finished triumphantly. "In fact, I might do it right about—"

"Wait!" I leapt up, my hands raised. "Alvin, stop." I came around the side of the slab, Kaden gaping at me as I did.

Alvin's eyes narrowed. "Ruby?"

"Lachlann's right, this isn't really about Saray," I reasoned. "Running off to the Breoch Guard…you did that because of me. You may be angry at all of us, but I'm the one you're most angry at. So how about you let Saray go, and…you can have me."

He frowned. "You mean, you'll be my girlfriend?" He began to toy with Saray's hair again, clearly trying to figure out if, somehow, his charm was working on me.

I sighed. "Look, maybe I was a little harsh with you the other day. Maybe I should give you a chance after all. But I'm not going to unless you let Saray go."

Saray stared at me. "Ruby, what are you doing?"

I ignored her. "Come on, Alvin. Put away the gun, let go of Saray, and let's get out of here. We can run away together, just like you said."

He stared back at me for a moment, then released Saray with a shove. Kip shot forward and caught her, and Alvin grinned at me wolfishly, alternating between toying with his own hair and fiddling with his earring. Now that I was close to him, I could see that his eyes were afire with gold tones once again. "Well. This is an unexpected surprise."

"I'm known to be surprising." I smiled sweetly at him. "Put that gun away. It's not very romantic to court a woman while you're holding a loaded weapon, you know."

He lowered his gun slowly, then took a tentative step towards me, taking my hand. "Ruby," he whispered. His eyes flickered to the right for a moment. "Do you mean it?"

"I do," I replied, my heart thudding in my ears.

"Good. Because we're running." With one fluid motion, Alvin spun me around and pulled me to his chest, and I gasped as the barrel of his gun jammed into my temple. "Nice try," he hissed in my ear. Then his head snapped up. "Jasper, put that gun away or Ruby dies."

My heart sank, and I felt my breath coming in gasps as panic set in. *Now what do I do?*

"You really think I was going to buy that?" Alvin sneered. "I'm not quite as stupid as you want to believe, my dear." He let out a soft laugh. "Now you get to run away with me, though, just like you said. Let's take a walk, shall we? We won't need Lachlann for this."

He pulled me backward to the edge of the portico, his eyes on the others and his arm firmly around me. I carefully considered my odds of getting away. *As soon as we clear Lachlann's anti-magic, he can go invisible.* There was a chance I could hit him with lightning, but with him holding on to me the way he was, I'd likely electrocute myself as well. And though his gun might not work in the rain, I was unarmed too. It would be a battle of brute strength to get away from him. *What have I gotten myself into?*

I let out an involuntary cry as we neared the edge of the portico; the anti-magic was beginning to fade away. Alvin stepped down into the rain, leaving me on the portico edge, the gun still pressed against my head. I squeezed my eyes shut. Then he leaned in and whispered in my ear. *"Dominae Araknae—"*

"I wouldn't do that if I were you."

My eyes flew open, and I gaped at the pigtailed girl in front of me. She had a green fairy perched on her shoulder, and she was holding on to a large amethyst pendant, her eyes fixed on Alvin. "S…Sophie?" I squeaked.

She ignored me, twirling her pigtail in the same pattern I'd noticed earlier. "Alvin, I really think you should let go of Ruby."

Alvin stared at her for a moment. "I…uh…yes, I suppose you're right." He let out a shuddering sigh and obeyed Sophie's commands.

I collapsed as he released me. "Good," Sophie said. "Now put the gun on the ground, come over here, and take a seat."

"It's probably best if I do that," he mumbled. I gawked at her as Alvin seated himself. *I was right— she's a charmer!*

Lachlann stared in astonishment at Sophie as well, his eyebrows knitted. Sophie put a hand on Alvin's shoulder, then met Lachlann's eyes. "Arrest him."

Lachlann's anti-magic released, and he snatched his gun off the ground. "Jasper!" he called out. "Help me secure him!"

I watched, my head spinning, as the two men put Alvin in handcuffs. "Can you try to track down some more guards to take him away?" Lachlann asked Jasper. His voice, I noticed, was shaking.

Jasper nodded. Then he turned to me and grabbed my hand. "Are you all right?" His eyes were wide, and his skin was ice cold.

"I…I think so," I mumbled.

"Ruby, I'm sorry, I…" I thought I heard his voice break. Then he shook his head. "Never mind. I'll talk to you about it later." He turned, then disappeared into the rain.

"I can watch Alvin," Sophie said to Lachlann. "You should go see Noelle."

Only now did I realize that everyone else was clustered around the slab. I followed Lachlann back into the room and came over to Kaden. She grasped my hand tightly, but her eyes were still on Noelle, whose face was pale, her breathing shallow. Marcus held her hand tightly, seemingly oblivious to the dark stain spreading above his own shoulder blade.

I heard Lachlann calling out more orders. "Cover for us," he said to someone. Then he closed the large double doors and came to join the rest of us. "Kip, can you get the bullet out of her?"

Noelle shook her head. "It's…too late," she rasped. "I'm too weak. I won't be able to heal."

Trina sobbed, and Lachlann's eyes went wide. "I…I'm sorry," he whispered.

"Don't," she said. "I…gave you an order."

"We have to try." Marcus's voice trembled as he spoke. "We have to do something to save you."

"No," she said firmly. "No life transfers, or…anything like that." She met his eyes. "Promise me."

Marcus shook his head. "Noelle, I can't…"

"*Promise* me," she repeated. "You need to let me go."

Saray took Noelle's hand on her other side. "We won't do any life transfers," she said, her own voice trembling. "Promise."

Noelle turned her head and gave Saray and Trina a ghost of a smile. "I…I love you girls." Then, turning back to Marcus, she said, "And you…you've been everything to me." Her trembling hand reached up and ran down his cheek. "I love you so much."

Marcus stooped to kiss her gently. "You're the most amazing woman I've ever known," he whispered. "I'm here with you 'til the end."

Lachlann put a hand on my shoulder. "Ruby, can you get Rayla to come help with Marcus's shoulder?" he said. "And Kaden, do a fly-over and see if you can find us a teleporter." We both nodded and left the room without a word. My head spun as I pulled open the door.

Outside, we found Jasper and Sophie watching the doors and several other guards busy with Alvin. "How is she?" Jasper asked.

"Not good," I said. "Sophie, you'd best come back to the other healers with me." Sophie nodded, and Kaden gave my hand one last squeeze before flying off.

Minutes later, I'd returned to the hall with a confused, wide-eyed Rayla in tow. Alvin was gone, the doors were still closed, and Jasper guarded the door. The shouts and gunshots of battle sounded in the distance, and smoke billowed from the charred ruins of the school.

"I think the battle is turning in our favour," Jasper said. "A lot of those folks who were trapped in the school were eager to get out there and do some damage."

A form in the sky caught my eye, and I saw Kaden approaching, accompanied by not one, but two figures. When they landed, Alisa and Shawnie bolted towards me, crushing me in their embraces. "I heard you got shot, and I thought it was over," Shawnie said, his voice catching in his throat.

"I'm so glad you're okay," Alisa put in. "What happened?"

"I'll explain later," Kaden told her. "But are we...supposed to go back in there?"

I crossed the portico and cracked open the door. Everyone was still gathered around Noelle. Marcus knelt, his head resting on her collarbone, Trina sobbed into Kip's shoulder, and Lachlann had an arm around Saray, who shook visibly. He glanced up at me and gestured that we should come in.

I slipped through the doorway, Jasper and the others close behind. Noelle's eyes were closed, her form completely still. The arm that she'd had around Marcus was now limp, and I felt a lump rise in my throat. Less than half an hour ago, she'd been vibrant, strong, and saving lives like she always did. *How does someone so full of life just cease to exist?* My eyes flickered to Saray, then Trina. "I...I'm sorry," I offered.

Rayla was staring down at Noelle, seemingly in shock. "What happened here?"

"There was a gunman," Lachlann said. "We weren't able to save her." He sighed then. "I'm sorry, we need your help with Marcus though; he got shot in the shoulder. And then we'll need as many healers as possible to make up for this."

"Of course," Rayla said, but her voice was weak.

Lachlann let go of Saray and crouched down next to Marcus, putting a hand on his uninjured shoulder. "I know this is terrible timing, but we need to get that bullet out of you, all right?"

Marcus nodded, his face blank.

"I'm going to help you up, and we'll see what we can do." Lachlann got Marcus to his feet and escorted him to a nearby chair. "Kip, I'm going to need your help over here."

Kip nodded and let go of Trina. "Jasper, come help me hold Marcus down," Lachlann said then. I watched as Lachlann cut the shoulder of Marcus's shirt and moved around to the front of the chair. He leaned down and locked Marcus's arms in place. "You hold his legs." Jasper nodded and got into position.

"All right, Kip, your turn." Kip stepped forward and muttered his spell, and I cringed, remembering how much pain this same action had caused me. Marcus squeezed his eyes shut, his face contorted, but he didn't struggle or yell.

"Got it." Kip held up the bullet a moment later. "Can you take a look at the wound, Rayla?"

She nodded and began to clean his shoulder. "I'll have to stitch this shut," she mumbled. "This'll hurt; you two had best hold him in place again."

Lachlann nodded, and he and Jasper moved into position again. Marcus let out a shudder as she worked. "I…I can't move my hand," he whispered.

"Sorry, what?" Rayla asked.

"My right hand isn't working," he repeated, his voice trembling. He lifted his right arm at the elbow, and only now did I see that the hand hung limp, useless.

Kip sighed. "Nerve damage. At least, that's what my knowledge from Kirilee tells me."

Rayla nodded. "Likely, yes. There, you're all stitched up." She began to bandage the wound.

"Will the nerve damage heal?" Jasper asked.

"I'm not sure," Rayla admitted. "I wish I could tell you otherwise."

"You've done what you can," Lachlann assured her. "Thank you."

"Yes, thank you," Marcus said. He leaned forward and covered his eyes with his good hand, and his shoulders began to shake. Then he let out a great, heaving sob and began to weep.

Lachlann knelt to put an arm around him, and Trina came over and met Lachlann's eyes. "Send him home. I'll go with him."

Lachlann stood and motioned to Alisa, who put one hand on Marcus's shoulder and another on Trina's, then mumbled a few words. All three of them disappeared, and Rayla excused herself to fetch more healers.

Lachlann sighed, grief etched into his features, then looked around at all of us. "All right," he said. "We need to make a decision."

"What do you mean?" asked Kip.

"We've all just faced one of the hardest things that can happen in war. In the army, we're trained to push past the pain of losing someone we care about in the heat of battle. But you kids aren't military, you don't have that training. So I'm going to give you a choice.

"If you want to stay and fight, that'd be useful. You're all valuable, and I can use every last one of you out there. But only if you can keep your head. If you don't think you can do that, I won't judge you. I can send any of you back to the house with Marcus and Trina. I know you're all hurting right now, badly, and I am too. But the battle doesn't care about our pain. So I need you to make a choice and stick with it either way."

We all stood in silence for a moment. Then Kip spoke. "Well, I'm certainly used to turning my pain into rage against my enemies." He smiled grimly. "I'll stay."

"Me too." Saray's voice trembled. "I'll…I'll fight to honour Noelle. She'd be proud of that."

"Are you sure, Saray?" asked Lachlann. "You look like you're about to faint."

She took a deep breath and nodded. "I'll be all right for now. But it's probably best that I don't fight out in the open, if what Alvin said is true."

Lachlann nodded.

"I'm in too," Jasper said.

I shrugged. "I'm a bit shaky, but I should be all right."

"If you're staying, then I'm staying," put in Kaden. Shawnie and Alisa, who'd reappeared in the room halfway through Lachlann's speech, both nodded.

"I suppose that settles it, then," Lachlann said. "Kaden, can you and Jasper go find Desmond and let him know what's happened here? Jasper, you report to him from now on, see where he needs you. Alisa and Shawnie, you can head back out there and do whatever you were doing before."

Kaden nodded and gave my hand a squeeze, then she and the others ventured out into the battle once more.

"Ruby, you stay with me 'til Kaden comes back," Lachlann went on. He glanced at Kip and Saray. "Are you two comfortable working together?"

They exchanged a glance, and both nodded.

"All right, how about you two go back into the school and search for anyone who wasn't in the courtyard. You'll have to look out for falling debris and pockets of fire, but I figure you can handle that."

Kip and Saray left the pavilion, and I was alone with Lachlann. "Are you sure you're all right to keep fighting?" he asked. "You don't look much better than Saray."

"I don't feel great. But if I can get somewhere high and use lightning, I should be all right."

Lachlann nodded. "Perhaps you and Kaden can work together. You can control the lightning, and she can fly you wherever you're needed."

Kaden returned to us a few minutes later with two folks I'd never met before. "This is Sage and Shiloh," she said. "Both healers. Desmond has more coming."

Lachlann greeted the two newcomers, then repeated to Kaden what he'd said to me.

"We'd best get moving," Kaden said. She frowned when she looked me over. "Are you all right, Ruby?"

I took a deep breath. "Not completely. But I can keep fighting for a little longer."

She nodded and put an arm around me. "If you need to stop, you tell me, all right? I'll fly you home."

"Sounds good," I said. "Let's go."

CHAPTER 34

BEFORE I KNEW it, we were airborne again. A flyover of the school showed us that the telekinetics had succeeded in punching a hole in the wall; now, the magikai who'd been trapped inside were sitting near the school's ruins, dazed and covered in soot but mostly unharmed. We landed on a roof near the fighting, and Kaden glanced over at me. "Should we keep moving?"

"I suppose that's best. I don't want to fly out in the open too much though."

"Right. We'll stick to the rooftops."

We began moving, gliding quickly from roof to roof. Kaden's night vision was better than mine, so she looked out for isolated Breoch Guard members for me to strike at with lightning. Occasionally, she flew down and engaged a cluster of them, her short sword glinting as she attacked with fluid strokes while tumbling about in midair. The tide seemed to be turning in our favour. I heard shouts of indignation rising as word of Noelle's death spread, and the citizens of Dundere attacked with a new vigour. Someone had directed the formerly trapped mages to Lachlann, and he was busy giving directions to those well enough to fight. The teleporters darted in and out of visibility, slitting throats and pulling Witch Slayers off of civillians; the vanishers did the same, remaining invisible while they attacked.

The firebrands had turned to using their flames as a weapon, and the other stormbrewers followed my lead, calling down lightning. Trina seemed to have left commands for some of the animals before her departure; I watched as birds dove ferociously at guards and dogs hurled themselves with teeth bared. A single bear wandered out of the forest and began chasing a cluster of terrified guards who took off running, only to be trapped in a tangle of vines that Starla summoned from the ground. Shawnie appeared in cougar form, attacking Witch Slayers whenever he could catch them.

The police engaged a large cluster of the Breoch Guard while another batch of telekinetics disarmed them, turning the Guard's own weapons against them. I watched this take place through a haze of exhaustion and shock, calling down lightning mechanically, unable to think much beyond my next strike.

It felt like hours had gone by before I heard the captain of the Breoch Guard calling his men to retreat, and they began filing back towards the portal. A collective cheer rose up from the people of Dundere. The guards clustered around the building where the portal was located, and I turned to Kaden. "Didn't Kip say that Willem closed the portal from the other side?"

"You're right. We should go find Kip. Perhaps he can teleport back to Willem and have him reopen it."

As she spoke, I noticed a pair of Breoch Guards who refused to go and instead stayed crouched over Gabrielle's still form. "You find him," I told Kaden. "I have something I need to deal with.”

Kaden flew off to find Kip, and I scanned the area for Jasper. Once I’d located him, I flew down. “Father and Jade are here,” I told him. “They’re with Gabby. Do we speak to them?”

Jasper closed his eyes, then nodded slowly. “I suppose we should. Come on.”

We wove our way through the masses together to where Father and Jade were hunched over Gabrielle. Father did not look up when we approached. Jade, however, saw us coming and stared at us, his blue eyes steely with hatred. “You traitors,” he snarled, meeting my gaze. “I should’ve listened to Gabby. Should’ve killed you when I had the chance! And you.” His gaze shifted to Jasper. “This is all your fault, you know.”

“My fault? I didn’t kill—”

“Yes, you did!” Jade leapt up and shoved Jasper, sending him stumbling backwards. “If you hadn’t run off to rescue your witch of a sister, we wouldn’t be here today, and my *wife* would be alive. *You* did this. You and your elfieblooded friends.” He stared down at Gabrielle’s body. “She was right,” he murmured then, his voice catching as he spoke. “Folks like you and your friends should be butchered.”

“Jade.” I shook my head, tears welling up in my eyes. “I’m your sister.”

“You’re nothing to me anymore. I don’t want to see either of you ever again.” He stalked off, leaving us there in grim silence.

My eyes fell on Gabrielle’s still form once more, then shifted to Father, who had been watching the exchange. Father let out a deep sigh, then spoke. “Jade is right, you know, Jasper. You set something off when you ran away from home to track down your sister. You began something on that island. A revolt. And that’s what led us here.” He met my eyes. “You two have lost your family today.”

I stiffened. “We may have lost Jade. But you could still let us back in.”

“No, I can’t.” He shook his head. “I am Angus Jameson, second captain of the Breoch Guard. I have a hundred men following my orders. If I let my witch of a daughter back under my roof, the consequences would be unimaginable.” Then he frowned. “Though I suppose I could consider it if you renounced your magic and vowed to never use it again, like your mother.”

My eyes widened. “Mother was a magikai?”

“Where do you think you got your magic from?” He sighed. “Yes, she had magic, but she realized at a young age how damaging it could be. So she sealed it away and vowed to never use it, and she didn’t. You could do the same.”

I shook my head. “You’d ask me to deny a part of who I am in order to rejoin the family?”

“You’re asking me to do the same in order to take you back.”

“No. It’s different. The things you mentioned about yourself, those are…titles, job descriptions from a career you chose. My magic, it’s in here.” I patted my chest. “It’s a part of me, Father. I didn’t choose it, and I’m not giving it up.”

“I could take you back to Breoch with me and have you made into a krossemage again, you know.”

“No, you couldn’t,” Jasper spoke up. “You can’t arrest someone for being a magikai here in Dundere. And if you want to take her, you’ll have to go through me. Not to mention all of them." He glanced back, and only now did I see that our friends were watching the exchange. Saray allowed her fire to dance freely on her hands, Lachlann clutched the pommel of his sword, and Kaden and Alisa stood poised beside Shawnie's fearsome cougar. "And you'd have to face Ruby herself. I've seen what she can do with lightning, Father. You don't want to cross her."

Father's eye moved to Saray. "There is one way you could persuade me to let you back into my life, son. Finish what you started four years ago. Bring me *her*."

There was a sharp intake of breath from the crowd of magikai, and Lachlann moved in to defend Saray, whose eyes were wide.

"We were promised that you'd be here for the taking," Father told her. "My men may have retreated today, but trust me, we're not finished hunting you." He regarded Jasper coolly then and asked, "Well, son? You know what you have to do now to be part of this family again."

Jasper met Saray's gaze. Her eyes were still wide with fear, and fire danced wildly on her hands. Lachlann stayed where he was, holding my brother's gaze.

Jasper turned back to Father. "I'm not who I was four years ago," he said. "I don't believe that magic is evil anymore. I've seen it used for good. I saw it heal my sister. And I already have a family." He came to stand tall beside me. "Ruby is my family. I'm done hunting magic users. Saray has been kind to Ruby, and she's given me a second chance, despite everything. I'm not going to do anything to destroy that, just so I can be part of your world again."

"You would side with the folks who killed your sister-in-law?" Father asked softly.

"That…wasn't Saray." Jasper squared his shoulders. "There's no reason to punish Saray for something she didn't do. I've chosen a side, and if you try to hurt Saray again, I will fight to defend her."

"Well, I suppose we're done here, then." He reached down to lift Gabrielle's body, grunting as he did. "Ruby, if you change your mind, let me know. And Jasper, you know what you must bring me in order to be forgiven. Until then, neither of you are welcome under my roof." He turned away from us, grimacing under the weight of Gabrielle's body, and began walking slowly towards the portal.

I heard Jasper let out a long, defeated sigh, and I put my arm around him. "I'm sorry," I whispered.

He nodded, blinking back tears, then turned to our friends, all of whom were still watching us. "Can I go home?" he asked Lachlann. "Am I still needed here, or can you folks…" His voice broke.

"Yes, go home. We'll be fine." Lachlann clapped Jasper on the shoulder. "I'm sorry about your father. You did well today."

"Can I go to your place? I need to be alone."

"Of course." Lachlann looked back over his shoulder. "Saray, you go home as well. Go be with Marcus and Trina. I'll be along shortly."

Jasper nodded again and left us, his head hanging low. Out of the corner of my eye, I saw Saray leave.

Lachlann studied me carefully. "Are you all right?"

I nodded. "I think it's harder for him than me. I realized long ago that I wasn't getting Father back. It still hurts, but…"

"I can only imagine." Lachlann gave me a grim smile. "Do you feel up to doing one last task before you head home?"

"What's that?"

"Can you and Kaden do an aerial sweep of the area to see if there are any injured folks we've missed?"

I nodded and joined Kaden, who gripped me tightly for a moment before sending us both skyward. When we found no others injured, we returned.

"Looks like we got everyone," Kaden said to Lachlann. "I suppose now we just need to—" She paused when she noticed the air near us become iridescent and begin shimmering. "What's that?!"

"Looks like someone's teleporting in," Lachlann said. His hand went to the pommel of his sword as he spoke. A moment later, he relaxed visibly as Willem, Hilda and Kip materialized.

"Willem!" Lachlann exclaimed. "Where've you been? We were worried about you!"

"I'm sorry," Willem replied. He looked disheveled, I realized; his hair was a mess, and his robes were askew. "Kip and I discovered the portal was breached about ten minutes after the attack began. So I summoned Hilda, and we held off all the remaining troops from the other side."

"How many were there?" Lachlann asked.

"A couple hundred, maybe."

My eyes widened. "You two held off a couple hundred troops all on your own?"

He chuckled and exchanged a glance with Hilda. "You're looking at likely the two most powerful magikai in Breoch, my dear. A couple hundred non-magical folk aren't too hard to handle."

"Where's Saray?" Kip asked.

"I just sent her home to be with her family," Lachlann said. "You can go join them if you'd like."

He nodded. "I'm not sure if she'll want me there, but I'd best check on them, at least." He started off in the same direction that Saray had gone.

Willem, meanwhile, was looking around at the damage that had been done to the city. His face fell when he saw the smoking remains of the school in the distance. "That's a shame. Did anything else of significance happen?"

"Yes, " Lachlann replied. "A lot. Take a walk with me, you two, and I'll fill you in." He glanced back at Kaden. "You likely need a place to stay tonight?"

She shrugged. "We all do. What will happen to the students with nowhere to sleep? And the folks from the island?"

"I'll need to think about that. Perhaps Starla can craft some buildings to shelter all of you?"

"Why are you making these decisions?" Willem asked. "Where's Noelle? And Marcus for that matter?"

Lachlann sighed. "Come on. Let's take a walk." He took Willem's arm and dragged him away before he could protest, Hilda following.

"You should go home," Kaden said to me. "You look awful."

"What about you? Do you want to stay with me tonight?"

"Maybe not tonight. I don't want to get in the way of the Westwoods, with all that's happened to them. Alisa and Shawnie and I will figure something out." She squared her shoulders. "Come on, I'll fly you home."

We took to the sky and began our flight to the governor's mansion. It was completely dark now, and my head spun as we flew above the burned, desecrated streets, over folks who likely didn't know where they'd sleep that night, and people crying for lost loved ones. Kaden kept a hand in mine, but neither she nor I spoke as we flew. What could possibly be said about the cruelties of war?

CHAPTER 35

WHEN I AWOKE the next morning, I lay in bed for a long time, not wanting to face all that had happened just a few short hours before. Everything after Kaden deposited me on my balcony was a blur. I vaguely remembered drinking the sleeping tea that Lachlann brought me, and then having a bath and washing the soot and blood off myself. Soon after, Trina had come up to her room on the other side of mine and cried herself to sleep. I hadn't been able to cry at all, and now I felt numb, barely capable of thought.

Eventually, the sounds of people talking downstairs got me out of bed. I tiptoed nervously, still uncertain how I'd respond if I saw Saray, Trina, or Marcus.

I was surprised to find Starla and Lachlann in the kitchen making breakfast. Both of them wore the clothes I'd last seen them in; Lachlann's were covered in dirt and ash, and Starla's long black hair was matted, the bottom of her skirt caked with mud. She turned when she heard me and gave a brief smile. "Morning, Ruby."

Lachlann looked over as well, and I studied both of them. "Where have you two been?"

"Out helping all the displaced magikai," Lachlann answered, stifling a yawn.

"Did you not sleep at all last night?"

"Not yet," he replied. "I'm going upstairs to nap for a few hours once we've made breakfast, then I'll get back out there to help with the repairs."

Starla nodded. "And I'm planning to do the same once I've seen Trina." She scooped some porridge into a bowl and offered it to me. "Here. Eat up."

"Thanks." I sat down at the kitchen table. "What sorts of repairs need to be done?"

Lachlann joined me with his own meal. "Dozens of buildings were damaged yesterday. The streets need to be cleared of rubble, and we're trying to figure out how to house all the students from the school of magic, along with the refugees from the island. It'll be a busy day."

I nodded. "Is it safe for you to be out there? Aren't you concerned that the Blackwells are going to come after you?"

He sighed. "If the Blackwells know what's best for them— and I suspect they do— they'll be keeping a very low profile right now, given that their son just murdered the governor and all."

My eyes blurred with tears. "I still can't believe he…"

"Me neither. I knew he was an angry kid, but everything he did yesterday seemed…extreme."

"I noticed this strange gold glint in his eyes. I saw it once before, when he cornered me in my room. I wonder if he's being affected by some sort of magic?"

"No idea. I'm not the best person to ask about those things."

"Right." I sighed. "Do you know what happened to him?"

Lachlann shook his head. "I know the guard took him away in anti-magic handcuffs. Not sure what became of him after that."

"Do you think he'll be executed?"

"I don't know. He's only seventeen, and I don't think they execute teenagers here. But he'll be facing a very long prison sentence." Lachlann poked at the food in his bowl. "Noelle had several attempts on her life in the past, you know. Most folks in Dundere loved her, but there were certainly exceptions. And there were some Candeshi folk who weren't too fond of her either. It's hard to believe that the person who finally succeeded was a kid with a grudge."

I nodded slowly.

"I only wish there'd been another way to find out where he was. If I hadn't used my anti-magic, we might still have Noelle with us."

"You're not blaming yourself for Noelle's death, are you?" Starla frowned. "Lachlann, she gave you an order."

"I know. And I keep wondering if I should've ignored it."

"If you'd ignored it, a lot more people might be dead, you and me included," I put in.

Starla put a hand on his shoulder. "When tragedies happen, everyone starts thinking it's somehow their fault. But it's rarely the fault of one person."

I nodded. "I could blame all this on myself if I wanted to, you know."

"How?" Lachlann asked.

"I was the one who insisted we go back to help the krossemages. If I hadn't been so set on doing that, the Breoch Guard might never have come here. And Noelle would still be with us."

"Yes, but then we'd all be dead," Starla pointed out.

"I know. And I'm glad we went back to the island for all of you, because of that. But still." I sighed. "Where…is Noelle? Her body?"

"In the backyard, under Kirilee's tree," Lachlann told me. "You can go see her if you want. Starla and I cleaned her up, and Willem put a spell on her so she won't start to…decompose. We figure folks will want to come say goodbye to her before she's buried."

"There's no way to bring her back then?"

"You heard what she said before she died. She doesn't want that. She was hesitant to bring Kip back using magic, even though she knew Kirilee only had hours left."

"What are you folks saying about me?" We all turned to see Kip walking into the kitchen, rubbing his eyes. He sat down at the table with the rest of us.

"Did you sleep over?" I asked.

He nodded. "Saray fell asleep on the couch in the parlour, and I stayed with her. I didn't have any faebane with me, so I dozed off a bit, but I didn't sleep much. Every time I started to dream, I woke up terrified that I'd cast. Noelle would've had my head if I threw her pretty china vases around in my sleep." He laughed, but I heard his voice catch, and he put his head in his hands to take a deep, shaky breath. Starla reached out and touched his shoulder.

"Sounds like you'll need to head home for a few hours as well. You'll feel a bit better after some sleep." Lachlann gestured to the stove. "There's porridge if you want some."

Kip nodded. "I shouldn't stay away from the Shrouded Woods for too long. Once Saray and Trina wake up, I'll use Trina's stone to summon Willem, and he can teleport me home. I don't want Saray to wake up without me here."

"Are things…better between you two now?" I ventured.

"I'm not sure. I knew she needed me last night, so I stayed. I don't think it changes my worries about us being together, but…"

"Now's probably not the time to try figuring that out," Lachlann said.

I nodded and dug into my porridge, and Lachlann and Starla began discussing what today's cleanup effort would look like. "What can I do to help?" I asked.

"I was hoping you could stay here with the others," Lachlann said. "Just make sure they're doing all right."

"Of course." I nodded. "I'm not sure what I'll say to them, but I suppose I'll figure it out. I've been through a similar loss, but with my mother it was more…gradual." I closed my eyes as I recalled my mother lying in her open casket, her frame emaciated and her skin yellowed from illness. The memory left me shuddering, though I doubted Noelle would look at all similar. "I, uh, suppose I'll go see Noelle now." I stood up, cleared my dishes, and made my way out the back of the house and into the garden, where a long bundle wrapped in cloth lay beneath Kirilee's tree.

I slowly peeled back the burlap to reveal Noelle's face. She looked much better than she had yesterday; she was pale now but peaceful, and no longer stained with blood. I blinked back tears.

"This'll be hard on Saray and Trina, Noelle being like this."

I startled, then turned to see Kip there behind me.

"It's not just because she's gone," he went on. "The way she's been laid out, wrapped in burlap and all? That's exactly what I looked like, or so I've heard. And I know seeing me like that was difficult for them." He sighed. "I think someone's coming by a little later to lay her out properly, put her in clean clothes and in a proper coffin and all."

"I didn't know her as well as the rest of you, but she seemed like an incredible person."

"She was. She was smart and generous and cared so much about her people. It's madness that it was one of the locals who…" His shoulders hunched, and I saw his hands ball into fists. "Alvin was always trouble, y'know. Everyone figured Saray and I didn't like him because he and Trina had a fight. But no, I always knew he was a bastard…" His voice broke, and he squeezed his eyes shut.

I reached out a tentative hand and put it on his shoulder. "I'm sorry," I whispered.

He nodded, then let out a long breath. "I didn't come out here to get all worked up about Noelle, ai."

"It's all right," I assured him. "You're allowed to be upset, you know."

"I s'pose so." He eyed me. "The girl who I shot yesterday— that was your oldest brother's wife?"

I nodded.

"Are you…all right? After all of that? Jasper didn't seem to take it so well."

"It's hard to explain. I have…all sorts of confusing feelings about it."

"And I imagine some of those feelings are about me."

I let out a sigh. "I guess so. More than anything, I'm grateful to you, Kip. You saved my life, likely two or three times yesterday. You caught me when I got shot out of the sky, you got me to Noelle in time to heal me, and you saved me from Gabby."

"You're not angry at me, then?" He frowned. "I s'pose I'm concerned that your older brother wouldn't have shut you and Jasper out like he did if I hadn't killed her. And I have no idea how you felt about her."

"Gabby wasn't much of a sister to me at the end, you know? And Jade wasn't much of a brother, either. He was the one who sold me out to the Guard." I shook my head. "I doubt Jade would've ever come around with Gabby influencing him, so maybe losing her will give him a chance to stop thinking like a Witch Slayer. Though, if he blames magic for her death, it might make him even more unreasonable."

"It's hard to say. Losing someone close to you can change you in all sorts of ways. I just hope I haven't made things worse between you and the rest of your family." Kip glanced toward the house then. "We'd best get back inside. You'll be okay staying here, with the girls?"

"I think so." I nodded. "Where's Marcus?"

"He hasn't come down yet. We think it's best not to disturb him, for now."

We returned to the house to find Saray and Trina both awake, eating their porridge silently. Kip stood behind Saray and put his arms around her. I shifted, feeling like I was intruding on intimate moments between family, and left the room for the parlour.

I sat down at the piano and began to play a soft, sad melody. It was one of my mother's favourite songs, and playing it on repeat was one of the things that helped me get through losing her. I found my mind wandering back to those terrible days leading up to her death, that gut-wrenching feeling of knowing the end was coming and being absolutely helpless to do anything about it. Then there were the days shortly after, wandering my home like a ghost, not sure what to think or feel, and the warmhearted smiles of sympathetic family friends, folks asking how I was doing, if I needed anything, and being unable to respond with much beyond "I don't know." Now I was on the other side of that, wanting to help Saray and Trina and Marcus. *Chances are they're just as numb and confused as I was,* I thought. I wasn't sure what to offer them, other than music.

Starla peered in some time later. "Saray and Trina are outside, with Noelle," she told me. "Kip's on his way home, and Lachlann and I are both headed upstairs to get some rest."

I nodded. "Do you want me to stop playing?"

"No, it's fine. If anything, your music is relaxing."

She left the room, and soon after, I heard Kip departing and doors closing upstairs. Trina did not come back inside; I assumed she was in the garden talking to the animals for comfort. Saray joined me in the parlour, though, and when I was finished playing through the song a third time, she gave me a wan smile. "That's beautiful."

"Thanks."

Saray shook her head slowly. "I…I can't stop thinking this is all my fault."

"Your fault? Why? If anything, it's mine and Jasper's. If he hadn't rescued me from the island, none of this would have happened. Father said so himself."

"But would a bunch of Breoch Guard really have marched all the way through a magical forest they're terrified of, and gone through a magical portal they were likely even *more* terrified of, if there wasn't the promise that I was on the other side?" She sighed. "I don't think they would've gone through all that trouble without me here. I'm a fugitive, and wherever I go, trouble follows me. I'm not sure where I'm going to go now, but I know the Guard will follow me anywhere. Sometimes I think I'm cursed." She took a long, shuddering breath. "Maybe I should just turn myself in so they don't hurt anyone else I love."

Saray buried her face in her hands, clearly trying not to cry, and I came to sit next to her. "Don't talk like that. You're not cursed. If anything, you're an inspiration." I frowned. "Did you know that back on the island, there were stories about you?"

"Really?" She swiped at her eyes.

"Absolutely. We'd all heard about the firebrand who could cast with her mind, who managed to run away from school before the Breoch Guard came for her and then outwit them two more times after that. I had no idea that my father and brother were the bad guys in that story, of course." I laughed.

Saray let out a shaky chuckle. "It's not like I outwitted them on my own. The only thing I figured out was how to escape that prison on the Guard ship, and even then, if Gareth and his crew hadn't come along, I'd be dead."

"I seem to recall you outsmarting Jasper at the end," I pointed out.

"Still. Couldn't have done it without a lot of people helping me."

"But the point is, you did it. And that was an inspiration to us on the island. It showed us that the guards *could* be outwitted. You were *hope* to a lot of people there, Saray. And apparently, so was I, after I got away."

She nodded slowly, then sighed. "I don't know what sort of hope I can offer them now. The school's burned down, they're without a home, and they don't have Noelle here to protect or heal them." Her voice caught again, and this time she gave in, leaning forward and sobbing into her hands. I held her as she cried, not knowing what to say but also aware that, right now, not much could be said.

The rest of the morning passed in a similar fashion. Saray and Trina came and went from the parlour to listen to my music, or talk about Noelle, or cry in my arms. In the early afternoon, Lachlann came downstairs, still looking tired but dressed in clean clothes, and Starla followed soon after. They began making lunch, and only now did I realize that the servants must have been given the day off. They, too, had a loss to grieve.

After we ate, Lachlann and Starla both went out to help in town again, and Saray and Trina ended up falling asleep on the parlour couches. Once I'd cleaned up from lunch, I decided to join them; I, too, was incredibly tired.

Some time later, I was awoken by a knock at the door. I answered and was surprised to find Willem, Kip, Hilda and Carmine staring back at me. "We're here to help," Hilda told me. "Where is everyone?"

"I haven't seen Marcus yet. Saray and Trina are sleeping in the parlour."

"Ah. Well, we won't disturb them for now. Can we make you folks some dinner?"

"We brought vegetables from home," Carmine put in, gesturing at the large basket of plump produce that she carried.

"That would be lovely," I said.

The four of them began working away in the kitchen, while I sat at the table and watched them, still half asleep. Dinner was ready by the time Lachlann and Starla showed up, both of them looking exhausted. "What's this?" Starla asked.

"Dinner," Willem replied, giving her a thin smile. "We figured you folks could use some help."

"We appreciate it." Starla nodded, then glanced at Hilda and Carmine. "I saw you around at the school after the rescue, but I don't think I've officially met you."

Hilda introduced herself and Carmine, and Starla smiled at them. "I've heard good things about both of you. You're the one who can speak to plants, right? Just like me."

Carmine nodded and gave her a broad smile. *"You can speak to them as well? I've never met someone else who can!"*

Hilda began to translate, and Starla laughed and shook her head. "Not necessary, I can sign perfectly well. I've heard about you, too, Hilda. Aren't you the one who Kirilee said Kip needed to talk to?"

Hilda chuckled. "So you folks have finally figured out that Kirilee's still with us, huh? I wondered how long that would take."

"I always figured she was in that tree, but I had no proof until Starla came along," Lachlann said. "I wish you'd told me earlier."

"We were under strict orders not to," Carmine explained. *"There's no point in arguing with a tree when it wants something. Stubborn things, they are."*

"Makes sense that Kirilee would want to be one, then." Lachlann grinned.

Trina and Saray appeared in the doorway then, both looking exhausted. Hilda and Carmine embraced them gently. Kip, I noticed, was hanging back, the tension between him and Saray evident once again.

"We should go pay our respects before dinner," Hilda said, and Carmine nodded.

"I'm going to go check on Marcus," Lachlann announced. He left the room, and the rest of us followed Hilda and Carmine out to the backyard, where we discovered that someone had come by to tend to Noelle's body. She was dressed in clean clothes, her hair was styled, and she was placed in a long wooden box.

"Hilda?" Trina spoke, her voice wavering. "There's no chance you can bring her back, is there? You managed it with Kip."

Hilda gave her a sad smile. "Well, I'm certainly not going to use a life transfer. I seem to recall her being quite opposed to what we did to Kip, even with the state Kirilee was in. She'd be furious if she woke up to find we'd done the same to her."

Saray nodded. "And she made us promise not to. Though what about that other way of bringing people back? Soul magic, I think it's called?"

Hilda sighed. "In honesty, I could try that. The trouble is, I might well end up losing my own magic if I did. You recall what happened to Claudi when she used that on Kirilee?"

"Not to mention what it did to Kirilee herself," Kip put in.

"That as well. She might return to us a very different person. And you need to understand that my primary responsibility is to the fairies. I'm meant to guard them. If I lost my magic, I could no longer fulfill that responsibility. Performing soul magic isn't an option for me."

"So there's no hope," Trina said.

"Not this time. I'm sorry, Trina. I won't be able to bring back everyone you love who dies." She gazed down at Noelle's still form. "Noelle wouldn't want people sacrificing their lives or magic to bring her back. I think this time it's best to let her go. It's a shame, though. She was deeply loved by the people of this land."

Trina nodded, blinking back tears, and Saray put an arm around her. Carmine, meanwhile, knelt beside the box and waved her hand over it. I watched as a small branch sprouted from the wood and snaked up Noelle's side. A large flower bloomed at the end of it, directly over Noelle's hands.

"Dinner's going to get cold," Willem said, coming out onto the porch a few minutes later. "Come eat. You'll all feel a bit better after a meal."

CHAPTER 36

AFTER DINNER, KADEN, Alisa and Shawnie showed up, and we headed for my room when Saray and Trina went to check on Marcus. Exhausted from the events of the past two days, we sprawled out on my bed.

"I'm sorry I haven't come to see you all," I said. "Lachlann asked me to stay with Saray and Trina today. What's it like out there? Where are you all sleeping at night?"

"Starla made treehouses in the grove just outside of downtown," Kaden said, idly toying with my hair as she spoke. "They're fine to live in for now, but I don't think we can stay there for long. Downtown is…a mess." She sighed. "I don't know what will happen to us now."

"Me neither. You can stay with me for the next little while, though we might all need to sleep in one room."

"You don't think Marcus will mind having a bunch of extra houseguests right now?" Shawnie asked.

"He and Noelle were always very welcoming. I think that so long as we give him his space, he should be all right."

There was a knock at the door then, and Trina popped her head in. "Hi." She gave us a small smile. "Just wanted to see if you were doing all right."

"We're fine. Come on in." I grinned and patted one of the last remaining spots on the bed. "How are you doing? Where's your mother?"

"I think she's outside with Lachlann. Apparently, Kirilee called her to come check on him. Sounds like he's having a hard time."

I nodded and peeked out the patio doors to see for myself. Lachlann sat with his back to Kirilee's tree, his shoulders slumped, and Starla was crouched next to him, her hand on his shoulder. Alisa and Kaden joined me by the door.

"Huh," Kaden said. "I didn't realize he was hurting. He seemed so strong yesterday."

"Lachlann does that," Trina replied. "Walks around like he's doing just fine, takes care of everyone else, and ignores his own feelings." She sighed. "He's like family to us, you know. So losing Noelle has probably hit him pretty hard, too. But he's not going to admit that to Saray or Marcus or me. I'm glad he can talk to my mom, at least."

Starla noticed us then and made a shooing motion with her hand. Alisa chuckled as we closed the door. "Do you think Starla's going to have a boyfriend soon?"

Trina's eyes widened. "My mom and Lachlann? I'd never thought of that."

"They do spend a lot of time together," I put in. "I'm guessing Kirilee's been trying to set them up."

"That sounds like the exact sort of thing she'd do." Trina gave me a half smile.

"Would it be strange having him as a stepfather?" I asked.

"Yes. But also no." She frowned. "I could get used to it. It'd give me some hope, too."

"Why?"

"Because if Lachlann's able to move past Kirilee and fall in love with someone new, then I'd be less worried about what's going to happen to Marcus now." Her shoulders slumped. "I've gone to check on him a few times, and he seems like a ghost. I don't know if he'll recover from this. He and Noelle were so in love, and I'm scared this will break him." Her voice shook, and a tear trickled down her cheek.

I crossed the room again, sat on the bed, and put my arm around her. Trina swiped at her eyes. "I feel so lost," she whispered. "People keep asking me how I'm doing and what I need, but…I don't even know."

I nodded. "I get it."

She blinked away her tears. "I suppose you would, after losing your sister-in-law and having Jade and your father walk out of your life. How are *you* doing?"

"Better than you, I think. Jade wasn't much of a brother to me at the end. I am a bit worried about Jasper though. I should probably go check on him."

Alisa nodded. "How about I teleport you over there, and then the rest of us can stay here with Trina?"

"Sure." I nodded.

When we reached the foyer, we were surprised to find Lachlann there, putting on his coat. "Where are you off to?" I asked.

"Going back to my place to clean all this and put it away." He gestured to his armour, which I now noticed was caked with dirt and blood. "Also, I figure I should check on your brother."

"I was heading over there for the same reason. Alisa was going to teleport me."

"Well, you're welcome to ride with me if you want," he said.

"Thanks, I'll do that. I suppose you can head back upstairs, Alisa."

She nodded, and I followed Lachlann outside.

Not long after, Lachlann and I walked into the apartment to find Jasper lying on the couch. He looked exhausted, and for a moment, I thought he was asleep. Then he opened his eyes. "Hi."

"Hi." I perched next to him. "How are you?"

"I've been better."

"Have you been cooped up in here all day?"

"I slept past noon, but yes. I wanted to come over and see you earlier, but I don't know if the Westwoods want privacy." He glanced at Lachlann. "I've been trying very hard not to drink all of this away, but it's pretty tempting right now."

"You'll probably feel less tempted if you're around people," Lachlann said, coming to sit in the chair across from us. "You should come join us at the Westwoods' place. Everyone else is there."

"Including Kip?"

"For now, yes."

"Well then, maybe I should keep my distance. I'm a little angry at him right now."

"You are?" I asked.

Jasper sat up and rubbed his eyes. "This is all so confusing. Kip could've just injured Gabby enough to make her stop hurting you, Ruby. But it's not Gabby I'm really upset about. It's that I've lost Jade, and Father too.

"I saw Jade earlier during the battle, and I was hoping to talk to him. I wanted to give him a chance to do better. Like you gave me." He was looking at Lachlann now. "When I came to your house all those months ago, I half expected you to try to kill me, you know. But you saw something in me. You saw that I…could be better than who I was when we first met. I thought similarly about Jade. He was raised in the same world as Ruby and me, and we've both stopped believing the lies about magic users. I hoped Jade could too. I hoped…" His voice broke.

Lachlann nodded. "I get what you're saying. You need to understand, though, that not everyone wants to escape that sort of thinking. Some people have their beliefs challenged, and they just dig in harder."

"You think Jade was one of those? That he was past saving?"

"I can't say; I didn't know Jade. I don't think Gabby would have come around though, and she had an influence on him." Lachlann shrugged. "Maybe he'll have a change of heart one day. I certainly wouldn't have expected you to change your beliefs when I met you four years ago. But look at you now."

"True." He sighed. "I just feel like…this was the last straw for me. I need to leave Dundere. I've had a rough time here…no offense." He glanced at Lachlann. "You've been a wonderful host."

"None taken. But where will you go?"

"I'm thinking I'll sail with Gareth for a while. It'd be a fresh start for me." He turned to me then. "Would you be all right if I left? Now that you have your friends from the island?"

I nodded slowly. "I'd miss you. And I'd hope you'd come back to visit. But yes, I would be okay."

"In that case, I might need to find out when Lady Liara will be in port next." He eyed me. "Hey, how'd your talk with Kaden go? I never got a chance to ask you, with everything that's happened."

I shrugged. "She admitted that she likes me. We're still trying to figure out where to go from here. What about your talk with Saray?"

"It was good. We realized that if we'd gone to the same school, I likely would've been one of those older boys who liked to tease her."

"Sounds about right. You were a bit of a troublemaker."

"Was I ever." He sat back. "It was interesting hearing about that incident on the ship from her perspective. I figured she'd be angry and spiteful toward me when I showed up here, but I didn't expect her to be *scared* of me, not after she burned half my face off, then outwitted me when I tried to catch her a second time. I didn't realize what that day did to her. I don't think she realized it either, until I showed up in her life again."

"Was she surprised at what that day did to *you?*"

Jasper nodded. "She knew some of it from when Lachlann forced me to tell the Westwoods my story, but she didn't realize just how badly it affected me." He sighed. "And I don't think I did either, until yesterday. Ruby, I owe you a very big apology for what happened at city hall."

"What do you mean?"

He took a deep breath, then began to speak very quickly. "After Alvin let Saray go, and before he spotted me, there was a minute or so in there where I could've shot him. I had the angle, I could have done it without putting you in danger. But when the moment came, I just…froze. The thought of killing someone again, even a bastard like Alvin, made me feel sick. I likely could've pushed through the feeling if I'd had a little longer, but next thing I knew, Alvin had a gun to your head, and he was dragging you away. I thought for certain that he would run off with you and it'd be my fault." He looked away. "If it wasn't for Sophie, I don't know what would've happened."

I nodded slowly, taking in his words. "I feel like I can't be angry at you for that, because if someone was trying to harm you and I was the one with the gun, I don't know if I could fire it either. I imagine that killing isn't for everyone."

"That's definitely true," Lachlann put in. "If shooting someone is easy for you, then I'd be concerned. It *should* affect you. You saw how shaken up I was after Aidan." He closed his eyes and shuddered a little.

"Yes, but your life depended on it," Jasper said to me. "And in the moment when you needed me the most, I couldn't do what was necessary." He sighed. "I've been beating myself up about it all day."

"Well, stop," I said. "You're not helping anyone by doing that. And even if Alvin had taken me, I have a feeling that between you and all the others, you would've tracked me down eventually. Or maybe I would've been able to get away from him. There's no point feeling guilty for what might have happened."

"I suppose not."

"And it's easier to fall into that sort of thinking if you're alone," Lachlann put in. "Come back to the house with us, Jasper. It's better for you to be around people than holed up in here."

"Even if one of those people is Kip?"

Lachlann snorted. "Kip won't be staying for long; he has to go back to the Woods. And you know my opinion on you and Kip. The two of you could likely do some incredible things if you'd work to put aside your differences. But you're both bloody stubborn, so I don't see that happening anytime soon."

"You're not wrong about that last part," Jasper said. "Fine, I'll come with you."

The following morning, Chase showed up at our house accompanied by a very nervous-looking Sophie and asked to speak with Lachlann and me. The green fairy was still with her, sitting placidly on her shoulder.

Trina led them into the parlour and went to fetch Lachlann. Sophie alternated between staring down at her shoes and throwing hesitant glances at me. I gave her a quick, reassuring smile as Lachlann came into the room.

"Chase," Lachlann said, "what can I do for you?"

"I'm hoping to get yours and Ruby's takes on what happened with my daughter the other day." He sighed. "I know this is likely not the best time, with everything else that's happened, but I need to know what we're dealing with here."

"Of course." Lachlann sat down and eyed Sophie.

"Word has gotten around that she somehow convinced Alvin to let go of Ruby, put down his gun, and allow himself to be arrested," Chase said. "Is that what really happened?"

I took a deep breath, willing myself to ignore the barrage of images that flooded my mind, then nodded. "That's…exactly what happened. Sophie saved my life." I gave her a smile. She didn't return it though; if anything, she slunk further down.

"Does this mean what I think it does?" Chase asked. "Is she…a charmer?"

I exchanged a glance with Lachlann. "That looks to be the case," he said.

Sophie let out a sob. "I don't want to be a charmer," she said, tears beginning to stream down her face. "I don't want everyone to be afraid of me. I don't want to end up like…like *him*."

I came to sit with Sophie and put an arm around her. "You won't," I assured.

"I'll tell you what I told Saray years ago, when she was just learning to use fire," Lachlann said. "No type of magic is bad in and of itself. Magic is a tool that can be used for good or evil."

"How can charming be used for good?"

I gave Sophie's shoulders a squeeze. "One of my friends had an aunt who was a charmer, and she was great at taking care of the family's kids. My friend and her cousins would get into fights, like kids always do, and her aunt would calm them right down."

Sophie sniffled. "People here don't like charmers. They think charmers are bad."

"And they're wrong," Lachlann said.

Chase sighed. "The charming bit is only half the issue," he explained. "You were using anti-magic while she charmed him, right Lachlann?"

Lachlann nodded.

"So what do you make of that?"

"She must have been using fairy magic somehow."

Sophie brightened a little. "That's right! Spirit here told me what to do." She glanced at the fairy on her shoulder.

"You can talk to the fairies?" Lachlann asked.

"Only this one." She shrugged. "It makes sense, because the fairies saved me when I was a baby."

He frowned. "All right, let's back up a bit. Have you ever cast before this, Sophie?"

She frowned. "I might've a few times before. I noticed a few weeks ago that when I played with my hair a certain way, people would do what I asked them. I thought it was just because I was being cute, though." One corner of her mouth turned up.

"You're what, twelve? That's usually when gifts show up. Tell me what happened with the fairies."

"Weren't you wearing a pendant when you charmed Alvin?" I asked. "I wonder if that had something to do with it."

Sophie frowned, then slowly pulled the amethyst pendant I'd seen her wearing out of her dress pocket.

"Can I see that?" Lachlann asked. Sophie gave it to him, and he flinched when he took it. "That hurt for a moment. Sort of like…" He glanced down at his metal arm. "Fairy magic. It has to be."

"Spirit only began following me around once I got the pendant," Sophie said.

"Now, how does a twelve-year-old girl end up with a pendant of fairy magic?" Lachlann mused. "This item is incredibly powerful."

"A man gave it to me when I visited the Shrouded Woods," Sophie explained.

Chase frowned. "A man in the forest gave you a strange pendant, and you just…took it? You should know better than to take gifts from strangers."

She averted her eyes. "He said that I would need it someday, that the fairies had told him as much, and that a fairy would tell me when to use it."

"What did this fellow look like?" Lachlann asked.

"He was taller than you, with long black hair and a really fancy beard. And his clothes were really…interesting."

Lachlann nodded. "Alexander."

"Who is he?"

"A friend of mine. He uses fairy magic in potions and charms that he and his spouse make."

"Did the fairy tell you when to intervene, like Alexander said?" I wondered.

She nodded. "After you told me to go help the doctors, I did what you said until I heard the shooting. Then I snuck back onto the porch to see what was happening."

Chase sighed. "This is the part where you could have easily been killed."

"But I *wasn't*." Sophie glared at him for a moment, then turned back to Lachlann. "At first I was scared, and I was going to go back inside, but then Spirit was there, telling me which casting words to say and what to do next. So, I followed her directions."

Lachlann nodded and sat back. "You know, now that I think about it, if anyone can help you learn to use your gift, it's Alexander. He and Willem would likely need to train you together."

"Willem's from Breoch, right?" Chase said. "Am I going to have to send my daughter far away?"

"I'm not sure. Are there any practitioners of fairy magic here in Dundere?"

"I don't think so. There's certainly no fairy magic guild, so if there are practitioners, they're likely pretty quiet about their work." He frowned. "Some folks here don't like fairy magic, because we depend on anti-magic to properly govern our country. Fairy magic is the only thing that can counteract it, so many people see it as dangerous. And the wild fae here aren't likely to want to lend their magic to humans, either."

"I'd best see if Trina can bring Willem in." Lachlann stood.

"Can you have him bring Kip as well?" I heard Saray chime in. "I need to talk to him."

Lachlann nodded before leaving the parlour. He called for Trina, and a few minutes later, I could hear him and Willem speaking in the next room. Then Lachlann appeared in the parlour doorway once more. "Willem will be back in a moment. How open are you to having Sophie train in Breoch?"

Chase frowned. "Isn't that dangerous?"

"It certainly could be if she were caught," Lachlann admitted. "Though I doubt that's as much of a concern as..." Lachlann paused. "Ah, here they are. Chase and Sophie, meet my friends Willem, Alexander and Ember."

Alexander swept into the room wearing a long, jewelled frock coat and top hat. Ember followed, Mischief on their shoulder, then Willem, dressed in his wizard's robes. "Chase, it's a pleasure to meet you," Alexander said with a bow. He eyed Sophie. "And I hear you used my gift well."

She nodded. "I hope so."

"Well, given that you may have saved Ruby's life, I'd say you did." He smiled and then peered at the fairy on her shoulder. "Is that a Dunderi wild fae?"

Sophie frowned, cocked her head, then nodded. "Spirit says yes, that's what she is."

"My, my. You must be a special girl, befriending one of those."

"That is rather unlike the wild fae, from what I know of them," Willem put in.

"Indeed it is." Alexander smiled at Sophie and then turned back to the others. "Sophie, this is my spouse, Ember. And I'm not sure if you've met Willem before."

Sophie looked Willem over. "You were the one who led the rescue, right?"

"I am," he replied. "Lachlann tells me you're a charmer?"

"I think so." She shuddered. "It's a rather frightening gift, isn't it?"

"It's a splendid gift," Alexander countered. "I would know."

Sophie's eyes widened when she looked at Ember then, her gaze immediately drawn to Mischief. "Is that a fox? Can I pet it?"

"Absolutely."

Sophie gathered Mischief in her arms, and I turned to Alexander, frowning. "Wait, are *you* a charmer?"

He grinned. "It's my innate talent, yes. But my parents were very insistent that I learn to use my gift in ways that don't harm others. My use of charm is incredibly subtle. I can make people like me, and I can nudge prospective clients to buy my wares. But I only use it in a forceful way if I need to protect myself or folks I love. It's the reason no one has suspected our shop to be a front." He winked, then turned to Sophie. "This one is certainly not going to use her talents for ill. Or so Mischief thinks."

"Can you help my daughter?" Chase asked.

"I believe that between Alexander and me, we can help her a great deal," Willem said. "Would you like to come back to my place in the Shrouded Woods and discuss what this might look like?"

"I suppose so. Will she have to live in the Woods with you?"

"It's one option. But I'm a teleporter, so it may not be the only one. We just need to wait for Kip, and then we can head out." He smiled.

It was some time later that Kip appeared in the doorway, accompanied by Saray. I noticed they were holding hands. "I'm ready to go when you folks are," Kip said. "And Saray's coming with me."

Willem frowned. "You're bringing Saray back to the Shrouded Woods? I thought you said that was too dangerous."

"I did," Kip said. "But now the Breoch Guard is expecting to find her here, so it only makes sense that she leaves. And maybe it's not my place to tell Saray where she can and cannot live." He and Saray exchanged a glance.

"I'm realizing that I'll likely be hunted by the Breoch Guard no matter where I go," Saray said. "So I might as well go somewhere that allows me to be with the man I love."

"Good." Lachlann smiled. "Kirilee will be happy to hear that; she was a little upset that her advice to Kip caused a breakup."

"Does Marcus know you're leaving?" asked Willem.

Saray nodded. "I talked to him and Trina about it yesterday. They both agree that the Woods might be the safest place for me now. I'll come back to see them, of course; I don't want to leave Father completely alone with this sort of grief. I've given him a summoning stone so getting back and forth isn't too hard for us."

"Well, if that's what you both think is best, then so be it. Let's head back to my place, shall we? Stand in a circle and hold hands, everyone."

I watched as the mages all poured their magic into a single teleport spell, then disappeared. Lachlann let out a sigh once they were gone. "I'm so glad Saray and Kip managed to sort things out."

"Me too. Do you think Willem and Alexander will be able to help Sophie?"

"If anyone can, it's them." Lachlann smiled slightly. "That girl is powerful. I hope they can teach her well."

The next two weeks dragged by. A few days after Sophie's departure, I went to the swearing-in ceremony for Deshi, the deputy governor. Deshi came to the mansion that same evening with her husband and three small children and helped us with the preparations for Noelle's memorial.

The casket had been moved to the ballroom, and that section of the house was declared open to the public for the next two weeks so that people could come and pay their respects. As time went on, I watched as each person dealt with loss in their own way.

Marcus had finally emerged from his room, but he was nearly silent, his movements mechanical. His right hand remained useless, and I began to wonder if the damage was permanent. Lachlann and Starla threw themselves into taking care of the family and helping with memorial preparations. Kip and Saray visited frequently, and it was clear that Kip's initial shock and grief had turned into anger toward Alvin. When he wasn't with Saray, he could often be found in the backyard shooting his bow or trying to find one of us to sword fight with him in order to burn off some of his anger. Kaden picked up on this and challenged him regularly. Both of them possessed a natural grace in their movements that mixed well with a fierce, competitive streak, and though Kip had more formal training with the sword, Kaden was quickly becoming a force to be reckoned with. Some afternoons I would sit in Kirilee's tree and watch the two of them moving in what looked almost like a dance as they sparred, Kaden occasionally smirking at Kip as she resorted to flight in order to make an unexpected attack.

Trina began composing a tune on her pipe to honour Noelle, and she asked Jasper, Kaden, and me to help her with it. The four of us spent hours in the parlour coming up with harmonies and accompaniments to her song, which she hoped to play at the memorial. Alisa spent a good amount of her time helping out in the makeshift village that most of the Yarel Island folk were living in, and near the end of the second week, she invited Kaden, Shawnie, and me to come with her.

The village Starla had crafted from the grove was incredible. Trees that had once been difficult to scale now bore low-sweeping limbs, making it easy for folks to climb into them. Boughs were flattened and broadened to create a semblance of floors and walkways in amongst the trees, and foliage grew in hanging clusters for privacy. Some of the houses had been fashioned on the ground from shorter trees and hanging vines.

It was the sort of arrangement that could be livable, given time to build and improve upon it all. But it was cramped, and there were few of the luxuries that the school dorms had offered. Deshi supplied the encampment with blankets and extra clothing and food, but that didn't change the fact that there were several hundred people now crammed into the grove. I recalled the eagerness with which the citizens of Dundere had fed and clothed and helped these same people mere months ago. Now there were few Dunderi citizens here, if any.

After our arrival, Alisa and I helped make a large pot of soup for everyone, while Shawnie helped one of the men haul in mattresses that had been salvaged from the school dorm. Kaden distributed warm drinks to everyone. *They can't live like this for long,* I found myself thinking. Kaden, Alisa and Shawnie had gotten lucky; they were all camped out in my room now, the four of us somehow managing to sleep on one bed. The rest of these folks didn't have friends in the governor's mansion, though.

After the meal, Kaden gave me a shy smile. "You want to fly somewhere today?"

"I'd love to," I replied. "It'd be good to get out of here for a while."

Kaden grabbed my hand and mumbled her spell, and we rose into the sky together. "Where do you want to land?" she asked me.

I looked down at the world below me and selected a green, moss-covered outcropping that overlooked the city. "How about there? But let's fly around for a bit first."

"All right." She grinned. "Make us go faster."

I shifted the wind so it was at our backs, and we picked up speed. Kaden let out a whoop. She let go of my hand and did a somersault in the air; I attempted to copy her and failed miserably.

The worries of the past few weeks seemed to drop away like the ground beneath us as we flew; for the first time in a while, I felt carefree. "We need to do this more often," I exclaimed breathlessly.

She nodded and grabbed my hand again, and wound her fingers into mine. I felt my heartbeat pick up; now seemed like a good time to finally vocalize the thoughts I'd had every night when I fell asleep wedged up against her. "Let's go sit now," I suggested. "We can fly more after."

I shifted the wind once again, and we soared down to the cliff and landed gently. Kaden let out a sigh as we settled on the soft cushion of moss. "The city isn't nearly as pretty as it was the last time we flew together."

I looked out over Dundere and nodded gravely. Plenty of work was already done to rebuild the school, but even so, its blackened walls were visible from here, an ugly scar against the green trees and shining spires. Other parts of downtown stood soot blackened as well, and many buildings were boarded up, shops that remained closed because of the Breoch Guard's pillaging or because their owners were killed in the battle. The twisting trees of the park where the mages camped added an interesting feature to the landscape, neither good nor bad, just unusual.

I sighed, then turned to Kaden and gave her a grin. "I'm not sure if this is bad timing, but you and I were in the middle of a pretty important conversation right before all this happened. Do you want to talk about that now? About whether we want to be together?"

Kaden brightened. "I…thought you said you needed to think about it."

"I did. And I have." I studied her, noticing how her dark eyes glowed amber when the sun hit them just right. "Kaden, I don't think I ever realized how I felt about you because you didn't come with fireworks."

"Fireworks? Wait, is this about what happened on Banishing Day?"

"No." I laughed. "Sorry, that didn't make much sense. When I was dating…my ex," I wrinkled my nose, not wanting to say his name, "it was all about these grand gestures. Fancy picnics and dinners at restaurants and such. He was always trying to impress me, you know? And I was trying to impress him back. With you it doesn't quite feel like that. I don't feel like I have to prove to you that I'm worthy."

"Because I already know," Kaden said.

"And I feel the same about you. Maybe this love stuff isn't always about trying to sweep the other person off their feet."

Kaden nodded slowly. "I get what you're saying. Though, you have to admit that I'm pretty good at sweeping you off your feet." She gestured to the ground far below us and grinned.

"That you are." I grinned back at her, then looked out over the city again. My shoulders hunched a little as my gaze landed on Starla's tree village. "There's so much uncertainty right now. I have no idea where we're going to end up, Kaden. But maybe it'd be easier if we decided that we're going to face it together."

"Is that your fancy way of saying you want to date me?"

I laughed. "I suppose it is."

Her smile widened, and she stared at me for a long moment, then ran a finger slowly down my cheek. "Good," she whispered. "It's about time."

I laughed again and put an arm around her, and she rested her head on my shoulder. "Ruby? Can you promise me something?"

"What's that?"

"I'm, uh, new at all this. Dating and everything. Can you promise me that you won't do what, uh, certain people did to you?"

"What, that I won't use my magical charm to make you fall for me?"

"No. Just that you won't push me to do anything I'm not ready for."

"Of course." I pulled away and met her eyes. "Kaden, I promise you that much. And if I do make you uncomfortable, you need to promise you'll tell me."

She nodded. "You know, I'm curious about kissing. But I think I need a bit of time to get used to the idea of us dating before I want to do that."

"That's fine. We'll go at your pace, all right?"

"Thank you." She reached up and took my hand, and together we looked out over the beautiful, broken city that we'd called home. I wasn't sure how much longer we'd have here or where we'd go next.

But we would do it together.

CHAPTER 37

JUST LIKE BREOCH, large memorial ceremonies in Dundere were rare. When a person died, they were usually celebrated by loved ones, then buried on the family property or in the large public graveyard just outside of the city limits. Only important officials and influential people were honoured publicly.

Noelle, of course, was one of them.

There was a huge outdoor amphitheatre in the centre of town used for most public meetings, and next to it stood what I'd always thought was a small park. This park, I quickly learned, was actually special a graveyard for important officials, and the Dunderi folk were known for planting trees over the burial sites of their deceased.

The people of Dundere crowded onto the carved stone amphitheatre seats, most of them quiet, subdued. I sat a few rows back with Kaden, Alisa and Shawnie on one side of me, and Jasper on the other. Starla sat in the front row with the Westwoods, her arm around Trina. The Yarel Island folk had shown up to pay their respects, and I saw that they stayed far in the back, clustered together, with few Dunderi folk sitting near them.

Sophie sat with a group of the Yarel Island teens; most of them seemed less fearful of her gift than the local population. The Blackwells sat separate from most others as well, their faces impassive. I'd recently heard that the family officially disowned Alvin and in no way condoned his actions, but the stigma surrounding them remained. No one wanted to be near the family of Noelle's murderer. Ashlynn sat a little ways apart from her parents, accompanied by a fellow who looked slightly older than her, and whose hair was more red than strawberry-blond. He kept a hand on Ashlynn's shoulder and conversed with her in low tones, and I had to wonder if this was Arquinn, the eldest of the Blackwell children.

A small group of musicians began to play as the casket was carried down the aisle. Kip and Lachlann were among the casket bearers; I noticed that Lachlann studiously avoided looking at the Blackwells as he walked. There were tears from many as the procession passed them, and I gripped Kaden's hand tighter, blinking back some of my own.

As the new governor, Deshi was to lead the ceremony, and she stood quietly to cast a spell that would amplify her voice. Then she looked the crowd over, her dark eyes solemn. "Friends and family, people of Dundere, we are here to honour the life of Noelle Westwood, our beloved governor and healer, who was taken from us at far too young an age." I didn't miss the way her eyes flickered, just for a moment, to the Blackwells as she spoke. "I would like to begin by sharing my own memories of Noelle, and what I learned from her."

Deshi began to speak at length about the wisdom and courage that Noelle had modelled for her over the years, and I found myself relaxing as she spoke. As uncertain as everything was right now, I could rest assured that Dundere was in good hands. Deshi was younger than Noelle, perhaps in her late thirties, but I could see a similar mix of the courage and compassion in her that I saw in Noelle.

Several others rose to speak. Noelle's older brother, who lived on the Candeshi mainland, had been brought in for the service, and he shared stories of their childhood, of the absolutely determined and brilliant child that Noelle had been, and how she'd initially scorned her healing abilities in favour of her political aspirations, before finding a way to balance both aspects of herself. A few Candeshi officials were at the service, and one of them spoke of Noelle's ability to handle governorship from a relatively young age. Noelle was only thirty when she'd been sworn in, and she'd led the people of Dundere for nearly twenty-five years.

After a few more people rose to speak, I was surprised to see Saray stand and make her way to the stage. She took a deep breath as Deshi cast the voice-amplifying spell on her, then she began to speak.

"A little over four years ago, I came here to find Noelle," she began. "I came because my best friend needed healing, and I needed safety. I certainly wasn't seeking her out because I was trying to find family, but that's exactly what she became.

"I don't know my birth mother. When I found out that Marcus was my father, and then when he and Noelle offered to adopt Trina and me, I had doubts about how it would go. I didn't doubt that my father would do everything he could to adjust to having me in his life, but I was unsure if it would be as easy for Noelle. She'd never had children of her own, and I wasn't hers. I wondered if she would resent me, because I was taking up my father's time now, because I was a reminder of his past, and because she now had two unruly teenagers running around her house when she was trying to govern a country." She paused, and a few people chuckled. "I was absolutely amazed to discover how wrong I was. Noelle was so kind to us, so ready to help us figure out this new life we had, but at the same time, she never tried to smother us. The first year or so took a lot of adjusting for both Trina and me. We'd been through a lot in the months before we arrived, and now we had to adjust to life in a governor's household. Noelle was always there when we needed her…" Her voice broke, and she took a deep breath. "Noelle taught me that there are people out there who can be trusted, who can be depended on.

"And at the same time, she was such an example when it came to strength and courage. If you know me at all, you probably know I can be a bit stubborn and determined and…well, fiery." She smiled. "Back when I was in Sylvenburgh, I was always made to feel like these were bad things. Nice young ladies weren't supposed to have strong opinions or stand up for what they believed in. My grandmother Kirilee was one of the first women I knew who was all those things and wasn't ashamed of it. But it was Noelle who taught me to see these things as strengths, as tools that can be used for good when they're handled properly. She knew how to be stubborn and passionate, but she could also be gentle and understanding and wise at the same time." Her voice broke once more, and she swiped at her eyes. "Noelle was incredible. And I will miss her dearly."

When her speech was finished, Saray took a seat, and then Deshi stepped forward again. "I'd like to invite Trina and her friends to play a song in honour of Noelle. The rest of you may come forward and bid Noelle farewell in your own time."

Trina stood, and Kaden, Jasper and I followed. We took to the stage, and Kaden and I sat on the piano bench. We would be playing like we used to, me handling the low notes and her taking on the higher, more complex melodies. Only now, there were four hands playing instead of two; the songs we could create were far more intricate than before.

All because of the woman we honoured today.

Trina cleared her throat. "Hello, everyone," she said. "I'm not as good at speaking in front of people as Saray is, so I won't give a speech. But I am going to play a song for the woman who was a mother to me when my own mother was still a captive, who took me in and..." She trailed off, and tears began to stream down her cheeks. She sank to the ground, sobbing.

I exchanged a glance with Kaden. *"What do we do?"* she signed to me.

I was about to respond when I saw Jasper put down his fiddle. He walked over to Trina and crouched to tentatively put a hand on her shoulder, only to have her bury her face in his shirt while she wept. The audience began to murmur and look at one another.

Jasper hugged her carefully, then met my eyes. "Play something," he mouthed.

I nodded and began to play the bass section of a song that Kaden and I were known for back at the farmhouse. Kaden caught on and came in with the melody. The Yarel Island teens began to whisper amongst themselves, remembering the tune. Meanwhile, Jasper led Trina off to the side of the stage and sat with her, his arm around her shoulders. Saray and Starla joined him, and I couldn't help but notice that Saray was standing directly next to my brother, seemingly unbothered for once.

Trina stood a few minutes later, and Kaden effortlessly changed her tune to reflect the beginning of the song that Trina had written. I followed her lead, and Jasper returned to pick up his fiddle. Trina lifted her pipe to her lips, took a deep, shuddering breath, and began to play.

The song Trina composed was both mournful and infused with hope. It started slow, melancholy, then slowly built over several minutes to crescendo into a bright, buoyant ending. I watched as attendees filed past the casket, paying their final respects to Noelle, many of them in tears.

A few tears trickled down my own face as well, and I ignored them, focusing carefully on getting the notes of the song right. When it was finished, Kaden and I continued to play together, trying to somehow comfort the mourners with our melodies and harmonies, the same way we'd tried to comfort a farmhouse full of scared teenagers.

When the last of the mourners had filed past, we left the stage and approached the casket, where Shawnie and Alisa both stood waiting for us. Kaden slid her hand into mine, and together we gazed down at Noelle's still form. A preserving spell was keeping her intact until the burial, so she still looked very much like herself, but she also looked nothing like what I was used to. It was strange seeing someone so full of life reduced to an unmoving shell.

"I'll miss you," I said to her. "Thank you for everything."

Jasper stood behind us now, and he put a hand on my shoulder. "We should go," he whispered. "Only family is allowed at the burial."

I nodded, and Kaden squeezed my hand. Then we turned and walked out of the amphitheatre in silence.

The following Monday, I woke to find most of the inhabitants of the house gone. My friends were still around, as was Jasper, but Marcus and Trina were absent, as well as Lachlann and Starla. Alisa, who was up before the rest of us, shrugged when I asked where they were. "Something about a meeting with Deshi and some council members from Candesh," she told us.

"Why was Starla invited, though? And Lachlann?"

"No idea. I'm sure we'll find out soon enough."

When we had seen no one by lunchtime, I headed up to my room, thinking about a nap. I was more than a little surprised when I glanced out the window and saw all three of the Westwoods, Kip, Lachlann, Starla, Willem, Deshi and a few others I didn't know gathered around Kirilee's tree. Lachlann had his hand on the trunk and his head tilted, and I watched as he turned to say something to the others.

"What's going on?" Kaden asked, coming into the room.

I glanced back at her. "Looks like they're consulting Kirilee about something."

"I wonder what it is." She breezed past me and pushed open the balcony doors, only to be noticed and waved away by Willem. She huffed and sank down on the bed. "Fine. Leave us out of your conversations."

"I'm sure they'll share with us later," I assured, then flopped back onto the bed. "I think I need a nap. I'm exhausted from…everything."

She nodded. "I'll join you."

We lay there, her back pressed up against me, and I ran my hand through her soft black curls. "My hair's getting too long," she said. "I'm going to see if someone will cut it short for me again."

"You like it better short?"

"I do. Yours looks good now that it's getting longer."

I nodded. "I was actually pretty sad about losing my hair, of all things. I was proud of my curls."

"They suit you." She rolled over and tugged on one, grinning. Her face was inches from mine, and I tensed, wondering if she was getting curious about kissing. Last time I'd kissed someone in bed, things hadn't gone well.

But she rolled back over and snuggled up against me, and I relaxed. I must have fallen asleep, because the next thing I knew, Alisa was shaking me awake, telling me that we were needed downstairs.

We stumbled into the living room, bleary eyed, to find Marcus waiting for us. "We need to call a meeting at the Yarel Island camp," he said. "Something has come up."

Deshi had managed to organize everyone at the camp into a large semicircle by the time we arrived. The refugees whispered amongst themselves, several of them shooting suspicious glances at the new governor. Marcus walked over to stand next to her, and Saray and Kip stood off to the side, looking like they might be involved in whatever was about to happen. "All right, folks, we have some difficult news for you," Deshi began. "I recently had a visit from a few Candeshi councilmen, and it turns out that the Candeshi empire doesn't look favourably on Noelle's choice to rescue all of you without obtaining permission first. And the people of Dundere are frightened. They believe that having you here means there will be more attacks."

"So what?" someone spoke up from the crowd. "You want us all to leave then?" A few others murmured in protest.

Deshi held up a hand. "It isn't my decision whether you leave or stay, unfortunately," she told them. "If the empire orders you to leave, I'll have to comply. I've asked for three months to make the arrangements for most of you to depart. We're not just going to abandon you, though. We have a plan."

She turned to Marcus, who stepped forward and cleared his throat. "If you're hoping to return to Breoch and be reunited with your family, this will be the time to look into that. There's a fellow we know who owns a ship that offers free passage to anyone willing to work, so sailing with him may be the best option. You're also free to move on to other lands if you wish. You can make a home on one of the other Verdant Isles, or head to the Candeshi or Cherinese mainland if you so desire."

"But we can't stay here?"

"If you're able to secure housing and a job within the next three months, then you can stay," Marcus replied. "But the Candeshi government would prefer we limit those numbers to about fifty. They don't want to attract that sort of attention here again. As for the rest of you, here's what we are planning. Myself, my daughters, and my soon-to-be son-in-law would like to invite you into the Shrouded Woods, to create a new village where we can all live without fear."

My eyes widened at his words, and I glanced over at Kaden. *A village in the Woods?*

Several of the Yarel Island folk began muttering to themselves. "How is that safe?" one person called out. "Aren't the Woods full of bandits and criminals?"

Saray stepped forward. "I used to think that too. And yes, there are some bandits in the Shrouded Woods. But there are also incredibly lovely people, many of whom live there to avoid their gifts being discovered."

"Would these people accept us?" asked one of the teens.

Lachlann nodded. "The woods-folk aren't likely to turn away fellow magikai in need. But having an influx of this many newcomers might be overwhelming to them, so that's why we're going to build our village a short distance from the primarily populated area. There's a particular grove that was suggested to me. It's fertile and good for building, but in order to get there, you have to cross a river. And no one has built a bridge as of yet. We'll fix that, of course."

"That'll take some time," put in a red-haired woman whose name I didn't know.

Lachlann nodded. "We plan to send a few of us to this grove ahead of time to start building the new city. Starla's going to fashion more homes and start up some crops and gardens, Kip is going to use telekinesis to help with building, Willem and Saray will work on getting Willem's school of magic ready for the younger folk, and I'll be there to help with any odds and ends. It'll be a bit of an undertaking, but I don't doubt we can make it happen."

"What's this about a school of magic?" Shawnie asked.

Saray turned to him and grinned. "Willem is going to reopen the school of magic that his parents once ran, to house and teach the younger folk," she explained. "I'm going to help him with that."

An awkward silence fell over the assembly for a moment, and then the redheaded woman spoke again. "If we're going to have a village of our own, who will lead us?"

"I will," Marcus replied. "I imagine I'm the only one here with much political experience, so it falls on me to lead, for the first little while at least. If anyone wishes to challenge me after a year or so, we can put it to a vote." He grinned a little.

"And he'll have lots of help," Lachlann put in. "We're planning to set up a council. I'll be recruiting a small guard to maintain the town's security, Starla will preside over farming and gathering, Kip will train hunters, and Saray and Willem will oversee magic schooling. And we're hoping Kip's friend Ambrose can help us set up a trade system with the other occupants of the Woods."

Jasper frowned. "How do you know the Breoch Guard won't find this new village?"

Willem responded with a sharp laugh. "Do you know how terrified the Breoch Guard were to go through that portal? They have no desire to venture into the Shrouded Woods again anytime soon. And even if they came looking, it would be mighty hard to find the village unless they had specific directions."

"You know," Saray said, "I've heard rumours that you folks told stories about me on the farm, because I managed to outwit the Breoch Guard. Well, after this, there will be stories about how an entire *people* managed to outwit them, how they vanished under their noses and were, hopefully, never discovered again. Once we make this move, all your questions about where you're going to end up can be put to rest. We can build a new home together. We can have hope for a good future. It'll take some work, but I think it'll be worth it."

"Saray's right." Marcus put a hand on her shoulder. "We also think it's best that I lead you folks because I understand you. I know what it's like to be enslaved, to have your dignity taken away, and to have no hope for a good future." Several of the assembled nodded, and Marcus clapped his hands together. For a moment, I saw the light return to his eyes. "*This* is our hope, my friends. This is proof that they *lost*. They called us krossemages because it means 'shattered mage'. Well, you know what? They may have hunted us down, mutilated us, and forced us to do their bidding; they may have tried to burn us alive and scare us into submission; and they may have taken us away from our families…" His voice broke, and he swiped at his eyes before continuing. "But despite all this, they haven't taken our hope. They may have tried, but they have *not* shattered us."

An impromptu cheer rose at the conclusion of Marcus's speech, and I leapt to my feet with the others, whooping and throwing my fist in the air.

When the cheering died down, Marcus grinned and turned to Willem. "Do you know how to say 'not shattered' in Cherinese?"

Willem frowned for a moment, thinking. *"Ankrossi."*

"Ankrossi," Marcus repeated. He looked over the crowd once more. "That's what we're going to name our village."

There was another round of cheering, and then Deshi concluded and dismissed the meeting. She came to Marcus and put a hand on his shoulder. "You sure managed to get them excited about being deported."

Marcus chuckled. "I do that sometimes."

"You're definitely the right person to lead them."

Lachlann turned to me then. "Ruby, can Starla and I chat with you and your friends quickly?"

I nodded, and Kaden, Alisa, Shawnie and I followed him to where Starla stood. Starla grinned at us. "You folks have already been to the Shrouded Woods once, right?"

We all nodded. "I've been twice," I told her.

"Perfect. How would the four of you like to come along with the group that's going to prepare our little village?"

I exchanged a confused glance with Kaden, and Alisa frowned. "Us? What would we do?"

"I'm sure you could all find ways to be useful. Ruby, we'll need someone to keep the weather relatively clear while we're making preparations, especially during the winter. Alisa, you're a teleporter, right? And Kaden, you can fly?"

They both nodded.

"Those can be useful skills when you're building a city. Shawnie, I figured you'd be interested in helping Willem and Saray with the school of magic."

"Absolutely." Shawnie nodded. "Though, if you need help hauling things in town, I can do that as well. I've spent most of my life on farms. And if wild animals get too close, well, I know how to scare them off." He grinned.

"Of course." Lachlann replied. "Sophie will be coming with us as well. I hope you kids don't mind looking out for her when she's not learning from Willem."

My eyes narrowed. "She's going to live in the Woods? Chase is allowing that?"

"Initially, she was meant to be teleported home each day after training with Willem and Alex. But now that the school is reopening, Chase thinks it might be best for her to live in dorms with the other kids. She'll go home on weekends."

I nodded. "I think that's for the best as well. She seemed pretty lonely before."

"Exactly. The plan is to leave in two weeks, assuming you are all interested in going."

"How will we get there?" Alisa asked.

"Willem's planning to redirect the Shrouded Woods portal to the grove and open it two more times— once to let our advance crew through, and once more to allow the entire population of the new village to pass. After that, it will be closed permanently. I'll be leaving the same day as you folks by ship, and I'll hike into the Woods on foot from Flavalan, then have Ambrose bring me the rest of the way. I believe Jasper plans on accompanying me on the Lady Liara."

"Will he be joining us in the grove?"

Lachlann shook his head. "Jasper wants to go to sea for a while. Though I'm sure he'll be more than willing to visit all of you."

"What about Kirilee?" I asked. "I suppose you'll be leaving her behind?"

Lachlann exchanged a look with Starla, who shook her head. "Not if I can get a particular spell right. Kirilee thinks there's a way to confine her soul to one limb of the tree, cut it off, and replant it on the other side." She sighed. "I hope we don't have to leave Kirilee behind. But if we do, she's instructed me to find someone with a gift like mine to allow her to speak to Deshi when needed. She'll be valuable in either setting."

"I'm sure you'll figure it out," Lachlann assured her. Then he looked to the rest of us. "Let's head home. The next few weeks will be busy."

CHAPTER 38

"WHAT DO YOU think it'll be like, living in the Shrouded Woods?" Kaden asked me later as we perched on a branch of Kirilee's tree, staring up at the luminescent blooms.

"I think it'll be something like camping. Very peaceful."

"Won't we freeze in the winter? Those treehouses aren't going to keep in much heat."

"I suppose I'll have to make sure it's not too cold then." I put an arm around her. "We'll be fine, Kaden. It'll feel strange at first, but we'll adapt."

"I hope so." She sighed. "I'll miss Dundere."

I nodded. "Me too. It's been amazing, learning about politics and leadership from Noelle. I don't know Deshi very well, but I suspect I could learn a lot from her too."

"Perhaps you could join the village council that Marcus was talking about when you're a bit older."

"Maybe." I stared up at the stars. "I always wondered where we were going to end up, but a hidden village in the Shrouded Woods was never on my list of guesses."

"Me neither. But at least we'll be together." Kaden reached over and toyed with my hair for a moment before sitting up to peer down at me. "Uh, Ruby? Could we...try something?"

"What's that?"

"Well, I suppose I'm feeling extra adventurous tonight, with all this talk of moving, and I was wondering if maybe you felt the same way, because, well, I've really been wanting to kiss you."

My heartbeat picked up. "You...have?"

She nodded and smiled at me shyly. "Only if you want to, of course."

"I...I definitely want to, Kaden. I've wanted to since we started dating, but I was waiting for you to be ready. I think it'll be a little awkward up here in this tree, though."

"It would be for most people. But don't forget my gift." She mumbled her casting words and rose off the tree limb, then floated around so that she faced me. Resting her knees on the branch, one on each side of my legs, she used her flight to maintain her balance. "How's this?"

I laughed. "That's incredible," I said and reached forward, trailing a finger down the side of her cheek.

Kaden's lips were hesitant at first, brushing against my own lightly, tentatively. I leaned in and kissed her just a little bit harder, and she giggled, wound a hand into my curls and kissed me more decisively.

Then she jerked back, nearly throwing me off balance. "Why do I hear piano music and thunderstorms when I kiss you? And why does it smell like rain on cobblestones?"

I laughed. "When two magikai kiss, they can sense the other's magic."

"Huh. I've never heard of that before." She frowned. "What's my magic like?"

"Come here, and let me figure that out." I smiled, then leaned in to kiss her again. Kaden relaxed slightly, her hand sliding into my hair once more. A minute or so later, I pulled back, resting my forehead against hers. "Your magic," I whispered, "is light and fluffy and carefree. It makes me feel…weightless. And it tastes like cherries."

"Cherries?" She grinned.

I nodded. "I like it. I want to taste it some more."

Kaden nodded and kissed me again, and I slid a hand around her waist, her form so tiny and delicate compared to what I'd been used to over the past few months. I found myself relaxing in her arms, but unlike with Alvin, there was no seductive sweetness that caused me to abandon all reason.

With Kaden, I was lighthearted and free but fully in control of myself.

Eventually, she pulled away and rested her head on my shoulder, and we stayed like that, nestled in each other's arms, until sleep bid us to head inside for the night.

The following weeks were a blur of preparation and planning, and finally the day for our departure arrived. Lachlann and Jasper would leave earlier than the rest of us, and we crowded into the foyer to bid them farewell. Kaden and I were accompanying them to the docks.

In the doorway, Jasper stood clad in a travelling cloak and the rough tunic and breeches he'd worn at sea. "Well, I suppose it's time I say goodbye to you all." He gave the group a tense smile. "Thank you for everything. Taking my sister in, giving me a second chance, all of it."

Trina took a step forward, and Jasper gasped in surprise when she embraced him. Then he laughed and put his arms around her. "I never thought I'd say this," she mumbled, "but it was good seeing you again."

"Good to see you as well, Trina," he replied. "You're always welcome to come visit on the ship. Ruby has a summoning stone." He looked up at the others then. "That goes for all of you."

Shawnie and Alisa stepped in to embrace him next, and both Marcus and Starla offered him handshakes and words of thanks. Then I saw Saray whisper something to Lachlann, and she came forward, Lachlann following. "Jasper," she said, "I know this hasn't been easy for either of us, but I'm glad you showed up. I might even miss you when you're gone." She smiled, then took a deep breath and extended a hand. "I hope you find what you're looking for out there at sea."

Jasper stared at her hand for a moment, then looked at Lachlann, who nodded. "Thanks, Saray," he said, his voice turning rough as he reached forward to shake her hand. "And congratulations on your wedding. You as well, Kip."

Kip nodded and gave him a tight smile and a wave. "Thank you, Jasper. Good luck out there."

Jasper squared his shoulders. "I'll be waiting in the carriage. Come with me,

Ruby, Kaden?"

I nodded and followed him out the door, Kaden trailing us.

Lachlann joined us a couple minutes later, having said his own farewells. As soon as the carriage was moving, Jasper let out a laugh. "I did *not* expect Saray to shake my hand."

"Me neither." Lachlann chuckled. "That was brave of her. And brave of you, being willing to accept it."

"I wouldn't have done it if you weren't there." He shook his head. "You know, I might miss them all too. Well, maybe not Kip, but the rest of them. Even so, I think spending some time away at sea might be best for all of us."

I nodded and then turned to Lachlann. "So, what's your plan for when you get to Breoch? Are you going back to the farm?"

"I'll visit, but I'm not going to stay," he said. "I got a letter from Tom recently telling me that Mother has hired some farmhands, which means that he and I won't need to be as committed as we were. And I think this is coming at a good time for me. I'm needed in the village."

"You're going to move there then?"

"I think it's about time I settle down and actually get my own place. I'll have Starla grow me one of her fancy treehouses. It's funny, you know. I've spent all these years thinking I'd never really settle in one place, but this feels right. Also, I feel a bit obligated."

"Why?" asked Jasper.

"Because there's a chance none of this would've happened if I hadn't agreed to help you and Ruby. We wouldn't have rescued an entire colony of magikai, and they wouldn't be needing to find a permanent home in the Woods." He frowned. "I had a part in making all this happen, so I think I need to see it through, help establish the village and such."

I nodded, taking in his words. "That's all true," I said. "And I owe thanks for all that." I smiled at him. "Thanks for being willing to bring me here. For giving Jasper another chance, and for taking a risk like that. It mustn't have been an easy choice, letting a fellow who shot one of your friends travel with you."

"It wasn't." Lachlann eyed Jasper. "I'm glad I did it though."

Kaden grinned. "You know, I doubt it's *just* feelings of obligation making you want to live in the village."

"Oh?" Lachlann raised an eyebrow.

"Don't think we haven't noticed. There's a certain someone you want to spend more time with." She winked.

"Ah." I thought I saw Lachlann blush ever so slightly. "Yes, there is that."

"You do realize that if you break Starla's heart, you're going to have about fifty teenagers with magical abilities all out to get you," she went on.

"Well, it's a good thing I have anti-magic." He smirked at her, then sobered. "Don't worry. I make no promises that Starla and I will work out, but I'll treat her well, no matter how things go. She's a lovely woman, and she deserves that much."

"Trina told me once that her mother wants more kids," I said. "Do you think you'd be up for that?"

He chuckled. "Well, now, I think you're getting ahead of yourself. We aren't even officially dating yet."

"Which there's no point in doing if you don't want the same things in life," Kaden pointed out.

"True. I spent a lot of years thinking I'd never have children. And I don't think that I'm someone who needs to have them to be happy. But I'm not opposed to the idea either. It took me several years of taking teenagers through the Woods to realize this, but perhaps I'm better with kids than I once thought."

We pulled up to the harbour and parked the carriage, and Kaden grinned at us. "I'll stay with the horses. You three go." She embraced Jasper and Lachlann, then sat back in the driver's seat and shooed us away.

Lachlann, Jasper and I made our way down the dock to the waiting ship. It was hard to believe it had been less than six months ago that the three of us had set out on our journey. I remembered the tense silence of that first day, the distrust that hung in the air between us and Lachlann. Now it felt like he was practically family.

We reached the base of the gangplank, and Lachlann turned to us. "I'll let you two say your goodbyes." He smiled and put an arm around my shoulders. "I'll see you in a month or so, Ruby. Stay safe."

"You too. See you soon, Lachlann."

He let go of me, nodded to Jasper, and made his way up the gangplank. Jasper turned to me. "You'll be okay without me, right?"

I nodded. "I have Kaden, and Alisa and Shawnie. And Starla. And…all the others. I'll miss you, but I'll be all right."

"Do you have your summoning stone?"

I nodded and closed my hand around it. "I'll try not to summon you when you're halfway up the shrouds."

"I appreciate that." He smiled. "And I'll try not to get you when you're in school. But I might call you out for an occasional weekend sail."

"I'd like that." I sighed then, tears pricking at my eyes. "I don't know how to thank you, Jasper, for rescuing me. If you hadn't, I might not be alive."

He nodded and pulled me into an embrace. "I'm glad I could finally be a decent brother," he said softly.

"You've been more than decent."

He held onto me for a moment longer and then let me go. "Well, I'd best be going. Hope to see you soon, Ruby."

I nodded and waved goodbye, a lump rising in my throat. Then he turned and made his way up the gangplank.

I went back to the carriage just in time to see the Lady Liara pull away from the dock. I waved at the ship one last time, uncertain whether Jasper or Lachlann could see, then turned to Kaden and kissed her on the cheek. "Let's go home," I said.

It was time for a new adventure.

EPILOGUE

Eight Months Later

"HOW DO I look?" Kaden asked me, spinning around in the middle of my room. "Dashing?"

I took in her dark trousers and bright red waistcoat. "Absolutely. Though I think you'd look even more dashing with a top hat."

"I'll have to borrow one of Shawnie's, then." She stepped toward me and twirled me in a circle. "I can't wait to dance with you later."

"Here they come!" Alisa squealed, leaning out my bedroom window. I quickly joined her to stare out at the two figures making their way across the network of bridges and walkways that spanned our small village. *Ankrossi.* It was still hard to believe we'd built this, that our little hideaway was real. That it was our new home.

I wasn't sure what we'd be able to create from the large, fertile grove when we first set foot in it all those months ago. I certainly didn't envision something this complex. Starla had grown the trees that surrounded the meadow into a community of small houses connected by walkways, most of them draped with hanging plants for privacy. They were not perfect, as far as houses went— a large communal tent on the ground served as the kitchen and dining hall for nearly four hundred people, and baths mostly took place in a pair of pools that Kip and Marcus created by redirecting water from the river. But the treehouses gave each of us some privacy.

Starla's was one of the largest in town; she had grown it with several rooms to host guests and folks in need. Right now, she shared it not only with Trina, but also Kaden, Alisa, Shawnie and me. Most of the other teens lived at Willem's school, but we decided to stick around town and teleport to our classes each day instead. My stormbrewing skills were more needed here in town than at Willem's, and Kaden wanted to stay with me. Alisa and Shawnie, however, were considering moving to the school next fall after their graduation; they were both interested in teaching magic with Willem and Saray.

The village also contained several small shops, some nestled into the bases of trees and others in large tents, where various members of the community sold their wares. The group from Yarel Island had a large variety of talents amongst themselves, and Ankrossi was now home to several seamstresses, a few leatherworkers, a baker, a healer who used herbs and salves, and a couple of blacksmiths. Recently, a tavern had opened in one of the larger tents, and beyond our circle of trees were fields of grain, vegetables and fruit. At Trina's insistence, animals were not farmed here, but Kip had several hunters trained, and the river was teeming with fish. Beyond the fields was the bridge that connected us to the rest of the Woods. And in the centre of our grove, two trees stood tall and intertwined, creating a structure that could shelter us from the elements, house council meetings, and host guests. One of these trees was a massive oadek, native to Dundere, its trunk sturdy and red barked and its leaves trailing nearly to the ground. This tree represented the steady, gentle force that Noelle had been to all of us.

The other tree, of course, was Kirilee's.

Starla had succeeded in her attempt to bring Kirilee to Ankrossi, and the new viletta that housed her soul was far larger, stronger, and more colourful than the original. Its branches twisted around the more solid oadek, its colourful blooms mingling with the other tree's vines to create canopies and curtains. Our town council met under this tree monthly, with Kirilee occasionally chiming in with her insights. Guests could be housed in the many small rooms that were fashioned from branches and hanging vines. Children slid down the sturdy limbs, folks hung hammocks off the branches to rest on hot days, and a large rope swing served as entertainment for both young and old. At night, the viletta infused our grove with subtle illumination.

It was under these two trees that, later today, Saray and Kip would be wed.

I could see Saray now, her bright hair contrasting with the deep greens of the forest as she and Trina made their way to our home, chattering excitedly. Alisa turned to me. "Shall we go downstairs and meet the bride?"

"Absolutely," I said, and we left the window and headed for the stairs.

In the main room, Starla sat on a couch fashioned from tree branches and topped with furs and cushions, drinking tea and chatting with Lachlann. We were all accustomed to Lachlann's near-constant presence in the house by now; he had his own place nearby, but he and Starla had been nearly inseparable for the last several months. They both looked up when we entered. "Morning, bridesmaids," Starla greeted us. "You all look lovely."

I smiled as I took in Kaden's outfit once more— which she had completed with a top hat stolen from Shawnie's room on her way downstairs— and Alisa's soft pink dress that hugged her curves. My own dress was navy blue and sleeveless, tied behind my neck in a fashion that was common in the Shrouded Woods. Alisa's hair was done in soft waves that just brushed her shoulders, and my curls were piled on my head and secured with a few brightly coloured feathers. "*They* look lovely," Kaden corrected. "I look *dashing*."

Lachlann chuckled. "That you do."

The door swung open then, and Saray and Trina stepped into the room. Trina huffed when she saw Lachlann. "What are *you* doing here? You know the rules— you're not supposed to see the bride ahead of time!"

"I believe that rule applies only to the groom," Lachlann countered. "Besides, my house has been taken over by unruly young men who stayed up most of the night drinking and swapping rowdy stories. I find this company much more pleasant." He grinned and put an arm around Starla.

Saray grinned. "You two are so cute it's disgusting."

"Try living in the same house as one of them," Kaden put in.

"Hey, now, don't talk to *me* about being disgustingly cute. Only one of us in this room is getting married, and it's certainly not me," Lachlann replied, standing.

"Yet," Trina countered.

Lachlann grinned and exchanged a look with Starla. "You're likely right about that. But my point still stands." He took Starla's hand, leaned down, and kissed it. "I'll see you at the wedding." Then he turned to Saray. "And I'll see you at the altar." Since weddings in the Shrouded Woods were not yet legal affairs, anyone could perform the ceremony. Kip and Saray had chosen Lachlann, as he'd known them the longest.

Lachlann strode out, and Starla stared after him, a grin playing on her lips. "All right, ladies," she said after a moment, "let's get Saray ready for her wedding."

A few hours later, Saray stood in the middle of the main room, flanked by Alexander and Ember. Trina, who was the maid of honour, had retreated upstairs after Lachlann left, and returned wearing a dress that was similar in style to Saray's, but was a soft lilac, its colour deepening to violet at the hem.

Saray's dress had short bell sleeves and a fitted bodice inlaid with sky-blue stones. The dress was white until it reached her knees, where it darkened to bright yellow, then orange, and then a brilliant, fiery red along the hemline. The dress was the brainchild of Alexander and Ember, who were the only non-wedding-party folks allowed in Starla's house right now.

I watched as Alexander adjusted Saray's dress so it sat properly on her hips, while Ember applied a subtle layer of eyeshadow to her lids. Trina had done her hair up in an intricate, braided crown and finished it off with a delicate tiara fashioned by Lachlann. "You look incredibly striking, my dear," Starla said to her.

Saray grinned. "I can't wait to see what you folks have done with Kip."

"I think you'll like it very much." Alexander chuckled. "But for now we must run along. We'll see you out there soon enough."

We bid them farewell, and they left. Trina took Saray's hands and twirled her ecstatically in a circle. "Are you nervous at all?"

"Nervous? About marrying Kip?" She laughed. "Not after all these years together."

"What about the Joining ceremony?" I asked. "I'd be nervous about that." I exchanged a glance with Kaden, my heartbeat picking up. We'd already discussed partaking in that ceremony ourselves if we did decide to marry.

"Maybe a little," Saray admitted. "But I've had stranger spells cast on me. I think I'll survive."

"And if you don't, well, there's a few spells for that as well," Trina added. "Not that we would *ever* be involved with those, of course." She winked.

Starla chuckled. "Speaking of which, Kirilee sends her congratulations to both you and Kip. She's excited for the two of you— as excited as a tree can be, anyway."

There was a knock on the front door then, and Trina answered. Marcus stood outside, dressed in his best tailcoat. His eyebrows lifted when he looked his daughters over. "Wow. You both look stunning."

Saray laughed. "You don't look too bad yourself, for an old man."

He grinned, then closed his eyes. "I wish Noelle could see you like this," he said, his voice wavering. "She'd be so proud of you."

I felt the mood in the room shift as the sadness that always lurked just below the surface of all our minds reared its head. I remembered how nearly all-consuming it had been for Saray during our days of building the village. She tried to put on a brave face, attempting to distract herself by helping Willem and Shawnie create the school of magic, but there were many days when she was quiet and withdrawn, and it was obvious enough that she was grieving.

My own feelings of grief were not as strong as Saray's, of course, but they were certainly real. On the day of Alvin's trial, when we heard the story of Noelle's death told again and again in detail, the sadness was excruciating for all of us. Alvin was locked up for the rest of his life, unable to hurt anyone else, but that only barely diminished our pain.

Moving to Ankrossi was good for the Westwoods, I thought; Marcus had a village to run, Saray and Kip had the magic school, and there were plenty of animal friends to keep Trina distracted. Marcus was mostly back to his normal, quirky self now, and Trina and Saray were smiling nearly as much as they did before all this. For me, the grief only came in small waves now— when I saw the tall bellflowers that reminded me of Noelle's room of tropical plants or heard a laugh that sounded like hers, and during moments when I knew she would've offered poignant advice. But I still missed her.

"You're right, she would be proud," Saray agreed.

He gave her a watery smile, then took a deep breath. "Today's not a day to mourn though. It's a day to celebrate. And they're ready for you." He offered his daughter an arm. "Shall we?"

When we arrived a few minutes later, my eyes grew wide. The massive chamber that was formed by the broad, twisting limbs of the two trees was decked out in finery. A rich, embroidered runner that was almost certainly the work of Alexander and Ember was laid out on the ground, and people were seated in rows on either side of it, on benches formed from raised tree roots. The cavern was adorned with flowers of all kinds today; twisting vines bursting with colour had grown up among the limbs of the trees, and wildflowers blossomed on both sides of the runner. Light emanated from the viletta blooms and from torches that had been placed around the room, as well as from the dozens of fairies that accompanied Hilda and Carmine to the occasion. A rich, melodic song began— Gareth had agreed to play for the processional and the reception, on the condition that he was accompanied by Jasper.

I certainly wasn't expecting Jasper to be part of the wedding. But Gareth insisted that my brother was the best fiddle player on the ship, and so here he was, dressed in a fine blue and silver waistcoat, his blond curls smoothed down a bit more than usual. He'd shown up with the rest of the crew from the Lady Liara last night, and I'd given him the grand tour of Ankrossi, his eyes wide as he took it all in. Kaden and I had used my teleportation stone to visit Jasper on the ship quite regularly over the past few months, often accompanied by Alisa and Shawnie, or, more recently, Trina. But this was his first time visiting our new home.

Jasper met my eyes and gave me a brief smile as I started down the runway, behind Alisa and followed by Kaden and Trina. I looked from him to Kip's men, who were poised in a row, each dressed in their own finery. Ambrose ended up as Kip's best man, and Shawnie was one of his groomsmen, along with two other fellows who lived here in Ankrossi, Tobias and Kyler. Then, finally, I looked at the groom himself.

Alexander and Ember had done wonders with Kip. The coat that they'd fashioned for him was dark brown with green and gold leaves embroidered into it. The shoulders had pauldrons of golden brocade that were made to look like leaves, and the coat was trimmed with the same iridescent golden fabric. A simple leather belt held the coat in place, and his hair, which hung just past his chin now, was smoothed out and had been topped with a simple silver circlet. His dress was formal enough, but it suited him, unlike the fancy waistcoats he'd worn during his Dundere years. I saw his eyes widen and his face erupt into a smile, and I knew that Saray had entered the chamber behind us.

We took our places as the music faded, and I watched Kip step forward to meet Marcus and Saray. Kip took Saray's hands in his and whispered something to her as they came before Lachlann.

"Friends and loved ones," Lachlann said, "we are gathered here today to join Kip Robinson and Saray Westwood together in marriage." He looked at the couple and grinned. "Finally."

A chuckle rippled through the crowd.

"I've known Saray and Kip since they were teenagers," he went on. "I was asked by my late wife Kirilee to help accompany them to Dundere. Two days into the endeavour, they were already squabbling like an old married couple. There was accidental fire magic, betrayal, and even some punches thrown, and I remember wondering what exactly I'd gotten myself into." He smiled. "As time went on, I watched them go from being rivals to friends, and then to lovers. I saw them learn to forgive and let go of prejudices, and begin to use their strengths to help one another. They transformed from a pair of awkward, volatile teenagers to a couple rich in courage and kindness.

"A very long time ago, I had a conversation with Kirilee that was meant to be private; only, a pair of very curious young women decided to listen in." He grinned, and Saray and Trina exchanged a smirk. "While we were discussing our future, I said something to Kirilee that I think fitting. She'd been without a permanent home for many years, and I suggested to her that perhaps *home* doesn't always have to be a place; perhaps home could be another person. Saray and Kip, your journeys thus far have taken you to many unexpected places. And who knows if you'll be able to stay here forever. But my hope is that, no matter where you go next, you can find a home in one another."

Saray and Kip both nodded, and I felt the mood in the chamber dampen ever so slightly. A few months back, Saray had confided in us that, realistically, it was only a matter of time before the Breoch Guard discovered her location. Someone in Dundere might tip the Guard off, or they might come looking and have an innocent passerby give them directions to our grove. We might even experience another betrayal. No one in Ankrossi was certain if the Guard would risk venturing this deep into the Woods, or whether they would succeed in locating our village, but Saray said that she needed to be prepared for the possibility that she and Kip might have to run one day. It was part of why they'd elected to undergo the Joining; it made sense to have both of them as powerful as possible if they were to come up against the Guard in the future.

"With all that in mind, I ask you this question," Lachlann continued. "Saray, do you take Kip to be your husband, to share a life and find a home with him, no matter where fate takes you, as long as you both shall live?"

Saray gazed into Kip's eyes and smiled. "I do."

Lachlann turned to Kip and repeated the question, and Kip smiled broadly as he repeated Saray's response.

Once he'd led them in their vows, Lachlann addressed the audience. "Kip and Saray have chosen to undergo the Joining of Magic, and I'd like to invite Willem and Hilda to come forward to perform the ritual."

Willem took Lachlann's place and looked upon the couple solemnly. "Saray and Kip, you have requested to be Joined not only by life and love and body, but also by magic. This bond will last so long as each of you lives, whether or not you choose to stay married. Do you both agree to be Joined in this way?"

Saray and Kip exchanged a long, nervous glance, and the both of them voiced their agreement. Hilda passed Willem a small cushion that bore a ceremonial dagger. "I will require one lock of hair from both of you, then one drop of blood."

They each used the dagger to cut off a piece of hair. Willem held out a small golden bowl between them. "Now you will each work your magic on these strands of hair."

Kip nodded and waved his hand, and I watched as his lock levitated in front of him. He took hold of Saray's lock next and used his telekinesis to tie both in a knot. Then Saray set fire to the knot, letting the ashes fall delicately into the bowl. When the hair had completely burned away, Willem offered the knife to Saray again. She pricked her thumb, then let a drop of blood fall into the bowl. Kip did the same.

Willem handed the bowl to Hilda, who poured a vial of liquid into it while singing a spell, fairies floating effortlessly around her. Then Willem put his hands over the bowl and mumbled his own spell, and a sweet-smelling plume of smoke rose from it. Hilda dipped a small brush and painted the mixture onto Saray's lips, then onto Kip's.

Lachlann stepped forward again. "Kip and Saray, I now pronounce you husband and wife. When you kiss, the Joining will be complete, and you will be bonded in life, love, body, and magic." He smiled. "You may kiss."

The two of them stared at one another, both their expressions ever so slightly nervous. Kip smiled at Saray, ran a finger down her jaw, and lifted her chin. Then he leaned in.

The moment their lips met, a tangible wave of power swept through the room. I gasped as it hit me, and for a few fleeting moments I could sense both Kip's ferocious, pine-scented magic and Saray's fiery, cinnamon-flavoured power. Their two gifts melded into a single, much stronger form of magic that was all fire and forest, hot and cool, and utterly fierce. I shuddered as the spell faded.

Kip and Saray were suffused in a pure white light now, and I watched as they pulled away from each other, both gasping. Saray grinned as she looked Kip over.

"I…I think it worked."

"I'd say so," he agreed.

Satisfied, Lachlann turned to address the crowd. "Friends and loved ones, may I introduce you to Mr. and Mrs. Kip and Saray Robinson." He grinned. "Now, let's get this party started!"

Growing up, I'd attended countless balls and social functions. I'd danced at birthday parties, been swept off my feet at many weddings, and celebrated holidays and important occasions with large, sometimes raucous gatherings of extended family.

Yet it was hard to recall a celebration as merry as the one that followed Saray and Kip's wedding. We feasted until we were stuffed, while Kip and Saray attempted to eat and drink using only their minds to lift their dinnerware. After we ate, the entire population of Ankrossi, plus a few more, took to the floor of the tree cavern for wild dancing, the music led by Gareth on his pipe and accompanied by a few of the other musicians from our Moon Dances. Most of the dancing I'd done in my lifetime had been a bit more composed than this, but here, there was no need to hold back, and Kaden and I whirled and laughed ecstatically.

We occasionally danced with other partners too, trading off with Alisa and Shawnie for a few songs, or pairing up with some of our classmates. Jasper cut in during one of the faster melodies, and he and I launched into the Angry Squirrel Dance, much to the amusement of those nearby.

When we were done, Jasper glanced over at the refreshment table, where Saray stood sipping a drink and watching the action. Kip was dancing with his aunt at the moment, and Jasper turned to me. "I, uh, should go congratulate Saray."

"Do you want me to come with you?" I asked, recalling how nervous Saray and Jasper had been around one another when he'd showed up in Ankrossi the night before.

"Please." He smiled at me, and I followed him to the table.

Saray saw us approach, and I noticed her tense up for just a second. Then she smiled at us. "Hi."

"Don't worry," Jasper said, standing a reasonable distance away from her, "I'm not going to ask you to dance."

"Good. I would have to politely decline."

"Politely decline?" He chuckled nervously. "I could have handled that. I was more worried about you setting something on fire and throwing it at me with your mind."

Saray raised an eyebrow. "I'll keep that in mind for next time I'm dealing with unwanted company."

He laughed again and shifted from one foot to the other. "I just wanted to say congratulations. I'm happy for you and Kip. And I'm happy you have such a wonderful place to live, too." He glanced at me. "Ruby showed me around last night; Ankrossi is incredible."

"Well, you're welcome to come visit again," she told him.

I grinned as I picked up a slice of cake from the refreshment table. "That's what I keep telling him."

"And you're welcome to visit the ship if you want," Jasper said to her. "Trina's been enjoying herself when she stops by."

Saray nodded. "I hear she's thinking about joining you folks for a few months."

"She mentioned that. It'd be good for her, I think."

"And what about you? Where do you see yourself ending up once you're done with sailing?"

He shrugged. "I'm not sure. I can't go back to Breoch, I know that much."

"Have you considered moving here?"

"Possibly. As I say, I do like it here. And Ruby and her friends have been trying to convince me that it's a good idea. I'm just not sure that I'm welcome."

"Well, I can't speak for anyone else, but I'm sure I could get used to having you around again," Saray told him.

"It wouldn't make you nervous?"

"Oh, it might. But I could adapt." She frowned. "Truth be told, Jasper, I'm rather impressed with you."

His eyes narrowed. "Impressed?"

"I don't fully understand what it must have been like, growing up in a home like yours. But questioning things that were so ingrained into your beliefs and standing up to your father when he ordered you to hunt me down, that took courage." She sighed. "I may be a little nervous around you, but I have a lot of respect for who you're becoming, Jasper Jameson."

He smiled and shrugged. "If it means anything, the feeling is mutual."

"You respect who I'm becoming, or you're nervous around me?"

"Both. I'm terrified of you, remember? You said so on the ship all those years ago." He smirked.

"Right." Saray closed her eyes for a moment, and I saw her hands tense up. I glanced at Jasper and shook my head.

"I'm sorry, I shouldn't have joked about that," he said.

Saray breathed deeply, then opened her eyes and shrugged. "I also seem to recall you telling me I hadn't seen the last of you. Which was true, though not in the way I expected. I figured you might come back to finish what you'd started, but I certainly didn't think you'd show up with a krossemage sister in tow, begging our forgiveness."

Jasper raised his palms. "What can I say? I'm full of surprises."

"What you did for Ruby, that took courage as well."

"I just did what I had to." He looked over at me. "You know, I'm more impressed with Ruby than myself."

"Really?" I asked, my eyebrows lifting.

He nodded. "After what happened with Alvin, I was worried you'd get all timid again. But, well, look at you. Out there, helping everyone get used to living in a place you hardly know yourself, running for village council, and falling madly in love."

"Who's madly in love?" Kaden asked, sauntering over. She put her arms around me and then snatched the cake from my hand to take a bite of it. "Oh, us?"

Jasper laughed. "I was surprised I even had a chance to dance with my sister. I thought you'd be keeping her to yourself all evening."

"Well, I've come to take her back. If she wants to be taken back, that is."

I laughed. "Of course I do."

Jasper turned back to Saray. "Speaking of dancing with sisters, if I ask yours, do I need to worry about you or Kip throwing flaming projectiles at my head?"

"That depends." Saray crossed her arms and smirked at Jasper. "What are your intentions with Trina? I hear rumour that you're— what was it again— a bottle-sucking skirt-chaser?"

"I'm never going to live that down, am I?" Jasper shook his head. "Trina is lovely, but she's only barely eighteen. I'm just asking for a dance."

Saray chuckled. "I'm teasing. It's not exactly up to Kip or me who Trina dances with, you know. Though you'll have to get in line. She's become quite popular here over the past few months."

"I've noticed. That fellow with the dragon— Ambrose, is it?— seems pretty sweet on her."

"Oh, he definitely is," Kaden put in. "Likely because she can talk to Spark. I wonder if Spark is the one trying to set them up."

"You think a dragon could pull that off?"

Saray shrugged. "Lachlann and Starla got set up by a tree. I've seen some strange things in my life."

Another dance was starting, a slower one this time, and I saw Kip making his way across the floor towards us. Jasper noticed too and turned to Saray. "Well, I think it's time for me to get back to my own dancing. Have a good night."

He disappeared into the crowd, and Kaden grinned and offered me a hand. "Shall we dance?"

We headed back out onto the dance floor, and Kaden grinned as she pulled me into position. The light of the viletta blooms caught on the gems in her waistcoat as she moved, and I laughed.

"What is it?" she said.

"Oh." I reached out and ran my fingers over the jewels. "You're just sparkling, that's all."

"Like the magical creature I am." She smirked. "Speaking of which, I have something very important to tell you."

"What's that?"

She dipped me low and then whispered, *"Incantus Momentus Gravita."*

I let out a squeak as we floated off the ground. Kaden grinned and propelled us higher, until we were just a few feet below the tree canopy that formed the cavern's roof. A few fairies began to flit around us. "I figured the dance floor was a little crowded," she said.

I glanced down at the people moving below and saw a few of them looked up at us. "Do you think they can see up my skirt?"

"Not at this height. But there definitely is an advantage to trousers." Kaden twirled me around, seeming to walk on the air as if it were something solid. "This has been quite the day, hasn't it?"

"Absolutely." I looked down at Saray and Kip, who were staring into one another's eyes as they swayed together. "I'm happy for them."

"What did you think of the Joining? Did you feel their magic merge when they kissed?”

I nodded. “I wonder what our magic would be like if it was combined.”

“Me too.” She grinned. “Thunderstorms, piano music, and…cherries, right?”

“That’s right. It sounds lovely. And being able to control the weather while flying in it at the same time could be pretty fun.”

“Fun and deadly.” Kaden frowned. “I know Saray and Kip were Joined because they’re worried that they might have to run someday. Do you think we’ll have to run as well?”

“I have no idea,” I said. “I could see the Breoch Guard trying to locate Saray, but I’m not sure that they’d want to attack an entire village, especially with the amount of magic we have.”

“I didn’t mean that they’d come for all of us,” Kaden said. “I meant that they might be looking for you or Jasper.”

“Why would they do that?”

She shrugged. “Your father might decide he wants you to come home after all. Or, more likely, Jade may be looking for revenge.”

“Right.” I sighed, thinking back to the last time I’d seen my other brother. “I suppose it’s possible. But even if that did happen, why would *we* have to flee? You could stay here.”

“No way.” Kaden shook her head. “I’m not losing you again, Ruby. If you run, I’m running with you.”

I felt a shiver course through me. “You mean that?”

“Definitely.” Her dark eyes were sincere, and she gripped me harder, as if trying to make her point. “We stay together always. Promise?”

“I promise,” I responded, grinning.

She leaned in and kissed me fiercely. I relaxed into her as she held me close, suspended above the dancers and surrounded by the fairies and viletta blooms. We had no idea where things would go from here, or what newfound dangers and challenges awaited us in the days and years ahead.

But whatever came our way, we would face it together. And that was enough.

THE END

ACKNOWLEDGMENTS

TO MY HUSBAND, Dave- thank you for sharing your love of fantasy with me. Also thank you for letting me ignore you when I'm on writing binges, and being an incredibly wonderful and supportive husband in general.

TO COLTON NELSON- thank you for continuing to work with me on this project. Thank you for the many hours of work put into formatting, cover design, and publication. Thank you also for the hilarious phone calls, the nonstop memes, and the Firebrand prank book. You are a one-of-a-kind publisher!

TO ETHEL NEWBERRY- thank you for taking the time to edit my manuscripts, for having an incredible eye for detail, and for the awesome open communication. Thank you also for geeking out about birds with me. You're the best.

TO MY FAMILY- my parents John and Penny, my siblings Alice and Ash, my brother-in-law Teko and my grandma Enid- thank you all for supporting me along the way, being willing to read my works and encouraging me to keep going. To Alice and Ash specifically, thank you for putting up with you forcing me to play make-believe with you as kids. To my nieces, Ebi and Mae, I look forward to the day when you are old enough to read my stories. Love you all.

TO MY INCREDIBLE team of beta readers- Gen Moore, Christie-Anne Dear, Meghan Walker, Alicia Zigay, Kelly Port, Abby McCallum, Ash Morgan, Zoe Baker, and Alissa Schactman- thank you so much for being willing to read through my manuscript and give honest, thoughtful feedback. My book is better because of all of you!

TO ASH, MY witty and insightful younger sibling, thank you for being my consultant on all things queer for this novel. Thank you also to the members of the Batcave who Ash consulted for feedback, and to the Batcave in general for being a delightful, welcoming, and chaotic group of humans.

TO ROWAN SMITH, thank you again for your wonderful map of my world.

TO JARED QWUSTENUXUN Williams, thank you for allowing me to borrow from the magic system of Medieval Chaos Productions to create my own.

TO MY WORKPLACE, Accent Inns and Hotel Zed- thanks for being some of my biggest fans, being willing to let me host release parties in your lobby, and supporting me in more ways than I would have expected. Special thanks to Trina Notman for your enthusiasm and marketing advice.

TO STEVIE BARNES, my international bestie- thanks again for supporting me in my writing journey and encouraging me to keep going. Your friendship, listening ear, and insight are so valuable to me.

TO THE WILD Ones- most of my stories involve the trope of the found family, and you folks are definitely mine. Thank you for all the laughs, support, and many years of friendship, and for constantly challenging me to grow and learn. As one!

AND LASTLY, TO everyone who went out of their way to pick this book up and read it, thank you. I hope you enjoyed Stormbrewer, and look forward to giving you more to read in the future.

ABOUT THE AUTHOR

MARY WALZ WAS born and raised on the west coast of British Columbia. She's been writing stories since she was a child, and wrote her first novel-length story at sixteen (spoiler: it wasn't very good). She's participated in several writing communities over the years, and has won a few prizes for her short stories. When she is not writing, she can be found tending her garden, feeding the neighbourhood crows, baking delicious goodies, or running around in the woods dressed as a fairy or a wizard. She lives in Sidney, BC, a sleepy seaside town with one main street and about a dozen bookstores, with her husband Dave and her plant babies.